One Ordinary Day at a Time

Sarah J. Harris is an author and freelance education journalist who regularly writes for national newspapers. Her debut adult novel, *The Colour of Bee Larkham's Murder*, was a Richard and Judy Book Club choice and won the breakthrough category in the Books Are My Bag Readers Awards 2018. Sarah lives in London with her husband and two children.

www.sarahjharris.com

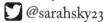 @sarahsky23

 @sarahjharriswrites

KT-164-597

Also by Sarah J. Harris

The Colour of Bee Larkham's Murder

D1486591

SARAH J. HARRIS

One Ordinary Day at a Time

HarperCollins*Publishers*

HarperCollins*Publishers*
1 London Bridge Street
London SE1 9GF

www.harpercollins.co.uk

HarperCollins*Publishers*
1st Floor, Watermarque Building, Ringsend Road
Dublin 4, Ireland

Published by HarperCollins*Publishers* 2021

1

Copyright © Sarah J. Harris 2021

Sarah J. Harris asserts the moral right to be identified as the author of this work

A catalogue record for this book is available from the British Library

ISBN:
HB 978-0-00-837733-5
Export TPB: 978-0-00-837734-2

This novel is entirely a work of fiction.
The names, characters and incidents portrayed in it are the work of the
author's imagination. Any resemblance to actual persons, living or dead,
events or localities is entirely coincidental.

Typeset in Adobe Caslon Pro by Palimpsest Book Production Ltd, Falkirk, Stirlingshire

Printed and bound in Great Britain by CPI Group (UK) Ltd, Croydon CR0 4YY

All rights reserved. No part of this publication may be
reproduced, stored in a retrieval system, or transmitted,
in any form or by any means, electronic, mechanical,
photocopying, recording or otherwise, without the prior
permission of the publishers.

MIX
Paper from
responsible sources
FSC™ C007454

This book is produced from independently certified FSC™ paper
to ensure responsible forest management.

For more information visit: www.harpercollins.co.uk/green

For all the children who were told
they wouldn't amount to anything in life.

Now, what I want is Facts. Teach these boys and girls nothing but Facts. Facts alone are wanted in life. Plant nothing else, and root out everything else. You can only form the minds of reasoning animals upon Facts: nothing else will ever be of any service to them, and this is the principle on which I bring up these children. Stick to Facts, sir!

Thomas Gradgrind in *Hard Times* by Charles Dickens

Love is in all things a most wonderful teacher

Our Mutual Friend by Charles Dickens

Prologue

'*Memory boy, memory boy, memory boy!*'

The audience chants my nickname as I step forward, willing my heart rate to slow and my hands to remain steady. William is behind me on the stage, just out of the spotlight, along with Bai and Francesca. He gives an encouraging nod and crosses his fingers for luck as I glance back. We've both been up since 4 a.m. as usual, revising for tonight's televised final of *Little Einsteins: Britain's Brainiest Kids*. I've aced the mathematics and memory rounds, as expected – not even my brother can come close to beating me in these fields. My fortes are complex equations along with memorizing the order of three fifty-two-card decks in sixty minutes.

My fellow competitors have caught up in logic, history and geography; they remain my weakest areas despite extensive drilling from Father. We're in a tie going into the sudden-death round. If I can get through these English Literature questions without making a single mistake, the prize will belong to me. However, one wrong answer could cost me the whole contest.

The camera zooms in as I walk up to the podium. I lower the microphone, which one of my previous rivals had adjusted before being eliminated.

'Let's give a warm welcome back to twelve-year-old Simon Sparks,' *Little Einsteins'* host, Jon Dolan, says to the camera, flashing a mega-watt smile. 'He joined Mensa at the age of five and has a genius level IQ of one hundred and sixty-four, which makes him cleverer than Albert Einstein and Professor Stephen Hawking. Simon wants to study maths at Cambridge University and crack the Riemann Hypothesis – a problem that has baffled mathematicians for more than a hundred and forty years. We believe he can do it – Simon is a genius, destined for greatness!'

The audience whoops and cheers.

'Simon has blown us away with his stunning performance throughout this contest,' he continues, 'but can he survive the sudden-death round? Let's find out!'

Jon's forehead is shiny under the bright lights even though the makeup lady dabbed his face with powder in the break.

'Are you ready?' He mops his brow with a tissue as the camera pans to me.

I look for Father in the front row. He's sat next to Mother, who's staring at her lap. Father's lips are moving. The spotlight blinds me but I know what he's mouthing: *Bright sparks create fires*, the Sparks' family motto. Beside him, Mother's lips remain tightly pressed shut.

I turn to the host. 'I was born ready!'

Jon fires his first question about Shakespeare's plays.

I close my eyes and search for the answer from within the rooms of my Memory Palace; a structure Father is teaching me to build inside my head to store information.

'*Romeo and Juliet*,' I say confidently.

The audience claps.

I step back into the shadows. The spotlight shifts between William and Bai as they each walk up to the podium, and finally lands on Francesca. They all successfully answer their questions. I take a deep breath as the light sears my face once more.

'Right, Simon,' Jon announces with a flourish, 'it's back to you. The line: "I had no advice, no counsel, no encouragement, no consolation, no assistance, no support, of any kind, from anyone, that I can call to mind," is said by a character in which novel by Charles Dickens?'

I look down at Mother. Her shoulders are trembling; her fingers brush something from her cheek. Is she crying? She pulls out a handkerchief from her pocket but, before she can dab her face, Father catches her hand. He places it firmly in her lap and pats it. His hand remains on top of hers.

I hesitate. I've lost my focus.

'Please can you repeat the question?'

This is a useful delaying technique.

'I'm afraid that's not possible in the sudden-death round,' Jon replies. 'I need an answer.'

I scour my Memory Palace, but I can't find the answer in any of the rooms. Where is it? I know it's here somewhere.

I stare at Mother. Tears are rolling down her face. Father's leaning forward, jaw clenched. His fists are hard, tight balls.

'Simon? Can you give me an answer or would you like to pass?'

Desperately, I run along the corridors of my mind, trying door after door. None of them will open.

'*Great Expectations*?'

I hold my breath.

My ears are buzzing.

I hear a stifled gasp behind me and, in that moment, I realize I've failed.

'I'm sorry,' Jon says finally. 'The answer I'm looking for is *David Copperfield*. You are eliminated from the final.'

I turn around, searching for William's usual support, but a wide grin stretches across his face.

For the first time ever, he's celebrating my defeat. The stage is finally his.

I

Eighteen years later, November 2018

SIMON

'HEY, EINSTEIN! GET A move on with those French fries! Shovel them. It's not rocket science!'

I jump as Ed appears at the fry station during the Monday lunchtime rush. He's caught me daydreaming again. I was deep in thought, concentrating on a new prime number theory that looks promising. I shake the baskets, which are submerged in spitting golden oil. Dark brown splinters bob to the surface creating interesting formations of Roman numerals.

'You've burnt them, you blithering idiot!' he barks. 'We can't serve those. Start over!'

'I'm on it,' I confirm.

'I'd prefer you to bloody well fry it!'

This is my boss's feeble attempt at humour, but none of my co-workers laugh; he's marginally less popular than me, albeit for different reasons. Ed possesses a rat-like face, a short fuse and an IQ level, I suspect, of 79, which is borderline deficient. His features would not be out of place within the prison population, yet they have inexplicably propelled him up the management ladder of this Prince Burger branch in West London. His professional success is possibly even more difficult to fathom than the Riemann Hypothesis.

Unfortunately, Ed hasn't returned to the sanctuary of his office and is still hovering.

'Something's attached to you.'

Before I can stop him, he whips off my Post-it, containing a series of complex variables. I'd surreptitiously attached it to my uniform, allowing me to cast my eye over the mathematical workings during quiet spells.

'What *is* this?'

I shrug. He wouldn't understand if I attempted to explain the complicated concepts.

'And more to the point, what the hell is this?' He hoists up a heavy white sack from the counter.

Despite Ed's unfortunately low IQ level, I thought he would definitely recognize the bag's contents. 'Those are frozen French fries. Pre-cooked, they are pale in colour.'

'Yes, I know that, you moron!' Ed trembles with rage. 'But why have you left the bag out instead of putting it back in the freezer? They've started to defrost! You've wasted at least thirty batches! What have you been doing all morning?'

I can't admit I was horribly distracted, and not even by my mathematical equations, which require urgent attention. On arrival at Prince Burger, I discovered that Archie – the stray cat whom I have named in honour of Archimedes – had a nasty cut above his left eye. After finally coaxing him out from behind the dustbins, I tended to his wound and provided saucers of water and leftover chicken scraps.

'Sorry. I was somewhere else.'

Ed's face turns an unflattering beetroot red – and that's before he notices I've also accidentally left out a pack of frozen burgers. I moved them to get to the fries.

'You mean like yesterday and the day before that? Exactly how many batches of burnt fries have you binned in the last week because you were *somewhere else*?'

He doesn't wait for the correct answer, which is three and three-quarters. One portion was salvageable if you like fries *very* well done. He's shaking his head faux-regretfully as he bins the bag.

'I thought that docking the number of stars on your badge would make you buck up your ideas, but I was clearly wrong. I've given you enough chances.'

No, no, no.

Being relegated to Ed's lowest possible staff ranking – one star out of a possible five for work ethic, teamwork and good hygiene – was humiliating, but not completely unexpected.

'I'll try harder, Ed. I'll stop . . . thinking about other things.'

'Honestly, this is pretty much the last straw. You're costing me money and have zero people skills. Two employees have lodged complaints over your insensitive IQ level comments. I'm interviewing for new recruits tomorrow – you're definitely replaceable. You won't be missed by anyone.'

I flinch at the accusation.

'Please don't fire me,' I whisper.

My pulse quickens with panic. This is one of the few jobs that allow me to pursue my true passions while earning a living wage. Looking for alternative employment will adversely affect my quest to discover the hidden pattern within prime number sequences, thereby solving the Riemann Hypothesis. Plus, there's only one thing more embarrassing than working at Prince Burger for someone with my IQ level, and that's being fired from Prince Burger. My brother William would never let me live it down.

Ed glares at me. 'Why not? You clearly want to be *somewhere else.*'

'I need this job. I have to pay my rent, my bills . . . I promise I'll work on my productivity and people skills. Please, Ed. You'll see massive improvements, I swear.'

He sighs deeply, weighing up my fate.

'I'm begging you. I can do better. Give me another chance. Think of all the times I've suggested new and better shift schedules and assisted with reordering stock. Plus, I'm the only employee you trust to fix mechanical glitches.'

Ed sighs again, and I feel a glimmer of hope.

'OK, but this is your final, *final* warning, do you understand? If I don't see improvements in the next few weeks, you're out.'

He screws up the Post-it and bins it, stalking off before I'm able to thank him. I exhale slowly. Ed respects only the swift supply of customers' food yet for me it's a means to an end. However, we appear to have reached an uneasy truce – at least for the time being. After scooping out the burnt detritus from the oil and discarding the bag of rapidly defrosting burgers, I take another sack from the freezer and refill Fro-Bot – my pet name for the mercurial robot who refuses to work unless she's handled with respect. She dispenses exactly one kilogram of uncooked potato chips, which her mechanical arm picks up and places in the fryers, to be cooked for precisely three minutes at 171 degrees Celsius, shaken halfway through.

'We're having a run on fries, Prof!' Marta calls over from the counter. 'You'd better get moving!'

'It's coming!'

Marta claims to be a *Game of Thrones* enthusiast, dyeing her long dark brown hair blonde to look like the Mother of Dragons for fan conventions. But she always appears uninterested whenever I test her on trivia from the hit TV show or facts about Poland, where she grew up. Although she never invites me to drinks after work along with everyone else, I'm grateful for her continuing deference to my superior abilities. That's what they call me here: *Prof* or *Einstein*. Not *Memory Boy* or *Freak* although Ed, admittedly, does call me *Shithead Simon* whenever I screw up.

Pam – one of Prince Burger's more mature employees – swings by my station. She's only just begun work so she can't be after her usual break-time fries. Her eyes are red; maybe she has an infection.

'I have a massive favour to ask, Prof. I'm looking for someone to cover the last two hours of my shift. I need to be gone by four p.m. Something urgent has come up at home. Please can you help?'

My schedule is proving increasingly challenging despite rising at 4 a.m. each day. William has named my conundrum 'Simon's Equilateral Triangle'. It's a never-ending battle to ensure all three points – working here, my preparation for general knowledge contests and mathematical research – remain balanced. I wince, though. Pam, at least, has never rolled her eyes at my conversation openers or called me a derogatory name even in jest.

'Sorry, I have too much to do outside of work.'

She sighs heavily, her shoulders drooping. 'I thought you'd say that, but it was worth a shot.' She looks around the kitchen for someone else to approach.

'Good luck, Pam.'

I turn away, remove the fries, shake again and dispense in the pan, before transferring to the bagging station for seasoning and packing. There's a glorious monotony to the routine, which allows me to think about more important things. I enjoy the constant hum of machinery and voices and the physical proximity of people around me – the flow of customers drifting in and out of the restaurant and the frantic racing around by my co-workers. Sometimes, like Pam, they'll speak to me briefly or accidentally brush against my body. The warmth of human contact almost takes my breath away.

I'm still repetitively shovelling fries towards the end of my shift when a fracas breaks out. A tall man with a shaved head and tattoos on his knuckles has homed in on Marta at the counter. He is our Worst Customer, or 'The Worstomer' as I have renamed him. He deliberately disrupts our routine at least once a week, sometimes by randomly ordering a Princely Whirl at 7.30 a.m. when he knows the ice-cream machines are switched off. Other days he demands 'off-menu' choices with ingredients we don't stock. These encounters seem to enable him to let off steam. I suspect this is his idea of therapy or post-prison rehabilitation.

'I didn't order that, you moron! Take it back!' The Worstomer hurls the box across the counter. It shoots off, the burger spilling onto the floor. 'Don't you understand English, you stupid bitch? I ordered a cheeseburger!'

This is his favourite trick – changing his order and pretending it's the server's fault. The Worstomer likes to make women cry, the younger the better. He glances past Marta and I make the mistake of catching his eye.

'Oi, mate! Do we have a problem?' His jaw locks, his fists clench; he's daring me to stop him.

My mouth dries painfully; my limbs turn to stone.

I know a million and one facts that come in handy during my successful quiz championship participation – the average bullet travels at around 1,700 mph; it is illegal to own only one parrot or guinea pig in Switzerland; and J and Q are the only letters that do not appear on the periodic table. But I cannot defend Marta from this monster.

Jerkily, as though rusted at my joints, I turn away.

I can't get involved. I'm only ever a bystander.

I return to my duties: restocking Fro-Bot, reviewing my prime number theories and stacking packets of fries as the shouts become louder. Marta flees the counter in tears. Carlos abandons flipping burgers and goes after her, and The Worstomer directs a tirade of abuse at Ed, who's trying to calm him down.

As a young child, William taught me how to turn off from frightening confrontations by retreating into myself. I close my eyes and enter the Memory Palace, which is constructed inside my head. I use this visualization technique to store everything I must remember. I attach facts, theories and formulae to specific objects in the rooms. A list of Japanese emperors is kept in a green, crackled sixteenth-century Ming vase in a first-floor living room while the formula for Newton's Second Law dangles from a crystal chandelier in a third-floor drawing room.

I picture it as a large Victorian mansion, with many floors and rooms. It has numerous places to hide.

I imagine running into a heavily fortressed ground-floor room. A sturdy oak door slams shut behind me.

I lock it.

Slide two bolts into place.

Put a chain across it.

I won't open this door until it's safe to come out again.

2

JODIE

'Can I come in now?'

Zak has insisted I wait outside our bedsit door while he gets my birthday surprise ready. I ignore pervy Steve who shuffles past in the corridor, while simultaneously scratching his groin. *Nice.*

'Soon, Mummy!'

I hear a series of thuds, followed by a muffled 'Aagh!'

'Are you OK in there?'

'Yup,' he says, breathlessly.

What *is* he doing? I dread to think what he's creating, or more like destroying. But then again, I might as well let him go for it. He can't really make our shitty bedsit look any worse than it already does.

I check my watch. 'I can't wait to see this, Zak, but I need to drop you off at Sandra's before school and catch the bus. I mustn't be late for this interview.'

I picture the leftovers in the fridge; if I don't get a new job today I'll need to visit the food bank. I lost my cleaning gig last month when the Duffin family moved from Clapham to Switzerland, and every interview I've been to since has been a dead loss. I'm in debt and next month is Christmas.

Today's interview is the most promising thing I've had in ages. The Prince Burger shifts are flexible; I can work around college and school hours and the staff benefits look great – the food vouchers will help in tight weeks.

'Now, Mummy, but you have to keep your eyes closed.'

I turn the handle. The familiar scent of damp drifts into my nostrils as I feel my way into the cramped, cold room. I can't mask the strong, musky odour however many joss sticks I light.

'Ta-dah! You can open them now. Happy birthday!'

The first thing I see is my gorgeous son – all beaming smiles, freckles and crazily tousled light brown hair. His toy dog is tucked beneath his right armpit as usual. Next, I spot the 'Happy Birthday' banner, made from three pieces of scrawled-on A4 paper roughly taped together. It's draped across my towering piles of novels, which had been neatly stacked against the wall and now look precarious. Beneath the sign, he's formed a big letter 'M' for 'Mummy' on the threadbare, stained carpet using books including *The Bell Jar*, *Wide Sargasso Sea*, *A Christmas Carol* and *To Kill a Mockingbird*.

'Wow! Amazing!'

I move closer, pretending I'm inspecting his handiwork, and straighten a leaning skyscraper – if one book comes out of place the whole thing will come tumbling down. I don't want to damage the spines or bend the pages.

Zak hops from one foot to the other with excitement. 'Look at this!'

He gestures to the table; we eat here and it also doubles as my desk and Mum HQ. My college files, swear box and home-made heater have been pushed to one side, along with the iron; I need to change the fuse. Centre stage is a chocolate cake with glossy frosting. My stomach rumbles. I'd settled for toast last night so Zak could have an extra big helping of veggie slosh – his description of the stew, not mine.

'Mmmm. That looks yummy!'

'Sandra bought it for us after school yesterday. We got candles from the pound store!' Zak holds up a packet. 'I didn't know how many to put on the cake.'

'How old do you think I am?'

'Forty? Or maybe forty-five?'

Jesus. I glance at the wardrobe mirror, taking in the dark violet rings beneath my eyes and the hollowed cheekbones. Most days I still feel like a kid – stupidly expecting someone else to tell me what to do – but, in this cold daylight, I look ancient, like I've lived several lives already. Maybe I shouldn't be so hard on myself. I got up at 4 a.m. again to reread a few chapters of *Great Expectations* and make notes for my latest essay. How else can I get everything done?

'I'm twenty-five,' I say, sighing.

'Phew! That's better than forty. Billy says when you're that old, you may as well be dead.'

I swallow a snort. *Cheers, Billy.* That's something to look forward to. I thought this birthday was bad enough – it isn't exactly how I'd pictured myself turning twenty-five when I was growing up in the children's home. I figured I'd have made it by now. I'd have a good job, a lovely flat and enough money to go out with friends at weekends. *Where the hell have all the years gone?* I've nothing to show for them really . . . apart from Zak who makes everything worthwhile.

'Here's your present. I got it specially.' He passes me a brightly wrapped package, which feels book-shaped.

'Oooh. What is it?' I pretend to shake it.

'Open it and see.'

I rip off the paper and pull out *Great Expectations*. I sneak a look at the table; my copy is absent from the pile of notes.

'It's your favourite book. I thought I'd wrap it up for you.'

'That's a great idea, thank you! Very thoughtful.' I draw him in for a hug, but he struggles beneath my arms.

'No time!'

Sadly, he's stingy with his cuddles and thrusts a card at me instead. This is what he was secretly making on Saturday while I studied for my tutorial. A stick woman is holding hands with a stick boy, who's clutching a stick dog. Beneath the picture, he's written:

For The Best Mummy In The World. Happy Birthday. I luv you, Zak.

I open my eyes wide to prevent tears from forming. How can I be a great mum when we live here? The bedsit is always cold and clammy, even though I've resorted to homemade double-glazing – cling film tacked onto the window – to keep in some warmth. But the mould continues to grow up the far wall in the shape of a fat man, which Zak has nicknamed Hairy Mo. I squint at it now. *Bloody hell.* Zak's used a red crayon to give him birthday balloons. Thank God our useless landlord never visits.

Obviously, I'm not as bad as my own mum, but Zak deserves more than *this*.

I clench my fists. I swear I'm going to give him more than I had growing up. Next year, on my twenty-sixth birthday, things could be different for both of us. I *have* to believe that.

'Let's light the candles,' I say, opening the packet.

'Have we got twenty-five?' he asks.

'No, but why don't we use the number we had on *your* birthday cake as you've made today so special?'

'I'm seven and nine months. Let's have eight and break a bit off the end of one.'

I do as he says, despite the waste, as it's quicker than arguing. 'There.' I throw the small chunk of wax into the bin.

Zak grins. 'Does that mean I get to blow them all out? Sandra says they're lucky candles and make all wishes come true.'

'I don't see why not.'

'Cool!'

I take the large clay flowerpot off the muffin tray and place it next to the cake. Beneath it is a smaller flowerpot, a piece of metal sealing the hole to keep in the heat from the four tealights beneath. This is a neat trick, one I was taught at the hostel – it takes the chill off the room when I can't afford to top up the meter. I use one of the tealights to light the seven-and-a-bit candles.

'Go for it, Zak!'

He takes a deep breath and takes out most of the candles in three puffs, which he clarifies means three wishes.

'What did you wish for?'

'A lightsaber that changes colour like Billy's.'

I gulp. I'm pretty sure his friend's lightsaber cost almost £40 – which is far more than I have to spend on food in a week.

'Or that big Star Wars Lego set for Christmas,' Zak adds, hedging his bets.

'Hmm. Did you wish for anything cheaper or, preferably, free?'

'Global warming.'

'You mean you want it to stop?'

'Of course! I want to save the polar bears.'

'That's a very noble wish. What's your third one?'

'I want Daddy—'

'Is that the time?' I flick a look at my watch. 'We need to get a move on.'

No way are we talking about Jason on my birthday. I have to look forward, not dwell on the past.

'But it's your turn,' Zak says, frowning. 'I *almost* had all my wishes.'

'I'll do it when you're ready. Get your backpack.'

'Do we have to *make it snappy*?'

The cheeky monkey's imitating my voice. 'Yes! Remember, we're a team?'

I put on some upbeat music, which usually makes him get his butt in gear. We run around cleaning teeth, brushing hair and having last-minute trips to the toilet down the corridor. While Zak searches under our double bed for his spelling book and other shoe, I tidy up the books, slipping *Great Expectations* into my handbag for the bus journey. I open the bedside table, pulling out the email I had printed off in the library. I reread it, even though I can recite the letter off by heart after receiving it this weekend:

Dear Jodie

Lucy Cavendish College has shortlisted your application for interview and is pleased to invite you for further assessment as detailed below.

Daring to hope, I grip the piece of paper tightly until my knuckles turn white. But that old, familiar voice in my head swiftly returns, chipping away at my self-confidence.

Why are you putting yourself and Zak through this? You're wasting your time. You're definitely going to fail.

My doubting, inner voice is right. Far better candidates than me all want the same thing: to study English at Cambridge. Only six undergraduate places are up for grabs at this college next autumn. Everyone else will know what to do. I've read all sorts of things about the interviews – they'll try to catch me out with offbeat questions, to see if I can think on my feet. I'll be up against people with good school records who can afford private tutors to prep them. They'll have watched Shakespeare per-formances, whereas I've never seen a live play.

I scan my wall planner, where I've flagged all my looming deadlines. The Cambridge exam and interview are both on the same day next month. I'll need to prepare like mad for the assessments as well as juggle college with looking after Zak and, hopefully, working at Prince Burger *if* I get the job. I'm knackered already.

Can I really do this?

When I look in the mirror again, I recognize that familiar spark of defiance in my eyes. I catch a glimpse of the young girl I used to be – someone who put up a fight. I had to look fear-less at my old comp; it was Jodie Brook versus the world. I punched kids who called me a 'skank'. I swore at the teachers who expected nothing from me because I came from a children's home. They wrote me off from the day I arrived, putting me into bottom sets, and I lived up to their low expectations, giving them lip and playing truant.

'Jodie is unlikely to amount to anything in life unless she changes her poor attitude,' Mr Chalker wrote in my report card. 'She is more suited to vocational options than university.'

The only person who ever believed in me was Lizzie, the school librarian who later became my friend. She'd help me with my English homework in the library and recommend books she thought I might like. A lump rises in my throat as I pick up the picture of us linking arms at school from the mantelpiece. The pile of books on the table in the photo hides my bump. The picture was taken shortly before I was kicked out of the sixth form without being allowed to sit my exams and Lizzie lost her job; the head teacher axed her library to make room for a new IT suite. Lizzie salvaged the novels that had been thrown into the skip in the staff car park; most are here in this room now, along with her own personal book collection. I hold the photo to my heart. I still can't quite believe she's never going to walk into this room again and ask me what I'm reading.

I close my eyes and feel the warmth of one of her reassuring hugs.

I remember her words:

Believe in yourself, Jodie. Don't give up. Aim high.

Although she's gone, her voice conquers the doubting one that squats bad-temperedly inside my head, ambushing me in dark moments. She's right. I'm going to prove all my old teachers and social workers wrong, even my own mum – everyone who ever doubted me, put me down or didn't give me a chance. I'm finally going to make something of my life; I want to become the kind of English teacher *I* never had at school. I need a degree first – and why shouldn't someone like me aim for the best, for Cambridge?

Don't I deserve a chance along with everyone else?

I light a single candle on the birthday cake to appease Zak otherwise we'll never get out the door. The flame looks small and insignificant. It flickers feebly; it may not be strong enough to keep going.

'I've been ready for ages and you still haven't blown out your candle and made a wish.' Zak sighs and crosses his arms. 'You're daydreaming again.'

He's re-emerged from under the bed, coughing and clutching three lost socks and a sweet covered in fluff. He's actually done his coat up without me having to nag him to death, although he's only wearing one glove and odd socks.

I glance back at my birthday candle. The flame flutters determinedly and has grown in strength – the only light in our dingy room.

I blow it out and make the wish for both of us.

3

SIMON

THE LIGHT BLINKS AND reluctantly flickers on in the storeroom. As I step inside, rain hammers loudly onto the skylight above my head. I hope Archie the cat has made it to dry shelter in time. I heave a drum of cooking oil into the doorway and place the keys in my pocket. These are necessary precautionary measures – during my last stocktake a mischievous co-worker locked me in here as a prank. It took fifty minutes to get out and Ed docked my pay when he discovered I'd constructively used my captivity to write a series of calculations on the wall with a pencil.

His formal warning yesterday – presented in writing at the end of my shift – plays on my mind as I inspect the neat shelves, jotting down gherkins and ice-cream toppings. My equilateral triangle is in danger of becoming distorted due to the extra effort I must now make for my boss. I weigh up various options such as getting up even earlier as I lock up and head to his office to return the keys and paperwork. Sitting on a chair outside his room is a young woman. She has damp, shoulder-length white-blonde hair with pronounced dark roots, heavily pencilled eyes, bright red lips and a small silver nose ring. A tattoo peeps out from the sleeve of her blouse; I can't make out the design. She's searching for something inside her handbag.

She must be one of the interviewees Ed mentioned yesterday. Just from her appearance, I'd estimate her IQ is around 89 – below average intelligence – but it's hard to tell for sure without engaging her in conversation. If I'm right, this IQ score will not prevent her from securing shifts here – I suspect that ninety-nine per cent of Prince Burger's workforce falls between the range of 80 to 109. Obviously, I am the exception.

I look around for something to test her motor skills and reaction times and seize upon a doorstopper that resembles a brick in both shape and structure. Admittedly it is on the heavy side, but a test is a test, after all, and Ed did something similar to me in my own interview, two years ago. This will prepare her for the drive-through; she mustn't drop the orders that the team will throw at her. I would have been grateful for assistance ahead of *my* assessment.

'Here, catch!'

The woman shrieks and ducks, missing the doorstopper. It smacks into the wall, leaving a large dent, and thuds to the floor. All this occurs within the space of four seconds, which is a respectable time, I have to grudgingly admit.

'What the actual fuck?' She leaps to her feet, knocking over her handbag. 'You almost hit me, you dickhead! Why the hell did you do that?'

I shove my hands into my pockets, suddenly sheepish. I can't possibly admit that I'm attempting to calibrate her IQ, adding points for her ability to respond quickly and effectively and deducting points for profanities. She obviously wouldn't under-stand – or take kindly – to a truthful explanation about my experiment. Thankfully, I can recall the interview techniques and training manual I was introduced to when I first started here.

'I was trying to prepare you,' I explain, attempting to keep my sentences simple.

'Prepare me for what?' she snarls.

'For life,' I say, waving my arm to demonstrate the expanse of Prince Burger.

'Is that supposed to be a metaphor or something?'

My eyebrows rise slightly. I can one hundred per cent guarantee that the word 'metaphor' has never been uttered by anyone within the walls of Prince Burger before, myself included.

'Well, yes, you could interpret it as a metaphor for life. Having to dodge life's trials and tribulations.'

The woman nods slowly. 'Yes. That's one interpretation.' She walks towards me – she's a tiny, malnourished thing, I realize. 'Or,' she says, 'could another simpler interpretation be that some stupid wanker attempted to assault me with a brick?'

'For the record, I'm not stupid or a wanker and it's a door-stopper that resembles a brick.'

'It's a brick that resembles a fucking brick and if you can't see that, you're far stupider than I first thought.'

More stupid, I think, but do not say out loud for fear of antag-onizing her further.

'I think we'll have to agree to disagree on the semantics,' I say, attempting to gain ground. 'I was trying to equip you for your imminent interview and subsequent career at Prince Burger.'

'People are going to throw heavy objects at me?' she asks faintly.

'During my interview, Ed hurled something to test my reaction times. He wanted to make me think on my feet and see how well I could catch a Merry Prince Meal at the drive-through. It's wise to be prepared for all eventualities in any interview situation. You never know what curveballs you might face.'

She looks aghast. 'The boss threw an *actual* brick at you?'

'Not a real brick, obviously; that would have been assault.'

'Oh, obviously,' she snorts, returning to her chair. She bends down and picks up the items that have spilled from her handbag: a purse, phone and a book.

'Well, best of luck with your interview,' I say cheerfully. 'Consider this a special welcome from the Prince Burger crew.'

She looks slightly dazed, probably by my display of people skills, and doesn't reply. Her eyes widen as the door swings open and Ed peers out.

'What's that brick doing under the chair and why is there a dent in my wall?' He glowers at me suspiciously before switching his gaze to the woman. 'And who was shouting and swearing while I was on the phone?'

Despite yesterday's threat regarding my employment, I'm about to own up to my anthropological pre-interview test and selflessly claim responsibility for the profanities when she replies: 'The brick was here when I arrived and I have no idea who was swearing.'

She *is* quick-witted, I'll give her that. But so are psychopaths, who make up approximately one per cent of the general population. However, my curiosity is piqued now I can see the title of the book in her hand: *Great Expectations*. My childhood nemesis! I wonder . . . Is she actually reading this fine example of nineteenth-century literature? In which case I might test her on Dickens' use of food to portray greater social themes. Or did she simply find the book lying around and plan to take it to the local charity shop? I'm keen to discover the truth, but Ed has other ideas. He glares at me as he takes the storeroom keys and paperwork.

'Don't stand there gawping, Simon. Log the damage in the maintenance book and get back to work.'

He turns to his potential new recruit.

'Come in, Jodie. Let's get started.'

I smile brightly to bolster her spirits. She returns my pleasantry with a rather ferocious scowl. The woman – Jodie – approaches the door cautiously, as if expecting to be ambushed by a wild animal. She is full of surprises, which may prove a hindrance during the interview. Ed hates surprises as much as late shift workers, wasted orders and burnt Prince Burger buns.

The door shuts behind her with a conspiratorial click.

4

JODIE

'So, Jodie.' Ed dangles my CV between his fingertips. His hair colour and freckles remind me of the ginger nut biscuits Zak likes. 'What do you believe you can bring to the Prince Burger family?'

I'm tempted to say 'sanity', because who in their right mind lobs a brick at someone? If this is a family, the guy outside with one star on his badge must be the mad uncle everyone tries to avoid sitting next to at Christmas dinner. My heart rate is still beating through the roof. I shift uncomfortably in my seat. My blouse is damp and sticking to my back. I forgot to pick up my umbrella and had to run through the pouring rain to get here on time, as the bus was late as usual, and then being almost clobbered to death has made me break out into a fresh sweat.

'I'm a people person and a team player,' I parrot stiffly, remembering the generic interview tips I read on the internet.

'Hmm. Yet there's no evidence of that on here,' Ed points out. 'You appear to lack experience of working in a team and collaborating with others. Unless, of course, you mean you're currently developing those skills at . . .' His eyes scan up and down the page. 'Kensington College, right?'

I grab the lifeline he's dangling, even though I spend hours alone each day in our bedsit and local library studying for my Access to Higher Education Diploma.

'Yes, absolutely! I'm all about the networking. At college . . . in the workplace.'

Ed squints at the piece of paper again, searching for something that isn't there. My CV is lacking in most departments and my employment record is unimpressive to put it mildly. I've spent the last seven, almost eight years, looking after Zak, claiming benefits and working part-time gigs – a lunchtime supervisor at his school until cutbacks meant the post was axed, cleaning houses, waiting tables, helping out on a friend's market stall and, in between, reading every book I could get my hands on and dreaming of something bigger and better.

I pick at the skin around my fingernail. 'Well, I regularly help out at my son's primary school for the Parent Teacher Association – you know, organizing the Christmas raffle and the summer fete.'

That's a lie. The mum mafia doesn't let me anywhere near it even though I've volunteered twice; I didn't pass their secret initiation test.

'That should be on here,' he says, tapping the piece of paper. 'Sorry.'

'I think you require a few sticking plasters, don't you?'

'Absolutely! I need to cover up all the gaps in my education and employment record, but I firmly believe everything can be fixed!' I smile brightly at him.

'I meant for your fingers. They're bleeding.'

'Oh!'

I look down. I've gnawed my nails and surrounding skin; an old childhood habit I've been unable to break. As Ed fetches a first aid box, I look around the tidy office. A poster from the old TV series, *The X-Files*, hangs above his desk, featuring an alien and the words: 'The Truth Is Out There'. He's crossed out the word 'Truth' in a thick black pen and written 'Customer'. In the Prince Burger family, Ed must be the dodgy second cousin who bores everyone to death with his alien abduction theories.

'Here you go.'

He returns with plasters and runs through the job requirements, the daily routine and hygiene rules as I get myself sorted. I can't do anything about my blouse; I've smeared flecks of blood down it. So much for dressing smartly. When I turned sixteen, a personal adviser was assigned to prepare me for being booted out of the home and moved into semi-supported accommodation. She helped me with budgeting, cooking meals and interview practice, but that feels like a lifetime ago. She also stressed the importance of looking presentable and making a good first impression. I've failed on both points, but there's still time to salvage this.

When Ed pauses, I warble on about how hard I'm prepared to work. He cuts in, sounding exasperated.

'How exactly would you describe a Princely Whirl to an alien?'

My mouth drops open. What do aliens have to do with anything?

'Come again?'

'I've got enough basic info from your CV and online application. I like to make potential recruits think on their feet, or rather, outside of the box.'

'Erm, please can you repeat the question?'

He asks again, but I'm still stumped. I revert to Plan B: humour.

'Did I say repeat the question? I meant replace it with a completely different, easier one. Ha ha ha!'

He stares back, stony-faced. 'Fine. How would you describe a cucumber to an alien that's landed in my restaurant?'

Oh God.

I've applied for dozens of part-time jobs but this is the only interview I've been invited to. Zak needs new shoes and a backpack for school. The one he has is held together by safety pins and I know it embarrasses him – he keeps 'accidentally' leaving it on the bus or in the stairwell in the hope that someone takes it.

I take a deep breath. 'I'd ask the alien why he wants to eat a cucumber when there are so many other delicious things on the menu here. Plus, what's the point of cucumbers anyway? They're green, full of water and don't taste of anything, right?'

Ed's face doesn't give anything away. After a thoughtful pause, he returns to talking about the gaps in my skills set, which 'require urgent development'. More like CPR. I stare despondently at his poster of *The X-Files*, wondering where else I should drop off my CV. I passed a few betting shops, cafés and pound stores further up the road. It'd be a shame to waste the bus fare while I'm out and about.

'How did it go?' Sandra's face brightens as she opens the front door to her flat. Her pixie haircut is red this week, matching her lippie and the pair of parrots dangling from her ears. Changing her look cheers her up and takes her mind off turning seventy next year. She stands aside as I mock-stagger into the hallway.

'That bad?'

'It was horrific.' I shrug off my coat, hanging it on the rack next to hers, and sling down my bag and a lightsaber I picked up for Zak in the pound store on the way home. 'Well, beyond horrific, really.'

'Oh, I am sorry. Come here, pet.'

I close my eyes as she envelops me into a hug, inhaling her comforting floral perfume. She should bottle it – this is how every grandma should smell. Meeting her in the corner shop while Zak was having a meltdown and discovering we live on the same street is definitely the best thing to come out of moving here two years ago. Sandra's a retired nursery assistant so she's seen her fair share of kids' tantrums and ailments. She's become my closest friend who believes in me and always has my back, the way Lizzie did. I don't know what I'd do without her.

'There now, pet,' she says, releasing me. 'It's nothing a good cup of tea won't sort out.'

'I could do with something stronger.' I check my watch. 'Ugh! It's nowhere near lunchtime.'

'Well, it is your birthday. It must be lunchtime somewhere in the world.'

I smile, despite everything. 'True!'

I collapse onto her green velvet sofa in the lounge while she heads to the kitchen. I discover one of Zak's missing gloves tucked behind a cushion, along with his spelling book. One of these days, I swear I'm going to find a pair of his skiddy pants. I glance at the mantelpiece and spot the picture of Zak and me. He's pulling a silly face as usual. Photos of Sandra's late husband, Frank, who died five years ago, have pride of place along with those of her three sons and their partners, and seven grandkids. I'm always insanely flattered that Zak and I have made it up there too.

I hope someone remembered to call her this weekend; her lads are rubbish at staying in touch. The grandkids are scattered around the country after her eldest sons' marriages broke down and she doesn't get to see them as often as she'd like. That reminds me, I need to do something for her before I leave – like bleed the radiators or fix the broken drawer in the kitchen. Frank used to do all the odd jobs.

She returns, carrying a tray with two glasses, along with a present and card.

'Here we are. Pink gin.'

'Ooh! This is a treat!'

'Happy birthday!'

We clink glasses. I take a large swig as I read her card and open the present – sparkly fingerless gloves. She'd remembered my complaints about the cold when I get up mega early to write essays. After another hug, Sandra almost wets herself as I give my best impression of Ed from the interview.

'Cucumbers? What's the point of them?' she laughs. 'They don't taste of anything!'

'That's what I said!' I sink deeper into the sofa, feeling nicely woozy. I'll need to pace myself; I'm drinking on an empty stomach as I didn't have time for breakfast.

'I don't know how you could have prepared for a question like that.'

'That's the problem, Sandra. It's scared the crap out of me. What if the tutors ask questions like that at the Cambridge interview? I'll freeze again. I'll be up against people who come up with the perfect answers to every question.'

'You could practise with me. I used to help my manager interview for new staff at the nursery.'

'You're far too nice. I need a rottweiler who can teach me how to dodge curveballs and lob them back at the tutors.'

'Where are you going to find someone like that?'

I stare at the bottom of my glass.

'I don't think the answer's in there,' she points out.

We both laugh.

'Don't take this the wrong way, pet, but are you sure you want to put yourself through applying to Cambridge? I know you like books and everything, but all this stress can't be good for you or Zak.'

I put my glass down firmly on the coffee table. 'I *have* to do this.'

'But why?'

'This is all I've ever wanted to do – it's just having Zak stopped me from trying when I was a teenager. I feel now he's older it's my time to give it a shot. I love English Literature more than anything, apart from Zak, and I want to study it with the best of the best. I want to learn, *really* learn and improve myself.'

'Still . . .' Sandra takes a large slurp of gin. 'University isn't really for the likes of us, is it? Particularly a dead posh one like Cambridge.'

'Why shouldn't I have the same opportunities as other people? Lizzie was pushing me to apply before I got pregnant, even though it would have been an uphill struggle with my grades at the time. She showed me college prospectuses and even took me on an open day to Pembroke on her day off because that's where her brother used to study English.'

I blink as my eyes well up. 'She looked past my rebelliousness and could see some potential. She drilled it into me that I *was* bright enough, not just to go on to university, but to get into one of the best in the world. She told me not to listen to the teachers who said it wasn't for me, that I'd enjoy proving them all wrong when I finally got my degree. Well, that's what I'm going to do.'

'But you could do a college course in retail and get a job in a shop instead – work your way up to manager level and get a good salary before you even graduate. That would prove all your doubters wrong and you wouldn't get into so much debt.'

I shake my head. 'I've done my research and I know what I'm doing. I'll get student loans that I'll only start paying back once my income reaches a certain level. I'll apply for hardship grants while I'm at Cambridge; the university and college have different pots of money I can tap into. We'll also live in far nicer accommodation than here; the college's family flats are beautiful. It will be a better life for Zak.'

Sandra begins to argue, but I cut in. 'This makes sense, career-wise. I need a degree to get onto a teacher training course so why shouldn't it be from Cambridge? I'm going to become the teacher I *should* have had at school – someone who encourages all pupils to achieve, whatever their backgrounds. I'll never write off kids who need support, particularly those in care. I can help them to succeed and become like Lizzie was to me – their biggest supporter and cheerleader.'

Sandra bursts into tears. 'Well done! You passed the interview, pet. I could really see your drive and commitment. I'd definitely give you the place at Cambridge.'

'Bloody hell, Sandra. You're a rottweiler in disguise!'

'Thanks, I'll take that as a compliment. I'm sorry I couldn't help you with the Prince Burger interview too.'

'Actually, that's something I wanted to talk to you about . . . I got the job at the madhouse. They're short-staffed. I start tomorrow – as long as you don't mind having Zak after school again?'

She thumps me with a cushion. 'Of course I can have him,

but I can't believe you didn't tell me straightaway. Now I don't know whether to congratulate you or commiserate!'

'Maybe both?'

'Either way, we need another drink.'

'Can my alien friend have some cucumber with his gin?'

We dissolve into giggles again. I really need to sober up before school pick-up otherwise the mum mafia will look down on me even more than usual.

'Never let other people get in the way of what you want to achieve.' Sandra raises her glass. 'Here's to proving all your doubters wrong and getting into Cambridge!'

'And to surviving becoming a member of the Prince Burger family!'

We clink glasses for about the millionth time.

'To family,' Sandra says, her eyes misting up.

5

SIMON

'ARE YOU TRYING TO avoid me?' William asks.

I'm speaking to my twin brother as I hunt for a snack in the kitchen. He's the only family I have left, but I've been dodging him for the past couple of days. The problem is he's very persistent. Unfortunately, I've learnt from experience that he won't give up until he gets through.

'Of course not! I've had shifts that clash with yours *and* the time difference.'

Like myself, William faces unpredictable, long hours – but rather than working at a greasy fast-food joint, he's a neurosurgeon at the Mount Sinai Hospital in New York, a position he never lets me forget.

'To be honest, now isn't a good time.'

I don't feel up to talking tonight. William has a habit of weaselling things out of me and I don't want to discuss my final warning at Prince Burger: he'll dine off it for months. My job is probably in further jeopardy. On closer inspection, I realized the object I threw at the female interviewee – Jodie – earlier today *was* an actual brick. She could report me to Ed, the police *and* sue. I've let down Marta, by not defending her against The Worstomer, and Pam, by refusing to swap shifts. To top it all, Archie's wound may become infected without the application of antibiotic cream. It hasn't been a great start to the week.

'Could we catch up on Thursday or Friday night?'

William continues as though I've not spoken.

'I'll go upstairs so we can talk properly. It's feeding time at the zoo here.'

In the background, the TV is blaring; the show sounds distinctly non-educational. Victoria, a former model, shouts her usual '*Hello, Simon!*' She's kind to me and extends invitations to visit each summer. William describes her as high-maintenance, but that's probably because she doesn't let him push her around. She calls out again, reminding me to let her know my Christmas plans ASAP. Now she's yelling at the kids to stop fighting and come into the kitchen for tea. '*No, you can't bring your iPads.*' I grin. Not only have Harper and Lucy been allowed to watch TV after school, they are multi-screening with their new devices. What would Father have said?

William breathes heavily as he climbs the stairs to the newly refurbished study on the fourth floor of their town house. He should eat less junk food and exercise more, but he never listens to advice from Victoria or myself. Maybe it's another belated act of rebellion.

'That's better. Peace and quiet.' I hear the study door click shut and the squeak of expensive leather as he sits down. 'Something's wrong, Simon. I can hear it in the tone of your voice. You sound troubled. Are you having the same old nightmares about Mother?'

I steady myself against the kitchen table, the question catching me off guard. William sleeps like a baby; *his* conscience never keeps him up until the early hours. Or if it does, he'd never admit it to me.

'No, I'm just tired from work.'

I hate myself for constantly attempting to impress him, but I can't help it. 'My shift gave me a chance to expand my general knowledge: I learnt one hundred and thirty-three new facts while I cooked approximately nine thousand French fries.'

William makes no attempt to disguise his loud yawn.

'*Wow.* You were busy. By the end of my shift, I'd removed a tumour the size of a golf ball from a seventeen-year-old girl's skull. She'll make a full recovery.'

'*Wow*,' I shoot back. 'Father would have been proud.'

Medicine has never interested me despite Father's former occupation as a surgeon – if anything, that put me off. William channelled his efforts into the specialism despite a similar lack of initial enthusiasm. We attended Cambridge together just before we turned fifteen, with William opting for this subject. However, my loyalty has always resided with mathematics; I couldn't bring myself to betray a true calling just to curry favour with Father.

'Seriously, Simon. Talk to me. I hate the thought of you being on your own when you're feeling low. I have Victoria to speak to when I've had a bad day but you've got no one apart from me.'

Wincing, I attempt to enquire about his children's latest achievements, but he doesn't give up. *He never does.*

'Today is the second anniversary of you starting work at Prince Burger, right? I remember because I was giving the keynote speech at the American Association of Neurological Surgeons' annual conference.'

I stare at the calendar on the kitchen wall. I'd completely

forgotten until now. No one remembered at work either – Ed usually plays music over the speakers on my colleagues' birthdays and start-date anniversaries. I'd requested 'We Are the Champions' in advance but it wasn't played today.

'I can't believe you're still there after two years. It was only supposed to be a stopgap. It's such a waste of your talent and potential. Honestly, Simon, what *are* you doing with your life?'

Good question.

I can't answer it and, therefore, opt to remain silent.

'Have you asked your boss for a promotion or more pay? Or, better still, updated your CV and applied for another post, a *professional* job?'

I sigh heavily as I retreat to the bedroom. A lecture on careers is all I need. I glance at the Post-its on the wall, containing crucial dates and facts in preparation for Thursday's quiz and the rows of academic trophies and certificates arranged across the shelves below in chronological order, from my first win aged five in a school mental arithmetic contest, to the Prince Burger 'good hygiene' medal that Ed presented me with three weeks ago.

'You know I haven't done anything yet. I'm busy with quizzing and my mathematical work. How could I do all that on top of a demanding, time-consuming career? It's impossible.'

I don't need to see William face to face to know he's shaking his head.

'You're drifting. You have to get your career back on track. Start earning a good salary that will allow you to invest in your future before it's too late. You're up against a fresh round of competitive, thrusting young graduates every year.'

It's my turn to shake my head. William will never understand my extra-curricular commitments as he judges success in terms of monetary gain. While I don't, it doesn't hurt that the Clay

Mathematics Institute has offered a million-dollar prize to anyone who solves the Riemann Hypothesis, or any of the other Millennium Problems. So far, only one of the seven – the Poincaré Conjecture – has ever been cracked. The prize money would be welcome, but being named the victor of a second theory would earn my place in history – and gain the respect of my academic peers and, *possibly*, my brother. That's how *I* judge success.

'I know you think I'm being harsh, but it's because I care. I want you to be happy.'

Does he? Still?

I stare at the framed photographs of Mother, Father and William and myself growing up and William with his own family in New York. I focus on the pictures before *Little Einsteins* – this was the period of my childhood when I felt closest to him. I remember his arms around my shoulders after I'd struggled with a French test that he'd breezed through; how he'd rubbed my back when I fell off my bike, comforting me again when Father confiscated it. Sometimes he whispered rude words in my ear about Father at the dinner table and pulled faces behind his back to make me laugh.

But from the age of twelve onwards, the competitive glint in his eyes is visible in every photo. William had always got off lighter, but he'd finally worked out that siding against me helped him escape Father's wrath. I wish we could return to the days when he was my staunchest ally, not my chief competitor. I long for a rapprochement.

While my attention has been wandering, William has launched into a misguided attempt to console me by describing the stresses of *his* life with a high-powered job and dependants.

'Victoria spends a fortune on handbags and, when I challenge her, she says: "So what? You earn hundreds of thousands of dollars a year. We can afford it." Can you imagine Mother ever speaking like that to Father?'

I shudder, my gaze still lingering over the family photos.

'It's left to me to support her spending habits and the kids – the expensive beach holidays at five-star resorts in Barbados, skiing in the French Alps at New Year, the astronomical school fees, plus saving up for Harvard or Yale. Sometimes I dream about having a simpler life without any responsibilities whatsoever.'

'Ha! Of course you do! And when you wake up, you're thankful for your six-figure salary and fancy holidays; the letters after your name; your research, which is regularly published in scientific journals, and the high esteem of your peers.'

William sighs. 'I've upset you again, haven't I?'

It's become a habit, sadly. I stare at last year's photo, taken by an obliging tourist on my phone. We're all pictured together on Gapstow Bridge in Central Park. I'm standing apart from the group – William is laughing, Victoria and the children look puzzled and I'm fighting back tears. William had just jokingly asked when I was going to get a family of my own instead of relying on his.

'I'm sorry, Simon. I'm not trying to rub your nose in it.'

Ha! Really?

'Remember, you could still have a successful, fulfilling, well-paid career *and* a family.'

I turn the photo over. I've resigned myself to the fact it's impossible to have it all – women have never been interested in me and, even if they were, inflicting my regime on others would be unfair. I know the sacrifices I have to make to become a successful mathematician.

'I should go,' I say, curtailing the conversation before it takes a further nosedive. 'I have hundreds of analytic continuations to verify.'

'Don't work too hard,' he replies.

'Back at you, brother.'

I close my eyes and picture the scene in William's house now he's off the phone: the kids jostling each other as they sit at the large antique oak table, which my brother bought to host his legendary dinner parties, and the smell of Victoria's meat bolognaise sauce. They'll exchange stories about each other's day as they eat together as a family.

My chest tightens painfully. My empty stomach rumbles. I head to the kitchen. Scouring the fridge, I grab a bran muffin, but the *Sparks' Family Guidelines for Success* stare reproachfully at me as I begin to close the door. This document was stuck on our fridge door when we were growing up. I dutifully return the muffin to its shelf and opt for a handful of blueberries. I study the laminated rules again.

1. *Wake up at 4 a.m.*
2. *Only cold showers allowed.*
3. *No junk or processed food.*
4. *Room temperature to be no more than 15 degrees Celsius.*
5. *TV and pop music banned.*
6. *No friends allowed over.*

Father explained to us at the age of five that the brain is lazy and needs to be retrained. Whenever faced with a problem, it automatically searches its archives for a solution based on previous learned behaviour, like a computer search engine.

It looks for the easiest, least challenging routes and has to be punished until it learns something new.

I shiver.

I reach for my stopwatch and packs of cards to distract me. Memorizing decks and reciting the suits in order is my preferred recreational pastime. William has been unable to beat me in this pursuit since our time on *Little Einsteins*.

He no longer enjoys competing in IQ challenges, but remains a formidable adversary who mustn't be underestimated. We both know some competitions will never be over, however much I want them to end.

It's only the rules of the game that change.

6

JODIE

I T'S MY FIRST DAY at Prince Burger and I haven't had a chance to flick through the hundred-page rulebook Ed gave me when I arrived, let alone memorize it as ordered. He's thrown me in at the deep end, rotating me around different workstations. I've just joined Pam, a glamorous sixty-something singer in her church choir, who has five stars on her badge. We're on the counter and I'm trying to get to grips with the temperamental tills as the Wednesday lunchtime queue of customers doubles in size.

Behind me is the fry station, manned by One-Star Simon. I'm avoiding him like the plague, despite him attempting to make eye contact, in case he uses me as brick target practice again. Next to him is burger production – an assembly line of toasting buns, cooking the patties in the clamshell grill, squirting sauce from a contraption that resembles a grouting machine and then assembling: adding salad, onions, gherkins, topping off with the crown (the lid of the burger) and sealing into a box. The orders are put onto a conveyor belt, which runs across the workstation. At the front of the kitchen, the 'runners' and 'initiators' pick them up and deliver to the counter.

After three non-stop hours, my legs are aching, I have a splitting headache and I'm desperate for a wee. When Marta starts her shift on the counter, I use my timed rest break to nip to the toilet but, as I pass the fry station, One-Star Simon swings around.

'Jodie? May I have a minute?'

He deserts his fryers before I can say no.

'I have re-examined the object I threw at you and have come to the conclusion you were right – it was a brick. I apologize for the misunderstanding and do not wish to enter into protracted legal proceedings. Perhaps this is something we could settle privately without Ed, the police or lawyers becoming involved?'

'Eh?'

He stares at me intensely. His eyes are a startlingly deep blue that stand out even more due to his black hair. They remind me of cornflowers; Lizzie's favourite flowers.

'The brick I threw at you.' He talks slowly, as if I'm an idiot.

'What . . . about . . . that . . . bloody . . . brick?' I say, even more slowly.

'I'm sorry I threw it at you. I thought I was being helpful.'

I accidentally laugh and snort at the same time. 'I'll admit I was tempted to punch you over Brick-gate, but it hadn't crossed my mind to sue you.'

He winces.

'Don't worry! Just joking. I'm not going to do either. I have to run.'

As I turn around, a muscly guy with a black goatee beard and hairnet from burger production steps in front of me, blocking my path.

'Hey. How did *you* get onto the counter so quickly? I've been trying for six months.'

I glance at the door to the toilets, swallowing a sigh, before dragging my gaze back to my new colleague.

'Ed says I need to develop customer relations skills to improve my CV.'

'That's where you're going to stay? Permanently?'

I shrug.

He glares at me fiercely. 'How did you pull that off?'

'Erm . . .'

'I know why.' One-Star Simon edges closer. 'Hasn't Ed ever explained his counter system to you, Carlos?'

He shakes his head. 'I try to avoid talking to him. I pretend my English isn't so good. *Es mentira.*'

One-Star Simon turns to me, smiling. 'That means *it's a lie.* Carlos is fluent in English and can swear at me in at least three languages, including his mother tongue, Spanish.'

I cross my legs. I only have two and a half minutes left to get to the bathroom and back before my break is up.

'Ed likes to relate management concepts to alien theory,' he continues. 'For example, how would you describe a cucumber to an extraterrestrial and would your description tempt the alien to take a bite?'

I laugh despite my discomfort. 'He asked me something similar in my interview yesterday!'

One-Star Simon nods appreciatively, but Carlos looks baffled.

'So for the counter, Ed asks himself this: if an alien landed in Prince Burger would it find this person objectively attractive for a different species? If the answer is "yes", that person, such as Jodie, goes straight onto the counter.'

Carlos' mouth falls open.

Simon continues. 'Jodie has lost her nose ring from yesterday, presumably on hygiene grounds, toned down her makeup and her hair and nails are groomed. She is presentable and, dare I say, objectively more attractive. Well, attractive enough for an alien.'

I glance around the kitchen, hoping to spot something heavy to lob at him.

Who the hell does he think he is? He's not exactly an oil painting himself – yes, he has nice eyes, but he's got a very smackable face.

'However, if he or she fails his Alien Test, they're on fry or grill, like you and me,' One-Star Simon adds. 'Permanently and with no chance of parole.'

Carlos continues to gape at us. I want the floor to open up and swallow me, or preferably One-Star Simon. He has less tact than Zak.

'You shitting me, Prof?' Carlos asks finally.

'I most certainly am not. You and I, my friend, were rejected from the counter because we couldn't even attract an alien. There's something vaguely anarchic about that, don't you think? The Alien Reject Club. Hey, we could get T-shirts together!'

Against my better judgement, I step in between One-Star Simon and Carlos, who looks as though he wants to swing a punch.

'Is something burning?' I nod towards the fryers.

'Oh dear!'

One-Star Simon scarpers, leaving me with Carlos. Judging by his dark mutterings, I don't think he found One-Star Simon's explanation – and what I suspect may have been a woefully bad attempt at male bonding – much comfort.

He shoots daggers at me again before returning to the grill.

'If you need anything else explained, feel free to ask,' One-Star Simon says over his shoulder as I dart past on my way to the loo. 'I'm always here for assistance.'

Yeah, right. Hell will freeze over before I come to you for help.

The rest of my shift passes in a blur until someone behind me hisses: 'The Worstomer's back!'

I wish I'd read the rulebook because I think that's code for something. Ed scurries towards us and Pam shudders, muttering: 'Please not me.' I carry on serving my last customer even though my aching legs feel like they're about to give way. I'm not used to standing for so long, but at least I'm nearly done for the day. As I log out from my till, I hear Pam's customer order a double Prince Burger with fries and two Coke Zeros.

Suddenly, she shrieks and I catch a glimpse of glinting coins as they shower over our counter and onto the floor. I bend down to help pick them up. As I stand, it's clear that the customer has dumped a mountain of loose pennies to pay for his nearly ten-quid order. Pam's eyes are like a rabbit caught in headlights, as she scoops coins onto the counter and slowly tries to sort them into piles as the customer smirks and her queue grows.

Ed beckons to her other customers. 'I'm opening a new till over here.'

'Aagh!' Pam exclaims, as one of her lopsided coin towers collapses.

One-Star Simon bounds over. 'Do you want me to check you're adding it up right?'

'It's OK, I can do it,' I say quickly. 'I'm here already.'

'Thanks, Jodie.' Pam moves along the counter, making room for me.

I begin to line up the coins into neat columns, as One-Star Simon continues to hover.

'It's probably best if I take over, seeing that I've got a degree in mathematics.'

'Yeah, because you definitely need a maths degree to count pennies,' I shoot back.

'A maths degree helps with the three P's: problem-solving, patience and perseverance.' He lets out a snort of laughter. 'Actually, it's four P's if you include these pennies.'

I raise an eyebrow. 'I'll take your word for it.'

'You should – I was one of the youngest people ever to go to Cambridge when I was almost fifteen and went on to gain a double first. That was a *long* time ago, but the skills I developed during my degree course prove useful every day.'

'Wait.' I stop counting and stare at him. 'You went to Cambridge? As a *kid*? Is that why Carlos called you Prof? I thought he was being ironic.'

He nods. 'Everyone here uses that name, but Ed also calls me Einstein or Shithead Simon depending on his mood.'

'Can you get a bloody move on, before my frigging order gets cold?'

I ignore Pam's snappy customer. 'Why are you working here if you've got a double first in maths from Cambridge?'

One-Star Simon flinches.

'Sorry, I mean—'

'Are you done counting or what?' the man demands, drumming his fingers on the counter.

'Yes, sure.' I stack coins quicker.

Wow, Cambridge. I can't believe my luck! Surely One-Star Simon can give me some advice – although, of course, he would have to be the oddest, most annoying man in the universe.

48

I make a quick guesstimate and push the customer's change towards him along with his meal, forgetting to make eye contact.

'I'm sorry, sir. Here's your forty-five pence change and your lunch. Have a great day!' I turn to One-Star Simon. 'Now, about Cambridge . . . I have so many questions. How—'

'Don't you ignore me, you dumb cow!'

The customer – a tall, hulk of a man with a shaven head – is still at the counter, scowling menacingly. My gaze rests on his bruised, tattooed knuckles flexing on the tray and suddenly I'm short of breath. My stomach lurches; my legs are leaden weights as he picks up the cup of Coke Zero. I know what he's going to do with it before it even leaves his hand. I remember that fraction of a second, which always felt like a lifetime, before the impact of Jason's first blow – the bitter taste of fear in my mouth, realizing I was powerless to stop what was coming.

The drink hits my forehead and splatters down my uniform.

'Have a *fucking* great day, you stupid bitch!'

The counter and kitchen fall silent. The other customers stare at me wide-eyed before glancing away, embarrassed. Some study their phones.

Inside I'm screaming, but nothing comes out of my mouth as sticky Coke drips down my chin and ice slips inside my shirt.

I can't speak.

I can't move.

At my old comp, I'd decked kids who'd chanted: 'In care, nobody cares!' But my years with Jason made me revert back to the mouse I was as a little girl, creeping around the discarded needles on the floor – learning never to make a noise, antagonize or be noticed by Mum whenever she needed a fix. I disappeared into myself and became lost. *Invisible.* It was safer that way, and the same urge to shrink, to disappear from view, has come over me now.

Take a deep breath, Jodie. Pull yourself together. That wasn't Jason. He's still in prison.

He can't find us.

I look down at my sodden uniform and up at One-Star Simon. I want him to say something, *do something*, but he's curiously white-faced and shaking as if the drink had struck him instead of me . . .

The customer has been sniggering, looking from me to One-Star Simon, but now – probably infuriated by our lack of reaction – he picks up his lunch and swaggers out. Ed follows him, muttering about calling the police if he visits again, but it's too little too late. The exit of The Worstomer – *I get it now* – breaks the moment, and everyone starts moving again.

'Oh dear, you poor thing. Let's get you cleaned up.' Pam dabs at me with serviettes. 'I'm so sorry this has happened – on your first day too. You only get one uniform, so we'll have to dry you off in the crew room.'

I nod, numbly. Everyone carries on as if nothing has happened. Carlos continues flipping burgers, Marta smiles and serves the next customer, a young man leaves the restaurant and a mum and her two kids enter. Life continues for everyone except me. And One-Star Simon. He remains rooted to the spot, trembling violently.

'Simon?' Pam says, glancing up. 'Are you OK? You should get back to work before Ed notices you've burnt the fries again.'

He sways on his feet, eyes fixed on the floor.

'Did you hear me, love?' She tries to steer him away, but he doesn't move.

He's a tall guy – not solid like the customer, but gangly and thin like that sad, tatty scarecrow I saw as a kid when the care workers took us on holiday to Norfolk. It was the first time I'd ever visited the countryside and I'd cried when I saw the scarecrow – it had been left forgotten and flapping in the cold, empty field as birds slowly pecked away at its stuffing.

Pam has to push One-Star Simon quite hard to get him to the fry station.

'No idea what's up with him.' She shakes her head as she returns. 'He lives in a different world from the rest of us.'

As she leads me to the crew room, I instinctively touch the tattoo that stretches from my wrist up my arm: a flock of birds soaring into the air, escaping from the dangers on the ground below. It seemed fitting at the time and it partially hides the scar, the one that's visible to most people.

I wonder if One-Star Simon has his own scars that no one else can see.

I recognize his paralysis in the face of an ugly confrontation – not daring to show distress because it will only make the outcome worse. I have a hunch we have something in common: I think he knows exactly what it feels like to be deliberately broken into tiny fragments by someone else.

Maybe my strange co-worker is secretly trying to figure out how to put all the pieces back together too.

7

SIMON

WILLIAM WAS RIGHT *AGAIN*: I have no one else to talk to after a bad day. That's one of the main problems of being single and friendless; he's my sole confidant, apart from Archie, who can only tell me he loves me with slow, lingering blinks. After joking about us speaking two days in a row, I recount the incident with The Worstomer – just talking about it makes it feel like a smaller part of the day. And . . . part of me wants to see if the encounter jogs William's memory too, if it makes him think about our early childhood ahead of the looming festive season. Perhaps if I can get through to him today, we might find our way back to each other in a pre-Yuletide miracle.

'I didn't do anything to help.' I sink into the comfortable armchair I use whenever I revisit my Memory Palace. 'I should have comforted Jodie, the way . . .' I stall, take a breath, 'the way you used to comfort me.'

When we were younger William was far quicker to pick up new concepts than me and could concentrate for longer, thus escaping much of Father's censure. I remember his small arm around my waist after Father had told me off for not achieving a hundred per cent in my maths test. I felt the warmth of his hug after being released from my locked bedroom for failing to accurately recite a long list of history dates. He placed towels around my shoulders after all those cold showers designed to improve my focus.

'You knew the right things to say to make me feel better whenever I was punished.'

'Not *always*,' he says quietly. 'I wasn't a miracle worker.'

'But when you did, it worked. I wish I'd told Jodie that things will get better.'

'Will they?' William sighs.

He's exhausted after performing a particularly tricky six-hour craniotomy on a seventy-two-year-old diabetic female with a heart complaint. I know the Prince Burger drama is the last thing he wants to hear when he's 'resting' after a stressful shift; Victoria had to cajole him into speaking to me.

'Probably not. She'll get used to people treating her like dirt. She'll learn to let her mind drift away and imagine herself in a place far away, the way I do. Eventually, she'll end up feeling nothing.' I pause, placing a cushion behind my back. 'I should have told her it's amazing how much the body can withstand if it's been subjugated for long enough. It's always the soul that's destroyed first, never the flesh, don't you think?'

'Ha! Thank God you *didn't* comfort her. That little motivational speech wouldn't exactly have cheered her up. Pushed her over the edge, more like.'

'My people skills need some work, apparently.'

William chuckles dryly. 'Anyway, realistically, what could you have done? By the sounds of it, the customer's built like a brick shithouse and you, on the other hand, have the physique of a rubber band.'

'Thanks.'

'What I'm trying to say is that it would hardly have been a fair fight. He'd have knocked you out flat had you tried to intervene on her behalf.'

'But at least I'd have stood up to him. The guy's a psycho. He does this every week – he enjoys the confrontation. Today, he deliberately bought two drinks so he could throw one, and still have a Coke Zero with his burger; he didn't want his violence to interfere with his meal. It's the kind of thing Ted Bundy would have done before he went on a murder spree.'

'The world is full of terrible people who manage to get away with murder,' William replies quietly. 'Not *all* of them are locked up in prison.'

I gasp, unable to speak.

His words float around the ether like dust motes trapped in an air current, circling and spinning out of control, but never allowed to rest.

He breaks the painful silence first.

'Sorry, I didn't mean . . . Honestly, that just slipped out. It was an accident.'

I knead my eyes with my knuckles. It's always *an accident* with William, like the time he sliced open my wrist because he wanted to study the skin cells beneath the surface. He claims he didn't mean to cut so deeply. I still have the scar, which curls up my skin in an ugly, competitive smile – a permanent reminder of our apparently unbreakable sibling bonds.

'I'm sorry, but I honestly wasn't referring to . . .' He pauses. 'You know I love and support you one hundred per cent.'

I bite my lip, until I can taste blood. How did we get here?

Once so close, now trying to communicate across an unspeakable chasm.

'Stop reading bad thoughts into everything I say! You always look for hidden meanings in my words, Simon. It's like you wilfully *want* to misunderstand me.'

'So, this is my fault again? I'm the villain?'

'No one is the villain, but you *are* being oversensitive.'

I wipe my lips, staring at the red stain on my fingers.

'I know it's hard.' His voice softens. 'But neither of us can change the past, however much we might want to. You have to stop beating yourself up and try to finally put it behind you. Accept what happened and move on, the way I have.'

A heavy weight presses on my chest. It's easy for him to say – he never takes responsibility for anything, whereas I carry this pain around with me at all times, an unwelcome passenger, which I know I deserve.

'You know it's not healthy to start obsessing about things, like you did with Mother,' he says abruptly. 'I don't want you to go back to—'

'I'm not!'

'That's good because Father always said—'

'Please don't!'

I don't want to think about Father tonight.

'Someone's at the front door! I think it's my Amazon delivery. I have to go, sorry.'

'Really? Another one?'

'Bye, William.'

I cut him off. Talking to him was a mistake. Our relationship reminds me of Father's old model railway – a locomotive going round a track. It loops to the beginning and repeats the same mistakes over and over again. We never move forward to a new destination.

I need to put the conversation – the week so far – out of my head. After memorizing and recalling in order a single deck of cards in two minutes forty seconds, according to my stopwatch, I close my eyes and commence a tour of my Memory Palace. I warm up my brain by dipping in and out of rooms containing subject matter on the Iranian Revolution, the complete works of Charles Dickens and Quantum Theory. It's tempting to revisit my favourite floor, which contains prime number theories, but I have to prepare for tomorrow night's general knowledge contest. I study the contents of the room, which houses statistical geography, before performing a tour of European history from 1400 to 1900. After memorizing thirty-three new pieces of data and consolidating fifty-two facts and figures, I'm ready to move on.

But the conversation with William nips at my concentration. I find myself in a closed-off area of my Memory Palace that I usually try to avoid.

There's a panelled door licked with sharp, white paint.

Number thirty-six.

Inside is a poorly executed imitation of a John Nash oil painting and a charcoal drawing of a clown on the wall. I hear the faintly threatening clickety-clack of Father's Midland Pullman locomotive making yet another lap around the track laid out on the floor.

A shameful hotness crawls across my cheeks; pain gnaws deeper and deeper into my chest until I'm left gasping for breath.

I never enter this room. I'm too afraid.

I daren't even imagine myself touching the handle because I know that if I enter this tiny, cramped chamber, the door will slam behind me.

I won't find my way out again.

8

JODIE

'I'M HERE TO SAVE you all from Kylo Ren! This is a rescue mission – follow me to my starship!' Zak flies through the door of Prince Burger and runs between the tables, swinging his lightsaber at unsuspecting customers. Sandra follows slowly after him, large neon lightning bolts swinging from her ears.

They're a welcome sight. My shift wasn't as bad as yesterday's – no one threw a drink – but I'm knackered. I had to drag Zak to the launderette before school to wash my uniform, which meant getting up even earlier than usual.

He spots me and waves the lightsaber. Maybe he's figured out his new present isn't *so* bad after all. He'd burst into tears on Tuesday night because, apparently, the toy isn't as good as Billy's. Who knew when it only cost £1? Anyway, he seems to be enjoying annoying people with it now.

Dammit. I spot Dog under his armpit: he's tricked Sandra into letting him bring along his favourite toy. He knows he's not allowed to take it outside; he loses *everything*. Dog is the only possession that's survived since he was a baby; we've moved around since he was little and things have been lost along the way. He can't go to sleep without that toy. It's splitting at the seams and falling apart – the way I feel most days – but Zak doesn't care. He loves Dog, whatever he looks like.

Zak searches for something in his tatty backpack before yanking out a piece of paper. Mud has spattered his football kit and freckled nose. I come out from behind the counter to hug him, dirt or no dirt.

'Whoaa!'

He pretends to leap up for a big hug but as I open my arms he falls to the floor, scrabbling around like a crab.

'What *are* you doing?'

'Breakdancing. I learnt how to do it today.'

'Cool.'

He leaps up again, a ball of energy as usual. 'You smell like a bag of fries. I'm going to eat *you* for my tea.'

'Thanks. That's exactly the perfume I picked out for myself this morning – Eau de Prince Burger.'

I wish there were showers here – I'm dreading the bus journey home in case other passengers can smell the grease. I don't know how the other staff put up with it. I look back at the kitchen. One-Star Simon glances away quickly. If Sandra can keep Zak occupied for ten minutes while he eats his tea, I could lay my cards on the table and ask about Cambridge – it's quiet and One-Star Simon must be off shift soon as we started at about the same time. Carlos isn't lurking around either, after being moved on to the fry station today. He apologized after 'accidentally' splashing me with hot oil when I attempted to collar One-Star Simon earlier, but I swear he deliberately swung the pan in my direction. It's not my fault Ed judged me attractive enough for aliens.

'A bag of fries is a treat. It's not going to be your regular tea, yeah?'

Zak nods, holding up the piece of paper again as I lead him over to Sandra. 'I've been invited to Billy's Star Wars sleepover birthday party. Can I go?'

I hesitate for a fraction of a second. 'I don't think we can make it, sorry.'

'You haven't looked at the date.'

'Yes, well, I know we're busy.'

Classmates' birthday parties mean buying a present; Billy's mum would expect an expensive one. I change the subject and tell Zak off for tricking Sandra into going back for Dog and his lightsaber after football club. After sitting him down, and fetching a cup of tea for Sandra, I dig out the staff meal vouchers from my pocket and make a beeline for One-Star Simon.

'Can I have two large fries, please? My son's here for tea with my friend.' I nod over my shoulder at Zak, who holds up the party invite, scowling.

'Oh. Of course.'

One-Star Simon dumps a load of fries in the bin and begins making a new batch.

'You didn't need to do that. Aren't you about to go off shift?'

'It's no trouble,' he replies gruffly. 'They taste better fresh.'

He's methodical, carefully loading the machine.

'Is this your new boyfriend?' a small voice asks.

A lightsaber jabs at One-Star Simon's bum, making him jump. Zak glares accusingly up at him.

'God, no,' I say, before I can stop myself.

The black cloud lifts from Zak's face and his mouth cracks into a gappy smile. 'Oooh, harsh!'

I feel my cheeks redden.

'I mean, this is One-St— This is . . . Simon. He's someone I work with, that's all. He's clever – he studied maths at Cambridge, a university you could go to when you grow up if you want to.'

One-Star Simon's cheeks are bright red too.

'Sorry, it's nothing personal,' I say hastily. 'He's started asking every man I talk to whether they're my new boyfriend – the newsagent, his teacher, the man on the till in the supermarket. It's become a *thing*.' I frown at Zak. 'You're not allowed back here. Do you want to get me fired?'

He ignores my question and hops from foot to foot, watching curiously as One-Star Simon shakes the basket, making the fat sizzle and spit like a dragon. But unlike Carlos earlier, he shields us from the fryer, careful not to splash either of us.

'Don't worry,' One-Star Simon says. 'Ed's doing paperwork in his office. You could get a Princely Whirl while you wait if you want?' He points at the ice-cream machine. 'Everyone helps themselves when he's not around.'

'Yes, please!' Zak gasps. 'With extra sprinkles!'

I take Zak over to the machine and he makes what must be the biggest, sloppiest, sickliest creation ever, with multiple vividly coloured sauces oozing over the side. He races back as I collect a tray, spoon and serviettes, scattering toppings in his wake as if feeding pigeons in the shopping precinct again. By the time I return, he's quizzing One-Star Simon.

'How clever are you exactly?'

'I know millions of facts. I store them in here.' One-Star Simon taps his head. 'Inside my Memory Palace.'

Zak looks distinctly unimpressed as he licks the sprinkles from his ice cream. 'Must be a small, lame palace. Your head's not much bigger than mine.'

One-Star Simon guffaws. 'My Memory Palace is vast, and

always expanding. That's how I remember things – I make new floors and rooms to store facts.'

'Cool! Like what?'

He steals a look at Zak's team shirt. 'Inside room seventy-five I can find the name of the footballer who kicked the fastest-ever shot.' He closes his eyes and reopens them for dramatic effect. 'It was Ronny Heberson in 2006. The ball travelled at one hundred and thirty-one miles per hour.'

'That's dead fast,' Zak says. 'I love football. Do you play?'

One-Star Simon shakes his head. 'I've never kicked a ball in my life.'

'What, like, as in never ever ever?' Zak gasps.

He turns to the fryers. 'I wasn't allowed to play football when I was a child. Father said it would distract from my studies. After that I got too old to learn.'

'Your dad sounds like a jerk. Like mine. He's in prison.'

'Zak!'

I shake my head at him.

'What?' He glares up at me. 'It's true!'

'Can you sit back down, please?'

Zak ignores me and focuses on One-Star Simon.

'What is twenty-five plus eighty-six times seventy-six?'

He barely misses a beat. 'Eight thousand, four hundred and thirty-six.'

'Wow! That was quick. You're a genius!' Zak's eyebrows have disappeared into his fringe. 'I reckon I could work that out eventually, but it would take me longer and I'd probably have to write down my workings out.'

'You like maths?'

'Yep! There's a right or a wrong answer, not something confusing in between.' Zak chews his lip. 'I love it, but I can't

61

tell anyone that at school or put my hand up in class. I keep quiet even when I know all the answers.'

One-Star Simon frowns. 'Why?'

'The other kids would call me a geek and a show-off.' He looks at his feet. 'They think maths sucks.'

'Your teacher said at parents' evening you always put your hand up in maths class,' I point out.

Zak kicks his lightsaber, trying to pick it up before it drops. 'Yeah, well. Now I don't.'

Before I can challenge him, One-Star Simon leaps in.

'I never put my hand up at school either but I was still called a swot . . . among other things. But that's because I was top of every subject at my primary and high school and won so many trophies and certificates in my spare time. Father insisted that my head teacher presented them to me in assemblies.'

Zak nods thoughtfully, leaning on the lightsaber. 'You sound like a mega swot. Did the other kids do mean stuff like trip you up and kick your shins?'

I could swear One-Star Simon's bottom lip trembles.

'There's nothing wrong with working hard and winning things,' I say quickly. 'It's far better to be a swot at school than end up . . .'

I swallow the end of my sentence. I was about to add: *working here*.

'End up with no qualifications,' I finish.

'I know, I know. I need to *do well at school* and *go to university*.'

Zak rolls his eyes – he's heard me say this millions, if not trillions, of times. I've been drilling it into him since birth, so he doesn't screw up his education, the way I did.

He turns back to One-Star Simon. 'Bet you don't know everything!'

'Try me.'

Zak points at his lightsaber. 'How was the sound of a TIE fighter engine made in Star Wars?'

One-Star Simon closes his eyes and thinks for at least fifteen seconds, before opening them and lining up orders for the counter.

'Hmm. You've got me.'

'Ha! It's a mixture of a car driving on a wet pavement and an elephant bellowing.'

'I didn't know that.'

'Bet you don't feel so clever now!'

'Zak! Don't be rude.'

One-Star Simon stretches out his hand, and Zak shakes it triumphantly.

'Thank you for teaching me something new,' he says, solemnly. 'I won't forget it.'

Zak beams at him. 'Now you know one million and one facts, Mr Mega Swot. You should open another room in your Memory Palace and name it "Zak's The Ultimate Champion".'

I laugh as One-Star Simon puts two packets of golden fries on the tray. I hadn't expected him to be so good with Zak. He can't talk to anyone here without causing offence, but somehow – *miraculously* – the pair of them have hit it off.

He winks at my son. 'Competing against you has been an honour.'

Zak giggles. 'Maybe I'll build a Memory Palace in *my* head. It'll be bigger and better than yours. I could do my Show and Tell about it at school. I can't do it about my lightsaber. It's way too lame.'

He shoots a pointed look at me. I ignore the jibe, so he dips a fry into his ice cream and licks it to annoy me.

'OK, that's gross. Can you give Sandra her fries before they get cold? I need to talk to Simon about something.'

'Are you trying to get rid of me so you can ask him out?'

'For the love of God, no! Now scoot!'

He saunters away, juggling the tray precariously along with the lightsaber tucked beneath his armpit. I don't know where Zak's sudden obsession with my love life, or lack of it, has come from – I haven't dated anyone since leaving Jason. I can't handle another shitty relationship, but I'm not exactly beating off a pack of good-looking, interested men either. Aliens are a different matter, of course.

Ed appears from the back office to help out with clearing trays. I need to speed this up before he comes this way and sees me loitering. Marta said he's looking for someone to work a double shift as Pam's called in sick.

'I wanted to ask you something about Cambridge.'

'What about it?' One-Star Simon says sharply, his shoulders curving inwards.

'I'm after a tutor to help out ahead of the interview and exam. I could pay you for lessons . . . I mean, not much, because I'm broke.' That's the understatement of the year. 'Simon? Did you hear what I said?'

There's a faraway expression in his eyes as if he's shrinking within himself, his uniform swamping his thin frame. He sways, steadying his hands on the counter, reminding me again of that scarecrow stuck in the field.

'Zak's bright,' he says faintly. 'How old is he? It could be too soon to provide an accurate estimation of his IQ levels.'

'What?' I'm thrown off balance by the change in subject. 'He's almost eight.'

'Some might argue your son's on the young side to prepare for

Cambridge, but my father always claimed you should start early. He used to play Mozart symphonies and read Dostoevsky to my mother's pregnant stomach. Studies have shown this can enhance foetal development.'

My jaw drops.

'By Zak's age I'd started an intensive after-school timetable of drilling in mathematics, science and languages. Father also regularly tested me on spelling, spatial awareness, logic, verbal skills, puzzles and made me spend hours memorizing packs of cards and the periodic table.'

'I don't mean Zak! He's a kid. I mean *me*. I want you to tutor *me*.'

'*You* want to go to Cambridge?'

One-Star Simon's eyebrows shoot up as he rocks back on his heels. Anyone would think I'd offered to strip off all my clothes and run naked laps around Prince Burger.

'That's right! I've been invited to an interview at Lucy Cavendish. I've got about four weeks to prepare.'

He continues to stare at me, as my blood pressure rises.

'Well? What do you think?'

'But you work *here*. In a low-skilled, low-paid job. In a fast-food restaurant. In Prince Burger.'

His words come out in sharp staccatos, wounding me with every beat.

'Yeah – and so do you! Anyway, this is temporary until I get my diploma and find something better.'

'Yes, but—'

'My life's ambition isn't working here: it's studying English at Cambridge and becoming a teacher. I want to better myself – and help other kids from my background get the chances I missed out on. But I need to improve my exam technique and try to control my nerves for this interview. I can't get that kind of one-to-one help at college.' I pick at my fingers. 'I'm worried the tutors will catch me out the way Ed did. You told me I should be prepared for all eventualities because you never know what curveballs you might face.'

'Did I say that?'

'Those were your exact words right after you lobbed that brick at me. Well, you were right. I have to be prepared. I don't have a good education, like you or the other students I'll be up against. I need help. *Your* help.'

One-Star Simon closes his eyes, shaking his head. Is that a nervous tic? I plough on even though this feels like a battle I've lost.

'I thought we could meet before or after work every day? Or maybe every other day?'

Silence stretches between us.

'Twice a week?' I'm getting desperate. 'Perhaps once—'

One-Star Simon leans on the counter, winded, as if I've punched him in the stomach. His face is grey, making his cheeks appear even more hollowed.

'Are you feeling OK? You look awful.'

I fetch him a cup of water and notice a pad of Post-its next to the fryers, which is an odd place to find them. Quickly, I dig out a pen from my pocket and scribble down my mobile phone number.

'At least think about it,' I say, passing him the scrap of paper, along with the cup. 'Please.'

He takes a swig of water. 'Look, I can't possibly help. You wouldn't understand. Working here . . . my research and quiz participation . . . my equilateral triangle can't take more strain.'

'Simon . . . what triangle are you talking about?'

We both jump as a kid drops her tray of food out in the

restaurant. Ed snaps into action, launching a military-style clean-up operation. He leads the small, teary girl over to the kitchen, promising a complimentary ice cream and a fresh order. After I've helped make a Princely Whirl, I turn back to try again, but One-Star Simon has disappeared.

His apron dangles precariously from the edge of the counter, about to fall.

'Can I have pocket money?'

We're walking to the bus stop after saying goodbye to Sandra. She's meeting up with the friends she goes swimming with each week.

'My classmates get dosh and they don't even have to do any chores. It's not fair.'

'We'll see.'

'Is that a "We'll see, yes" or a "We'll see, no"?'

I sigh and don't reply. It's definitely a 'We'll see if my numbers ever come up on the lottery scratch cards.'

My phone vibrates. 'Hold on.'

Could this be One-Star Simon? My heartbeat quickens. He *did* take the Post-it with my number before he scarpered. Maybe I'm in luck for once; he's had second thoughts. I fish out the mobile from my bag and open the message.

I want to see my son.

Six words. That's all it takes to paralyse me.

I hear Zak asking why we've stopped walking and the rumble of cars and feel people brush past.

'What's wrong? You're shaking.'

I take a deep breath. 'Nothing. Let's go. The bus will be here soon.'

'Do we need to *make it snappy*?' Zak tugs at my sleeve. 'Mummy?'

I nod numbly. As we reach the stop, a double-decker pulls up.

'So, about pocket money . . . Can I have five pounds a week? Also, can we check the calendar when we get home to see if I can go to Billy's birthday party?'

Zak's words wash over me as I follow him up to the top deck, clinging onto the rail, trying to remember how to put one foot in front of the other. If I fall, I'll never be able to get back up.

Everything is pushed from my mind apart from these two questions:

How did Jason find me?

And what the hell am I going to do?

9

SIMON

'ARE THERE ANY SECRET geniuses amongst us tonight?' Quizmaster Philip bellows into his microphone. 'Don't be shy! We'll flush you out! There's no hiding place in here. I'm going to find you!'

I keep my head down as I walk into The Rising Sun. I cannot admit I'm a member of Mensa and a former star of *Little Einsteins* due to the unwanted attention I could receive. The TV show has had a recent resurgence; the reruns have gone on to a streaming service and weirdly become a cult favourite, according to newspaper articles. It's now being rebooted in the New Year with a famous actor as its host.

I quickly buy a pint and settle into my usual seat, on the outskirts of the quiz participation. Conducting a last-minute tour of my Memory Palace should be my priority, but my mind wanders back to Jodie. My colleague is clearly far brighter than I first thought and enthusiastic about learning. Yet, how can I possibly fit her in? I have no spare time in my schedule. My equilateral triangle of work, study and quiz preparation is being twisted into painful contortions that could snap one of its sides, like a bone that has a fault line after previously being wrenched and fractured.

Plus, I don't want to revisit my time at Cambridge. It is another door in my Memory Palace that must remain tightly shut.

I straighten the blue-and-purple-striped waistcoat I wear for competitions as Philip runs through his usual series of weary jokes.

'Get on with it!' a member of the audience shouts.

I concur. Competitions are serious. They do not require amateur dramatics.

'Fine, fine,' Philip says, laughing. 'Don't expect me to take it easy on you lot tonight. I'm warning you, it's going to be tough. Let's play!'

Cheers ripple from the crowd as I pick up my freshly sharpened pencil – I bring my own each week, along with my lucky pad. I twist the pencil around my fingers three times for luck and repeat our family motto: *Bright sparks create fires.*

Philip has a very different idea of 'tough' questions to me. Tough is unsolved maths problems such as P versus NP, the Hodge conjecture and, of course, the Riemann Hypothesis. It doesn't involve citing the third sign of the Zodiac to be associated with water other than Pisces and Cancer (Scorpio, obviously). Likewise, the Manhattan Project refers to the development of the atomic bomb and light travels at 186,282 miles per second. My mind is ticking over nicely.

By this halfway stage of the quiz – the comfort break – I like to imagine my neurons as glittering lights. I dim them to save energy as I replenish my pint at the bar and study my rivals to prevent myself from dwelling on Jodie and Zak. The greatest competition, as usual, comes from tables five and six. In ninety-five per cent of the quizzes here, they are the highest scorers, according to my spreadsheet at home. Both groups are obviously well educated, with at least half a century separating each.

Team Victorem, on table six, are in their mid-twenties and come straight from work – probably the City – in sharp suits, and order bottles of Prosecco and Pinot Grigio. They wear a uniform of sorts – the women have glossy blonde hair, perfect white teeth and wear huge rocks on their engagement fingers. The men have silk ties that denote their old schools of Eton, Harrow, Marlborough and Rugby. I became familiar with their colours and stripes at Cambridge, the secret codes of acceptance that allow you to join friendship groups or remain forever banished into the social wilderness, where I resided for three long years.

Table five interests me the most. Their quiz name is the Three Wise Men. They sport a fine collection of nostril and ear hair between them and come equipped with pencils, as I do. They appear to be aged seventy-five and above and, like myself, are smartly dressed in shirts and waistcoats – but unlike the people on table six, their ties do not represent old boys' clubs. To judge from the breadth of their knowledge, I'm guessing they attended redbrick universities and their former careers spanned sport, engineering and the arts. Interestingly, this team has the smallest number of members in the contest, which suggests this pursuit may not be purely academic. The rollover jackpot has reached £1,600 tonight. The pensioners' motives could be financial – they would only have to split potential winnings three ways, instead of six and above, like the others.

They sit quietly, studying the half-empty pint glasses on their table, gathering their thoughts before the second round, which I respect. William and I learnt early on that conversing mid-competition disrupts concentration levels and reduces optimum performance. Some competitors know this and will deliberately engage rivals in conversation in a bid to undermine them, using a technique that is colloquially known in our business as 'fucking with other people's heads'. Members of Victorem have cottoned on to this tactic and are currently taunting the performance of another, less successful, team sitting opposite them.

The leader of table five suddenly fixes me with a stare that is more direct and soul-searching than any stage spotlight I have faced throughout my competitive career. I blink first and look away – mind games have always been William's forte, not mine.

The second half of the quiz includes the categories of sport, food and drink and television soaps, which are my least favourite general knowledge topics. Visits to these rooms inside my Memory Palace are purely perfunctory, enabling me to jot down my answers without hesitation. As soon as Philip has finished reading out the answers for both rounds, I make a note of the final total, tear out the paper from the pad and place it face down on my table. The teams have also marked their own duplicate answer sheets, with the top copies collected by the bartender.

I am an active participant in these quizzes each week, but remain a neutral observer from here onwards. That's why I sit at a table on the outskirts of the Venn diagram I imagine inside my head when I gaze at the pub's interior. Philip stands in the centre, with eight to ten participating tables in the overlapping circles around him.

A particular quiz rule prohibits me from paying the entry fee, sitting within the Venn diagram and competing for the jackpot:

The answer on Philip's master sheet is the correct answer – even if it is wrong!

How can a wrong answer be judged right? How can a right answer be marked down? It's ludicrous. Philip threatened to have me thrown out of the pub one evening after I'd vociferously challenged him over his assertion that what makes us human is our DNA. I'd pointed out that the human genome is ninety-nine per cent identical to a chimpanzee's and fifty per cent to a banana. He wouldn't listen to the other factors I wanted to cite. The unfairness, *the unjustness*, of his judgement still makes my blood boil. Something is either right or wrong. It can't be a mixture of the two.

The team captains shout out their results and, as expected, the Three Wise Men officially achieve the top score tonight with 42 out of 50, which earns them a round of applause. Philip checks their answer sheet and confirms their claim. Team Victorem is in second place with a score of 41.

'Bravo,' Philip booms into the microphone. 'There's life in the old dears yet.' He winks at table five. All three men flick their middle fingers up at him in perfect synchronization. 'Now, now, I'm only joking,' Philip says, mugging at the audience. 'So, what would you gentlemen like to do? Take the cash or gamble?'

Conversation at the bar lulls, people pause mid-pint. The room takes a collective breath and waits for the answer. The winning team can collect half of tonight's entry fees and a £30 bar tab, or gamble and receive a tough sudden-death question. If they answer correctly, they get the entry money plus the jackpot. But if they get the answer wrong, all the cash goes into the bonus jackpot and the team will receive only the bar tab. For weeks, the winners have gambled, leading to tonight's substantial prize, which is attracting participants from across London.

'Gamble, gamble, gamble!' the crowd shouts.

I feel a trickle of sweat drip down my back as the team leader leans heavily on his stick, finally making it to his feet.

'We wish to gamble, sir!'

The crowd hoots and cheers. Drinkers bang their glasses on the bar in appreciation, the noise drilling malicious little holes into my temples. I straighten in my seat, smoothing my waistcoat to calm myself. I remember that walk across the *Little Einsteins* stage; it took forever to reach the microphone. I felt the weight of the audience's eyes upon me, my father's fault-finding gaze and silent instructions:

Don't mess this up.

'Sudden death' is an inaccurate description of this process. It was always a long and agonizing torture, from the moment the question was read out and way beyond the uttering of the answer. The awful ramifications of a wrong reply could last for days, weeks – a lifetime, even.

My heart pounds against my ribcage; my throat is dry but I do not have time to replenish my drink a third time. The overhead light blinds me, burning my eyeballs. Alcohol swills around my empty stomach, which churns like an unseaworthy boat.

I can do this.

'Here goes,' Philip says, picking up a card. 'No help from the audience, please. For the £1,600 jackpot, can you tell me the length of the Hundred Years' War?'

Philip pretends to drumroll as the man bends down and confers with his teammates, but I'm silently reeling off the answer.

One hundred and sixteen years from 1337 until 1453.

I imagine the deafening applause, which will make my ears

ring for days afterwards. But everything happens in slow motion, the way it always does.

The team captain straightens up and adjusts his tie. 'One hundred and fifteen years,' he says, confidently.

Everyone is frozen in time. *Waiting.* No one apart from the quizmaster and myself appears to realize that the answer is wrong.

'I'm afraid that is incorrect,' Philip says. 'The right answer is one hundred and sixteen years.'

'Buggeration!' the team leader says loudly, sitting down.

Groans ripple across much of the room. The man's teammates shake their heads with disappointment while members of Team Victorem make loud, celebratory whoops. They'll be back next week. The Three Wise Men huddle together, conferring about their loss. I pick up the pencil and tuck it into my jacket pocket. I neatly fold up my piece of paper listing all fifty correct answers and leave it next to my empty glass.

After visiting the bathroom to splash water on my clammy forehead and wrists, I battle through the drinkers to reach the exit. Before I reach the door, I'm almost tripped up by a walking stick between my ankles.

'Hold on there, young man,' a deep, cracked voice says.

I take in the steely blue eyes, white hair and formal dress. It's one of the Three Wise Men.

'I'm Arthur,' he says, reaching out a gnarled, veiny hand.

I suppress a shudder as I shake it; Father used to have pronounced veins, which snaked up his hands and arms like bulging, well-fed serpents.

'The barman told us your name. You're Simon and you never miss a quiz night.'

I attempt to wrestle my hand away, but he has a surprisingly firm grip. His eyes narrow and he leans closer.

'We've been watching you for weeks and know your secret.'

He waves his walking stick in the direction of his team members. They raise their glasses, as if they're confirming Arthur's story, even though they are out of earshot and cannot possibly hear.

My heart is racing. I want to run away, but if I do I'll never return for fear of being ambushed again.

'Is that so?'

'Yes, indeed.' He pushes large, black glasses up his bulbous nose.

Patience is a particular prowess of mine so I wait him out until he clears his throat.

'You're bloody good at quizzes, aren't you, eh?'

I let out the breath I've been holding and shrug noncommittally.

'Each week you fill in your own sheet of answers and leave it behind,' he says, leaning on his stick, 'and do you know what happens next?'

I freeze.

Don't blink. Don't swallow.

'Me, Winston and Trevor collect your papers and have a good look at them. Each week you get the answers one hundred per cent right. That's your secret: you're a bloody genius and no one here knows it apart from us!'

I'm speechless. I have massively underestimated the wiliness of the Three Wise Men. I've been watching them for weeks, but had no idea *they* were spying on *me*. I should have taken far greater care and thrown away evidence of my quiz participation.

'You never compete even though you could win each week. Is that because you don't get on with the quizmaster? Or is there another reason? We're curious.'

No words are better than the wrong ones.

'You're a private man who likes to keep himself to himself,' he continues. 'We respect that. But we have a proposition for you.'

I stare at him, my brow furrowing. 'A proposition?'

'We always bloody well fail at the final hurdle. The sudden-death question fells us every time.'

I do *not* like where this conversation is heading.

'I should be going—' I start to say.

'We're inviting you to join our team. How do you fancy that?'

My head's spinning as I look for the door.

Arthur points with his stick. 'That's Trevor, with the dodgy comb-over and big gold rings. He's a gobby West Ham fan, but don't let that put you off. He's our wingman in sport. Winston has the red handkerchief in his top pocket – a reminder of his lovely Tashina, God rest her soul. He's our secret weapon in geography and a good all-rounder from watching TV quizzes. I'm the man for history, but we're weakest in science and maths. That's where you come in.'

He looks at me expectantly, but I don't fill the silence.

'We *know* you never get any of those questions wrong. That would make you a valuable team member. You wouldn't be carrying us, if that's what you're worrying about. We may look old, but we're young at heart – Winston swims all year round at an outdoor pool, Trevor's running a half marathon next year and I play chess and poker to keep my mind active. We're ready to take on those young'uns and beat them in the sudden-death round next week.'

I sigh.

'Well, what do you say?' Arthur persists, nudging my foot with his stick again. 'Can you help us?'

Tap, tap, tap.

Bang, bang, bang.

For the second time today, someone is raining blows on the doors in my Memory Palace that I do not wish to reopen – this time, the room containing details of my participation in *Little Einsteins*. The stress . . . the unrelenting pressure . . . the public humiliation . . . the fear of letting someone down. It's all safely packed away.

Allowing Jodie and the Three Wise Men to mine the vast array of information within my head could open further doors, which must also remain tightly shut.

'No, I'm sorry. Please excuse me.'

I lunge away, vomit rising in my throat.

The heat from Arthur's gaze bores into my back as I flee, managing to make it outside before I throw up. Breathing heavily, I stumble up the road and glance at my reflection in a shop window. Dabbing my mouth with a tissue, I repeat our family motto: *Bright sparks create fires.*

Father had wanted the Sparks to blaze through the world in medicine or mathematics. But he had never meant his adage to be taken literally.

Unfortunately, we had no idea how a single spark could cause such terrible pain and destruction – until it was far too late.

10

JODIE

'**D**OES YOUR BACK HURT?'
Zak's pulled his usual magic trick of appearing behind me while I'm getting changed. I thought he was reading on his side of the bed. He chose a pile of library books this morning – mainly non-fiction about football, cars and animals, along with *Harry Potter*. Quickly, I pull the pyjama top over my head, the cotton brushing the familiar welts on my back. He's too young to remember the gory details, thank God, and I'm not going to enlighten him.

I turn around, producing a wide smile. 'No, of course not.'

'That's good. So can I touch your dragon skin then?'

I wince. I hate it when he calls it that. Sometimes, when he presses me, I claim the scaly scar is a birthmark. When I'm lying in bed worrying about how we'll manage, I imagine the tattoo I'd design to cover my disfigurement if money were no object. But there's no way I can afford it without a big win on the scratchcards.

'Let's have a bedtime story instead. Shall we read *Harry Potter* together?'

Zak sighs and passes me the book as I climb into bed next to him. I've read this novel many times; it's like returning to an old friend. As I begin the familiar story, my mind wanders.

How did Jason get my new phone number?

I changed it after we fled three years ago, but he still has contacts outside prison. He'll have wheedled it out of someone, pretending to be charming. That's how he hooked me in when I was seventeen. I'd met him in the park after bunking off school one afternoon. Jason was five years older and cool. He made me feel special. I thought he was my knight in shining armour – someone to rescue me from my shitty life.

How wrong could I be?

My gaze slides over to my mobile on the bedside table.

'How about you take over reading now? I need to send a quick text.'

'Okey dokey,' Zak says, taking the book.

As he begins a new chapter, I message a neighbour from our old estate.

Have u heard any news about Jason? Can u let me know ASAP?

I stare at my phone, willing Jez to respond as Zak reads on. A few minutes later, my phone vibrates. Heart thumping, I open up his reply.

Will ask around. Hope yr both keeping safe.

Thanx. Pls be careful, I text back.

'Did you hear what I said?' Zak asks belligerently.

'What?' I surreptitiously wipe my sweaty palms on the duvet as I put my phone down.

'Harry has to live with the horrible Dursley family when *both* his mummy and daddy die. He hates it, but there's nowhere else for him to go!'

'Well, he's happy when he gets to Hogwarts because the school becomes like another family to him. Shall I take over again?'

Zak frowns, crossing his arms. 'I don't want any more *Harry Potter*.' He points at the book on my side of the bed. 'Why do you like *that* so much?'

'*Great Expectations*?'

He nods as I pick it up.

'This is the first book Lizzie ever gave me to read, which makes it important. It changed my life, really.'

The memory comes rushing in . . .

I'm sitting behind a bookcase in the library after Mr Chalker humiliated me in English again. I managed to make it here with the laughter of my classmates ringing in my ears before I burst into tears. No way could I let anyone see me cry.

'Are you OK?' a voice asks.

A short woman with greying braids, tied into a bun at the nape of her neck, appears. She's carrying a pile of books. I roughly wipe my wet cheek with the sleeve of my pullover.

'Go away!'

She doesn't move.

'What's wrong?'

I flinch. No one's ever asked me that at school, but if I tell her she'll take Mr Chalker's side the way everyone else does.

'Like you care!'

'I do.'

'Bullshit. No one does!'

'That's not true. Tell me.'

'Fuck off and leave me alone!' I grab a book from the shelf

and throw it in her direction. The novel lands at her feet. Now I'm in more trouble. I stand up, bracing myself to be yelled at and sent to the head teacher's office again.

Slowly, she bends down and picks it up, carefully smoothing the bent cover.

'I never enjoyed The Pickwick Papers *either, but you shouldn't give up on Dickens,' she says. 'Come back and I'll find something else you might prefer to read.'*

'Yeah, right!'

'I mean it.'

My heart beats quicker as she smiles. Is she for real? I don't wait to find out. I flee.

I'm not called to see the head teacher so I go back to the library later that week. I'm sitting behind the bookcase again when Lizzie eventually finds me. My shoulders tense as I wait for her to lecture me about swearing and damaging The Pickwick Papers, *but she doesn't say a word. Instead, she places* Great Expectations *on the floor next to me and walks away. Inside, is a note saying:* 'You won't want to throw this book at me! Have a read and tell me what you think. Love, Lizzie.'

I put my arm around Zak's shoulders, drawing him closer, as I finish my PG version of those first few encounters with Lizzie.

'I couldn't believe how kind she was! No one had ever been interested in what I thought or given me a present before – *Great Expectations* felt like mine, even though I had to return it eventually.'

His forehead crinkles. 'But why's it so good?'

'I guess I could relate to the main character, Pip. He was hard on himself and had lost both his parents, but in a different way to me.'

Zak shudders. 'Not another orphan!'

'I'm afraid so.'

Pip had been forced to rely on a substitute family, whereas my mum was judged unfit to look after me by social services and I'd never met my dad, a drug addict who'd done a runner before I was born.

'Pip wasn't perfect and had made some bad decisions, like me, but he also wanted to improve himself. I read the novel with a torch under the bedclothes. And do you know what I realized?'

'That being an orphan really sucks?'

'No . . . well, yes. That does suck. But I knew that Pip had succeeded. Change *was* possible. After that I borrowed two books a week if I knew there were no group activities in the home that weekend. I couldn't wait to visit different lands, to travel backwards and forwards in time and see new sights.'

I wanted to end up anywhere, as long as I avoided the world I lived in.

'I spent each break and lunch hour in the library talking about books with Lizzie – some lessons too, if I couldn't stand the teacher and didn't see the point in turning up for their classes.'

'Tut, tut,' Zak says. 'You were bad at school.'

'I was *very* naughty because I was unhappy and no one tried to understand me, apart from Lizzie. She persuaded me to sit on a proper chair to read my books instead of hiding at the back of the library. She said I'd earned my place at the table along with everyone else and insisted I could go on to make something of my life.'

I describe another book that Lizzie had lent me – *Mister Pip* by Lloyd Jones. 'Reading *Great Expectations* had changed the life of *that* book's main character, Matilda. She'd faced terrible problems but had gone on to university and become a teacher and an expert on Charles Dickens.' I pause, inhaling deeply. 'When I'd finished it, Lizzie said I should apply to Cambridge to study English, that I could become a teacher, like Matilda. That really lit the fire inside me and made me think about university for the first time ever. No one had mentioned it before.'

'Can I see the photos again?'

He reaches over and grabs my phone, eagerly scrolling through the pictures of the guinea pigs that live in a hutch on the lawn of Lucy Cavendish. Famous feminists or their works inspire the animals' names – fitting for a college that was opened originally for mature female students.

'Emmeline Squeakhurst, Virguinea Woolf, Oreo and Ruth Bader Guineasburg.'

He rolls off the names; he knows them by heart.

'I like Emmeline the best. She's so soft and cuddly.'

I'd taken Zak along to the open day in the summer. He'd run around the grounds and stroked the goats, rabbits and miniature pigs – the college had hired a temporary petting zoo. It's something the tutors also put on before exams to help students relax, apparently.

'I can't wait till we go back again.' He sighs. 'Finally, I'll have pets. I'll feed the guinea pigs with dandelion leaves every morning. I want to spot a black squirrel *and* a muntjac deer.'

Both animals can be sighted in the grounds, a second-year English student told us. Sometimes the college also gets a sparrowhawk and an escapee peacock from St John's. It was at that point Zak declared we had to move there *immediately*. The animals had won him over, but it was the tutors who impressed me most.

They seemed normal and not at all snooty. One of the tutors had been a single mum throughout her degree course. She stressed she was looking for potential and enthusiasm for literature, not a well-trained parrot who could only recite quotes from A-level texts.

As I walked away, I realized I'd found a new family that actually wanted me. I could almost feel Lizzie squeezing my shoulder with encouragement. Later, I thought I spotted her among the people milling around the lawn and my heart leapt. I was about to run over, until I remembered that it was impossible. Lizzie had died of pancreatic cancer months earlier. When I blinked away the tears, I realized it was just another potential mature student. But I'd sensed Lizzie's approval – this was somewhere Zak and I could finally call home, *if* I were lucky enough to get in.

I glance at the stack of past papers I printed off in the library this morning while Zak chose his books. Luck doesn't have anything to do with it. I have to earn my place at the table.

'Is Simon going to help us get to Cambridge?' Zak murmurs, his eyelids drooping.

'I don't think so. He says he's too busy, but I can do it myself, anyway.'

He yawns. 'I like Simon.'

'Really?' *God knows why.*

'Yup. He's cool. Can I see him again soon? I want to test his Memory Palace and beat him a second time. I'll also tell him about the guinea pigs and make him change his mind.'

'We'll see.'

Zak's eyelashes flutter as his lids close. I wait until his breathing becomes heavier before climbing out of bed. I pad over to the table, pulling on my dressing gown and Sandra's fingerless gloves before draping a blanket around my shoulders. I need to prepare for the Cambridge exam. I open the sample test paper from last year.

The following extracts are all linked by the theme or imagery of mothers.

Seriously? My mum wore long-sleeved tops to hide the track marks and pretended I had leukaemia when her comedowns got so bad they'd make her miss work. I remember her sweating and shivering on the sofa as I was taken away by a social worker and two police officers. I shake the image out of my head and focus on the paper. It's a ninety-minute test; students should spend thirty minutes reading and making notes for their essay. The paper cites six pieces of poetry, drama and prose including Helen Dunmore's last poem before her death, 'Hold Out Your Arms', Barbara Kingsolver's *The Poisonwood Bible* and Jamaica Kincaid's 'Girl'.

Students should pick two extracts to compare in detail, for example focusing on imagery, mood, structure and language.

My heart sinks. I haven't read any of these extracts before. The paper says you're not expected to, but I bet the well-educated candidates who sat this exam last year had known them all. They would have recognized the symbolism and probably would have started to make detailed notes by now. Sure, my college tutor, Monica, awarded me distinctions for my latest essays about the similarities between *Macbeth* and *Dr Jekyll* and *Mr Hyde* and the theme of isolation in *Jane Eyre* and *Wide Sargasso Sea*, but I'd spent hours poring over the texts, getting up at 4 a.m. to perfect my arguments. I'm not good under time pressure. Never have been. The thought of sitting an exam at my age makes me wants to hurl.

Which extracts should I pick? How should I compare them?

We're covering study skills at college, but it's my weakest unit and Monica needs to move on to another topic soon; we've got a lot to cover on this course. Back when I sat GCSEs, I fucked up most of them, apart from English and maths, even though I thought I'd prepared. I was knackered after getting hardly any sleep because a nutter kept banging on my door – I'd been moved into a post-sixteen dump after getting too old to stay in the children's home. I'd kept going over my answers and altering them. I flick through the mark scheme. What if I keep changing my mind about which extract to use in this exam? I could end up in band four: '*Struggles to make meaningful comparison and cannot adequately structure a cohesive argument.*'

I breathe in deeply, trying to stay calm. I repeat Lizzie's mantra under my breath: *The world is your book, Jodie. You have to open it, keep reading and find your way to the last page.*

Oh God.

What if I don't know how to answer the questions in the interview either? What are they going to ask me about anyway? It's not like I've achieved anything over the last seven years that could help me win a place. I didn't exactly shine in the Prince Burger interview. My mind drifts back to One-Star Simon. I take a deep breath, clutching the exam papers to my chest.

I'm going to pester him until he agrees to become my personal tutor.

I can't, *I won't*, give up.

II

SIMON

'VICTORIA IS PESTERING ME to get a firm answer from you about Christmas,' William says.

On cue, I hear her muffled voice in the background. '*Say, yes. Please, Simon!*'

'We'll pay for your plane ticket, of course,' he adds hastily.

'I'm not sure—'

'Is this because of our last conversation? I'm really sorry. I honestly hadn't meant to make you feel bad.'

I wince. 'No, it's OK.'

He knows I've never been able to hold a grudge for long.

'It's just that I haven't received next month's rota yet so I don't know if I'm working Christmas Eve and Boxing Day.'

That isn't a lie. Usually, I volunteer for unpopular shifts across public holidays to accrue extra lieu days for quiz preparation. But in all honesty the prospect of a prolonged lecture about 'Moving on from Prince Burger' isn't a particularly attractive proposition after turkey lunch either.

William sighs. 'Well, let me know when you can. We'd both love to see you – the kids too.'

I make a noncommittal humphing noise as he heads upstairs to his study. Maybe I should make more effort, the way he seems to these days, albeit mainly driven by Victoria. I fill him in on Jodie's request for me to help her with Cambridge and the approach from the Three Wise Men – he'll appreciate my sharing, it's an olive branch of sorts.

'Couldn't you help?' he asks, as I make my way to the kitchen.

'Who? Jodie or Arthur's team?'

'Either. Perhaps both?'

There's the squeak of what sounds like a drawer opening and then shuffling as he rifles around, looking for something. He's the expert in multi-tasking.

'I'm guessing you're shaking your head, but have you considered the possibility that you've been hasty in your rejection of those old men and Joanne?'

'Jodie.'

The click of a table light being switched on; more papers rustle. 'Whatever. They all clearly need you. Would it be so bad to say "yes" for once in your life?'

'Bad? It could be a total disaster!'

'You say that . . . but if you think about it, what's the worst that could happen if you tutor Jodie? You're more than qualified for the job and we both know you could do with the company. It could be a godsend.'

I flinch as I study the *Sparks' Family Guidelines for Success* on the fridge.

'You know what could happen.' I open the door and peer at the shelves, slamming it shut without retrieving any sustenance. 'You've seen it all before. We've . . . *I've* lived through it. The memories are too much to bear. I don't think I can go back to those days – not after what happened at *Little Einsteins* and during that Easter holiday before my finals.'

After what you did to me both times.

Those are the words I long to say. I hear William's breath catch even though I've only lined up my weapon. I haven't fired it. Not yet, anyway.

'Let's not talk about any of this when you're so stressed and anxious.'

The silence grows between us once more, in the same way we have allowed resentment to take seed over the years; the strong and durable taproot from a dandelion, which reaches deep into a perfect lawn, ruining it, and resisting all attempts at removal.

'But it could be different this time. You're older and stronger. You've come through so much. You're better equipped to cope than you were as a kid. Remember, you only have to discuss subjects that are relevant to this young woman's application. You don't have to tell her *everything*. The same goes for those old men: stick to the quiz, but don't get bogged down in the past.'

That's easy for you to say!

Protective shutters roll down over the windows of my Memory Palace; ugly, grating metal that disfigures the glorious Victorian building. The structure quivers at the unwanted intrusion. Its security has been rigorously tested over the last few days.

'Impossible,' I whisper. 'It doesn't work that way *and* you know it. A simple crack in my guard causes fissures, which creates large, unfixable cracks. Eventually the whole structure will come tumbling down and all my secrets will come out.'

What happened before my finals ... Mother's death ... Father ...

Silence.

'William? Did you hear what I said?'

'I'm thinking.'

I hold my breath, waiting for the verdict like an accused man in the dock.

'I know you don't want to hear this, but I honestly believe you should just tear down the shutters from your Memory Palace. In fact, knock down the whole bloody thing. It's holding you back. You're using an artificial structure to hide away from the world instead of living in it. You could be making friends and personal connections, the way I do.'

I swallow a sob.

I promise to let Victoria know soon about the Christmas rota and terminate the conversation. My ears buzz and a narrow band tightens across my forehead. I squeeze my eyes tightly shut to prevent tears from forming. The doors containing memories of *Little Einsteins* and Cambridge must be safely secured. But I haven't been quick enough. A series of old images from Magdalene College flash into my head.

I'm standing at my window, watching the braying freshers head out to a club at the end of the Easter term. They wake me with their drunken yells and illicit antics on the lawn on their return. Fellow guests on my candle-lit table at formals snigger among themselves and later become louder and abusive, leading me to flee, my face scorched with hot, salty tears. I can't turn to William – he's making new friends at Jesus College.

I'm alone in the library, behind a pile of books every day; sitting by myself in lectures – there's always space on either side. I'm trudging to my room after supervisions. Apart from the compulsory teaching hours and visits to the cafeteria, I go for days without properly interacting with any fellow students, except for William.

Each week involves the exchange of information with people far older and even cleverer than me – my tutor, Dr Spencer, regularly emails to check up on me or report other people's observations about my habits.

'Someone has spotted you near a college bar. If true, please ensure this does not happen again. You are not allowed entry to any premises serving alcohol.'

Instead of helping me settle in, I feel like I'm constantly being watched.

Dr Spencer asks for my opinion during supervisions. The sound of my voice surprises me each time I answer and after a few months I barely recognize the tone. It's altered, as if I'm metamorphosing into something, someone, completely different.

I've been wrestling with tough calculations in my college room for hours. I reach for my compass and accidentally prick my finger. I hesitate as I see the tiny dot of blood. Instead of bringing the sharp point to the page, I long to draw it along the length of my bare arm.

My eyes fly open, my mouth is horribly dry.

I grab a pack of cards from the table as a distraction from my recollections. After drinking several glasses of water, I sit down at the table and set my stopwatch. I memorize three-quarters of the deck in record time, but am thrown off guard when I unpeel the next card: the king of diamonds. He glares back. I've always hated his judgemental sideways glance, along with his lack of compassion and mercy, turning away in the face of suffering. I stare at the card, rubbing my fingers around the sharp edges. I should have prepared myself for his arrival.

The king of diamonds' presence in my life is inevitable – one I can't ignore however much I want to. I put him aside and continue, despite my stopwatch indicating I have lost precious time. I won't beat any world or personal records tonight. The queen of hearts, the jack of hearts and the jack of diamonds are among the final few cards to reveal themselves. I dutifully place them next to the king of diamonds. That's where they're supposed to belong: the members of a happy family.

Who am I kidding? The battle lines were drawn long ago.

Hearts versus diamonds.

Diamonds versus hearts.

I didn't tell William *everything* about Jodie; he always wants me to himself and has sabotaged any friendship I have ever attempted to strike up with a woman. For years I haven't even tried to establish one. The truth is I feel protective over her. I can't forget the distraught look on her face when The Worstomer attacked. The loving relationship I witnessed between her and Zak in Prince Burger is also engrained in my mind, the bonds between Mother and Son that can never be broken.

I shiver as I turn over the last card – the ace of spades, the highest valued card in a deck. It's also associated with death.

The fine hairs on the back of my neck prickle.

How can I possibly help Jodie – and by default her son – after what happened to *me* at Cambridge?

12

SIMON

A MIRACLE HAS HAPPENED – I'm not sitting alone as usual in the crew room during my break: I'm having a *conversation* with Marta and Carlos about *Game of Thrones*.

'Did you know that George R.R. Martin had a cameo in the original pilot?' I say. 'The scene was never aired. The pilot was axed when the actress playing Daenerys was recast with Emilia Clarke.'

Carlos sighs heavily and Marta stares blankly.

Out of the corner of my eye, I notice Jodie walk in. She ambushed me as I arrived for my shift, offering to swap days or do my cleaning jobs in return for tutoring, and has attempted to return to my workstation twice this morning. Ed had to shoo her back to the counter.

I lock eyes with Marta again. Surely, Jodie won't try to butt in if she sees us deep in discussion? Carlos leans towards Marta, probably to offer his own opinion on castings, but I quickly rack my brains for another interesting fact.

'Did you know that mathematicians used network science to calculate the show's main lead, based on the number of their interactions with other characters?'

'Fascinating.' Marta glances at Carlos. 'What were you saying earlier about meeting up before karaoke night? Should I tell everyone else to come along?'

'No, I was thinking just the two of us, because—'

Jodie is edging closer, so I cut in.

'Mathematically speaking, Tyrion Lannister was the winner.'

'Thanks for the lesson, Prof, but we'd better get back on shift,' Marta says, standing up.

'Are you sure? Don't you have another fifteen minutes?'

She shakes her head and walks over to the coffee machine.

'Thanks a lot, mate!' Carlos snarls.

'What?' I say, bewildered.

He curses me in three different languages, before following her. Where am I going wrong? To help strike up debates, I carry out thorough research into my co-workers' interests:

Marta: Game of Thrones.

Carlos: Arsenal football club and weight training.

Pam: church choir, gardening, cookery.

I have memorized a list of facts on each topic as possible conversation openers to help improve my people skills, and am trying them out sequentially, but my subsequent interactions have been unsuccessful. In Carlos' case, it's probably because I offered an estimate of his IQ level in his first week at Prince Burger and he's held a grudge ever since. In hindsight, I should have left it a few weeks. I watch as Jodie joins my colleagues. Carlos swiftly departs, probably due to residual ill-feelings over her swift counter promotion, but Marta remains, and they chat, apparently effortlessly. Jodie smiles and listens intently to what her colleague has to say. I know they have already bonded; Jodie has secured an elusive after-work drinks invitation from Marta despite having been at Prince Burger less than a week.

Marta exits the crew room as Jodie heads over with two coffees. Quickly, I grab a magazine and open it, pretending to be fascinated by what I'm reading. Hopefully, she'll take the hint and leave me alone. Instead, she peers over at the article before sitting down, pushing a cup towards me on the table.

'Personally, I think it's easier to locate the clitoris when you read "The Mysteries of Masturbation" the right way up,' she says, taking a sip of coffee.

My cheeks burn as I toss my upside-down copy of *Cosmopolitan* onto the table as she manoeuvres to block my escape route. Thankfully, she changes the subject.

'So, that went well – you know, listing all those facts about *Game of Thrones*. Marta must have had a real treat.'

'You overheard our conversation?'

'Was that what you call it?'

'I've never been good with people.'

Jodie's eyebrows shoot up. 'No way! You surprise me.'

I sigh. When I was at school, Mother took me to see an educational psychologist. He concluded I was *socially inept due to isolation and a lack of experience in personal interactions*, a weakness that has continued to adulthood.

'Ed says I need to improve my people skills. I was practising on Marta, but either she must have stopped going to Comic Con dressed as Daenerys or she's unable to engage with multi-layered information due to her moderate to low IQ level.'

Jodie places her cup firmly on the table. 'I'm pretty sure Marta still loves cosplay and she's definitely not thick. Did you know she's training to be a nurse? She's studying part time at university while working here.'

'Really? I had no idea. Well in that case, I don't get it.'

'That's right. You don't get it.' She leans forward in her seat. 'I've been watching you, Simon.'

I flinch. Am I under surveillance here, as well as at The Rising Sun?

'You reel off all these facts, but it doesn't make people want to talk to you. You sound like a show-off and it doesn't impress anyone . . . well, apart from Zak. He thinks you're cool.'

'Really? That's great.'

She fixes me with a look. 'And he's seven years old.'

I wilt slightly.

She continues: 'The problem is you always sound like you're doing a TED talk – a *really* boring one that gets no "likes" on YouTube. It needs to be a two-way conversation where you ask open-ended questions. You listen to the other person and let them speak instead of lecturing them.'

'So . . . you think I should include fewer facts?'

'Exactly! Assume *you* are going to learn something, rather than teaching the other person, and stop obsessing about IQ levels. It makes you look like a dick. Professor Stephen Hawking once said that people who boast about their IQs are total losers.'

My mouth falls open.

'Yeah, surprise, I don't live in a cave. I have heard of Stephen Hawking.'

'It's not that . . . I thought I was being helpful, but that's where I'm going wrong, partially anyway. There must be other reasons that I should identify and work on.'

'You know, I could help you,' she says eagerly. 'How about I teach you how to have a proper conversation – without people wanting to run away or punch you in the face?'

'You'd do that?'

'Sure, in return for you agreeing to prep me for Cambridge.'

I sit back. *Here she goes again.*

'I've explained already . . .'

'Look, this is a win-win for both of us. You get me ready for Cambridge and I'll make you sound like an actual human being instead of a robot.'

'Hmm. I'm incredibly busy.'

'Ditto. I work here, look after Zak on my own and study at college.'

'It sounds like we both have equilateral triangles.'

'I have no idea what your triangle obsession is about, but I could find time to teach you a few useful life skills.'

'*My* itinerary isn't easy to adapt.'

Jodie stifles a snort. 'You have an itinerary?'

'Of course. It's tightly planned, to the last minute.'

'This could stop you from being fired,' she points out.

My cheeks turn bright red again. 'You've heard about that?'

'*Everyone* knows you're on probation – and that's before Ed finds out you're looking after that mangy old cat by the dustbins. It attacks him every time he steps outside. He's threatening disciplinary measures against anyone caught feeding it.'

I open my mouth to protest.

'There's no point denying it – I saw you leave a fish burger and a saucer of water out the back door this morning.'

'What? Are you resorting to spying *and* blackmail now?'

'No! This is me, pleading, *begging*, you to help me. Plus, you'd make a small boy very happy. Zak wants to test your Memory Palace again. He reckons he can beat you a second time.'

'Is this your tactical game? To wear me down until I crumble?'

'You've figured out my cunning master plan! I never give up and I don't take "no" for an answer.'

I raise my eyes to the ceiling. 'I'm beginning to realize that.'

'How about a trial session? If it doesn't work out we can call it a day and I won't pester you again. No more ambushes, I promise.'

Aside from ruthlessly framing her for feeding Archie, this is clearly going to be the only legitimate way to get rid of her.

'OK, I give in. You win this match – the first round, anyway. I should be able to juggle my itinerary if you come over to my flat, saving *my* travel time.'

'Seriously?'

'I'm only agreeing to a single one-hour lesson each. That's all I can commit to.'

'Do you swear?'

'For a quiet life, yes, I'll provide sixty minutes of tutoring in return for a reciprocal people skills session. However, you have to fit into *my* schedule. Also, you must promise not to tell Ed about my personal relationship with Archie.'

'Who's Archie?'

'The cat.'

The corners of Jodie's mouth twitch. 'Sure.'

'I can start at four a.m. tomorrow at my flat in Shepherd's Bush.'

'Are you kidding?' She studies my face. 'Oh shit, you're not joking.'

'I always commence studying at that time. It helps stimulate my brain function and enables me to work on complex mathematical theories. You should instigate an early-morning routine. It could help improve your study skills.'

'Yeah, sometimes I have to when I have a college deadline, but I can't pull Zak out of bed at that time or leave him alone while I go out. I wouldn't even be able to get a bus or train at four a.m.!'

'Well. I *suppose* it's possible to temporarily adapt my itinerary. Perhaps, I could jog over to you as part of my early-morning exercise regime?'

'Oh, I don't think so.'

'I'm not a paedophile – in case you're worried about me being around Zak.'

'Thanks for letting me know,' she says dryly. 'That's put my mind at rest.'

An awkward pause follows, which I'm desperate to fill.

'I like women – not in an objectifying way, but in terms of my . . . sexuality . . . not that I'm that either at the moment. Sexual, I mean. What I am trying to say is that this would be a strictly professional relationship. I'm not a risk to your son and I won't hit on you. Not because you're unattractive because, of course, you *are*. Not just to aliens, but other species too. *Humans*. However, I make it a rule never to mix my professional and personal life. Also, I don't know how to woo women. I don't have much, if any, experience in matters of the heart.'

Jodie's face has turned beetroot in colour and she appears transfixed by a small, white globule on the carpet, which she's nudging with her shoe.

'This chewing gum will be a nightmare to get out.'

I peer at her face. I'm not sure I'm getting through. She appears distracted.

'I thought it was important to tell you that.'

She looks up, frowning, and folds her arms defensively.

'Well, maybe not tell you all of that,' I add quickly. 'But this is virgin, I mean *new*, territory for me. I've never tutored anyone before and I think it's vital to lay out the ground rules from day one. Do you agree?'

'Absolutely! I promise I'll never try to get off with you either.'

'In that case, may I add—'

'No!' she says vehemently. 'Look, can we make the *tutoring* later in the day? You know, at a time when actual human beings are up and public transport runs?'

'OK, what about five p.m. at mine? I'll have had time to do my own work after my early shift. But we'll have to finish at six. I'm heading over to the British Library before it shuts.'

Jodie appears to be working out her schedule in her head.

'Yes, that's doable,' she says finally.

We swap telephone numbers; I've lost the Post-it note with her contact details. I promise to text her later with my address, and remind her to bring past Cambridge papers for us to peruse together.

'I look forward to teaching you everything I know,' I say, shaking her hand firmly.

She smiles back confidently. 'And *I* look forward to re-educating *you*, Simon.'

13

JODIE

'I NEED THE LOO!' ZAK hops from foot to foot, clutching
his crotch with one hand and his lightsaber and Dog in the
other. We're standing outside One-Star Simon's door; a neighbour
buzzed us in and we've pelted up the stairs to the third floor, as
the lift was taking too long. It's 5.25. We haven't missed him,
thank God. I can hear him talking loudly to someone. I think
he's on the phone.

I knock, kneading the stitch in my side.

'Simon? It's Jodie!'

There's a scrabbling noise as he fumbles with bolts and a chain.
It's like Fort Knox. Eventually, the door's thrown open and One-
Star Simon appears, frowning and clutching his mobile. Before
he has a chance to lecture me about my crappy time-keeping,
Zak streaks past, dropping Dog, which he's snuck out again.

'I have to wee!' he hollers.

'The bathroom's not down there!' One-Star Simon roars. 'It's
the other way!'

'Charge!' Zak zooms off, with his lightsaber outstretched.

'You're twenty-five minutes late,' he says stiffly, turning to me as I scoop up Dog. 'I was specific about the time slot I had available. I must finish at six otherwise I won't be able to study the book I've ordered at the British Library.'

'I know. I'm sorry. Ed made me work over because Pam called in sick again and the bus was late. Then I got delayed at the after-school club. The manager called me in to speak about Zak's artwork.'

Zak had drawn gruesome pictures showing stick figures being ripped apart by a giant serpent. Apparently that wasn't 'acceptable art', whatever the hell that is. He'd also upset a younger kid by talking about death. The snooty cow that runs the club is flagging her concerns with Zak's teacher, which is all I need.

'All I'm hearing are excuses that won't be tolerated at Cambridge,' One-Star Simon replies. 'Tutors will regard tardiness as an indication of an untidy mind and a lack of commitment. That's my first lesson leave plenty of time to get to the interview and test so you're not at a disadvantage, arriving flustered and untidy.'

'Thank you for being so sweet and understanding.'

I scrape away the tendril of hair plastered to my sweaty forehead. Either he didn't hear or the sarcasm was lost on him. I hadn't wanted to tell him the most important reason we were late, which was the long detour I'd taken to and from Zak's school in case one of Jason's mates has been tasked with tracking me down.

The temperature plunges as I step into the hallway.

'Jesus, it's cold in here. Has your heating broken down?'

He shakes his head. 'I purposefully keep it cool to optimize my learning.'

'How can you learn if you're freezing to death?'

One-Star Simon stares at me silently. *Ha!* That's one question he can't answer. Shivering, I pull out the sample papers from my bag. 'I printed off all the old tests I could find on the website. The question is always worded the same, but applied to different themes and texts. It's still a bloody minefield though.'

'Lesson Number Two: don't swear. It'll look terrible if you let slip expletives like that in the interview. You mustn't be overfamiliar or act casually with tutors.'

Before I can thank him for stating the *bleeding obvious*, Zak's voice echoes from further down the hallway.

'Look what I've found in here!'

'Aagh, sorry. Zak's nosy. We don't go to other people's places very often.'

One-Star Simon races after him.

'This room is off limits! You shouldn't be in here!'

I find Zak standing, open-mouthed, in the centre of a death-cold, soulless room. The only furniture is a wardrobe and a double bed, covered in a wafer-thin sheet and blanket. In the corner stands a small, folded-up stepladder, next to a flipchart covered with equations. The shelves are stacked mainly with medals and trophies as well as picture frames and maths books.

'Look, Mummy!' Zak waves his lightsaber. 'Lots of facts!'

I step closer, eyes widening. From a distance, it looked like peeling yellow wallpaper, but these are Post-its with red and green ink scribblings. They're so densely arranged, it's impossible to see the colour of the wallpaper beneath.

'This is cool! Simon has a facts factory!' Zak jabs his lightsaber at the wall. 'This one is about animals. It says there are around thirty thousand rhinos left in the world.'

'Please don't touch my Post-its!' One-Star Simon cries. 'They're precious and need to be kept in order. If one's dislodged, they could bring dozens down.'

Too late.

Zak swipes his lightsaber away, but one of the delicate pieces of paper I was secretly examining flutters off. It lands in my palm, butterfly-like. It lists all the Pulitzer Prize winners from 1925 to 1930. A diagram of polygons and a series of algebraic equations, written in impossibly tiny print, join another Post-it on the carpet.

'Tut, tut. Didn't you hear, Mummy? You're not supposed to touch anything.'

I try to stick the notes back, but they steadfastly refuse to attach. The white patches of exposed wall glisten unhealthily, slick with damp. The wet chilliness beneath my fingertips is all too familiar in our bedsit, but this is One-Star Simon's choice – to keep his flat as cold as a morgue.

'Here, let me fix that.' One-Star Simon grabs the Post-its off me and manages to reattach them on the third attempt. 'My bedroom is private! Neither of you should be in here. I explained in the crew room the need to establish ground rules.'

'Sorry. That's my bad. Zak, come out of here, please.'

He ignores me, making a beeline for the shelves. He's a total magpie, spellbound by the impressive display of glittering gold.

'Did you win *all* of these?' He picks up a medal, examining it carefully in his palm. 'This is *so* cool.'

'Yes, I did.' One-Star Simon's tone softens. 'I began competing when I was a child – even younger than you. If you like that medal, look at these. They're my favourites.'

He points to the top shelf. Zak stands on tiptoes beside him.

'They're amazing,' he breathes.

I move closer to study the framed exam certificates. I do quick calculations from the dates they were awarded – One-Star Simon gained his maths GCSE aged five, computer science GCSE aged seven, a bunch of other GCSEs at thirteen, A-levels including maths and further maths at fourteen. He was a Spelling Bee winner, a *Little Einsteins* finalist, International Geography child photographer of the year, Computing Olympiad bronze medallist, an International Mathematics Olympiad and a Junior Language Challenge finalist, specializing in Zulu. He also has a clutch of 'kindness' certificates from his primary school. He must have hoovered up every award going as a kid. The only honour I ever received was for the highest number of detentions in a single week.

I spot a few trophies engraved with 'QuizSoc' – Cambridge's quiz society – but the awards appear to stop abruptly post-university. Why hasn't he won a single trophy since graduating? He mentioned he competes in quizzes; I'm not sure what kind. Maybe he stores more up-to-date cups and plaques in another room. His only recent accolades are a Prince Burger Employee of the Month certificate from last year and one of Ed's 'hygiene' medals dated three weeks ago, which I'd have dumped straight in the bin.

Family photos are lined up on the fourth shelf. In each photo, from the age of about four upwards, One-Star Simon is standing next to his doppelganger along with – I'm guessing – their mum and dad. I shiver, not only from cold. No one is smiling in any of the pictures, not properly anyway. They remind me of those Victorian family portraits where everyone was told to glare at the camera, treating the lens like an unwelcome intruder into their lives.

'Having a twin must be fun. Did you ever do naughty things like pretend to be each other?' I pick up a photo of One-Star Simon dressed in his black graduation gown, next to his virtually identical brother who is wearing a suit and tie.

One-Star Simon almost loses his balance as he turns around quickly. 'No! Be careful with that picture! The frame is expensive.'

'Oh sorry, sure.'

I've got a similar one from the pound store, but whatever . . . I'm about to put it back when Zak pulls my hand down to have a look.

'Cool! If I had a twin I'd make him do all the stuff I didn't want to do, like sit tests for me. Did people mix you up at school?'

He shakes his head. 'Even though we're twins, William and I have different personalities and interests. It's easy to tell us apart, particularly now. William's heavier than me – he doesn't exercise much due to his shifts.' He points at another photo on the shelf of William with a blonde woman and two cute kids. One-Star Simon is on the outskirts of the group. He's right – the buttons on his brother's blue shirt are straining over his rounded stomach.

'What does he do?' I ask.

'William studied at Yale after Cambridge and is now a neuro-surgeon. He resides in New York with his family. We lead different lives but we're still close. We talk most weeks. Usually. And I sometimes visit. This picture was taken on Gapstow Bridge in Central Park last year. William had taken the day off from surgery to show me the sights with Victoria and the kids.'

I try not to let the shock register on my face. I bite back the questions I'm dying to ask. Why did the brothers' lives take such a dramatic turn after Cambridge? How did one twin land a high-flying job and gorgeous family in America and the other end up alone, working at Prince Burger and living in a mausoleum of facts?

'Your cheeks are red,' Zak helpfully points out. 'You should take off your coat if you're hot.'

'I think I'll keep it on for now.'

Zero chance of overheating in here.

I look closer at the graduation photo in my hands. As in all the other pictures, both boys are frowning at the camera, dark smudges beneath their eyes. One-Star Simon looks sad, maybe even afraid of something. William's expression is harder to read. There's something off about him, but I can't put my finger on what's wrong. Maybe it's because his features are slightly out of focus.

'How old were you both here?' I hold up the picture.

'Seventeen. I'd finished my degree, but William was only halfway through his medicine studies.'

'You look way older.'

One-Star Simon takes the frame off me, repositioning it correctly on the shelf.

'We were studying alongside older students and had to grow up fast, particularly in our third year. You see . . .'

His hand lingers on the picture.

'What is it?'

He takes a deep breath. 'Our parents died in a car crash shortly before my finals. It was—' His voice cracks. 'It was hard for both of us.'

'Oh God. That's awful, sorry.'

I swallow hard as a lump comes to my throat. This must explain, at least partly, why his life took a downward route to Prince Burger: he couldn't cope with his parents' death while William somehow managed to turn his life around and carry on post-Cambridge.

'Why did the car crash?' Zak pipes up, losing interest in the medals. The conversation has touched on a couple of his most asked-about topics: cars and death. 'Was it speeding? Did it hit another car or a tree?'

One-Star Simon's face pales. His hands tremble.

'You can't ask questions like that!' I scold.

'Why shouldn't I ask?' he says huffily. 'You say I should question everything that goes on in the world.' He looks up at One-Star Simon, who is ghostlike, melting away before us. 'Who looked after you and your brother when your parents died? What happened after the funeral?'

'Stop it! That's enough with those kinds of questions.'

'No one looked after us,' One-Star Simon says finally. 'We were all alone in the world.'

'But—' Zak begins.

'I never discuss the death of my parents. It's too painful. I keep those memories locked inside room thirty-six in my Memory Palace.'

Shutters roll down behind One-Star Simon's eyes.

14

Easter 2005

SIMON

'MOTHER!' I shout her name as the fire brigade battles to pull her free from the burning car. A uniformed man emerges from the billowing smoke, carrying her in his arms. Mother's eyes are closed. While her face and body are untouched by the flames, her arms hang limply. The firefighter lays her gently on the ground and checks her pulse before starting resuscitation.

William cries hysterically, 'Save her!'

'How long for the ambulance?' The fireman pushes on her chest again and again.

'Three minutes,' another replies.

'No, no, no, no.'

My fingers claw helplessly at my hair, my face. This was never supposed to happen.

Father staggers towards the firefighters, clutching his chest. 'Is it too late?'

'You need to keep back, sir. We're doing all we can to help your wife.'

'Let him concentrate on Mother!' William yells.

The firefighter puts his mouth to Mother's and blows. Her chest rises obediently and falls. He repeats before touching her neck.

'Still no pulse.'

Breathe, Mother.

I crouch, wrapping my arms around my head. William stays with me; I wish he would step away.

'This is your fault,' he whispers. 'You should never have tried to hurt Father.'

'It was your plan! You told me to do it.'

'I have no idea what you're talking about, Simon. This is all on you.'

I fall forward, small stones stabbing my hands.

The sheer scale of his lie expands before my eyes – a serpent gathering strength before the fatal strike.

Noises merge into one and branch off again, magnifying in volume.

I hear Father telling one of the firefighters about the pains in his chest; he thinks he's having a heart attack.

More sounds: a dull thud and a firefighter calling for help with a second casualty.

Sirens in the distance draw closer.

I try to focus. An ambulance pulls in, followed by a police car. The paramedics run over to Mother and Father.

William backs away as the police officers walk slowly towards us.

15

JODIE

WE'VE MOVED TO THE kitchen to find something for Zak to eat, but One-Star Simon's eyes are still vacant. It's like no one's at home. I dump my bag down along with Zak's lightsaber and Dog. I look around and see a piece of paper tacked on the fridge door: *The Sparks' Family Guidelines for Success.* What the hell? I can't resist taking a closer look. *Wake at 4 a.m., Only cold showers allowed* and *Room temperature to be no more than 15 degrees Celsius.* Who thought up this torture? More to the point, is One-Star Simon obeying the rules? His flat is voluntarily freezing, so that's one ticked off the list. But the guidelines about TV being banned and no friends allowed over have black lines drawn through them.

I peer inside the near-empty fridge and back at the laminated list.

No junk or processed food.

'Erm, you said you'd find a healthy snack for Zak,' I say. I forgot to bring some nibbles in the rush to get here. 'Do you have any ideas?'

I'm hoping to at least find a non-mouldy carrot. There's a carton of milk, a bag of wilted salad and a couple of avocados that have seen better days – nothing that's likely to tempt Zak.

'Simon?'

'Sorry.' He pauses. 'You were saying?'

'I was asking about snacks.'

'Yes, snacks,' he says robotically, but doesn't budge.

'I'm starving!' Zak says accusingly. 'I want my tea!'

'When we get home,' I whisper.

One-Star Simon silently heads to a cupboard and pulls the doors open. He has a few cans of tomatoes, a packet of dried spaghetti and a row of gourmet cat food in a variety of flavours: duck in tomato sauce, salmon fillets and tuna. This feline has sophisticated tastes – and eats far better than One-Star Simon.

'Do you have a pet?' Zak asks, spotting the tins.

'No, unfortunately. This is for Archie – a stray cat I feed at work.'

'You didn't tell me Prince Burger has its own cat!' Zak's mouth parts into a wide smile.

I'd thought it best not to mention the vicious fleabag; he might take Zak's hand off if he attempts to stroke it.

'Well, he's not a pet exactly . . .'

'Not everyone knows about Archie,' One-Star Simon says. 'It's a secret.'

'Cool,' Zak says. 'I'm good at keeping secrets. Can I meet him?'

'Maybe.' I nod towards the cupboard. 'Do you have anything apart from cat food up there?' I ask One-Star Simon.

He pulls up a chair and rummages around on the top shelf.

I'm half expecting him to find 1950s cans of condensed milk and corned beef. Mugs, glasses and bowls are neatly lined up and the surfaces are spotless, but the kitchen smells damp and musty. On the table lies a pack of cards, two pads and pens. Either this is where we're having the lesson or One-Star Simon wants to challenge me to a game of poker.

'Aha. Here you go!' He climbs down from the chair and presents Zak with a dusty bottle.

'Are there sweets inside?' he asks, hopefully, peering into the murky glass.

'Black olives. They're high in vitamin E and contain antioxidants, which help prevent heart disease.'

Zak's mouth drops open.

'Oh, wait. It's past its best.' One-Star Simon frowns as he examines the label on the bottle.

'I know the feeling!' I wink at Zak, hoping he'll understand the joke and not have a hunger-induced meltdown.

He stares back at One-Star Simon, speechless.

'Let me see if I can find something buried in here.' I grab my handbag and have a rummage, triumphantly producing a packet of emergency raisins.

'Da-dah! Mummy performs miracles!'

'Can you pull out a chocolate bar or a bag of crisps?' Zak asks sulkily. 'I prefer *those* kinds of miracles.'

'Sorry.' I ruffle his hair. 'We won't be here for long, I promise.'

'Nineteen minutes to be exact,' One-Star Simon says abruptly. 'The time slot must end at six as planned.'

Shit. We'll get hardly anything done.

'I heard you say *shit* under your breath.' Zak glares up at me. 'Now I've said a bad word, but I can't put anything in the swear jar because I don't get pocket money.'

'Maybe we should introduce a swear jar here,' One-Star Simon suggests.

Zak's face brightens up. 'Good idea! You'll get rich from Mummy. You could buy a house as big as your Memory Palace.'

I have the distinct impression I'm being ganged up on. 'Shall we get started?' I glance down at the pads and pencils. 'Maybe Zak could get set up in the sitting room if we're working in here? Can he watch TV?'

'Yes, of course.'

'Great!' Zak throws a handful of raisins into his mouth. 'Have you got Netflix?'

My heart sinks as we follow One-Star Simon. I can guess the answer.

'I've got something better!' he announces, opening the door.

'No way! You've got a one-hundred-and-ten-inch TV?'

'That was launched by Samsung in 2013. It was given a price tag of one hundred and fifty thousand dollars a year later in the US.'

'Yeah, but where is it?' Zak looks around the room. It's sparser than his bedroom, containing only a table, settee, an uncomfortable-looking armchair and a large, ugly lump of a TV that looks like it belongs in a museum.

'What is *that*?' Zak points to the corner of the room, horrified.

'It's a TV,' One-Star Simon says matter-of-factly.

'Are you sure?' Zak wanders over and peers down the back of it. 'Why's it so thick? Is there another TV inside it?'

'This is a cathode ray television, which was the only kind you could buy in the 1950s.'

'Yeah, but why would you want *this* when you could have a modern one like everyone else and watch Netflix? My friend, Billy, says it's the best thing *ever*.'

'Aleksy, my neighbour, was upgrading his TV and asked if I could take it off his hands; he has mobility problems and couldn't get to the tip. This suffices for my needs. I rarely watch it – only to catch interesting documentaries or the news.'

Zak shakes his head in despair. 'We had a better one than that, didn't we, Mummy?'

I give a tiny shrug. I bought our small flat-screen TV second-hand from a mate after we moved out of the hostel, but it breaks down all the time. It's way beyond my DIY skills to fix it and I can't afford to repair or replace it at the moment, even though it's close to the top of Zak's pestering list – after the sacred cow of pocket money.

'I've recorded a documentary about the rise of the Ottoman Empire on the video cassette player, which you might find interesting,' One-Star Simon says. 'I'm sure you can get it on Netflix too, but I don't need to stream it. I simply press the "record" button on this remote control.'

Zak stifles a giggle. 'Are you sure you can record on that thing?'

One-Star Simon nods. 'Of course! Or if you'd prefer, you could cast your eye over some old eleven-plus test papers from the 1950s?' He picks up a thick brown file from the table.

'Why the *beep* would I want to do that?'

'Zak!'

'You said you enjoy maths. This will give you an idea of the rigour of old grammar-school entrance questions in the post-war period. Didn't you mention something about a Show and Tell? You could talk about the difference between maths in the modern day and the 1950s.'

Zak looks up at me beseechingly, silently begging to be rescued.

'I'll fetch *Harry Potter* from my handbag.'

Zak fixes One-Star Simon with a cool, hard stare. 'Also Dog for company and my lightsaber in case you need protecting.'

'Sure,' I say, laughing, 'but I don't think Darth Vader is planning to attack the rebels tonight.'

I glance across at One-Star Simon whose shoulders are drooping. 'But it was a nice idea, thank you,' I add. 'Very thoughtful.'

'Well, if you change your mind, Zak, give me a shout, and I'll set up the documentary. You won't be able to work this on your own.' He holds up the remote that's the size of a brick. 'It's complicated, with lots of buttons.'

Zak's bottom lips quivers dangerously. I think he's about to burst into tears, but instead he throws himself onto the sofa, howling with laughter.

'Ohmigod, Simon! You're so funny!' He takes a gulp of air in between snorts. 'Everyone knows how to work a remote! I have so much to teach *you!*'

Ten minutes into our 'lesson', One-Star Simon is explaining how to memorize a pack of playing cards. I check my watch. We're wasting time and I've only managed to recall five cards in a row so far. My mind feels creaky and old as if I'm trying to force my way through a freshly painted door that doesn't want to be cracked open.

'Are you sure this is necessary?' I glance at the test papers on the table.

'This is practical – and a necessary first step,' he insists. 'We have to tackle the basics before moving on.'

I don't get it. How is this going to help on assessment day, unless the tutor tries to calm my nerves by suggesting a game of Snap? I swallow my sigh.

'Can you explain it again?'

'Assign a person to each card. Zak could be the jack of hearts. You could associate other family members with cards. For example, your mum becomes the queen of hearts and your dad the king of hearts.'

'I don't think so,' I reply. 'Hearts aren't what spring to mind when I think about my parents.'

Something flickers behind his eyes, a look of painful yearning and regret. I recognize that haunted expression – I've seen it stare back from my own mirror.

One-Star Simon dabs the corner of his eye, as if removing an irritation. 'Well, it doesn't have to be family. You could think of close friends or other people who have made an impression on you for good or bad reasons.'

I flick through the ranks of suits and decide to make Lizzie the queen of hearts, and Sandra the queen of clubs. I divvy up the cards between friends at college, work and from back in the home, but the kings and jacks are harder to fill. The children's home was single sex and Jason didn't let me have male friends. The only men in my life since I left him have been found between the pages of a book – Pip, Atticus Finch, Heathcliff – apart from Zak, of course.

I follow One-Star Simon's suggestion and make Zak the jack of hearts.

Mr Chalker, my English and worst-ever teacher, has to be the king of diamonds. I should turn One-Star Simon into a card, but I can't decide whether he is a jack, or a king, or which suit is best: hearts or diamonds? Spades or clubs? He's been kind to Zak, but he has strange, sharp edges like a decagon. I recognized the shape he'd sketched onto one of the Post-its in his bedroom. I'm still studying the mystery of One-Star Simon when he tries to explain the next step of his memory method.

'Once you've done that, go through the rest of the cards and try to associate them with other people, so the two of spades could be a celebrity you like or a neighbour and so on. After they're all memorized, I'll show you how to recollect them in sequence by associating them with different objects inside a room.'

'It sounds like a really interesting and fun exercise . . . but can we do something more practical first?' I tap the test papers. 'I want to go through some exam questions.'

'Improving your memory will help you in the test. You'll have to recall the definitions of different literary techniques such as pathetic fallacy and metonymy if you're going to spot them in the unseen texts.'

My jaw drops. 'You've read the exam questions?'

'I had a cursory look through all the exemplars on the website last night.'

'You did that . . . For me?'

No way had I expected him to make so much effort.

'I like to be prepared. I have a spare pack of cards you can practise with at home. Sharpening your memory means you'll have something to fall back on in the exam – even if you panic and go blank, you should at least remember the names of a handful of literary techniques to look for in the extracts.'

I'm too stunned to speak. One-Star Simon has taken the trouble to work out a battle plan.

'Jodie?'

I'm about to thank him, when Zak bursts through the door, covered from top to toe in Post-its, waving his lightsaber.

'Guess what I am?' he shouts. 'Guess! Guess!'

One-Star Simon's face turns ashen.

'I'm Obe-Post-it-note-Kenobi!'

I spring to my feet. 'Zak! Stop!'

'This isn't a game!' One-Star Simon's voice sounds strangled.

'Yes, it is! I'm fighting miniature droids!'

'I have ground rules—' he begins. 'I have a system!'

'No, Zak!'

Before I can reach him, he waves his arms and turns like a spinning top, making the notes fly off. He swats them with his lightsaber.

'I destroyed another droid!' he shouts excitedly.

We scurry about, trying to grab the pieces of paper, but the faster we pick them up the quicker Zak turns around. Notes flutter beside him like moths circling a flame.

'Stop!' I shout.

'But this is fun!'

'You have to respect the facts!' One-Star Simon says hoarsely.

Zak lurches from side to side dizzily as the last Post-it drops off his pullover. I grab his arm to steady him.

'Apologize to Simon and put them back!'

Zak turns to One-Star Simon, swaying. His gaze lowers to the floor.

'Sorry, Simon.' He sighs heavily before looking up at me. '*All* the notes?'

'Every single one.'

One-Star Simon is rooted to the spot, staring at the scattered Post-its.

'They have to be in the right place,' he spits out eventually.

'You're no fun, Simon,' Zak sniffs, on the verge of tears. 'Everyone says so.'

'Who's everyone?'

'Mummy.'

Typical. Throw me under the bus, why don't you?

'Life isn't about having fun!' One-Star Simon says loudly.

'Yes, it is!' Zak insists.

'No, it isn't.'

'Why don't we—' I begin.

'Haven't you heard of Darwin's theory about survival of the fittest?' One-Star Simon shouts. 'Life is about knocking out your competitors.'

He catches me flinching. 'It's true! Forget about having fun if you want to get into Cambridge. Father always used to say the world is only interested in winners, not losers. History never remembers the person who came second. It spits them out into obscurity.'

What the hell?

One-Star Simon's chest is heaving; his eyes are dark blue pools of overwhelming sadness again. My mouth opens but I can't find the right words to say.

'Spitting's bad,' Zak whispers, 'and I don't know what obscurity means.'

I put my arm around him. 'I'll explain while we clear up this mess.'

Fifteen minutes later, we've managed to fix the Post-its back onto the bedroom wall.

'Sorry again,' I tell One-Star Simon as he marches us to the front door.

'The damage is done,' he mutters.

'Really? I'm pretty sure we managed to put the notes in the right order.'

'I meant to my Memory Palace.'

He slams the door behind us without another word.

16

November 2004

SIMON

I'M WORKING HARDER THAN ever. Loneliness gnaws at me like lice in rotting wood, burrowing this way and that, finding points of weakness and bedding in deeper. I purchase a guitar as I've always wanted to learn to play; it will help fill the dreadful silences in between studying. I peruse the local newspaper for a music teacher who will take on a mature novice.

'Is that wise?' William asks, after spotting the instrument propped up in the corner of my room.

We've returned from our brisk Saturday afternoon walk along the River Cam behind King's; a weekend ritual we've pledged to keep up despite the mounting pressures of my final year. William has made himself comfortable, lounging on my window seat with his feet on the upholstery. He would never dream of doing that at home or in his own room at Jesus. It's the fourth week of the

Michaelmas term and we have not yet been allowed to see Mother. She's attempted to arrange a clandestine visit. However, Father found out and refused to sanction the reunion, claiming it would prove too much of a distraction.

You will see her at Christmas, which must suffice, he wrote in his letter, stamped with second class on the envelope.

I shrug my shoulders, pretending I'm unconcerned about Father's reaction, but I can't fool William. Father might have previously permitted a violin or a cello as they enhance personal statements for university applications, but guitars are non-educational, he claims, and therefore a waste of time.

'Father will punish you, *when* he finds out.'

On my return from the music shop, I thought I'd caught a glimpse of Father in the crowd and again outside my college, but it was only my mind playing tricks on me.

'Are you hoping he does discover my secret? Because I think you like it when I get into trouble.'

'Don't be daft! That's not true.'

Isn't it? Without fail, it always takes the heat off him.

'Can't I have some fun for once? Isn't that what life's about?'

'Ha! You know what Father will say: "The world is only interested in winners, not losers. History never remembers the people who came second. It spits them out into obscurity."'

'Well, he relaxes with the model railway. Why shouldn't I have an outlet to help me wind down when I need a break from work?'

'Father will point out the educational experience that goes into researching and planning models – the woodworking, engineering and electrical skills.'

'I don't care what he says. I'm doing this.'

'You do care and you know he'll put a stop to it.' William shudders. 'Is it worth the risk? Personally, I wouldn't take the chance.'

Of course, he wouldn't. He never stands up to Father.

We're both experts in predicting the mathematical probability of outcomes. For example, if someone chooses a playing card from a pack without looking, the probability of picking the suit of clubs is 13/52, reducing to 4/52 for picking a ten. The chances of Father reacting well to this situation are far, far lower, as William has no doubt predicted. He stands up, pacing the room.

'Have it your own way, but I know what you're doing. You're disappearing into your head. Take a leaf out of my book and get out and about as well as study hard – I regularly meet up with my friends and attend QuizSoc and Medical Society socials, which help take my mind off things. You can't keep hiding away in your Memory Mansion like this. It isn't healthy.'

'Palace,' I correct. 'It's my Memory Palace. You know that.'

It's true I have no friends and am scaling back on QuizSoc participation due to my heavy workload – something else I must keep from Father. The pressure is less for William – he has another three years of his degree course to complete.

'Whatever. I'll have to make myself scarce when Father finds out about your guitar, because he will. You'll be on your own. I can't keep watching you torture yourself. I won't be here to take the blame or to pick up the pieces afterwards, the way I used to when we were kids.'

I move to his window seat and watch the bursar chasing a tourist off the grass. It's a strict rule in our college: no walking on the green, even though the neatly cropped blades look springy and delightfully welcoming to a sprinter. I long to defy the warning sign and run across the lawn. I'll never stop, not once I've escaped from the confines of the college grounds, the entire city, the country. I'll keep running. I also know this won't happen. I can't leave Mother and William behind.

'How do you bear the pressure to succeed and the loneliness?' I ask quietly. 'Waking up to that feeling of emptiness, nibbling at the pit of your stomach every morning? Father breathing down our necks . . . Don't you ever want to escape?'

'I have no idea what you're talking about,' William replies coldly. 'Remember, I'm not *you*. We're twins but completely different people.'

'I know that!'

'Do you? I feel incredibly fortunate. My tutors are great. I'm on track for a first *and* I've got a great social life. I haven't had to give anything up and I don't intend to. It's all about finding the right balance.' He pauses. 'Don't throw away these opportunities by doing something stupid when you've almost made it. Father will never forgive you – or Mother – if you screw up now. It'll also make things more difficult for *me*, for the rest of my time here.'

I grip the windowsill tightly. One loosened finger and I'll fall down, down, down. Nothing – *no one* – can cushion my fall. Certainly not William. Not even Mother. She'll never dare disobey Father and come to my aid.

William's voice softens. 'Most important of all, I have *you*, Simon. You're all I really need to be happy.'

Is that true? Or is he telling me what he thinks I want to hear?

I suspect I'm simply another pawn in his strategy to come out on top.

William is the master of game theory – playing one person off against another until he gets what he wants. He always concentrates so hard on winning he never stops to question whether the game should be played in the first place.

I return the compliment, but deep down I feel lonelier than ever before.

17

JODIE

'I WISH I'D NEVER PLAYED that dumb game and messed about with Simon's notes!' Zak wails. 'I want Dog!'

He's lying next to me in bed, his pale face streaked with tears. We only discovered his toy was missing after he'd had a wash and changed into his Avengers pyjamas and it was too late to retrace our steps to One-Star Simon's flat. Zak hugs a pillow, trying to swallow the sobs that rack his thin chest. I brush the hair out of his eyes and wipe his bubbling nose, wishing I could absorb his pain into my body, osmosis-like. I'd take it all in a heartbeat.

'Have you rung Simon again?'

'His phone's still switched off. I'll keep trying him, I promise.'

Zak's bottom lip wobbles. 'It's my fault I've lost Dog, isn't it? I've ruined everything because I didn't like you being alone with Simon.'

'That's silly. He's only a work colleague. He's not my boyfriend.'

He takes another large gulp of air. 'Simon will do something bad to Dog to get his own back because I messed up his facts factory.'

I pick up his hand. 'I know I've said a few things about Simon—'

'You say bad stuff *a lot*. Our swear jar's half full because of him.'

'Look, Simon might be many, *many* things, but he's not a monster. Remember how kind he was the first time you met? He made a fresh batch of fries and told you about his Memory Palace. He wouldn't do anything to hurt Dog *if* he's found him.' I squeeze his fingers, which are laced between mine. 'The problem is, I'm not certain we did leave Dog at Simon's. Do you definitely remember picking him up?'

'I'm not sure, but I must have.' Zak's voice rises in panic before crumbling. 'Because if Simon doesn't have Dog, he's gone . . . I might never see him again. I wish . . . Wish I'd listened to you. Hadn't taken Dog outside.' I scoop him into my lap as he wails louder. 'Promise me we'll find Dog?'

I bite my lip. 'I promise I'll do everything I can to help find him.'

'That's not the same thing. Promise me, hand on heart, you'll find Dog and bring him home!'

I clutch him tighter. My childhood was littered with broken promises from people who were supposed to look after me.

We'll take care of you. We won't let anyone hurt you.

I don't want Zak's life to be built on lies too, even if they're told with the best intentions.

'I'm sorry, I can't promise something like that.'

He pushes me away roughly and dives beneath the bedclothes. 'You're rubbish! You can't do anything! *I hate you!*'

*

Zak's cried himself to sleep. I put down the photo of Lizzie I've been gazing at and walk over to the table. My pile of work stares back – a stack of test papers and notes for the college essay Monica has assigned on 'Use of Memory in the Narrative Technique of *David Copperfield* and *Great Expectations*'. I should get on with writing it and memorizing some literary techniques for the Cambridge exam, but I can't concentrate. If only One-Star Simon would turn his phone on – he must have forgotten after leaving the library or maybe he's not used to getting calls. Does anyone ring him apart from his brother and me?

I sit down and pick up his deck of cards, spreading out the suits. I'm struggling to remember which person I've allocated to each card, apart from Lizzie and Sandra. My memory sucks. How can I trust it? In the children's home I clung onto images of Mum pushing me on a swing and brushing my hair. Things would have been different if it hadn't been for the heroin, I'd tell myself while I lay in bed. We all made different excuses for our families. Anyone who contradicted us would be made to regret it. But were those memories of Perfect Mum just in my imagination? My real mum was probably too whacked out to do anything. She promised she would quit her *little bit of h*, but that was a lie; she worshipped drugs far more than she loved me.

My phone buzzes. Sandra's probably messaging about childcare, unless a miracle's happened and One-Star Simon has sensed the 'pick up your phone' vibes I've been throwing out to the universe. I catch my breath as I open the text. It's from Jez, my old neighbour.

Jason's out on licence. BE CAREFUL. Let us know if we can help again.

Adrenaline floods my body. My heart beats wildly. I lurch towards the window, almost cracking my head on the dressing table as my foot gets caught in a tangle of blankets. I peer down to the street. A man's stopped for a fag as he walks his dog. A car drives past, lighting up his face. I don't recognize him. No one sinister is lurking about, but fear gnaws at me. The scarred skin on my back twitches and itches. The birds on my arm take flight.

Run, run, run.

Where to? I have to calm down and think logically. Even if we hid with Sandra for a few days, we'd have to return eventually. I have my job and college and Zak has school. He's settled in his class. If we make ourselves *voluntarily homeless*, God only knows when we'll find another place to live. We could end up on the streets. Zak would be forced to drop out of school. I was always the outsider, never fitting in as I was shunted between foster and children's homes as a kid. How can I inflict that kind of upheaval on him?

I hear Lizzie's voice in my head, telling me to calm down and think things through. I force myself to breathe in and out slowly. I sit down, placing my palms on the table. Jason hasn't found our address; he'd already be here if he had. He's got my new mobile number, *that's all*. He's trying to get a response, even if it's a 'fuck off' before he tries to suck me in again. But he's run out of second, third, fourth and, God help me, however many more chances I gave him since we got together.

I'd stupidly thought it was true love when we first met – I'd regularly run away to his squat in Hackney. Anywhere was better than the supported housing I was dumped in. And when I discovered I was pregnant, keeping Zak had been a no-brainer. Jason's baby was someone else to love – and I knew I'd be loved unconditionally in return – even though it meant giving up on my dream of going to Cambridge. I thought I'd have something else I'd always wanted instead: a family.

And we *were* good after Zak was born, at first, anyway. Jason had moved into the council flat I'd been given. He told me he loved me so much, he wanted me all to himself. He didn't like Lizzie, or my friends, or anyone who tried to keep in contact from the home. He monitored my emails and phone messages and after a while it was easier to stop replying and avoid the confrontations. The violence crept up on me – a push and a slap here and there, before his fists started leaving painful bruises.

I shiver. Perhaps he's after money again. Or maybe he's looking for somewhere to live; jail time means he'll have lost my council flat. He forced me to sign over the tenancy agreement so it was in his name when we lived together. He knew I'd be trapped, with nowhere to go if he took control of the property. Still, I had tried to leave. A women's refuge had offered Zak and me a place.

I jump as I hear a door slam shut further along the corridor.

Bang, bang, bang.

Our neighbour's knocking on the wall again, to complain about the loud music. Jason's turned up the volume as usual so Zak can't hear what's going on behind the closed bedroom door.

I'm lying in a tight ball on the floor.

Jason is kicking me in the stomach, the back – any part of my body that I can't protect with my arms. I'm wheezing and fighting for breath, terrified Zak will come in. I have to protect him from this. He mustn't ever find out what happens in here.

Jason points to the packed holdall bag he's found beneath the bed after searching for a lost dumbbell.

'Try a stunt like this again – or talk to the police – and I'll take Zak abroad. You'll never see him again. Do you understand?'

His foot hovers above my ribs.

'Sorry.'

I brace myself as he flicks his foot, but he pulls it back in time. Now it's inches from my face.

'What did you say?'

'Won't. Happen. Again.'

'That's what I thought.'

Heavy thuds. Thank God. He's leaving the room. The front door slams shut.

A light patter of footsteps follows. Zak appears teary-eyed, clutching Dog.

'Mummy?'

Oh no. I can't move.

'Fell over,' I say, panting.

'Clumsy Mummy. Again.'

He passes me Dog to cuddle before lying down. He curls up next to me, his warm little body moulding into mine.

I push the chair back, tidying my pile of college notes and Cambridge test papers.

I examine the bird tattoo on my arm and feel up my spine, my fingers tracing the edges of the scar.

I glance down. Zak's large brown eyes stare sadly up at me from his pillow.

Before I can speak, he closes them again and rolls onto his side.

*

The following day at Prince Burger, a woman walks into the changing room after my shift. I turn around quickly, not wanting her to see my scar. I pull on my T-shirt and wrestle with my leggings, which are caught in a tight knot. Dammit. I've managed to rip a seam high up; commuters are in for a thrill tonight. I'll be flashing my inner thigh. It's been a crap day – Zak refused to eat breakfast and cried for Dog on the way to school. I called the bus company on my break, but the lost property department doesn't have his toy; the man on the phone suggested I keep trying. I check my watch. One-Star Simon should be finishing up. I haven't had a chance to grab him yet; Ed has been patrolling the counter and kitchen.

I throw on my charity shop designer anorak – Barbour will be delighted, I'm sure, to hear I'm endorsing their brand for the bargain price of £7.50 – and head out the door. I make a beeline for the fry station. Before I can speak, One-Star Simon cuts in.

'I'm sorry the tutoring didn't work out, but you did promise not to pester me.'

'This isn't about tutoring. I was trying to get hold of you all last night and again this morning, but your phone was switched off. Have you found Dog?'

'What?'

'Zak's lost the soft toy he brought round to yours. Have you come across it by any chance?'

'The raggedy thing that looks like it's been stitched together from dirty dishcloths?'

'It's his favourite toy,' I say defensively. 'He hardly ever lets me wash the thing because he can't bear to be parted from it. He loves Dog to death.'

'I haven't seen it, sorry.'

'Dammit. We must have lost it on the way back. Can you

check inside your building when you get home? Maybe Zak dropped it in the stairwell. I haven't had any joy from the bus company yet. I'm going to make posters and stick them up along our route home. Could you put some up in your block if I bring them into work tomorrow?'

'Have you considered buying a new toy? That might be quicker than going to the trouble of making posters.'

I fold my arms. 'You don't get it, do you? Zak loves Dog more than anything in the whole world. You can't replace that affection by buying something different. Love doesn't work like that.'

One-Star Simon shifts uncomfortably from foot to foot. 'Sorry, I had no idea.'

'Didn't you have a favourite toy that you'd have been distraught about losing when you were a kid?'

His shoulders tense as he grips the counter. 'We weren't allowed toys – Father claimed they had no educational value. He kept a large model railway in the double garage but he always said that was different. Designing the tracks and termini was an engineering feat that challenged his brain and improved motor skills due to the small tools required.' He takes a deep breath. 'William and I weren't allowed to play with his trains either in case we damaged them. Only card games were permitted in our house because they improve memory skills and increase competitiveness, both of which are important for success in quiz championships.'

I raise my eyebrows. So his dad's speech about winners and losers wasn't an out-of-character blip.

'Holy shit,' I say slowly. 'This explains a lot.'

'What, exactly?'

'The way you've turned out.'

For once, One-Star Simon doesn't attempt to correct me.

18

SIMON

Zak bursts through the door to Prince Burger and streaks past Jodie. A woman with bright red hair and rainbow earrings trails after him. I recognize Sandra; I cooked fries for her and Zak last week.

'What are you doing here?' Jodie asks loudly.

I notice Zak is wearing his school uniform today, not a football kit. The dark shadows beneath his eyes mirror Jodie's.

'I'm sorry, but he insisted we came!' Sandra calls after him.

'Zak, come back here! Don't bother Simon.'

He runs into the kitchen, waving a paper bag. 'I got you a present to say sorry for last night. Sandra gave me the money. Please can I have Dog back?'

I wipe my hands on my apron and look inside. I pull out a new pack of Post-its as Jodie joins us.

'That's a very useful present, thank you, but I don't have Dog.'

'Oh no! I must have left him on the bus or dropped him on the pavement.' Zak looks up at Jodie. 'Will I ever get him back?'

'Well—' she begins.

Luckily, a similar question has previously featured in a quiz at The Rising Sun. 'Three hundred thousand items turn up every year in Transport for London's lost property office and around one in five make it back to their owners. Some of the most unusual items ever found include a prosthetic leg, a judge's wig and fifteen thousand pounds in cash.'

'What? I only have a one in five chance of finding Dog?' Zak's bottom lip wobbles.

'Well, that's an optimistic figure. The chances are much lower if you dropped your toy on the street as opposed to on public transport. I'd say you have a one in five hundred chance. Maybe one in a thousand.'

'For God's sake, Simon!'

Jodie glares furiously at me as Zak's face crumples and fat tears roll down his cheeks. He throws his arms around her waist and wails loudly.

'Dog's gone forever!'

'Thanks a lot!' she snarls at me above his head.

I watch, mortified, as Sandra gently leads Zak over to the serviette holder. She pulls out a few tissues and dabs at his face, before sitting him down. He slumps over, resting his forehead on the table. His shoulders are racked with sobs.

'I'm sorry. I thought I was being helpful.' I take off my apron and place it on the counter.

'Well, I can do without that type of help,' Jodie hits back. 'You want to learn some people skills? First lesson: develop some bloody empathy. How about you read a book like . . . I know, how about *To Kill a Mockingbird?* In fact, that's a great idea! Check out what Atticus Finch has to say about having sympathy for others.'

I accurately recite the famous quote she's referring to about never really understanding a person until you climb into their skin and walk around in it; it's also been featured in another quiz at The Rising Sun.

'Exactly! So why don't you try considering what it means for a seven-year-old boy to lose something precious to him?' Jodie asks.

I inhale sharply.

'Or try climbing into *my* skin. You don't give a toss about his lost toy, but it breaks my heart to see Zak upset. Yes, big wow! You can recite off by heart what Atticus said to Scout, and I bet you can reel off hundreds of facts about *To Kill a Mockingbird*, but I don't think for a minute you really understand the importance of caring for other people.'

'Look, Jodie—'

A tiny hand squeezes my heart as she storms off.

My mind discovers a long-forgotten room in my Memory Palace.

I'm about Zak's age. Mother has secretly bought soft toys for William and I from a charity shop. She asked for a handwritten receipt that didn't specify the items, enabling her to pretend she's bought birthday cards when Father examines her expenditure as usual at the weekend. The toys – a rabbit and a monkey – join us for Friday supper while Father is away at a conference.

'Can you memorize the exact layout of the dining room table, Simon?' Mother asks. 'It would be nice for us to eat together in here for a change instead of at the breakfast bar.'

I nod confidently. We're not allowed to disturb the locomotives Father is mending at the far side of the table, or his revision documents that are scattered across two-thirds of the space. Once all the information is safely stored in my Memory Palace, Mother clears the trains, test papers and practice worksheets. We set the table for five, with the toys placed on their own mats so they can join in.

Mother's made everyone's favourite dinner: spaghetti bolognaise.

'Let's not talk about exams tonight,' she says. 'How about we pick a super power?'

None of us has ever watched a superhero movie, but I've heard other children talk about them at school.

'I want to fly!' William declares. 'I'll take you and Simon wherever you want to go in the world.'

'I'd like to be invisible,' Mother says. 'I could fade away and disappear whenever I want to.' Her voice drops to a whisper. 'No one would notice I was gone until it was too late.'

She rubs her eyes. She must be tired.

I agree this is a good super power, but opt for teleportation instead. 'But only if I'm allowed to bring you and William along.'

'That sounds like a plan,' Mother says, looking up. Her eyes are shiny. 'I don't want us to be parted.'

'The toys too,' I add hastily. 'They'd be sad if we forgot about them.'

I look around the table, smiling at Mother, William, Rabbit and Monkey – my perfect family.

I blink.

The memory has vanished.

As I look around Prince Burger, I realize that Jodie, Sandra and Zak have too. I can't blame them for wanting to leave. Quickly, I retrieve my coat and salad box from the crew room and go after them.

'Wait!' I shout, running down the street. 'Hold on a minute!'

The group stops further down the pavement. Jodie turns around slowly.

'What is it now? Did you forget to spout another fact about lost bloody property?'

'That's another pound in the swear jar,' Zak says quietly.

I shake my head as I squat down next to him. 'Look, I'm sorry. You have a *much* higher chance of finding your toy than the statistics I quoted.'

His face brightens. 'Your Memory Palace was wrong?'

'My facts are completely out of date.'

'Your Memory Palace sucks sometimes, doesn't it?'

I sigh deeply. 'It certainly does, but I could open a new room, devoted to finding your toy.'

'You'd do that for me?'

'Absolutely! I need all the relevant facts – the exact route home, any stop-offs and the public transport used. I'd suggest we start from the beginning: we thoroughly search my flat, the interior of the main building and immediate exterior before retracing your steps.'

'What?' Jodie asks. 'You're actually taking time out of your busy schedule to help us?'

I sense my equilateral triangle bending under the strain, but I ignore it.

'I've explained the importance of visual memory. Perhaps we can discuss how to adapt this technique to your exam along the way?'

'You're also offering to carry on tutoring me?' she asks faintly. 'After everything that's happened?'

'I've had a most unexpected opening in my schedule.'

Finally home after an intensive two-hour hunt, I kick off my shoes and slump onto the sofa, my feet aching. We had begun here at the flat – scouring the floors and stairwells and moving on to the route approaching the bus stop. This included making enquiries at a pub, where Zak had used the bathroom. Despite our combined forces, we were unsuccessful.

Dog is still missing.

On arrival at our final destination, Jodie's building, I would have welcomed the offer of a cup of tea and perhaps a biscuit, but she didn't invite me in. She was probably still annoyed at my earlier crassness. However, we drew up a plan of action: she will continue to ring the bus company and I will inspect the railings inside and outside my building as people often leave lost property on the staircase.

My stomach rumbles, reminding me I forgot to have lunch. I am at least three hours behind with my studies and must commence work, but I need to eat first. I pull myself to my feet, grabbing a plate and cutlery from the kitchen. I empty out my uneaten salad from the Tupperware box and pour myself a glass of water.

Before settling down, I retrieve my Kindle from the bedside table and download *To Kill a Mockingbird*. Within seconds the text pops up and I read the first paragraph about Atticus' son, Jem, suffering a broken arm. My mind wanders back to Jodie and Zak as I pick at my salad.

Why are you helping us? Jodie had asked, after I had agreed to design and print a missing toy poster and draw up an intensive tutoring schedule over the coming weeks.

Good question.

Fortunately, the arrival of a flurry of texts had distracted her. She'd turned quite pale attempting to read so many at once; at least a dozen. They were from her college tutor, she'd claimed, reminding her about an essay deadline, along with enquiries from a friend who was assisting in the hunt for Dog.

She forgot to repeat the question as Zak had burst into tears when he'd surreptitiously glanced at her phone. The truth is that, like Zak, I know what it's like to cry into a pillow for something I've loved and lost.

Father has discovered our soft toys' hiding place under the bed and confiscated them. He turns up the radio in the kitchen and closes the door while he scolds Mother for breaking the rules. We hear a muffled cry.

'This is your fault,' William says, weeping. 'You shouldn't have pestered Mother for toys. You've got her into trouble again.'

I don't argue with him. I know he's right.

Worse is to come the following day.

When we get home from school, I discover the toys' charred remains at the bottom of the garden. Father had thrown them onto the bonfire, along with the dead leaves he'd raked up from the lawn.

Even a hug from Mother doesn't make me feel better.

'Did it hurt Monkey and Rabbit?' I ask, sobbing. 'Did they feel the flames?'

'No, it was quick,' she whispers. 'They were asleep and didn't feel a thing. They slipped away peacefully.'

'I want my rabbit back! I didn't have him for long enough!'

'Life is short,' she says softly, stroking my hair. 'But you loved him deeply while he was here and that's what counts. Both toys are in a better place, far away from here, where they can't be hurt again. I think they'll be happier where they are now, don't you?'

I nod, choking back sobs. 'Can we join them?'

She holds me tightly. 'Soon, Simon, but not yet.'

19

JODIE

I T'S OUR SECOND OFFICIAL lesson and my phone is vibrating incessantly on the café table, radiating an intense, Chernobyl heat. It could practically light up the National Grid. It's Jason, of course.

Meet up with me. PLEASE!!
I want to see u and Zak. I miss u both.
Am sorry for everything. Am a changed man.
Things will be different this time. Promise.

I believed that way too often over the years. God help me.

'Jodie? Am I getting in the way of something urgent? A life-or-death emergency, perhaps?'

I jump and look up. *Simon* is frowning at me from across the table. I've dropped the insulting prefix; I feel he's earned that respect after he was kind to Zak and agreed to tutor me. Pam claims he has hidden depths – she must be right.

'No, sorry. It's the usual college reminders.' I throw the mobile into my bag. 'The tutors keep tabs on everyone to prevent dropouts otherwise it would look bad for the college.'

'You'll need to make sure your phone is switched off in the interview. Interruptions are rude and unprofessional. I'm sure you know that?'

Maybe Pam was wrong.

'I'm sorry—'

'Are you going to change your mind and get a coffee and something to eat before we get started?'

Simon's good side – *if he has one* – is currently well hidden at lost city of Atlantis-style depths. I take a sip of lukewarm tap water. Sure, I'd like a double espresso and a smoked salmon bagel, but he's picked one of those arty-farty places close to my college that charges £7 for a baguette. I insisted on paying as a thank you for the lesson, but I'm pretending I'm not hungry and am cutting out coffee and tea. It's a good job he doesn't know me better. Caffeine is my drug of choice.

He hands over a six-page document, the paper neatly lined up and stapled together. 'This is a small sample of literary techniques I found during a search of the internet. I also ordered these books on Amazon when I agreed to tutor you. They'll be useful for getting to grips with the vocabulary needed to approach unseen texts.' He passes over Stephen Fry's *The Ode Less Travelled* and John Lennard's *The Poetry Handbook*.

I look at the prices on the back of the books. 'Wow! That's very generous.'

Simon flinches. Oh God. Is he expecting me to repay him? That's almost £30! I could have borrowed them from the library. No way can I afford to pay him back. Cash is tight and I've put aside savings to bid on a Lego Star Wars set on eBay tonight – not the big box that Zak's got his heart set on for Christmas but the smaller and more realistically priced one.

'It's not a problem. I don't expect payment. They're second-hand and I can resell them at a later date.'

I sigh with relief. 'Well, thank you.'

'Why don't you have a look through everything and narrow down the list to fifty literary techniques you want to memorize for your first assignment?'

'Er, fifty?'

'Perhaps you're right.' Simon rubs the side of his face, before taking a sip of his extortionately priced espresso. 'That might not be enough. Shall we push to one hundred?'

'Can we round it down to ten? Unlike you, my memory's crap, plus I'm knackered. I can barely remember what I had for breakfast, let alone fifty words like a tricolon and . . .' I squint at the page. 'Anaphora and polyptoton.'

Will all the other candidates know what these things are?

We haven't covered literary techniques in depth at college. I scan the list with trepidation. Thank God, I know what an iambic pentameter is – at least that's a start.

'Did you practise memorizing your cards last night?'

'I was too tired to do anything after looking for Dog.'

'Tiredness is a state of mind. Barriers will always be in your way. How am I going to make my submission to the Clay Mathematics Institute by the deadline I've set myself on top of work, quizzing and now tutoring? I have juggled my schedule around and am rising an hour earlier to fit in everything. It's going to be difficult, but you'll have to make room in your itinerary.'

I chew my bottom lip.

'You have drawn up an itinerary, based on the suggestions I emailed this morning?'

The time stamp on his lengthy email said 3.15 a.m. Does he seriously expect me to be up at that time?

'I haven't had a chance. I had a bad night with Zak after he finally got to sleep. He wet the bed. I had to go to the launderette first thing and after that I was on the phone to the bus company – they kept me on hold for ages.'

I'm expecting Simon to scold me about making excuses, but he takes another sip of coffee.

'No news?'

'Nope. What about your end?'

'I surveyed the building again to no avail.' He fishes a piece of A3 paper out of his rucksack. 'But I got to work on this. When you approve the design, I will print off one hundred copies and commence distribution at the best strategic points along your route home.'

I stare down at the picture of Dog that I'd texted over. The headline above it is classic Simon:

'Please Assist Us in Locating the Whereabouts of this So-called "Dog" Toy.'

'How about simply, "Lost! Can You Help Find this Toy?"' I suggest. 'And maybe add my mobile number and something about how much Zak is missing Dog?'

'Good idea! But I'll set up a Gmail account for you, to avoid prank calls.'

Wow! He's surprisingly thoughtful.

'Thank you, Simon!'

Ten minutes later, we've sorted the final layout and I've moved on to studying his very long list of literary techniques.

'I was thinking about our first people skills lesson on empathy,' I say, glancing up. 'I thought I could give you suggestions of other books to read when you've finished *To Kill a Mockingbird*. Maybe Yaa Gyasi's *Homegoing* or Téa Obreht's *The Tiger's Wife*? Ooh, I know. How about *Great Expectations*? You could look at Pip's shoddy treatment of his brother-in-law and try putting yourself in Joe's shoes.'

Simon makes a choking noise. '*Great Expectations*?'

'You don't like Dickens?'

He chews his bottom lip. 'Well . . . this particular text brings back unpleasant memories of my competitive history on *Little Einsteins* as a child.' He sighs deeply, resting his chin in his hand. 'I got knocked out of the final after getting *Great Expectations* and *David Copperfield* mixed up.'

'*Little Einsteins*?' I say, frowning. Unlike Sandra, quizzes aren't my thing.

'It was a TV show that tried to find the brainiest child in the country. It's being rebooted early next year.' He shudders, shifting in his seat. 'Different host and kids, of course, but the same old torture.'

'Jesus. It was that bad?'

He struggles to find the words. 'Well, let's just say being watched and judged every week was excruciating. I lost on national TV and became a laughing stock at school.' He touches the centre of his forehead. 'I can still feel the heat of the spotlight right here, burning into my skin.'

His face clouds over as he stares into space.

'I'm sorry,' I say hastily. 'I had no idea. Of course, you don't have to reread *Great Expectations*. I'll suggest something else.'

He blinks away the moisture in his eyes.

'No, it's fine. Dickens might be helpful if he comes up in another quiz.'

'You do realize this exercise isn't about memorizing quotes and facts about Dickens, or Harper Lee? The point is to think about the messages the authors are trying to get across.'

He nods. 'I'm enjoying *To Kill a Mockingbird*, even though literature isn't normally *my thing*. I dislike the slippery vagueness of texts – the lack of a definitive right or wrong answer, as there is in maths. But it's made me think about the importance of standing up to bullies – you know, when Scout shames Mr Cunningham.'

'You've read that far?'

This is a pivotal scene about halfway through the novel when an armed mob arrives at the jail guarded by Atticus to lynch Tom Robinson. Scout recognizes one of the men – Mr Cunningham – among the crowd. She reminds him that she goes to school with his son, Walter. Mr Cunningham is so embarrassed he turns away, taking the mob with him. Bloodshed is avoided.

'I can't put the book down. It's made me think about how words can be more powerful than violence.'

I stare down at my bag. My phone is buzzing like an angry bee, preparing to inflict a fatal sting. My heart hammers in my chest.

'In fiction, maybe, but that's not true in real life.'

'I'm not so sure about that, Jodie.'

'Well, believe me when I say you're wrong.'

A frown line appears between his eyes. 'You clearly love English Literature so you *must* believe in the strength of the written and spoken word.'

'Oh, yeah, of course.' I breathe out slowly. 'But a fist is still more powerful than a sentence.'

'What—?'

My phone vibrates continuously, a call this time not a text. I can't take this any more. I scoop my mobile out of the bag and press 'answer'.

'Leave us both the fuck alone!'

Silence. A woman speaks.

'Miss Brook? Is this a bad time? I'm calling from St Joseph's. It's about Zak.'

'Oh God.' A shameful red flush travels up my throat. 'I'm so sorry! I thought it was someone else. What's wrong? Is Zak OK?'

I stare across the table at Simon, ice travelling through my veins.

'No, Zak is fine, but there's been an incident in the playground. Mr Silva wants a chat before pick-up. Can you come in?'

'Yes, I'm sorry. I mean, of course. I'm on my way.'

'Bad news?' Simon asks, as I hang up.

'Isn't it bloody always?'

He takes a breath.

'If you tell me one more time not to use bad language in my interview, I'll scream.'

He studies me carefully. 'I was going to ask who's upsetting you.'

20

JODIE

I PRESS THE BUTTON ON the gate outside St Joseph's. My heart beats a little faster as I wait to be buzzed in. The railings remind me of standing outside my new primary school after I'd been taken in by my first set of foster parents, Rob and Stella, in Birmingham. I hadn't known how to wash properly because I'd lived in filth for years. I wouldn't let Stella wash my hair. I didn't want to be touched. My classmates avoided me, gagging whenever I came close. I had no friends and I was behind for my age because I'd missed so much school. My teacher eventually forced me to sit on my own at the side of the classroom, making me feel like a leper.

That would never happen at St Joseph's.

The staff here genuinely care about their pupils. Things got better when I went to another primary school in Manchester. I caught up after being given one-to-one help by Njambi, a teaching assistant. I was sad to lose her when I moved on again; I've lost track of how many times I had to switch schools as I was shunted around foster placements and children's homes across the country.

'It's Jodie Brook here, Zak's mum,' I say into the speaker. The door swings open and I go through.

'Don't be mad,' Zak says, as I burst through the doors into reception. He's sitting on one of the red chairs, swinging his legs. I frantically study his little body for injuries.

'What happened?'

'I got into a fight, that's all.' He shrugs his shoulders.

'That's all?' I gasp.

'It's no biggie.'

'Fighting is a biggie!'

The receptionist interrupts, swiping us through into the main building. We walk past the library that has a woefully small number of books; the school is fundraising to stock it properly. She shows us to the seats outside the deputy head's office.

This must be serious.

I curl my hands into balls to stop myself from picking at the skin around my fingers. I regularly used to sit on this 'Row of Shame', waiting to see the head teacher of my old comp – usually sent here by my English teacher, Mr Chalker. He was rubbish – and I often told him so, in *far* stronger language.

'Sorry to have kept you waiting! Thank you for coming.' A tall, dark-haired man strides towards us. 'We can't use my classroom, sorry. This is the only spare office I could find for us to talk in private.'

Mr Silva shows me in while Zak waits outside. After some painful small talk, he finally gets to the point.

'Unfortunately, some older pupils taunted Zak in the playground. He threw a punch at a boy twice his size in retaliation.'

I bite my lip. I'm torn between being horrified that Zak lashed out and proud that he stood up for himself. I sigh, shaking my head.

'What were they having a go at him about?'

'Other children said the boys were laughing at his backpack and shoes. This isn't the first time this sort of thing has happened, but I want to reassure you that we're dealing firmly with the pupils involved.'

I catch my breath. I'd fixed Zak's shoes with glue again last night, but the sole must have come loose. His backpack is beyond hope; I can't keep putting this off. I'll have to hunt for one in a charity shop this week.

'We take bullying seriously at St Joseph's,' Mr Silva continues. 'We want Zak to know that he mustn't put up with being picked on. He can come and talk to me or another teacher if someone's upset him. That's far better than trying to tackle the problem himself.'

He's only seven. He was obviously scared. And it only made things worse for me if I ever ratted on another pupil.

'I've taught him to stand up to bullies,' I admit.

'That's great, but he also has to learn there are ways of doing it without lashing out.'

He's right, of course. I don't want Zak to grow up like his dad, thinking violence is OK.

'I understand. I'm sorry. I'll talk to him about it. He won't do it again.' I scoop up my bags from the floor.

'Actually, there's something else we need to talk about.' Mr Silva pauses. 'I'm a little worried about Zak. He's become withdrawn. He no longer participates in class – he rarely puts his hand up in maths and has refused to do a Show and Tell.'

'I guess he's reached that age where he's self-conscious about what other kids might say.'

'His artwork has also caused concern.'

'He drew some creatures, right? He's got a vivid imagination, which I don't think is a bad thing!'

Mr Silva pulls out pictures from a folder and pushes them across the desk.

I flick through the drawings; they're far worse than I imagined. A huge serpent towers in the air, ripping off the limbs of stick people who are spurting blood. His crayon scribbles are violent, almost tearing the pages.

'I had no idea . . .'

'The after-school manager also reported that he keeps asking the other pupils what will happen to them when their parents die. It's causing upset among the youngest children and several mums have complained.'

'I think that must be because he's reading *Harry Potter*. He was upset about Harry being an orphan. Maybe the book's too old for him?'

Mr Silva explains that this is an age when children often start to become more aware of their own mortality and worry about their parents' deaths – the worst-case scenario they could imagine.

'Do you remember fearing the same at his age?'

I shake my head. The worst had already happened to me; I'd been taken away from my mum and forced to live with strangers.

'We've previously discussed how you were in the care system,' he presses gently. 'I'm wondering if this could be exacerbating Zak's worries?'

My eyes widen. 'What? This is somehow my fault?'

'Not at all,' he says carefully, 'but have you considered the possibility that Zak fears the same outcome if anything happens to *you*?'

Not until now. I sink back into my chair. His statement has knocked the wind out of me more effectively than any punch Zak could swing in the playground.

'I think it would be beneficial for Zak to see an educational psychologist. The waiting lists are long, so it could be a few months before he's seen, but I can put his name down.'

I catch hold of the desk as I stand up. The signs I've been burying come into sharp relief: Zak's tantrums, his bedwetting. He's had a rough time recently – he's only just shaken off another chest infection from the damp and now he's lost Dog. No wonder he's feeling crappy. But there's no way I'm letting him enter 'the system', with endless referrals and people poking about in his life, the way they did in mine.

I force a small smile. 'I don't think Zak needs professional help. But don't worry – I'll make sure he stops drawing those pictures and doesn't, you know, punch anyone again. He won't talk to kids about death either.'

My mind drifts as Mr Silva points out there's less stigma about asking for help with mental health problems nowadays. I shudder at the thought of social services getting involved and finding out that Zak's dad is out of prison and trying to see him. They could take Zak off me if they suspect there's a chance we'll get back together.

'Thanks for your offer but, honestly, I can deal with this on my own.'

It's always been Zak and me against the world – it's far safer that way.

21

SIMON

'LOST!
CAN YOU HELP
FIND THIS TOY?'

I TACK THE APPEAL FOR Dog to a lamppost and move on to another along the route of Jodie and Zak's journey; I paid for a stack of posters in a printing shop nearby. I've allocated an hour to the activity, before I must continue my work on the Riemann Hypothesis, assessing the analytic continuation of the critical line reflected at the real value of 0.5. My phone rings in my pocket, but I ignore it. The wind is ripping the paper from the tree. Once it's safely secured, I listen to my voicemail.

'*Hi Simon! My name's Pippa Huxley. I'm a journalist for* The Herald. *We're planning a "Where Are They Now?" feature about the original contestants from* Little Einsteins *ahead of the reboot in February. We're interested in the people who reached the latter stages of the competition as kids. I'd love to arrange an interview with you. Can you call me back? My contact details are—'*

I cut off the message, steadying myself against the tree. My heart beats wildly, panic courses through my veins.

How did she get my mobile number?

I'm torn between fight and flight. Should I ring her back immediately and beg not to be included in the piece? Or will that make her suspicious, causing her to focus on me further?

I don't know what to do. My mind skips to William. Is Pippa Huxley interested in him too? The thought makes my heart beat even faster. I'm desperate to ask for his advice, but he has surgery all day. I'll have to wait until later. I must keep busy for now. After distributing more posters I check out the books Jodie has recommended from the library and stock up on cans of cat food. I notice an electronics retailer a few doors down from the supermarket, with large televisions in the window. A small boy is staring at the flickering screens, entranced by what appears to be a nature documentary.

On impulse, I decide to dip into my savings and order a new flat-screen TV, which will allow me to download Netflix. I figure the investment will be worth it if I'm able to keep Zak occupied during tutoring – and ramp up my general knowledge for The Rising Sun contests. I'll easily be able to afford it after winning the prize money for solving the Riemann Hypothesis.

When I look at my watch again, I realize a few hours have disappeared into the vortex. I'm too wound up to eat on my return home and instead place posters on each floor of my building, running up and down the corridors to increase my heart rate. Exhausted and hungry, I practise my cards and perform a quick tour of my Memory Palace before finally contacting William.

'How are you?' I ask tentatively.

'Bloody awful,' he replies. 'I've had a headache for days. Luckily, I'm the best neurosurgeon in New York, otherwise I'd have suspected an aneurysm and dialled nine-one-one.'

Despite my worries, I can't help smiling. Classic William.

'I wasn't expecting to hear from you so soon,' he goes on. 'My suggestion about tearing down your Memory Palace and living in the real world didn't exactly go down well. *Obviously*, I should have phrased it better.'

'I'm sorry for cutting you off.'

It's easier to apologize straightaway otherwise William will sulk throughout our entire conversation and refuse to help.

'You should know . . . I've been contacted by a woman called Pippa Huxley.'

'Who?'

'She's a journalist. She left a message on my mobile phone earlier today, saying she wants to do an interview for some piece she's writing about the reboot of *Little Einsteins*.'

'Oh God. That's not good.' The pitch of his voice rises. 'What if she's digging into our past? It could come out about Mother and Father. It could ruin you, Simon.'

You, not *us*. There it is again, the shifting of guilt solely on to me.

I hear faint music in the background; Victoria has turned on her favourite Coldplay album.

'Hold on,' he says. 'I'm going somewhere more private.'

Victoria says something to him in the background about Christmas.

'Yes, yes,' he mutters. 'I know flights are getting expensive. I'll mention it *again*.'

He climbs the stairs to his study, panting harder than usual. I must broach the subject of a regular exercise regime, but now isn't the time.

'Should I ring the journalist back?' I ask, when his study door clicks shut. 'I could tell her I don't want anything to do with the story she's writing.'

'Do you remember what the journalists were like back on *Little Einsteins*?'

I shudder. 'How can I forget?'

Words were often put into my mouth or later misconstrued, which had dangerous repercussions.

'Don't reply to her message and never answer your phone if you don't recognize the caller. The journalist is bound to lose interest and move on to someone else who's prepared to cooperate fully. Francesca Briley is probably dying to hog the limelight yet again.'

Ha, ha! He *still* hasn't forgiven Francesca for winning *Little Einsteins* all those years ago.

'You're right.'

'Of course I'm right. I'm always right.'

I don't attempt to disagree. I must give William this small victory. I'm grateful for his counsel. I'm actually glad we're on speaking terms.

'I mean, there's nothing to be gained by cooperating,' he adds. 'It must be a stitch-up piece. Think of the optics – a former child genius and Cambridge student who is now shovelling fries at Prince Burger. You're a journalist's wet dream.'

OK, I spoke too soon.

Luckily, William says he needs a lie-down to get rid of his headache.

'I'm not going to mention the journalist to Victoria. She'll only worry. It'll be our secret.'

I sigh heavily. I'm sick and tired of the Sparks' family secrets.

They sit heavily around my shoulders like a suffocating blanket I can never shake off.

My phone vibrates half an hour later. I check it tentatively, but it's only Jodie texting to arrange another lesson and update me about Zak.

He got into a fight at school. Don't worry, it's OK. We're both fine.

I walk over to the bedroom window, clutching my phone; it's raining hard. The glass vibrates beneath my fingertips from the violent strikes. Channels of water run down the street in a torrent; the drains have blocked. I reread Jodie's message. We have far more in common than I thought possible when we first met that day at Prince Burger. We're both adept at lying. She definitely wasn't receiving texts from her tutor in the café earlier. I'd noticed the slight tremble of her shoulders each time a disturbing message landed.

However, I can hardly lecture her about keeping secrets. Falsehoods trip easily off my tongue too. My entire world is based on an elaborate web of lies.

22

Easter 2005

SIMON

I BATTLE THROUGH TORRENTIAL RAIN after William, carrying my trunk with the help of the elderly porter, Cyril. Father's battered Volvo is parked further down the road. It's the last break before my finals and William's third-year exams. I pretended I'd receive one-to-one help if I stayed behind, but Father has seen through my deceit. He emailed my tutor, Dr Spencer, and told him I'm returning home as planned. He doesn't get out of the car to help as we open the boot, which annoys Cyril, who is drenched to the skin and muttering darkly. I'm relieved. Father might notice my trunk is suspiciously light. I've taken out most of my clothes and non-essential books and files to smuggle in my guitar, which is hidden at the bottom. I'll have to be extremely cautious, but I plan to practise during his evening runs.

'Not back there,' Father snaps, when I climb into the back seat next to William. 'Sit in the front. We can discuss the schedule I've drawn up. I'll give you a printout of the itinerary when we get home.'

I move listlessly to the front. Cyril turns up his collar and hurries back to the college. I want to leap out and run after him; I'd beg him to slide the bolt and not let Father in however hard he hammers on the door.

'Be careful where you put your wet feet,' Father barks.

My elation at being allowed to see Mother again after eight long weeks is dulled by the horrors that will inevitably follow. I watch the rain pouring in channels down my window as Father turns on the engine. The wipers flap backwards and forwards, a clock counting down to a test I will ultimately fail.

My chest tightens.

My ears buzz.

I feel empty and weightless. If I unfasten my seatbelt, I'm sure I'll float upwards. Yet, I know I'll never be truly free.

'Stop fiddling with that,' Father says sharply. 'What are your weakest areas? We should focus on those initially.'

This must be what it feels like when you drown.

I shrink into the leather and close my eyes.

I let his words wash over me.

I enter my Memory Palace and close the door behind me.

This is the only place where I'm safe from Father.

The car pulls off the road into our hidden driveway, past the house number that's obscured by shrubbery. The untrimmed branches discourage visitors, slapping and scratching the wind-screen, attempting to turn us back the way we came. Father is fastidious about the back garden, particularly in autumn, collecting leaves and twigs that have the audacity to invade his lawn. William and I agree the lack of pruning at the front is deliberate. He wants to hide us away from the rest of the world until a performance is required. The stones beneath the tyres grimace and cackle, setting my teeth on edge. We pass the large double garage that houses both Father's prized model railway and, at night, his car. I glance up and spot Mother at her bedroom window. I manage a smile – a real one – not the well-practised, fake type I use in QuizSoc competitions.

Within seconds Mother is running out as if fleeing a house blaze. Her black hair streams wildly down her back, a cardigan slips off her shoulders and falls to the ground, exposing her jagged collarbones. Her dress is looser than the last time I saw her. The car has barely stopped before she's pulled open my door and thrown her arms around me. I hug her tightly. She feels like a fragile origami bird, at risk of being crushed to death by my arms.

'I'm glad to see you,' she whispers. 'I know that's selfish. Half of me wishes you'd managed to stay at college over the break.'

'Help me unpack!' Father orders.

We spring apart and go our separate ways until lunch. Mother pushes salad around her plate, barely bringing the fork to her mouth. She stares into space after the plates have been cleared. Before I can ask if she's OK, Father says it's time to start revising. I head upstairs with William while he goes to watch the inaugural laps of his new, prized locomotive – the Midland Pullman – in the garage.

Colour returns to Mother's cheeks only when I show her my illicit guitar during Father's evening run. I play 'Stand by Me' for her and William in the sitting room and make only a few mistakes.

A smile lights up her face. 'That's the best thing I've ever heard. Listening to music makes me so happy.'

I place my hand over hers. 'I'll play for you every night, I promise.'

The next afternoon, my eyes are strained from studying and I'm flagging despite having consumed the energy drinks Father lined up on my desk. I watch from the window as he lights a fire at the bottom of the garden, before returning to the house. The flames lick dangerously closer and closer towards the fence. Our neighbour will complain again. Father re-emerges, carrying a large object.

'No!' I bang on the window as he strides down the lawn. 'Don't do it! Please!'

He's holding my guitar and doesn't look up. He's discovered the instrument under my bed. I've stupidly forgotten he knows all my old hiding places. Mother chases after him, begging him to stop, but he roughly shakes her off and throws the guitar onto the flames.

Bright sparks create fires.

I jump as William joins me at the window to view the ghastly cremation. We watch in silence. I don't cry, the way I did when Father destroyed our soft toys. By now, I've learnt that weeping achieves nothing; it can never breathe life back into ashes nor soften Father's steely resolve. Nothing will melt that, not even flames.

William squeezes my arm; he's comforting me the way he used to as a small kid. I'm grateful for his renewed support. We both know my punishment is only beginning. Father will strip my room – taking away the duvet, the bedstead and even the pillow – leaving only the mattress. I must earn everything back through additional studying. But this means nothing next to my fear for Mother; she will also be interrogated about my subterfuge.

I've got her into trouble again.

Would it have been easier for Mother if I hadn't been born and grown up to be such a disappointment? Sometimes, I definitely believe that's the case. She could have broken free far easier from Father without attachments.

Eventually, William steers me to the bed. He jumps as the back door slams shut, his shoulders relaxing only when the radio comes on in the kitchen. He sits next to me, telling me to whisper in case Father creeps up the stairs to eavesdrop.

'We can't go on like this.' His voice shakes. 'We have to teach him a lesson.'

I catch my breath.

'Do you really mean that? You're finally prepared to go against Father?'

A door clicks. William's eyes widen as he glances over his shoulder.

I place my hand over his – reassuring him, like he's done for me so many times.

'That was downstairs.'

He glances back, nodding. 'We *must* do something.'

'What?'

'Think, Simon, think. Search your Memory Palace. We have to find a way.'

23

JODIE

'MUMMY, IS IT POSSIBLE to charge a laptop by sticking the plug into a potato? Mr Silva says that they conduct electricity. How cool is that?'

I smile weakly and squeeze Zak's hand. I'm trying to find a way to bring up the 'what happens after I die' chat following yesterday's playground spat as we walk to a café for tutoring with Simon. There's no easy way to do this with a seven-year-old.

So about me dying . . .

Where do I go from there?

So about me dying after a freak electrocution involving a laptop and a potato. I pull Zak back onto the kerb as a van roars past.

I suppose not dying any time soon would be a start.

I chicken out and opt to raise the least contentious subject from the meeting with Mr Silva as we walk down Goldborne Road. The familiar smell of fried egg from the greasy-spoon trailer mixed with tagine spices from a Moroccan stall a few yards away drifts into my nostrils.

'What's all this about you not wanting to do a Show and Tell?'

Either Zak's daydreaming or he's ignoring the question. We walk silently past a boutique, which doesn't stock any dresses costing less than £500. I made the mistake of stepping inside once to ask if Zak could use the toilet. You'd have thought I'd queried whether he could smear shit all over their walls by the filthy look the assistant gave us. Only rich, size-zero women are allowed to enter.

We stop two doors down, to browse the clothes rail outside a second-hand shop. I need to find a suit for the Cambridge interview, as well as a backpack and shoes for Zak.

He shrugs as I repeat the question.

'Show and Tell is boring.'

'You didn't think that before – you were looking forward to doing one.'

'I've changed my mind.' He wanders off, distracted by a sign for ludicrously expensive organic cookie dough ice cream.

'And why's that?' I steer him back to the rack of clothes.

'You'll get mad if I tell you.'

'No, I won't. Promise.'

'You look cross already.'

'I'm not, honest.'

I try to rearrange my resting bitch face.

'Well, I've told you, my lightsaber's not like Billy's and my library books about cars and animals are lame. They don't even belong to me.'

'You don't have to own the books – you just have to pick something interesting to talk about.'

'I don't have anything interesting to say. Everyone else has cool stuff and I have nothing good. Nothing *new*. Everyone says so.'

He strops off down the street. I bite the inside of my cheek as I catch him up.

'Only the mean kids say things like that, but Mr Silva's dealing with them. Go to him if they cause trouble. Otherwise I'll sort them out myself.'

'Yeah, because you're so tough.'

He has no idea! I dished out a few black eyes and split lips to bullies at my old comp – before Lizzie helped me control my temper.

'Can we go to the pet shop?'

Zak darts off to his favourite store, without waiting for a reply. I find him inside, studying the fish tanks before scouring the shelves.

He glances up at me. 'Your hair looks pretty today, Mummy.'

'Thank you! You prefer it down like this rather than up in a ponytail?'

'No. I like it when it's blonde *and* dark brown.'

Dammit. I touch the top of my head. I really need to do something about my roots.

He clearly thinks he's successfully buttered me up, choosing a bag of dried pellets. 'Can we get this?'

'Why? Has your school decided to keep pets?'

He shakes his head. 'It's for the guinea pigs at Lucy Cavendish.'

'I haven't got in yet!'

'You will. I know it. Simon knows it too. You're the best.' He lifts the bag higher. 'Pretty please? You're beautiful *and* clever.'

Zak sure knows how to get round me. I take the packet to the counter and pay before I do any mental calculations about this week's budget and change my mind.

As we walk out of the shop, my phone vibrates in my coat pocket.

'Who's texting you?'

I know without looking, it's Jason again.

'Sandra, probably.'

'Aren't you going to check?'

'No, I can't be late for Simon again. He'll go nuts.'

Zak sighs heavily. 'I wish Dog was here. He'd look after us.'

'I know.' I squeeze his hand. 'I'm still looking for him. Simon says he's put up loads of posters. Fingers crossed he'll turn up soon.'

'I forgot my lightsaber. Can we go back home for it?'

'No, we're here now.'

I point to the café where I'd suggested we meet up as it's close to college; I need to pop in afterwards to pick up the books my tutor's lending me.

'You don't need it anyway. I brought your book. OK?'

'I guess.' Zak holds up the bag of guinea pig food, as I push open the door.

'This is our lucky mascot. It's going to keep us both safe until we find Dog.'

My phone burns in my pocket as more messages land.

I shudder.

We're going to need far more than mascots to help protect us from Jason.

24

SIMON

'OVER HERE!'
I wave at Jodie and Zak who are manoeuvring around tables, but they don't reciprocate. They both look downcast and in need of cheering up. Hopefully Jodie's spirits will be rallied by my newfound interest in literature. I finished reading *To Kill a Mockingbird* in the early hours today and will commence a reread of my nemesis text, *Great Expectations*, even though the thought of the novel causes tiny tremors to spread across my Memory Palace. However, I plan to strengthen its base by attempting to memorize a hundred of the world's greatest poems – an intellectual endeavour I feel much more comfortable with.

'How are you today, Zak?' I ask. 'I hear you've been using your right hook in the playground. Did you know Muhammad Ali was the only professional boxer to win the heavyweight championship three times?'

Zak manages a small smile, but Jodie's gaze is glued to her phone as she sits down.

'Which room do you keep boxing facts in?' he asks flatly.

'Room fourteen on floor two.'

'Cool.'

'What can I get you both to drink? It's my turn to pay.'

We have agreed to meet on mutual territory to avoid the risk of Zak destroying my flat. He opts for orange juice while Jodie has forgotten she's gone caffeine-free and chooses a double espresso, the same as me.

'This is a good opportunity to practise your people skills when you're at the counter.' She looks up from her phone briefly and nods at the lady on the till. 'Make eye contact, smile and ask how her day is going.'

'Why do I care? I don't know her.'

Jodie sighs heavily. 'Because it's polite and a good conversation opener. You listen, smile and think of something interesting to say back. If in doubt, talk about the weather.'

Why on earth would a twenty-something barista want to discuss drizzle and grey skies?

It's tempting to cite interesting facts about cirrus clouds, but I suspect this is not what Jodie means. At least there isn't a queue at the counter and no one will witness my attempts at conversation.

'We'll be watching and giving you marks out of ten.' Zak smiles mischievously. 'If you're terrible we might boo loudly and throw things at you. I have a good aim. I won't miss.'

I try to look unconcerned as I head over. When I look down, I realize I have company.

'Go on!' Zak hisses, as the woman finishes up with a customer. 'You're up. No pressure!'

Jodie's instructions fly out of my head. I focus on the trays of pastries as I attempt to improvise.

'How are you? The weather is, er, predictable for this time of year. Please can I have two double espressos and an orange juice?'

'Is that to drink in, Mr Weather Man?'

I look up. The barista is staring at me quizzically.

'Yes. Please.'

On impulse, I order a chocolate muffin for each of us after noticing Zak's hungry gaze.

I pay and wait at the end of the counter.

'I'd give you two points for that,' Zak says. 'You forgot to smile and make eye contact. Plus you acted like a robot and didn't wait for the lady to tell you how her day was going or what *she* thought about the weather.'

'Really? I thought that went well. I achieved the outcome I wanted.' I nod at the drinks, which are placed next to the muffins on our tray. 'We received our order in optimum time without delay.'

'You sound like a teacher.'

'Because I'm intelligent?'

'No. Because you do all the talking and you're not interested in what anyone else has to say. But don't worry – Mummy hasn't noticed you flunked her test. I'll cover for you.'

He picks up his carton of orange and saunters over to the table, where Jodie is fiddling with her phone.

'Simon did great! He's a real natural at this!'

'How's *your* day?' I say to Jodie in an effort of redemption. I make eye contact as she places her phone down on the table and lean closer to make sure I listen attentively to her answer, but she moves the chair back, glaring suspiciously.

'That's a little better.' Zak nods encouragingly. 'Although you're staring and smiling like an axe-murderer.' He takes a large bite of his muffin. 'Simon looks weird, don't you think, Mummy?'

Jodie stifles a giggle.

I sigh. 'Can we get on with the Cambridge lesson and leave my how-not-to-smile-like-an-axe-murderer tutorial for another time?'

'Sure.' She pulls out a book about cars and hands it to Zak. 'No interruptions, please. Mummy's working.'

He nods and wipes his fingers on a serviette, after polishing off the snack in record time. He's now eyeing up Jodie's muffin.

'I'm struggling with the whole memory thing,' she admits, retrieving a sheaf of papers from her bag. 'I've managed to remember two or three new literary techniques so far, but that's it. They're not going in here.' She taps her head. 'Well, they're going in and straight out again even though I've practised with the cards. I'm trying to put as many examples as possible in my essay, but I can't do it without looking at my notes.'

'Maybe that method doesn't suit you. Why don't you try making a journey?'

Zak's eyes flicker up with interest from his book.

'It's all about developing your visual memory. Assign a literary device to a place you can picture clearly and keep travelling. If you run out of locations, allocate a technique to a person you know well. For example, I could associate the word "exposition" with my childhood address, thirty-six Ember Lane, "enthymeme" with my old room at Magdalene and "catachresis" with my former tutor, Dr Spencer.'

'I don't understand the links?'

'You don't need to – they're personal to me, that's what makes them memorable. Now, whenever I imagine these locations or people, the literary techniques immediately spring to mind.'

'Thirty-six,' Zak pipes up. 'That's the number of the room you talked about in your Memory Palace – the one about the car crash. It must be a big room if it keeps a whole house *and* a car with people inside it.'

My cheeks flush. That was foolish. I'd forgotten that Zak is sharp; I shouldn't have used my childhood home as an example. I pretend I'm concentrating on my explanation as he repeatedly rolls the number over his tongue.

'*Thirty-six, thirty-six, thirty-six, thirty-six, thirty-six.*'

'Do you see what I mean, Jodie?'

She shrugs. I remember the little she's told me about growing up in care.

'Think about the journeys you've made throughout your life. For example, picture your childhood home and place a hyperbaton – an inversion of the normal order of words – inside it and move on to where you went next.'

'Hmm.' She sniffs. 'I'm not sure this method works for me. I don't like raking over all that old stuff. I try not to think about my childhood. I only want to keep looking forward.'

'You're not listening,' Zak interrupts, tugging on Jodie's sleeve. 'I want Simon to tell us about the number thirty-six.'

'Did I say thirty-six? I meant thirty-seven.'

'Liar, liar, pants on fire!'

'That's enough, Zak!'

He scowls. 'You say lying's bad but grown-ups do it *all* the time.'

Jodie picks at her finger instead of looking at Zak.

I shrug my shoulders. 'You're correct. I said thirty-six.'

'Why did you lie?'

'Forget about it, Zak!'

'No, it's OK,' I cut in. 'It's just that I don't have happy memories of living at that address.'

'Why not?'

I sigh, pulling back my shoulders.

'My father was hard on me, growing up.'

Zak's eyebrow shoots up. 'Did he ever hit you?'

'No, he didn't hit me . . .'

'Who did he hit?'

'Zak!' Jodie says sharply.

'What? This is important. We should talk about *things*. That's what my teacher always says.'

The foundations of my Memory Palace shake nervously; doors threaten to become unhinged.

'You're right, Zak, but not now,' I say. 'Thanks for the offer though. You're very helpful and insightful for someone of your age.'

Zak drums his fingers on the table and watches me expectantly. Will nothing appease this curious child?

'Look, if you have to know, I place everything that happened in my childhood home inside room thirty-six in my Memory Palace, along with the details of my parents' deaths. I like to keep the door shut. It means I don't have to think about it on a day-to-day basis. I feel safer that way. Happier. Well, to a certain extent. As much as anyone can feel truly happy in a world that will ultimately be destroyed by global warming or a nuclear war.'

To my surprise, my shoulders feel lighter after making this revelation, but Zak's eyes widen worriedly. Jodie rests her head in her hands.

'Obviously, you shouldn't worry about any of that,' I add quickly. 'Everything will be fine. For your generation, at least.'

'Tell me *exactly* how the Memory Palace works,' Zak insists. 'I want to build one inside my head. I'm going to store all my sad memories about . . .'

Jodie looks up.

'About losing Dog,' he adds quickly.

'Look, Zak,' she says. 'That sounds like a good idea, but I need to go through some practice test papers with Simon.'

'Actually, this technique could help.' I glance across the table. 'You could store your knowledge and preparation for Cambridge inside particular rooms if you don't wish to attempt the journey method.'

'Please, Mummy. Let him explain how he does it.'

'OK, if it's quick,' Jodie mumbles. 'But I want to get on with our checklist. We've so much to get through.'

I breathe a sigh of relief to be on slightly safer territory. 'Father was helpful in one respect. He taught me to build a Memory Palace using the powers of association and visualization.'

I explain the concept of deciding a basic layout of the building before attaching pieces of information you want to recall to distinguishable objects.

'Each of my rooms has a different coloured and textured door made from a variety of substances: wood, glass, plastic and steel. Behind each door lies specialized subjects, often stored in oak bookcases or cabinets and cupboards, ranging from eighteenth-century Queen Anne to modern-day Ikea.'

'Ikea? You have flat-pack furniture inside your head?' Jodie winks at Zak.

I resist the temptation to react to her leg-pulling.

'Again, it's about making things memorable. In other rooms, I associate facts and figures with everyday items like an umbrella or a slipper, or unusual objects, such as a leopard on a pink sofa, which helps me remember them.'

'Cool!' Zak exclaims. 'In my room I'll have a big bed that only *I* sleep in. Or maybe I'll let the leopard lie on it if he's good. The guinea pigs from Lucy Cavendish can sleep there too, so probably not the leopard because he'd eat them.'

Jodie laughs. 'We'll each have big beds and bookshelves lining every wall.'

I nod approvingly. 'I also try to make connections inside my head by creating internal doors to access other related chambers. For example, in a room dedicated to facts about Marie Antoinette, I place a single strand of forty-four natural saltwater pearls with a turquoise and diamond clasp on an eighteenth-century ormolu-mounted writing table. This is because the controversial French Queen once owned this necklace.

'On the right as I enter the room is a green door, which houses the history of the department store, Woolworths, its founder Frank W. Woolworth and the heiress Barbara Hutton, who was gifted Marie Antoinette's pearl necklace by her father as a wedding present in 1933. Ms Hutton subsequently went on to blow her entire fortune, leaving her bankrupt by death. The pearl necklace is, in fact, a symbol, connecting two wasted lives which never realized their full potential, but in different ways.'

Jodie is staring at me as if I'm mad, but Zak's smile could light up the street.

'I'll give you ten out of ten for that.' He takes another noisy sip of his juice carton. 'There sure is a lot going on inside your head, Simon, even though it never looks like it.'

'I think I preferred being told I resemble a crazy axe-man.'

Jodie laughs. 'Don't listen to him. It's impressive how you can remember everything, but I doubt I could.'

'You won't know until you try. Or attempt the journey method. Or both. Mix and match. Find out what suits your brain.'

Zak giggles. 'That sounds funny. It's like you're taking your brain shopping for new clothes. "Oh, those trousers suit you, *Brain*." "Oh, I love your T-shirt. It suits you, *Brain*.'"

He almost falls off his chair with laughter and, even though the joke's at my expense, the sound makes the grey skies appear lighter. Jodie's phone vibrates and Zak's smile disappears as swiftly as it arrived.

'Is that Sandra?' he asks in a small voice.

'Let me see.' Her face pales as she glances at her phone. 'Yes, she's texted to confirm she'll have you tomorrow after school.'

He shoves the chair back, rocking the table. 'I need a wee.'

I point to the rear of the café. 'The toilets are over there.'

Zak walks away, muttering under his breath. I raise an eyebrow at Jodie who jumps as another text arrives.

'Who's texting you? And don't say Sandra or your college tutor.'

She shoots a look over her shoulder. 'It's my ex – Zak's dad. I thought I'd got rid of him years ago, but he's found my mobile number and won't leave me alone.'

'What does he want?'

She shrugs. 'Jason claims he wants to see Zak, but he doesn't give a shit about him. Now he's out of prison, he'll be after cash. He doesn't realize I haven't got any.'

I push a sugar sachet away from a splash of coffee on the table as she explains that her ex-boyfriend was jailed for his part in a drug-dealing ring.

'What are you going to do?'

'Ignore him. I'm hardly going to meet up with the psycho, am I?'

'What does Zak think about it all? Does he want to see his father?'

She stares at me aghast. 'I haven't told him Jason's in touch and I'm obviously not going to!'

'You don't think he might have guessed? He was upset by the texts.'

'He probably thought it was his teacher. He's paranoid I'll be called back to his school. He puts on a brave front, but he hates getting into trouble. Zak doesn't know anything about Jason and I'm keeping it that way.'

She reflexively touches the tattooed birds on her arm. For the first time I notice crinkled, disfigured skin beneath the ink, which looks like a burn.

'What's . . .?' I stop myself, recalling her advice about listening. I mustn't blunder in with a question that will inadvertently offend her.

'Zak has no idea what went on when we were together,' she continues. 'He's too young to remember what a shit his dad was to me. If I admit Jason's been in touch there's a danger he might ask to see him. Zak doesn't understand the risks . . . He's at that age when boys want their dads, but I have to keep him out of our lives for good.'

'What's good?' Zak appears out of nowhere, like a will-o'-the-wisp.

'You made me jump!' Jodie exclaims, pretending to fall off her chair. 'Weren't you supposed to be having a wee?'

'I wee quickly. What were you talking about?'

She folds her serviette, smoothing out the corners. She appears to be playing for time.

'*My* mother,' I say, improvising. 'I was explaining how she thought she could protect me *for good* by keeping the peace in our house and pretending everything was OK. She meant well, but she was wrong. Ignoring the problem didn't make it disappear. Father was right there, the whole time. He wasn't going anywhere.'

Jodie's eyes narrow. 'And I was telling Simon how mums know

what's best for their own children and they don't like other people sticking noses into their business.'

'At which point, I argued that when you grow up you realize that mothers don't always know best. Sometimes they can't take advice. They make mistakes, even when they love you and think they're doing the right thing.'

'And I said—'

Zak yawns. 'I wish I hadn't asked. Grown-ups have *really* dull conversations.'

Jodie pushes her coffee cup, spilling it. 'Are we going to crack on with this tutoring or what?'

'Yes! Why don't I give you a quickfire test on all the literary techniques you've learnt so far? After that you can test me on the poems I'm memorizing.'

Jodie glares back. Zak looks from me to his mother, before disappearing behind his book.

'Now it's your turn to look like an axe-murderer, Mummy,' he mutters.

Her lips twitch.

Perhaps she's right. I can hardly lecture *her* about the need to face fears when I'm already quietly securing damaging cracks in my Memory Palace.

25

JODIE

I FEEL HOT BREATH ON my face and hands around my neck, squeezing the life out of me. Scorching white pain shoots up my arm and down my back. I struggle for breath. I'm going to die. I have to fight. I must reach Zak.

I claw at the darkness, battling with every ounce of strength left in my body.

No!

I clamber out of bed, gasping, and scramble for the lamp switch. For a split second, I don't know where I am or what's happening. Even when light floods the room, I'm disorientated and see demons. *Everywhere.*

Breathe.

Jason isn't here. He can't hurt you.

I focus on Zak's tousled hair on the pillow, his light snores that I find so annoying when I'm trying to go to sleep next to him, but are now the best sound in the world. His right arm, which he usually tucks Dog under, hangs limply by his side. The toy still hasn't turned up despite Simon's poster campaign. As I lean over and pull the bedclothes over him, I feel warm dampness beneath my fingertips.

Dammit. Zak's wet himself again. I change his pyjama bottoms, trying not to wake him. He curls up into a ball on the carpet as I strip the double bed. He can sleep through anything. I heave him onto the bare mattress; I don't have a spare sheet. He continues snoring as I bundle up the washing to take to the launderette tomorrow and check out of the window; the street is empty.

Even though we're safe, I can't settle. My heart is racing. I pad over to the table and tidy my papers: the list of literary techniques I'm trying to memorize, a practice Cambridge exam paper, the essay I've started writing and Simon's homework – to read and analyse an article in *Science* magazine. He said this will help me pick out relevant facts from an unfamiliar text, the way I'll have to in the Cambridge exam. I pull a newspaper cutting about a local company offering small, short-term loans to the top of the pile. It doesn't state a figure for the 'reasonable' interest rates. I'll check out the website on the library computer. Maybe I could borrow a couple of hundred quid. I was outbid on eBay last night, but with a bridging loan Zak could get a bigger, better Lego Star Wars set from Father Christmas.

I scrutinize my budgeting book to see how much I can afford to repay each week, anything to avoid thinking about my nightmare, which is still whirling around my brain. This is Simon's fault – questioning my judgement over Jason. How dare he? Sure, the tutoring is a great help and he's been kind to Zak over losing Dog, but that doesn't mean he knows us. What the hell does he think I should do about Jason anyway? If I report him to the police, they'll involve social services and I'll get regular visits. Social workers are the last thing I need.

I put my notebook away and warm my hands on the flowerpot; I lit the tealights inside it before falling asleep. My back prickles uncomfortably. The birds on my arm won't rest. I pick up a pen and pad, my hand itching to write. Sometimes, I did this in the home – jotted everything down that was scary or pissing me off – because there was no one I could talk to in the middle of the night when I thought I saw ghosts in the corner of my room.

You have to protect Zak. You must find a way to get rid of Jason.

I light the piece of paper using a tea candle and say a silent prayer. I can't risk Zak finding and reading this tomorrow morning. It'll only give him something else to add to his Worry List.

As the paper burns, I touch the tattoo on my arm.

I realize now, too late, that the birds aren't escaping from hazards on the ground below – they never managed to get away. They're simply frozen in flight.

I can't flee from my past either, however hard I try.

It's finally caught up with me.

I have to face it somehow.

I drop the paper in the metal bin.

Quickly, I douse it with a glass of water before the flames spread out of control and set the dimly lit room ablaze.

26

SIMON

'IT'S DARK,' JODIE SAYS, frowning. 'We're so far away from the centre of the quiz we're practically in the toilets. Shouldn't we move to a table closer to the lights? The barman said the quizmaster plans to show photos in the History of Art round. I don't think we'll be able to see or hear properly if we stay here.'

We've taken up position at a large table with four empty chairs in The Rising Sun. The lights have been dimmed to distinguish between the quizzing and non-quizzing sections. Jodie rang this afternoon, admitting she was struggling with my homework assignment, which involves extracting ten relevant facts from the study of wildfires in coniferous areas. I explained that the brain benefits from different stimuli and how quizzing often helps kick-start my mathematical studies. I let slip that my usual pub quiz contest was rearranged to tonight due to quizmaster Philip going down with a twenty-four-hour bug yesterday.

She talked me into letting her come along, claiming we could celebrate the end of a successful first week of tutoring. Plus we could work on my people skills 'and get merrily pissed' while Sandra babysat. By the end of our chat, she'd made it sound like this was all my idea; if she can manipulate the tutors this deftly she'll sail through the Lucy Cavendish interview.

'I've never had any problems sitting at this table.'

She scans the room. 'Shouldn't we get an answer sheet? They all have one.' She jerks her head at the tables nearest Philip, who is pale-faced and off the alcohol.

'We don't need one. We're not *formally* taking part. I disagree with some of the rules – that's why we're sitting in the "non-quizzing" section. But don't worry, I bring my own pencil and piece of paper each week so I can still take part.' I produce both items from my waistcoat pocket.

'Bloody hell, Simon. I hate to break this to you, but joining in a pub quiz actually involves *joining in*.'

'That's exactly what I'm doing from here, at a distance. I'm participating.' I straighten my waistcoat.

'This is observing from the shadows. You need to move closer to the action, to the lights.' Jodie points towards the brightly lit tables in the epicentre of my Venn diagram.

'We can't. There aren't any free tables.'

'Well why don't we ask another team if they want to join us? There's enough room and it's not *so* bad here. My eyes are adjusting.'

I bristle at her suggestion. 'No!'

'Come on! Lighten up. It's more fun to be part of a team. You're in your natural habitat here; you won't even have to think up conversation openers. And hey, maybe we'll even make new friends. I don't get out much. It'll do us both good to make an effort.'

'It's too late to sign up,' I snap. 'People have been registered in their teams for weeks. They aren't allowed to add new members due to the size of the jackpot.'

This is a blatant but necessary lie. I can't set myself up for failure as part of a team, I just can't. Jodie is bound to have something unflattering to say about the merits of being a sole competitor, but she has to play by *my* rules. She's a guest, not a teammate.

'Oh, that's a shame.'

Thankfully, she appears to believe my falsehood and settles silently into her chair as I enter my Memory Palace. I visit the literature, history and Impressionist art rooms as Philip has intimated they will feature heavily this evening.

'It's a big mix of people here, isn't it?' Jodie takes a sip of vodka, lime and soda water.

I reluctantly retreat from my Memory Palace as I notice her gaze resting on the Three Wise Men across the bar. They're smartly dressed in suits and ties as usual and armed with freshly sharpened pencils. Arthur's black glasses are slipping down his nose, Trevor's fingers glint with chunky gold rings and Winston's wearing his late wife's red handkerchief. Arthur lifts his glass and Jodie reciprocates.

'What are you doing?'

'Being friendly. Or is that against your quiz rules?'

I sigh. 'You'll only encourage them.'

'Encourage them to do what exactly? Storm the bar?'

I don't reply as the quiz is commencing. I haven't had time to do a full tour of my Memory Palace, but I *must* complete my routine. I rotate my pencil three times and recite the family motto. Jodie shakes her head and takes a large gulp of her drink.

*

Forty-five minutes later, I believe we have a clean sweep of twenty-five correct answers. Jodie is equally confident – and jubilant. She cited the Poor Law Amendment Act 1834 in answer to a Victorian history question and accurately gave key dates regarding the introduction of the Welfare State (1945–51). I also had these answers to hand, but her knowledge far surpassed mine in the literature round – naming Elizabeth Barrett's poem, 'The Cry of the Children'; *Sybil, or the Two Nations* by Benjamin Disraeli and the similarly titled *Sybil* by Flora Rheta Schreiber. The evening has not been unpleasant thus far, mainly because I've avoided mentioning the touchy subject of her ex, who is still texting judging by the look on her face whenever her phone vibrates.

'Another drink?' she asks during the break. 'My round.'

'Why not?'

She pops over to the bar, but inexplicably takes a detour to table five. Jodie ignores my frantic hand gestures, encouraging her to return, and talks animatedly with the Three Wise Men. Arthur stands up slowly and they embrace like long-lost friends. What is she doing? Finally, she returns to her original mission and orders at the bar.

'I have good news!' She sets down the drinks, spilling my pint.

Somehow I doubt that. I mop up the mess with a spare tissue.

She nods at the Three Wise Men. 'Those blokes are dead nice. Arthur told me there shouldn't be a problem with our teams joining up during the second half tonight. Apparently, the pub makes special arrangements for elderly participants.'

Yet again, I have underestimated the Three Wise Men!

I glare across the room. Arthur winks and raises his pint. He's a wily old thing.

'Well, I don't want to join up with them,' I say shortly. 'They've asked me before and I've politely declined.'

'Why? They're friendly.'

'This is how I always play the pub quiz. On my own.'

'Have you considered it might be time for a change?'

I shake my head. 'I'm happy as I am.'

'Are you?'

'Are *you* happy?' I counter, nodding in the direction of her phone on the table. 'Is Zak?'

Jodie's face reddens. 'Tonight is about *you*, not *us*. What if you could help those old guys win the jackpot? They said they've tried for weeks, but they gamble and always lose. I told them you're ex-Cambridge and a child genius from *Little Einsteins* so you're bound to sail through the sudden-death question.'

I raise my eyes to the ceiling.

'What now?'

'You're interfering with my system. I don't even know them properly. Why would I want to help?'

'Because it would be a nice thing to do? You could help them even though you don't know them yet. They probably need the cash, like me. The jackpot is huge! They said we could split it. I bet you could do with some extra money?'

'I don't compete for monetary reasons,' I point out. 'So there's precisely nothing in this for me.'

'Does there have to be? Kindness isn't a debt to be repaid. Lizzie, my old school librarian . . .' Her voice cracks. 'My friend used to say it's a gift to give away freely to others without expecting anything back.'

'Well, I shop on Amazon and they're fine about returning things I don't want.'

Jodie glowers. 'I'm sorry you feel like that, but somehow I doubt Amazon will accept your unwanted package tonight.'

'What do you mean?'

She stands up and beckons to the Three Wise Men. 'I've already told them they can join us.'

'You did what?'

I watch in horror as they rise to their feet and make their way over.

'I want to get to know them better. They tell interesting stories. It'll be fun, you'll see. Plus, *you* could benefit from being kind to others and letting your guard down for once.'

'But I—'

It's too late to protest. They've reached us in record speed despite their walking aids.

'Good evening, Simon!' Arthur booms. 'This is a pleasant surprise. Thank you for the invitation!'

He eases himself down next to me, followed by Winston and Trevor who drop their coats onto the empty chair. While quizmaster Philip fetches a last-minute soft drink, the Three Wise Men introduce themselves and explain their strengths in the quiz.

'My subject is English Literature – I've applied to study it at Cambridge,' Jodie explains.

As she fields questions from Trevor and Winston, she elbows me in the side.

'Ow!'

She nods surreptitiously towards Arthur. He's frowning and leaning forward with his left ear pointing towards the conversation. Jodie rams me with her elbow again. It's as sharp as a stick.

'OK!'

I have no idea what to talk to him about, but I could Google *popular sports for OAPs*. As I reach into my pocket to find my phone, this month's bundle of staff vouchers for free food falls out.

'Don't lose this.' Arthur hands me the thick wad, which is held together with an elastic band. 'My daughter's taking thirty-five kids for tea at Prince Burger after bowling for my grandson's fifth birthday. He loves the chicken nuggets there, does Harry. It's going to cost her a bloody fortune.'

'In that case, you should give them to your daughter.' I pass him the vouchers; they are of no use to me.

'What? Are you sure? You've got dozens.'

'Consider it a birthday gift for Henry.'

'Harry.'

'Yes, Harry and his friends.'

'Really? You'd do that for a stranger?'

I'm about to explain that I don't eat fast food – and neither should five-year-olds – when he squeezes my shoulder.

'You're a kind man, Simon – inviting us to join your team and giving me a present like this. It means a lot. Thank you.'

A warm glow creeps into my cheeks. 'You're welcome.'

I'm happy for the silence to remain until I've finished the internet search on my phone, but Arthur shifts uncomfortably in his seat. He coughs and leans towards me.

'Jodie tells me you were on *Little Einsteins* as a boy. I caught one of the recent reruns with my wife. We came in halfway through the episode but I couldn't believe the behaviour of some of the parents. Quite shocking.'

My phone drops onto the table with a clatter. Arthur gives it back, as if nothing's wrong.

'I can't stop thinking about one of the dads; he yelled at his kid from the audience because he got a question wrong. Awful it was. Car-crash TV. Wouldn't be allowed now, I'm sure. Poor lad was sobbing. Had to be helped off. Do you remember him? I didn't catch his name. He'd made it to the final.'

My Memory Palace is rocked with judders. Foundations splinter. Walls crack. Door frames shift and fall apart.

I rise unsteadily to my feet, knocking over an empty glass. My hands are trembling too much to right it.

Breathe in, breathe out.

'Simon?' Arthur says. 'Are you all right?'

Jodie glances up. 'What's wrong?'

Before anyone can stop me, I flee the pub as I did the *Little Einsteins* stage all those years ago.

27

JODIE

'I USUALLY ENJOY SEEING IF I can answer the questions, but I feel stupid today.' Sandra sighs heavily. She pauses the recording of BBC Two's *University Challenge*. Teams from Cambridge's Magdalene College and Oxford's Oriel College are frozen in competition: 155 points versus 120. We're chatting on the sofa while Zak has a sandwich and plays with Sandra's phone in the kitchen after our visit to the launderette.

My head's pounding after a few too many drinks with Arthur and the lads. It turned out to be a bit of a night, even though we didn't win the quiz. They stayed on while I picked up Zak. Sandra was on good form when I dropped him off last night – showing off her new lipstick and plum-coloured hair while I quickly repaired the leaking radiator in her bedroom. But today, her face is pinched and pale, drained of colour. It's the first time I've seen her without earrings or makeup. She usually puts on bright lippie even when she's coming over to mine.

'I wasn't looking where I was going,' she says, staring at her newly bandaged foot. 'I'd popped out to the shops this morning and the lift on this floor was broken again. A man brushed against me as he ran down the stairs and I lost my balance. My sons keep telling me to hold onto the handrail.'

I move the stool closer to prop up her sprained ankle.

'You're lucky you didn't fall more than a few steps. Do you think the man deliberately barged into you? Was he someone from this block of flats?'

'I haven't seen him around before. I think he was just in a hurry.'

My mind races to dark places. Once, Jason 'accidentally' knocked into a former friend from the home after a night out; afterwards he'd asked why we had to spend so much time together.

'Did he have tattoos?'

'Why?'

I haven't told her about Jason trying to find us; Sandra does enough for me without getting dragged into this mess.

'The local paper had a story about a man robbing old ladies around here. He had tattooed knuckles.'

'Less with the "old ladies", thank you! I'm still sixty-nine for a few more months, practically a spring chicken – well, a one-legged, daft one, anyway. And no, I think I'd remember that. But a nice young man gave me a lift to A&E. It was a good two-hour wait. I've never been more grateful to be at home.'

I swallow my fear. I have to get a grip. I thought I saw Jason outside The Rising Sun last night, and again I almost had a flash of him loitering by our building this morning. I'm going mad. I'm seeing him everywhere, torturing myself with imagined spectres.

'You're not daft. This could have happened to anyone.'

'But *I* did this.' Sandra gestures to her foot. 'I've no chance of getting on a train to visit my sons any time soon. I won't be able to see my friends from swimming. The days are going to be terribly long stuck here on my own.'

I squeeze her hand.

'Most of all, I feel awful about letting you down,' she continues tearfully. 'I'm no use to you as a cripple. I can't have Zak today or while you do college work tomorrow, like I promised.'

'Don't worry. I'll sort out play dates. The mum network at Zak's school is great – really supportive, even at weekends.'

That's a lie. They're a bloody nightmare.

'It won't be a problem. Give me your shopping list and I'll pick up your groceries before I head into work.'

After Sandra decides what she wants me to buy I press 'play' and her favourite TV show continues.

'*What number comes next in descending order after 8128, 496 and 28?*'

'Do you have any idea what the answer is?' Sandra looks at me, bewildered.

'Not a clue, but I bet my friend Simon would know.'

The captain of Magdalene College hits the buzzer, gaining ten points for the correct answer: six.

I frown as I realize the label I've given Simon. 'Well, he's not a friend exactly. He knows everything apart from how to be nice to people.'

I'm still fuming about how he abandoned Arthur's team last night. He ran out of the pub without saying a word to anyone, probably because he'd figured out a new calculation or stumbled across a dusty fact in his bloody Memory Palace. Or maybe he was still annoyed that I'd asked them to join us. Just when I thought he was showing a new, kinder side, he's back to acting like a jerk.

'That's good.' Sandra's not listening. She's concentrating on the next question in the maths and physics round.

I kiss her on the cheek and head to the kitchen to drag Zak away from her phone.

'What are we going to do this afternoon?' he asks, as we step out onto the pavement.

Quickly, I glance up and down the street. 'I need to find you a play date while I'm at work. Any ideas?'

I'm not a member of the 'in' group of mums who regularly organize meet-ups at each other's homes – I can't have kids over to our bedsit, which means that Zak hardly ever gets invited to anyone else's house.

'Billy?' he suggests.

I wince inwardly. Mrs Devine is patronizing as hell – sympathetically tilting her head to one side whenever she talks to me at the school gate. But it's a Saturday and most mums will ignore my text, as they want family time, not unreasonably. I have to swallow my pride and beg for a favour. Mrs Devine has a nanny, a cleaner *and* a housekeeper. One of them must be able to keep an eye on Zak until I've finished at Prince Burger later tonight.

I send the text into the ether, along with a silent prayer.

I know it sounds horribly selfish, but Sandra's fall totally sucks. It's come at the worst possible time in the run-up to my interview. I was supposed to work flat out on my essay tomorrow. My tutor, Monica, has offered to give it a look over this week and suggest things to improve before I submit it for formal assessment. I have no idea how I'm going to juggle working, studying and childcare now I can't rely on Sandra.

*

'My starter for ten is, what the hell did we both do to annoy Ed?' I ask.

Simon and me are imprisoned in a small, hot box – the drive-through cabin of Prince Burger. No one wants to work here; the customers are even ruder and more demanding in their cars than in the restaurant. There's no let-up and I'm knackered. After dropping off Sandra's shopping, I worked on my essay before Billy's nanny helpfully picked up Zak to take both boys to the park. I also made a quick detour, going on another short, fruitless search for Dog around the streets nearby.

'Ed's rotated the workstations,' Simon replies. 'He wants to make sure all employees have a range of skills to improve their CVs, which is a noble plan, but it's causing chaos. I'm worried about Fro-Bot.'

'Who?'

'My mechanical fryer. She's temperamental and might not survive Carlos' heavy-handedness. How will I cook the fries tomorrow if she breaks down yet again?'

He packs three cheeseburgers and fries plus drinks into a cardboard container, which I dangle out of the window.

'Here's your order! Have a great day!'

'Let me get this straight,' I say, as the customer drives away. 'You're worried about a bloody machine, but you couldn't give a toss about Arthur and his team? You ditched us last night. What was that all about?'

Simon freezes slightly, unable to look me in the eye.

'Let me guess. You were thinking about the Riemann Hypothesis?'

'Well, to be fair, I'm thinking about that all the time.'

'Typical! Arthur was worried he'd upset you, but I knew it was far more likely to be the other way around.'

He flinches. 'Sorry. How did you do?'

'We lost. Science was our weakest area. But the good news is that Team Victorem lost the sudden-death question on tactical warfare in Ancient Rome, which means we can go for it again next week.'

'You're returning?'

He sounds – and looks – horrified.

'Maybe. Sandra's sprained her ankle so it depends if it's better and she can babysit. You should join the team – apologize for your rudeness and make an effort. They're nice guys, smart too. You might learn something from *them*.'

Simon remains silent as six burgers arrive down the chute.

'Or maybe you should ask Fro-Bot to join *your* team. You could buy her a glass of wine and practise your people skills – you know, discuss the Battle of Carthage. If you're lucky, she might let you take her home.'

'OK.' He raises his hands in the air. 'You've made your point.'

My phone beeps. I abandon the burgers he's lined up and grab my mobile.

'Is that your ex who's going to miraculously vanish if you pretend he's not there?'

I glare at him as I resume the production line and pass the order out of the window to the driver.

'Touché. It was the nanny of a kid at school, arranging to drop off Zak before she finishes for the day. I'll have to ask Ed if I can do a half shift and leave at six thirty.'

'He's not in the greatest of moods today.'

'It seems to be going around!'

Simon pauses. 'I don't mind covering the rest of your shift if that helps.'

I'm slightly stunned. 'Really? You'd do that for me?'

194

'I'm making excellent progress with the Riemann Hypothesis. My zeta function theory looks promising. I can run over the calculations in my head here, before checking them later.' He pauses. 'Also, I want to make up for leaving early last night. Think of it as my way of apologizing.'

I shake my head slowly. 'Well, well, well.'

'What is it now? What have I done wrong?'

'You're a puzzle. I can't work you out.'

'That's because English Literature is your forte, not mathematics.'

'Funny! Thanks, Simon.'

The rest of my shift passes swiftly and without incident. Before I know it, Billy's nanny has brought in Zak on her way home. She turns down my offer of complimentary vouchers, saying Mrs Devine doesn't allow Billy to eat junk food, which is kind of predictable.

'Good day?' I kiss the top of his head.

'Brilliant! Can we go to the park tomorrow?'

'I have to crack on with college work, sorry. You could do some drawing or reading.' I lead him over to Simon to thank him again. He's been rotated back to his place of comfort: the fry station.

'All day? I don't—'

I change the subject quickly, sensing a looming meltdown. 'Simon is trying to crack the Riemann Hypothesis – it's a really tough mathematical problem. Someone called Bernhard Riemann proposed the puzzle in 1859. Simon told me that to solve it, you have to predict the occurrence of every single prime number. Do you know what a prime number is?'

'Don't know, don't care,' Zak mutters.

Luckily, Simon hasn't heard.

'It would make a great subject for your Show and Tell.'

'No it won't. Everyone in my class says it has to be about an object – something you can see, like a lightsaber. You can't see maths.'

'Actually, you can,' Simon says, turning around. 'Maths is everywhere.'

'No, it isn't. Maths is only in my textbook and in our classroom.'

Simon opens his mouth to argue, but I head off a potentially long lecture.

'Sorry, take no notice of Zak. He's in a bad mood because I have to write my essay tomorrow.'

'It's unfair! I don't want to stay in all day. I want to go outside and play.'

Simon chews his bottom lip, thinking. 'I could take Zak out for a couple of hours.'

'Really?'

'I've realized I may need more time to digest my workings out, before I return to them refreshed and revitalized next week.'

Hmm. Is that true? Or did my little lecture about helping others sink in at the pub quiz? Maybe he's making a superhuman effort to be kind.

Zak's face glows with excitement. 'Can we, Mummy? Please? Simon and me could go somewhere fun.'

'I'm not sure . . .'

I'm desperate to get on with my assignment in peace and quiet but I've only ever let Sandra babysit. Simon is great with Zak while I'm here, but what about when I'm not around? Zak is a handful who needs constant watching and, well, Simon's a liability himself sometimes.

'I have a seven-year-old nephew and a five-year-old niece, remember?' he points out. 'I'm not totally ill-equipped to look after a small child.'

'Please, Mummy! *Please, please, please, please, please.*'

'Well, if you're sure . . .'

'How hard can it be?'

I laugh. 'You're about to find out. But if you're absolutely positive – thank you!'

'Excellent!'

Simon and Zak beam at each other.

'Where are you going to take me tomorrow?'

'I've had a brilliant idea. I think you'll love it.'

Zak's eyes widen. 'Is it the cinema? Or a swimming pool? No, wait, is it a theme park?'

'It's a place my mother always wanted to visit, but never had the chance.'

'Australia?'

'No. Wait and see. I want it to be a surprise.'

I smile at Zak, all the worries pushed from my mind.

Simon may prove to be the biggest surprise of all.

28

SIMON

WE SHOULD REACH THE Charles Dickens Museum at 48 Doughty Street, Holborn, in eight minutes. We are running behind with our itinerary, as I had not factored in Zak's disorganization and last-minute trips to the bathroom while I waited outside their building this morning.

'I think you'll find it fascinating to peruse where a famous author once lived and worked at his desk,' I explain. 'I'm sure you've heard of some of his most famous novels such as *Oliver Twist* and *A Christmas Carol*?'

I interpret his silence as a 'yes' as I plough on down the street. I tell him that Dickens was a social commentator who highlighted the scandalous plight of the poor in Victorian England, particularly the mistreatment of children.

'However, letters have recently come to light, which show how the author had tried to banish his wife to a mental asylum to enable him to live with his mistress. The doctor who stood in Dickens' way was Thomas Harrington Tuke.'

I leave a dramatic pause, which Zak fails to fill.

'Dickens also expressed racist views in his personal life. I think both points raise an interesting question about how a modern readership should deal with such a legacy. What is your opinion on the matter, Zak?'

Silence yet again.

I glance down. To my surprise, he's not there. I spin around.

How long have I been talking to myself?

My head swims with panic as I look up and down the street; my chest cramps painfully. I think I'm having a heart attack. If that doesn't kill me, Jodie most certainly will. I've lost Zak due to a concentration lapse even before I've started musing about my promising mathematical theory. This is far, far worse than burning fries at Prince Burger. Zak could be frightened or injured or . . . My mind goes to terrifying places.

I dart down the road, frantically checking left and right, and head back towards the tube station. I hear a faint siren in the distance and run faster, fear rippling through me. Sweat beads under my collar and drips down my back.

As I turn the corner, I spot a small figure in the distance, leaning against railings. *Please let it be him.*

I squint harder.

It is! Thank God!

I sprint even faster. Finally, I reach him.

'Thought . . . I'd . . . lost you. Or . . . you'd been . . . injured.' I bend double, gasping for air.

'Are you, OK, Simon?' Zak asks. 'You look sweaty and weird.'

'Am fine,' I say, panting. 'Are. *You.* OK?'

'Of course! I'm fab! Can we go in there?' He points at a playground through the bars. 'It looks even better than the one I went to with Billy yesterday. It has monkey bars.'

A girl squeals with delight as a woman pushes her on a swing. Another height-challenged person sits inside a poor imitation of a locomotive, pretending to drive it. The engineering design is inferior, even for a model.

I rub the stitch in my side, attempting to gain my breath as Zak stares at the apparatus hungrily, the way I scrutinize a whiteboard filled with formulae. I check my watch. The guided tour will start in four minutes. If we spend two minutes here and increase our pace, we will not fall too far behind our schedule.

'I guess we have time—'

Before I can explain that visiting a playground is a useful educational experience, Zak has shot off. He clambers onto a swing.

'Give me a push?' he says, when I catch up.

I inhale deeply and out again. My breathing is finally back to normal.

'Certainly. Like I explained previously, maths is everywhere, not only in classrooms. It's all around us, wherever we go. Those tree branches show a pattern known as fractals.'

I point towards the large oak, but Zak doesn't look. I try again. 'This swing is a perfect example of a mathematical pendulum, whereby forces act on an inanimate object.'

'Higher, Simon! Higher!'

'But let me tell you first—'

'HIGHER!'

Perhaps a discussion about friction and speed calculations using the example of the slide will prove more entertaining.

'Now you can let go,' Zak shouts. 'I'm flying!'

'Yes, you are experiencing gravitational force or, as it's more commonly known, G-force,' I confirm.

'Get on next to me and we'll see who can go the highest.'

'Oh. No. I couldn't. Do that.' My cheeks flush as I try to speak in time with his accelerations.

'Why not?'

I move position to enable us to converse properly.

'Swings aren't for adults,' I point out.

'Mummy goes on the swings if no one else is waiting for a turn.'

This does not surprise me.

'Swings are for everyone. Not just kids. Dog used to come on with me, so you can too!'

I hesitate as my blush deepens. How does a full-grown adult do this without looking totally ridiculous? I've only ever been on a swing once as a child – Mother had sneaked me off to a park when I was three or four; it was only the two of us. William was doing a music class. I remember every detail as if it were yesterday . . .

The sun toasts my hair. I kick off my sandals, making Mother run for them as I swing higher and higher. She laughs each time she picks them up and attempts to slip them onto my socked feet.

'One more time, one more time!'

'Slowcoach!' Zak shouts. 'Bet I can go higher than you!'

I refocus my attention. I study the movement of his legs and upper body and tell him I'm calculating how to accurately adjust the moment of inertia with the motion of the swing before climbing aboard. By my fifth swing, I am managing to gather enough momentum to not look utterly ludicrous.

'You're doing it all wrong!' Zak calls over. 'Lean back further!'

I obey even though I'm afraid of letting go and falling.

I feel the breeze in my hair and the winter sun warming my face. When I close my eyes, I see Mother standing in front of the swing again. She's gazing at me, the way Jodie looks at Zak, and my heart feels as though it will burst.

She scoops me out of the swing, kissing my cheek. It's time to go home. I don't want the afternoon to end. I think Mother feels the same. She stops smiling when we get home. Father tells her off loudly in the kitchen. I hear a bang and a faint sob. When the front door slams shut, I creep in. Mother's sitting at the table, weeping. An overturned chair lies next to her.

'Sorry,' I whisper, as I climb onto her lap. 'Won't do it again.'

Mother hugs me tightly. 'Don't you worry, Simon. This wasn't your fault. I lost track of the time, which was silly of me. But we had a lovely afternoon, didn't we? I'm so glad we got to share it with each other.'

'Can we do it again soon?' I ask eagerly.

'Maybe.'

I put on my sandals each morning, lingering by the front door, hoping it will remind her. William waits with me and we whisper about Father's new idea to teach us Latin.

After a couple of weeks, I stop buckling my sandals. I push them to the darkest corner of the shoe cupboard. William does the same.

I lean back, kicking my feet high into the air.

'Don't you like being on the swing?' Zak asks.

'I think I may love it. It's the best thing ever.'

'Why are you crying if you love it?'

Am I? I let go of one hand and feel my cheek; it's wet with tears.

'I must have something in my eye – a fly or a piece of dust.'

'Why do grown-ups always lie about crying?' Zak shoots off the swing with a leap.

I slow down, dragging my feet across the concrete.

'Mummy does the same, but she always wants to know why I'm upset about things,' he says, scowling. 'I have to tell the truth but grown-ups *never* do.'

'Let's go on the seesaw. It's a good example of pivotal forces.'

'Mummy does that too.' Zak sighs heavily. 'She changes the subject.'

I follow him as he clambers onto the seat. I settle into mine, shooting him into the air.

'Tell me why you were sad, Simon, and I'll tell you what makes me sad.'

I close my eyes as I kick off the ground, rising up into the air. For once, I tell the truth.

'Being on the swing brought back a memory of my mother and some of the things that happened to me when I was a child. I wasn't prepared for the recollection as I thought I'd stored everything safely away in my Memory Palace.'

'In room thirty-six?'

'Yes, but sometimes memories hit you when you're least prepared.'

'I know what you mean.' Zak nods sagely, as he sails upwards. 'I get sad when I think about things that happened when I was a kid. What do *you* remember that's upsetting?'

Zak's impression of maturity makes me smile.

'My mother got into trouble with Father for taking me to a playground like this. He thought it was a frivolous activity. I heard him shouting at her in the kitchen when we returned.'

Zak chews his lip. 'I cry when I think about Mummy's dragon skin.'

I frown. 'I don't understand what that means, sorry.'

'The skin on Mummy's back is scaly like a dragon's. That's

where Daddy hurt her. She screamed and screamed, but he wouldn't stop doing it.'

My eyes widen. Bile rises in my throat. I don't know exactly what Zak is talking about, but he appears to have witnessed a horrific form of torture. I climb off the seesaw gently. Zak hangs limply at the bottom. I crouch beside him.

'Mummy stopped crying and closed her eyes. She didn't get up from the floor. I thought she was dead.'

I put my arm around his shoulders.

'That's awful. I'm so sorry. For you and your mother. I knew things had been bad, but I had no idea . . .'

We both fall into silence. Obviously, I'm no expert in dealing with traumatized children, but I remember what Jodie told me about using open-ended questions to develop conversations.

'How did that make you feel? Seeing what happened to your mother?'

'Scared. I tried to make Daddy stop, but the ambulance never came. That was my fault. I wasn't brave enough.'

'I'm sure that's not true. Why don't you think you were brave?'

'I found a phone and dialled nine-nine-nine because that's what Mummy taught me to do in an emergency. I gave our address and a woman asked what I wanted, but I was too scared to tell her what was wrong. My voice disappeared and it wouldn't come out again. A neighbour heard me crying. He took Mummy and me away.'

'It sounds like you were *very* brave. Do you talk to your mother about this?'

'She doesn't know I remember *everything*. She thinks I've forgotten, but I haven't.' He trembles. 'I'm worried her back still hurts, but she never wants to talk about it. Sometimes she says it's a birthmark. I think that's because she's sad. I don't want to call her a liar and make her cry. That would be bad.'

I recall wanting to talk to my mother about Father, but being afraid to raise the matter in case it distressed her. Instead, William and I would discuss him at length at night.

'Don't you think you should tell her what you remember? It could help you to talk about what happened that day.'

'No! Promise me you won't tell Mummy what I've said?'

'Oh, Zak. Secrets aren't good for us.'

I've lived my life with them and I wish I hadn't. They haven't made me happy. If I'd just been honest from the start, perhaps it would have saved me from so much misery.

'Please, Simon!' he cries. 'Don't tell her!'

What should I do? I Googled parenting advice for seven-year-olds on my phone before I picked up Zak but, unsurprisingly, helping youngsters keep traumatic memories from their mothers was not among the tips. I thought this jaunt would be straightforward. I mistakenly thought Zak would quietly and compliantly tag along, allowing my mathematical theories to percolate in my mind. But now I feel myself getting sucked deeper and deeper into his secret, which could damage long-sealed doors in my Memory Palace.

I take Zak's hands and squeeze them gently.

'I promise I won't, if you don't want me to. But you must talk to her at some point. I could be there with you when you do it.'

Zak looks uncertain. 'Would I have to tell her I took her phone and saw Daddy's texts?'

Oh God.

'Well, honesty is always—'

'Daddy says he wants to see Mummy and me. I'm scared she'll say "yes". That would be my fault. When it was Mummy's birthday I wanted to blow out a candle on her cake and make a wish that we never had to see Daddy ever again, but Mummy stopped me before I could do it because it was time to go to school.'

I pause, debating what to tell him. 'You will always be your mother's first priority. I know she wants to protect you from your father.'

'Dog used to protect us, but he's gone. I have to protect Mummy on my own and I'm not doing a good job. I keep making mistakes. I thought I saw Daddy outside my school, but it was only a workman. He had tattoos on his hands. I thought I saw him at the shops. But I was wrong. Most of the times I see Daddy in my dreams, but he doesn't look like a man. He's a giant serpent.'

He lowers his gaze, but I don't let go of his hands.

'This is why I'm convinced you should confide in your mother. She can reassure you better than me. Provide comfort, the way Dog used to.'

'Mummy doesn't always tell the truth. She says everything is OK, even when it isn't. She doesn't explain stuff.'

'My mother used to be the same,' I admit. 'I found that annoying.'

Zak smiles weakly. He pulls his hands away, placing them on his hips.

'Yeah, right? Mummy tells me not to think about death, but I can't help it after reading *Harry Potter*. If she dies, would I have to live with Daddy or would I be put in a children's home?'

I rub my forehead. Talking to Zak about his feelings has opened up a Pandora's box that I feel increasingly ill-equipped to deal with.

'Your mother is fit and healthy. She's not obese or a smoker – two factors that are known to cause cancers. The average life expectancy of women in the UK is eighty-one so I don't think you've got anything to worry about for a long time.'

'*Your* mummy died when you were a kid.'

His words stab at my heart, but I pretend I'm unaffected. 'Yes, but other factors were at play. Also, I was far older than you when it happened – seventeen. The council found me suitable accommodation; I was able to live independently after I'd left Cambridge due to my age, while my brother remained at college and continued with his medical studies. That was a long time ago, of course. I don't know the current rules, but I'm sure the child's needs and wishes would be paramount – above familial ties.'

Zak stares back blankly. 'Does that mean I wouldn't have to go and live with Daddy? Someone would help?'

'Social services would *never* let you go with your father, given his history of lawbreaking. They – along with myself – wouldn't allow such a move. I promise you, Zak. I won't let your father hurt you or your mother.'

'You're a mega swot, not a superhero.'

'I have hidden powers. Archie, the stray cat at Prince Burger, knows that. He only trusts me and scratches anyone else who ventures too close.'

'Cool!'

'Shall we go to the museum now?'

'Nah!' He points at a kiosk at the far end of the playground. 'After you've bought me a lolly, you can help me build a room in my head, where I can put all the bad stuff I remember about Daddy.'

'Well, if you're sure . . . ?'

He nods. 'First, can you give me a ride? I want to see the thing up that tree.' He points to the oak. 'The frrr-something-or-other.'

'Do you mean fractals?'

'Yes! Lift me up.'

I bend down and he clambers onto my shoulders.

29

JODIE

'WE'RE BACK!' ZAK RACES through the door into our bedsit, followed by Simon.

A neighbour has buzzed them in through the main door, which is a pain. I was going to come down as I hadn't wanted Simon to see how we live; I've managed to avoid letting him come up here until now. I'm not sure I can face him spouting off twenty facts about mould.

'How was your day?' I say.

'Awesome!'

'What about you, Simon? Did you survive?'

His forehead is furrowed, his cheeks pale. He's probably knackered after spending the day with this ball of energy.

'Today was . . . memorable.' He stares at Zak, opening his mouth to speak. He shuts it again.

'Oh God. What happened?'

Simon looks around, taking in the double bed that also acts as our sofa, the microwave, a portable hob for saucepans and our unwelcome mouldy guest – Hairy Mo, minus his balloons, which I've managed to rub off with washing-up liquid. Luckily, it's not a total tip. Once the rough draft of my essay was out of the way, I'd fixed the dripping showerhead in the communal bathroom down the corridor, folded up the washing and tidied our room. I've managed to crack open the window to air the place and lit joss sticks, but the smell of damp remains.

'Simon?'

He's staring at my bird tattoo.

'Should I be worried? Did Zak break something valuable? Have you both been banned from ever going back to the museum? Tell me!'

He breathes out, looking up.

'No, nothing like that, but the funny thing is we didn't go to the museum in the end. We stopped off at a playground and lost track of the time. I'm sorry about that, but it was still an educational experience for Zak. We learnt about gravitational force and pendulums.'

Zak translates for him. 'We went on the swings for ages and swapped stories about being little kids and had ice lollies.'

'*We?*'

I find it hard to imagine Simon in a playground, let alone sitting on a swing and eating a lolly.

'Yes, Simon joined in,' Zak says, 'even though he didn't want to at first. He said no one eats lollies in winter. After that, he got an insect in his eye and it made him cry.'

'I don't remember that,' Simon says.

'You blubbed. *A lot*. Other kids were staring and pointing. It was embarrassing.'

The frown lifts from his forehead as he laughs. 'That's *not quite* what happened!'

I ruffle Zak's hair, which resembles a bird's nest. 'Stop tormenting him. It's not nice, especially when he's given you a lovely day out. I hope you remembered to say, "thank you".'

'Thank you for not taking me to the museum,' he says impishly. 'I much preferred the playground.'

'We can go another time, if your mother allows it,' Simon replies. 'I honestly think it's worth a visit. You'll learn a great deal about life in Victorian England. There are hands-on elements, such as smell jars and soundscapes.'

'I'd prefer to learn about that thing you say is stuck on the slide.'

'You mean friction? Well, it isn't exactly *stuck*.'

'Simon was right,' Zak says, smiling. 'Maths is all around us, *everywhere*.'

'I had no idea!'

'Also, everything in life is possible. We talked about that too.'

'Wow! Maths *and* motivational speeches.' I turn to Simon. 'Thank you, I got lots done. Do you want to stop for something to eat or do you have to shoot off?'

I'm hoping he will leave. I haven't been shopping yet and there's only enough leftovers for the two of us in the fridge. It's veggie slosh again – I'm the Queen of Variety.

'I need to return to the Riemann Hypothesis. I managed to mull over some of my calculations on the way home. I'm excited to double-check my figures.'

'Talking of which, I was wondering if I could beg another favour?'

'What do you need?'

'Hold on a sec.'

I steer Zak over to the bed and help him take off his coat,

shoes and one glove. Dammit. He's lost another one; it's not in his pockets.

'Can you read your book while we have a chat about something?'

'Is this about me?' Zak shoots a worried look at Simon.

'No.'

'If you're sure.' He sneaks another furtive glance.

What happened today?

I gesture to Simon to follow me out into the corridor.

'Are you sure it went OK?' I ask, closing the door. 'There's nothing I need to know?'

He shakes his head. 'Zak is a delight, but you were right. Looking after a child wasn't as easy as I'd first thought. He doesn't stop running around. It must be hard being a single mother who . . .' He stops abruptly, his gaze shifting to the floor and then to my tattoo again. 'What do you need?'

'Well, tell me if this is a crazy idea, but I've been thinking about how you're a Cambridge graduate and a soon-to-be-famous mathematician who solves the Riemann Hypothesis. It could boost my Lucy Cavendish application.'

'Sorry, I'm not following you.'

'I want you to give me a personal reference.'

Simon swallows hard, running a hand through his hair. 'Why? Cambridge doesn't want personal references. They always have to be from an academic source – a teacher or tutor.'

'*You* are tutoring me. I've submitted my college tutor's reference with my application, but I have no idea what Monica's said about me. What if she lets slip something bad, like how I panic under pressure?'

'That's not likely. She wants to boost your chances, not harm them.'

'But—'

His phone vibrates with a call. He pulls it out of his pocket, his shoulders tensing.

'Hold on a second.'

He waits for the call to be diverted to voicemail before turning his back and listening to the message. I do the same when my phone flashes up as 'unknown caller' – Jason knows all the dark avenues to use.

Who is Simon avoiding?

'Is everything OK?' I ask.

He faces me again, the muscles in his face relaxing as he slips the phone into his coat.

'Yes! It wasn't who I thought it was. But actually . . . no, it's not OK, but in a completely different way.'

'You've lost me.'

'I forgot I've arranged a delivery for this evening. That was the driver; he's on his way to my flat. I need to shoot off otherwise I'll lose my slot.'

'But remember—'

'I can't tell you what's being dropped off. This is going to be a big surprise for both of you!' He waves over his shoulder as he strides away.

I can't let him off the hook about the reference – it *could* give me an advantage. I know I can make him realize that. I'm finally starting to see a person who understands more than the facts and figures he uses as a safety net.

Simon won't let me down.

30

SIMON

THE ARRIVAL OF THE flat-screen TV was a godsend; it enabled me to let down Jodie gently without upset. I cannot give her a reference, but I know she doesn't give up when she wants something. She'll keep pestering me in the hope I'll acquiesce as I did with tutoring. I must distract her, the way I managed to lead Zak on to discussion of lighter topics with the purchase of an ice lolly earlier.

But how?

I understand why she wants to do her best to impress the tutors. The miserable squalor of her existence left me speechless earlier: the condensation dripping in channels from the cling film stuck to the window, the mould crawling up the walls, the possessions in plastic bags and the double bed she and Zak must share. But I also spotted the piles of novels that are lovingly stacked. Jodie definitely deserves an escape route from that depressing room, Zak too. I simply have to make her realize she doesn't need my reference to achieve this freedom – indeed, it would do much more harm than good.

I open my laptop and stare at my calculations. I rub my eyes, barely believing what I'm seeing on the screen.

A glorious pattern slowly emerges from the prime number sequence I have spent months, *years*, creating.

Is this . . . Could it possibly be . . . ? I run through the numbers again.

Oh my goodness!

It is!

I slump back in my chair, stunned.

I'm right; I have made a major breakthrough! I simply have to follow the figures to their inevitable conclusion and success beckons. I'm on the brink of solving the Riemann Hypothesis with my unique zeta function theory; I can literally taste success. I think I can *finally* prove that for all complex numbers with a real number of 0.5 the zeta function is always zero.

I'm tempted to tell William, to announce my findings to the whole world! But I must keep a level head and check and double-check my figures again before typing out a submission to the Clay Mathematics Institute. Perhaps I could confide my looming success to Jodie; she's good at keeping secrets. I ponder the sequence of events leading to where she and Zak find themselves today. At the heart of their own disturbing pattern is Jason. He is the problem that must be solved, to enable them to succeed – and they *must*. I see something of myself in Zak. Despite having a mother who adores him, he thinks he has no one to talk to. Jodie would willingly sacrifice herself for him, but I know from painful experience this is not the answer.

They both have to escape from their past if they're to move

forward. I must somehow persuade Jodie to stand up to Jason without betraying Zak's confidence. This is the solution to all our predicaments – she will be distracted and have far bigger things on her mind than a reference. Getting rid of Jason will also be the first step to improving their lives, the beginning of a new, far more joyful sequence.

I have cracked the formula for their happiness. What a day!

My eyes settle on my calculations again, but I know their resolution isn't rooted in maths. Jodie turns to literature for answers. I catch sight of the Kindle by my laptop. I close my eyes and enter the newly opened room in my Memory Palace dedicated to the novel *To Kill a Mockingbird*. I revisit the pivotal scene when Scout confronts Mr Cunningham outside the jail. An idea begins to take shape.

Jodie is sitting at my kitchen table on Monday morning, her phone buzzing like an angry insect between us, as we focus on her personal statement. She's cited her interest in the novels of Charles Dickens, chivalry in medieval literature and the short stories of Katherine Mansfield.

'The tutors will definitely home in on these subjects, at least initially, before branching off to other topics,' I say.

She hasn't had time to ask me about the reference. In turn, I haven't confessed to making a breakthrough with the Riemann Hypothesis. After she's practised key points on each subject, we move on to interview techniques and breathing exercises.

'Do you remember the day of your interview, Simon?'

I close my eyes as she stares at her phone. I'm back outside that suite of dark-panelled rooms in Magdalene, waiting to be called in by the tutor. William and Mother were sitting either side of me; Father opposite. His eyes had bored into me, making my shoulders concave.

Don't forget everything I've taught you. Don't screw up.

I had to swallow repeatedly to prevent myself from vomiting.

'It was great,' I say finally. 'Very exciting!'

She shoves her mobile aside. 'Did the tutor ask any horrible questions to trip you up?'

He was abrupt and intimidating, but once I started studying I realized that was simply his manner. Dr Spencer was kind to his students.

'No, it was more like a supervision.'

'Yeah, because I have so much experience of whatever that is.'

'They're basically tutorials. The tutors are trying to find out if they can stretch your mind and work with you. You're not the finished article during the interview, that's only the beginning of your learning process.'

'Hmm.' Jodie's pen hovers over her notepad. 'What would be your number one piece of advice?'

'Don't be stubborn or proud about knowing when to ask for help. The tutors want to take you to your limits, and see if you're prepared to accept assistance to go beyond any learning you've ever imagined.'

She nods, making notes.

'Which brings me neatly to my next point. You need to know when to ask for help in dealing with Jason.'

The pen slips through her fingers.

'Hear me out. This isn't working – the whole trying-to-ignore-him business. It's a distraction from your studies, which is frightening you and . . . I believe you have to confront the situation, instead of hiding from it. For your sake and Zak's.'

'You think I should meet up with the guy who's scarred me for life?' She pulls up her sleeve, exposing the tattoo.

'I'd come with you – we'll go somewhere safe in public, away from where you live. There are things I believe you must say to Jason otherwise you will never have closure. I wish I'd confronted my father about his behaviour.'

Before it was too late.

I point at her vibrating phone. 'This is stopping you from moving on with your life.'

She shakes her head. 'You have no idea who I'm dealing with. Seeing him could make things worse.'

'How can it get any worse? He's controlling the situation and intimidating you with every message.'

'I don't think I can do it.'

'That's not the Jodie Brook I know. She never gives up, whatever life throws at her.'

She looks dubious, but I also see the crack of a smile.

'It's time to take the battle to him instead of waiting around, worrying about an ambush.'

'What are you suggesting?'

'*We* fight him with words, as Scout did with Mr Cunningham.'

'I've told you before. That's fiction and it's not going to work with Jason. You can't scare him off by talking about *To Kill a Mockingbird*. He'll laugh in your face before he beats you to a bloody pulp – think The Worstomer, but one hundred times more violent.'

'I'm not afraid. I'll be equipped with my secret weapons.'

'Oh Jesus. You're not going to threaten him with a blade, are you? I don't want to be involved in anything like that. I'm seriously anti knives.'

I frown. 'Who said anything about knives? Facts are my weapons. We're going to defeat Zak's father using my Memory Palace.'

31

JODIE

Two days later, my gaze flits over the smartly dressed businessman in a white shirt, lilac tie and dark blue, pinstripe suit as I scan the café for Simon.

'Jodie! Over here!' Pinstripe Suit Man waves at me.

'Simon?'

I'm used to the scarecrow version of Simon, not the groomed, freshly shaved one. He's had a haircut – a professional one, instead of his usual home hacking job. His face is a healthier colour, making his cheekbones look high and chiselled instead of sunken and hollowed. As I weave through the tables, I realize his suit is the perfect choice. It doesn't swamp him like most of his other clothes, and it brings out the colour of his eyes. He's surprisingly handsome. *For Simon*, I add quickly to myself.

'I didn't know you were serious about dressing up!' I stare at my shabby jeans as I sit down.

'I have to look the part – a modern-day Atticus Finch.' He tugs at his tie. 'What do you think of the suit?'

'It's . . . I don't know. I'm not a fashion expert. I guess it looks OK?'

He might fall off his chair if I tell him he looks like a slimmer version of Adam Driver. I notice a pretty woman at the corner table glancing over and trying to make eye contact.

'I bought it in a sale yesterday in preparation for when I get invited to the Clay Mathematics Institute. I'll have to do a presentation for the world's press shortly.'

'Does that mean . . . ?'

'I honestly think it does!' he exclaims happily. 'I think I've finally solved the Riemann Hypothesis! I'm double-checking to be thorough but I expect to make a submission shortly.'

'That's amazing!' I squeeze his arm. 'Congratulations! I knew you'd do it.'

He beams back. 'Anyway, I thought the suit would work for today.'

'Good plan.'

I try to press him on his breakthrough, but he insists we concentrate on meeting prep.

'Let me do the talking as your legal representative. I'm Simon Sparks from Sparks, Atticus and Finch solicitors' firm.'

'Atticus and Finch? That's too much . . .'

'Really? I thought it was a nice touch.'

'It sounds fake. Jason may be a thug, but he's not a complete idiot.'

'Don't worry. I'll make it sound believable, I promise. I've been getting tips from watching excerpts of *Suits* on YouTube. Interesting series, by the way.'

I shake my head. 'That does not reassure me. The US legal system is completely different to over here.'

Simon leans across the table, flinching slightly as his fingers tentatively find mine. 'I know. I've looked it up on the internet and done my research. I'll do a good job. I won't let you down. I've been practising for hours.'

'But—'

'This is going to be over soon, I promise. You'll be rid of Jason for good.'

I stare down at his hand, which is covering mine; it feels warm and comforting. His face flushes as he pulls it away sharply.

'Sorry, I—'

My face reddens. 'It's OK. I'm not going to sue my own lawyer.' I check my watch. 'We should probably get going even though he'll be late.'

Simon picks up his leather briefcase. '*Audentes fortuna iuvat.* Fortune favours the bold.'

'Couldn't you have found somewhere less posh?'

I look around the hotel lobby in Covent Garden from our table. Suited men and women sit on velvet-scalloped chairs and settees, tapping away at slim, silver laptops. A waiter has brought over a pot of tea, three cups and a plate of tiny cakes, which cost £15. What a rip-off! For that price I want to take home the china, maybe even a cushion or two.

'This is the perfect place. I've researched it extensively. It's nowhere near your home and it will put Jason at a disadvantage – he'll be out of his comfort zone. I want to put him on the back foot.'

'*I'm* out of my comfort zone.'

I feel even more conscious of my old jeans and scuffed trainers. Simon had suggested I wear a skirt and blouse, but no way could I give Jason the impression I'm making an effort to see him.

Now, I wish I'd at least put on my usual weaponry: winged black eyeliner, red lips and mascara. I scrub at the mark on my jeans where I dropped a minuscule éclair.

'You look fine.' He glances up. 'Is *that* your ex?'

Air rushes to my ears; a lump rises in my throat, choking me. A tall, muscular man with a shaved head, dressed in jeans and a black sweater, has appeared in the doorway. Jason hasn't changed much – a few lines beneath his eyes and a new scar on his forehead, but his eyes are still dark and cold. My gaze lowers to his tattooed knuckles: *Love, hate.* The disfigured skin on my back contracts and expands, like a creature breathing of its own free will.

'Take a breath,' Simon whispers.

I can't. He's walking over. I look around wildly for the exit.

'We're in control here, not him. We hold all the cards.'

I attempt to inhale and breathe out deeply, unable to reply.

'Mr Bishop?' Simon stands up, hand outstretched. 'I'm Mr Sparks from Sparks, Atticus and Finch. Thank you for agreeing to meet my client.'

Dammit. I'd told him to drop the Atticus and Finch.

Jason throws himself into a chair, ignoring Simon. His eyes are locked on mine. His body is tensed, anger simmering beneath the surface.

'Client?' He leans forward. 'Or lover?'

I force myself not to break eye contact, swallowing the vomit in my mouth. I shiver as he cracks his knuckles one by one.

Love, hate, love, hate.

Simon begins talking. 'Miss Brook has employed me due to your continuing harassment. My client plans to sue you in a civil suit if you persist. *De facto*, we will also make a formal complaint to the police and pursue a criminal prosecution to gain *jus naturale*.'

He removes a sheaf of papers from his briefcase. '*Ipso facto*, you should take this *in terrorem*.'

'What the fuck are you talking about?' Jason snaps.

'I explained in Latin, by that very fact, you should take this as a warning or deterrent, *orse*, otherwise, we will be *volens*, willing, to make a complaint to the police alleging coercive control under section 76 of the Serious Crime Act 2015.'

I shoot a look at Simon, silently pleading with him to tone it down. He sure as hell hasn't picked this up from watching *Suits*; he must have memorized the top thirty Latin legal terms off the internet, but solicitors don't talk like this.

Jason will know that. He's spent hours and hours with his legal reps over the years.

'Is this arsehole for real?' Jason jerks his head at Simon.

'He's completely serious and so am I. Stop texting me. Stop ringing. Leave me alone. *We've* moved on and don't want anything to do with you.'

'I'll take it from here,' Simon insists. '*Per minas*, by means of menaces or threat, you have attempted to control my client and I'm confident, *per curiam*, in the opinion of the court, you will be found guilty of harassment and coercive control. We have extensive evidence.' He holds up his papers. 'You have sent more than two hundred texts to my client in the last few weeks, which has caused her "serious alarm or distress" and had a "substantial adverse effect" on her day-to-day activities, as per section 76, 4b, of the Serious Crime Act. I am also confident we have met the required threshold under section 2 of the Protection from Harassment Act 1997.'

'There's no need for this.' Jason's mouth widens into a slash, but the smile doesn't reach his eyes as he stares at me. 'You don't need a lawyer. Can't we have a friendly chat?'

That's impossible with Jason.

I steel myself. *Keep breathing, Jodie.* 'We have nothing to talk about. I want you to stay out of my life and Zak's for good.'

'I'm his dad, remember?'

'You have no legal rights, regarding contact with a minor,' Simon chips in. 'Given your criminal record, no family court will ever give you access to Zak, should you pursue this matter further.'

'You've never been his dad, not a real one, who was ever there for him,' I add, gathering ammunition. 'The only reason you want to see us now is to take our benefits – Zak's child support – and anything else you can get your hands on. Well, here's the thing – we're broke. I'm in debt and we don't have a council flat. We were made homeless, thanks to you. We're still in temporary accommodation waiting for a permanent home.'

'You have enough money to hire a *so-called lawyer*,' he says silkily.

I feel a flush creep up my cheeks. Jason smells a rat.

'This is *pro bono* work,' Simon says. 'That means I'm working for free. My boss, Atticus, is a firm believer in social justice and helping those who are less fortunate – people who have been dealt a poor hand of cards in life.'

Jason studies him. 'What's the name of your firm again? It sounds familiar.'

Simon repeats it. 'Would you like a business card in case you have further queries about our proposed legal action?'

He shakes his head, leaning back in his chair. He strokes his chin, a deep furrow appearing between his eyes.

Oh no. We've been rumbled. We need to get out of here.

'*Ceteris paribus* – other things being equal – do we understand each other, Mr Bishop?' Simon persists.

Jason's gaze swerves to the teapot. *Hard porcelain; scalding water.*

My heart thumps wildly. I push the teapot further away and catch the eye of the waiter who heads over.

'We're done with the tea, thanks.'

'Leave mine.' Jason pours himself a cup. 'I think I understand *everything*. Thank you for making it so clear to someone as uneducated as me.'

'Excellent. *Cadit Quaestio*. The matter admits of no further argument.'

Simon places the papers in his briefcase and stands up. This time, he doesn't offer to shake hands.

'Goodbye, Jason,' I say.

He doesn't reply or look up. He remains seated, cracking his knuckles one by one, staring darkly out of the window as I walk away. I follow Simon out of the lobby onto the street. A gust of icy wind slaps my cheeks.

'We did it!' Simon cries. 'We pulled it off!'

I catch a look of pure joy on his face that I've never seen before.

'Absolutely!' I smile weakly. I don't have the heart to tell him otherwise.

'I wasn't sure if I went too far with the Latin?'

Time to lie.

'No. You were brilliant. Thank you.'

'There's no need to thank me. I enjoyed performing; it was a useful test of my legal and Latin facts.'

I open my arms for a hug, but he misunderstands the gesture and I walk into his outstretched hand.

'Ow!'

'Sorry!'

We shake hands awkwardly.

'Do you want to get a drink?' He coughs with embarrassment.

'I mean, to celebrate Jason and my breakthrough with the Riemann Hypothesis. I didn't mean in a . . .'

I interrupt before he launches into an excruciating speech.

'I can't tonight, sorry. I have to pick up Zak from school and I can't drag him out again later – he had a bad cough this morning. I'm worried it could go to his chest.'

'Oh, of course, sorry.' He looks downcast.

'But we should toast our joint success tomorrow? It's the pub quiz, remember? I could ask Sandra to take Zak if she's up to it and his chest is OK. Why don't you come along? Arthur mentioned you in his text. He'd love to see you.'

Simon's eyes widen with surprise. 'Really? Well, maybe . . .'

'I promise you that opening up to people will be nowhere near as scary as facing Jason.'

He exhales slowly. 'I guess *audentes fortuna iuvat* – fortune favours the bold.'

'Exactly! You've just earned an extra drink on me for being brave.'

I glance over my shoulder as we start walking, but the street is empty. I shiver.

'What is it?'

'Nothing. I'm just cold.'

I don't want to ruin his victory by admitting that something feels off.

Jason never used to let people walk away scot-free when he suspected they'd tricked him.

32

SIMON

I WASH MY FACE AND hands in the men's bathroom at Prince Burger and stare at my reflection in the mirror. I look different, not only because of the new, stylish cut I received at the barbers' shop. My skin has an unusually healthy glow and the shadows under my eyes are less pronounced. My face and figure appear fuller, yet I feel lighter than I have in years.

The Riemann Hypothesis is within my grasp!

I have vanquished Jason!

My heart flutters as I think about tonight. I put my hands back under the cold water tap to cool my wrists. Maybe agreeing to help the Three Wise Men tonight is a step too far; the probability of three consecutive successes is low. What if it goes to the sudden-death round and I freeze, letting them down? But how can I drop out now without causing offence?

I head out the back to surreptitiously feed Archie. I call out his name and see a flash of orange behind the dustbins. He creeps out, curling around my ankles.

'Do you think I should try to help the team win tonight? Or should I come up with a last-minute excuse?'

Archie purrs as I tickle him under his chin. His wound is healing up nicely after application of my antibiotic cream. I put down a saucer of his favourite salmon chunks and another of cream as a special treat.

He swiftly abandons his show of affection, prioritizing food over my problem; he is a cat after all.

Jodie is waiting for me on the street, shivering as she looks at her phone. I notice that her white-blonde hair is around her shoulders; it suits her worn down.

'How's Zak?'

'Much better, thanks. Sandra too.'

'Anything from Jason?'

'No, nothing.'

I smile back. 'Mission accomplished!'

She nods as we walk to the bus stop. 'Talking of Jason – with all that stuff going on, I keep forgetting to ask you something.'

'What?'

'You know – about that reference.'

'What reference?' I ask, playing for time.

'You know, the personal one I asked you to write. I could do with forwarding it on to the director of studies early next week if you don't mind banging something out over the weekend.'

I grind to a halt. 'I've explained this, Jodie. You don't need one from me.'

'But it could help.'

'Except it won't.'

'Well it can't hurt, can it? Please, Simon. Do it for Zak and me.'

'Haven't I done enough? Haven't I solved your Jason problem?'

She looks down and chews her bottom lip.

'Look, I really appreciate everything you've done for me. It's just a few glowing paragraphs, that's all. It'll take ten minutes tops to write and I'll do your cleaning duties or finish your next shift to say "thank you".'

I try to speak, but she cuts in.

'I know what you're going to say: *I'm wasting my time.* But so what if they delete the email? At least I'll know I've tried everything.'

I grit my teeth. I have to close this down once and for all – at whatever cost.

'Look, are you sure this is what you want? I'm not talking about the reference. I mean Cambridge.'

'Of course I'm sure! This is what I've dreamt about for years.'

'Don't take this the wrong way, Jodie, but Cambridge is, well, tough. The terms are condensed into eight weeks. It can be gruelling if you're not used to a pressured, high-stakes environment.'

'What? I'm not clever enough. Is that it?'

'No, of course you are. What I'm trying to say is that Cambridge might not live up to your expectations. You could be unhappy, mixing with people who are so different from you. I was a misfit. I don't want you to be one too.'

She clenches her fists tightly. 'You think I'm common as well as stupid? That I should give up because I haven't had a private school education and Daddy couldn't get me work experience with his mates at the investment bank?'

'No. I'm speculating, *wondering*, if you'd be better suited to somewhere less pressured, somewhere more accepting of people who are, well, different.'

She inhales sharply as I plough on.

'You could study part time at a higher education college or on a distance-learning course while you work and look after Zak. It would take longer to get your degree – maybe about six years – but you'll end up with less debt.'

'Would you want to work from home for six years in a depressing, cold bedsit or whichever shithole the council moves us to next? I'm guessing not! *And* I'll still have big debts to pay off.' Her body trembles as she stabs a finger in my direction.

'*You* of all people know what it's like to have a dream. The whole Riemann Hypothesis thing doesn't make much bloody sense to me and I bet there are a million easier paths you could take. But you're still chasing your dream whatever the hurdles, aren't you? Because it *means* something to you. Don't I deserve to follow my *own* dream?'

Her accusation opens a tiny, painful wound in my chest.

'I'm doing this, whatever you think. I want to get the best degree, *a Cambridge degree*, something that will make my mum . . .' She bites her lip, hard.

'What about your mum? You never talk about her.'

She shakes her head.

'Never mind. What matters is that you're trying to pull up the ladder behind you, which is shitty.'

'It would be remiss of me in my duties as your tutor if I didn't outline the huge challenges ahead.'

It surprises me how easily the lies slip off my tongue.

I step closer, but she backs away.

'You don't believe in me. That's it, isn't it? You're like my old teachers and social workers.'

'No, I definitely think you're capable of doing this, but I'm questioning whether you should.'

'Same difference!' she yells. 'You're so cold, Simon, I sometimes wonder whether you have a pulse!'

'Look—'

'Don't bother coming to the pub. I've got this.' She storms off down the road.

I've gone home to practise memorizing my decks. I can't face another outbreak of World War Three by turning up at the quiz.

Jodie's furious words hammer into my forehead as I flick over card after card.

Lick.

Flick.

Lick.

Flick.

Like the lashings from a whip.

I rest my aching head in my hands.

I'm in a no-win situation. If I do as she asks, the result would be catastrophic. But if I don't, Jodie could drop me. Our tutor sessions will be terminated along with the time I spend with her and Zak.

I close my eyes. The odds of me winning this new game are low.

The deck is stacked against me. Still, I must play. I will let the cards decide my next move. I shuffle my deck and turn over the top card, opening my eyes.

The queen of hearts.

33

JODIE

'Is Simon coming?' Arthur looks up hopefully as I slump into the seat beside him in The Rising Sun.

'I don't think so, sorry. He was on his way, but something came up. He had to go home.'

'That's a shame.'

I've replayed our argument over and over again on the way here. Maybe I misunderstood Simon and he was looking out for me. I know Sandra thinks I'm crazy trying to get into Cambridge. But I thought Simon, above anyone else, would understand why I'm going for it, even though I haven't told him one of the main reasons, which involves my mum. That's too personal.

Winston pats my hand. 'At least *you* made it.'

Is that enough to win? I glance at the empty chair next to me. I don't want bad blood between us. Simon's put himself out for me: tutoring, helping with Zak and trying to scare off Jason. I just can't work out why he's so reluctant to give me the reference for Lucy Cavendish. Am I overstepping the mark? Is it really too much to ask? Either way, perhaps I shouldn't have lost my rag. I grab my mobile to text him.

'Can you all hear me?' Quizmaster Philip taps his mic. 'The first round will be maths and physics, so get your thinking caps on!'

Arthur sighs deeply and Winston and Trevor take large gulps of their pints.

Oh shit.

These are Simon's strongest topics – and our weakest. We *really* need him.

Sorry for being such a cow, I type. *Please come to the quiz!*

As the barman distributes pieces of paper and pens around the tables my phone vibrates. I snatch it up, scanning the messages hopefully. *Yes!* It's Simon. He's replied by email.

Dear Jodie
I had a headache and wasn't thinking straight. Of course, you should set your sights on Cambridge. Why settle for less when you can aim high? I hope this reference suffices.
However, I don't feel well enough to compete tonight. Please extend my apologies to the team.
Yours sincerely,
Simon

My eyes scan down the page – Simon has gushed about my dedication, hard work and love of literature, declaring me 'a joy to teach'. He's signed it 'Simon Sparks Esquire, BA (Hons), Cantab.'

I can't believe it! What made him change his mind?

Quickly, I type out a reply:

Thank you so much! It means such a lot to me. Jodie x

On second thoughts, I delete the kiss in case he thinks . . . well, I never have a clue what he's thinking. I forward his reference to the director of studies, along with a short explanatory message before Simon changes his mind. Sinking into my seat, I feel warmth rise in my cheeks.

He may not be helping the team but he came through for *me*.

We're working together in Prince Burger's drive-through cabin the next afternoon. I've thanked Simon again for his help, but our silly argument is the elephant in the – very small – room.

'Some of the members of Team Victorem made paper aeroplanes from spare answer sheets and threw them at another team to put them off!' I say, before we lapse into another strained silence.

He grunts, but doesn't turn around.

'And you wouldn't believe it – not a single English Literature question came up!'

Simon continues to quietly line up orders.

'Anyway, we were beaten into second place by Team Victorem. They went for the sudden-death question, but couldn't name the first Millennium Problem to be solved. Of course, I knew it was the Poincaré Conjecture, thanks to you!'

Simon's shoulders tense. 'I'm sorry I wasn't there.'

Dammit. I'd meant it as a compliment. Instead, I've inadvertently made him feel bad. We both know that if he'd taken part we'd have sailed through the maths and physics rounds and won the sudden-death question.

'No one blames you, obviously. You weren't feeling well.' *Thanks to me ripping your head off.* 'Maybe next time?'

'Sure.'

The intercom blares to life – our connection to the booth that takes the drivers' orders, which is located thirty feet away. 'Heads up, The Worstomer's coming your way. He's ordered twenty Coke Zeros and one packet of fries.'

Simon grips the side of the counter. 'There's only one thing worse than The Worstomer and that's The Worstomer on wheels. Shall I take over?'

'No, I can do this.'

'Are you sure, because last time—'

'No! Honestly, I want to do this. I stood up to Jason and now I *need* to do the same with this psycho.'

I watch as the orders arrive and Simon places the Coke Zeros into holders. His hands are shaking. I look down and realize mine are too.

A black BMW, missing both wing mirrors, pulls up. The Worstomer is barking into his mobile phone. Sweat glistens on his forehead.

'Are you ready, Simon?'

'No,' he whispers.

'Yes, you are. We're both going to stand our ground today.'

I turn to the hatch and pass the first batch of four Coke Zeros. 'Here you go, sir!'

He grunts. The next four holders are safely delivered without The Worstomer responding, along with the fries. I smile over my shoulder at Simon.

'That went well!' I whisper.

I turn back as The Worstomer removes the lid from one of the cups. He glares at the liquid before clamping the lid on.

'This isn't what I ordered, dipshit! I wanted Diet Coke.' He leans out of the car and throws the cup through the hatch. From that point, everything seems to move in slow motion. I duck, but I see the drink sail past and reach its target: hitting Simon squarely on the forehead, exploding down his uniform.

A red mist descends before my eyes. 'What the hell did you do that for, you arsehole?'

'It's OK,' Simon insists. 'Don't worry.'

'No. It's not OK.'

'What the hell did you call me?' The Worstomer yells, hanging out his window.

'You heard me, arsehole!' I shout.

Men like him can't keep getting away with assaulting whoever they want. He tries to hurl another cup through the hatch, but misses. Brown, sticky liquid drips down the glass. Over the intercom, the guy in the neighbouring booth says he's dialling 999.

Simon steps forward. 'Working out the trajectory of a flying object depends on the speed and angle of projection. It's basic mathematics, taught in high school.'

'Do I look like someone who gives a fuck about maths?' The Worstomer's hand reaches for another drink from the trays on the passenger seat.

'You should, sir, because I can calculate the range by taking the square of the initial launch velocity, multiplied by the sine of twice the angle of projection, divided by the acceleration due to gravity.'

'Come again?' He leans further out of the car window.

'I have omitted an item from your order. I do apologize for the inconvenience, sir. I am sending it forthwith, using applied mathematics.'

Simon picks up the next order and throws the cup. It soars through the air, in a perfect arc, and detonates on The Worstomer's shaved head.

34

SIMON

'HOLY SHIT!' JODIE GASPS. 'What have you done?'
'I've delivered his order using a mathematical equation for trajectory.'

I try to keep my voice level, riding on the adrenaline of the moment, but my knees are trembling. I may throw up.

Oh dear Lord. What came over me?

I try to retreat to safety inside my Memory Palace, checking over trajectory calculations, but my mind isn't letting me in. I'm stuck in the real world where, as Jodie would no doubt succinctly put it, I'm in deep shit.

The Worstomer splutters and shrieks expletives as he dabs himself down.

'I should offer him a serviette or two,' I murmur. 'It would be the polite thing to do before he kills me.'

'No point. We haven't finished delivering his order yet.'

Before I can stop her, she seizes a cup and leans out of the

236

hatch so far her feet dangle from the floor. She hurls it into The Worstomer's car. The liquid spills over the man's crotch.

'You're dead, bitch!' he screams, fumbling with the door handle. 'You're so fucking—'

He tumbles out onto the ground and lunges towards us, a movement that threatens to turn my bowels to water. I'm rooted to the spot, but Jodie battens down the defences. Miraculously, she has found the key and locked the hatch. Despite the fact The Worstomer is hammering his fists on the glass, he cannot break through.

'That should hold him off,' she says, panting.

We watch as he runs to the rear of his car, lifting up the boot.

'This doesn't look good,' I note.

'No shit, Sherlock.'

He emerges with a jack, unfortunately not the playing card variety. *Surely not.* He pulls his arm back, lifting the jack, and hurls it at our window. I duck as the glass explodes, firing tiny sword-like shards. I've reached the door but Jodie still hasn't moved. She stands transfixed, white-faced, as The Worstomer clambers through. Her gaze is glued to his bloodied, tattooed knuckles.

'Run, Jodie!'

She remains statue-like. I dart back, grab her hand and pull her out of the cabin. Something's wrong with her legs, they're not moving properly.

Not moving at all.

I half drag, half carry her to the ordering booth as police sirens wail faintly in the distance. We've almost made it. I push Jodie through the door first. A hand grabs my shoulder and swings me around. Pain explodes in my face.

Sarah J. Harris

Bright sparks create fires.
All I see are flickering lights.
The whole world must be ablaze.

35

JODIE

'*I ENJOYED MYSELF.*'

I say the words under my breath in case anyone walking past Ed's office overhears and thinks I'm a psycho. I don't mean the part when The Worstomer chased us and thumped Simon, of course. That was awful. But I felt bloody fantastic after throwing that drink – invincible, like a character from DC Comics.

I stood up to Jason, with Simon's help, *and* The Worstomer.

Now, that adrenaline rush has stopped pumping through my veins and I've crashed back down to earth. It's me, Jodie Brook, a single mum with a kid who needs me. I'm not Superwoman.

Far from it.

I pull the jacket around my shoulders, catching the dressing on my hand as I perch on the edge of the chair. A paramedic has checked me out – Simon too – and applied antiseptic cream to the cut from the glass. I can't feel it. I'm numb. I'm waiting to go into Ed's office; the walls are thin. Simon has been in there for twenty minutes and Ed has barely drawn breath as he's roasted him, despite his injury. God only knows what he's going to say before he fires me.

I've spoken to the police and described basically what happened, glossing over our cup-throwing. The officer was far more concerned with dealing with The Worstomer anyway. He'd punched Simon and a customer who tried to intervene, before knocking out a policewoman with the car jack. But I'll have to tell the police *everything* when I give a full statement. Oh God, what if throwing the cup is technically an assault? I could be charged and go to court. If I get a criminal record I'll struggle to get *any* job, even a low-paid one. My interview at Lucy Cavendish will be withdrawn if Admissions find out.

How could I have been so stupid?

I turn around and shakily trace my fingers over the dent in the wall, the damage caused by Simon's brick. I'd thought the worst about him on interview day, but he's stepped up. When The Worstomer climbed inside the kiosk, I'd frozen yet again. The slick of sweat on the guy's forehead and the sight of his tattooed, bloodied knuckles had brought it all back. I was no longer stuck in the drive-through with Simon; I was trapped in the flat with Jason.

Despite looking like a puff of wind could knock him down, Simon had dragged me away, pushing me into the ordering booth. After being punched, he'd leant against the door, a waif-like barricade between a mountain of a man and me. Blood had dripped from his lip and his eyes were wide with shock, but he hadn't budged.

Ed's door bangs open and Simon flies out, looking about wildly. His lip is swollen and split. He runs along the corridor.

'Simon!' I shout. 'Wait!'

He keeps on running, banging through doors.

'Jodie!' Ed barks. 'In here, now!'

Oh God. *Here goes.* I drag myself into the room.

'This is unfortunate.' Ed stares at my bandage, before picking up a pen and notepad.

You think? I slump into a seat before my knees give way.

'The police have arrested the customer on suspicion of causing grievous bodily harm among other offences. He'll be charged, undoubtedly, and there will be a court case. That means bad publicity for Prince Burger.'

He pauses, expecting a response, but I have nothing.

'It will come out about our customer being pelted with soft drinks by an employee *before* he launched his attack. He could get off. I've spoken to head office's legal department – they say his defence could argue that he was provoked. They've ordered me to make a pre-emptive strike before this comes out in court.' He holds up his hands. 'I feel bad about it, but I don't have any choice in the matter. Head office isn't happy with me letting Pam have time off whenever she needs to look after her husband during his chemo. They say I should put customers first, not the staff.'

'Pam's husband has cancer? I had no idea!'

'Well, apparently, I've been too lenient. Head office claims I shouldn't have dished out so many lieu days or allowed staff to change shifts to fit in with college and childcare and *life* either.' Ed shakes his head. 'If I don't take decisive action, I'm going to be replaced by a management stooge who won't hesitate to sack Pam and probably half my staff.'

'I understand,' I mumble, standing up. 'I'm sorry.'

'Sit down. I'm not firing you.'

'Why not? This is my fault.'

'It's my understanding that . . . you're not the person who started this.'

I sure as hell don't like where this is heading.

'You understand wrong. This is my fault, not Simon's.'

'Yet he has taken full responsibility for the incident.'

'Well, he shouldn't have! He threw the first cup, but it was reactive, and then I—'

'*He threw the first cup.*' Ed jots down notes. 'So you are confirming the Prof's statement that he provoked the customer?'

'I'm not confirming anything. If you're going to punish anyone, punish me.'

'Head office has told me to think about what's best for Prince Burger, *who's* the best fit for our image. Simon has never fitted in here. I should have got rid of him long ago, but I made the mistake of feeling sorry for him.'

'But it's not fair,' I splutter. 'To let Simon take all the blame.'

'Look, there's no point contradicting what the Prof has told me. Head office doesn't think it looks good PR-wise to sack a single mum. I only need one person to take the fall for what happened today and Simon has admitted it all. Plus, he was on his final warning and I'm pretty sure he was the person feeding that vicious cat who's been causing trouble.' He points to a deep scratch on his hand. 'I'm sorry, but I had to sack him without notice.'

I grip the side of the chair, my eyes filling with tears.

'I gave Simon a good reference even though head office advised me not to.' Ed leans forward in his chair. 'Are you going to accept my decision and continue to work at Prince Burger, or should I type out a reference for you as well?'

36

SIMON

I FLICK THROUGH YESTERDAY'S POST – most look like utility bills – along with the familiar brown envelope containing the latest copy of *New Scientist*. Will I still be able to afford the subscription? Splashing out on the flat-screen TV and a new suit was hasty and extravagant. It's drained my savings and left me in the red. I'm unemployed and have no buffer. I throw the unopened envelopes onto the kitchen table and flip the calendar over to face the wall. I don't want to think about the long days that stretch ahead before Christmas.

My equilateral triangle has been badly damaged and left out of shape. I must return to the research on my laptop, double-checking my workings out before bashing out my submission. If I can convince the institute this theory is correct, my financial woes will be over forever. However, the assessment of my theory by mathematical peers could take months. In the short term, I have to find another job.

This is not how I expected such a promising week to end.

My cheeks redden with renewed humiliation at my firing yesterday, but how could I have responded differently to Ed's questioning? I squeeze my eyes shut, thinking of Jodie. She has a child to support and feed. And I couldn't let her suffer a damaging setback ahead of her Cambridge interview. I'm also getting better at reading between the lines after finishing the books on her reading list.

Jodie was fighting her ex again, not The Worstomer.

An image comes into my mind of her and Zak shivering in their freezing bedsit with no money coming in, no comfort or food. My heart pangs uncomfortably. No, it's far better I take the fall despite the financial pressures, the volume of my research and worries over who will feed Archie.

After taking a cold shower to stimulate brain function, I turn my phone back on. Only Jodie and Pam have left messages – Ed, clearly, hasn't regretted his decision. I check the email address provided on Zak's posters. I have three new messages, offering various sexual services, but no one has disclosed the toy's where-abouts. I spend the next six hours checking my calculations while William repeatedly tries to get in touch. Eventually, on his fifth attempt, I break off.

'What's happened? I haven't been able to get through.'

I take a deep breath. 'The thing is, William, I've been fired from Prince Burger.'

Even though I attempt to sound upbeat, the words echo dully, *joylessly*, through the corridors inside my head. Shame continues to crawl like damp up the walls of the most neglected floors inside my Memory Palace.

William remains quiet as I briefly outline the encounter with The Worstomer. Eventually he breaks his silence as I settle into my favourite armchair in the sitting room.

'I know this is hard, but you have to look at the positives. Try to think of this as the best thing that's happened to you in a long time.'

'I guess so.'

'You can't tell me you're missing it already? Surely you wanted to leave? It was a dead-end job!'

'Of course I'm glad to be out of that hellhole! I won't have to permanently smell like French fries.'

My mind drifts to Archie waiting for me by the dustbins; Pam asking me if I want a cup of coffee in the crew room; Marta and Carlos discussing theories about *Game of Thrones*; Jodie catching up with me after work.

'This is also an amazing chance for you to reassess everything – decide what you want and get your life back on track.'

'You mean on the Sparks' family track,' I mutter.

William swallows a sigh. 'I hate to see you waste your life like this, year after year in menial jobs – stacking shelves in super-markets, picking up leaves for the council and working in fast-food outlets. It's killing Victoria and myself to watch.'

'I don't consider my time at Prince Burger as a waste,' I say tightly. 'Working there gave me time to work on my prime numbers theories.'

'And that's going so well!'

'It is! I'm pretty sure I've cracked the Riemann Hypothesis!' I blurt out the words before I can stop myself.

William falls into an incredulous silence.

'You've said that before,' he says eventually.

'Well, this time I mean it.'

He catches his breath. 'I believe in you, Simon.'

'Really? It doesn't sound like it.'

'Of course I do! If anyone can solve the Riemann Hypothesis, it's you. But the point is, it's been *years*, and the world has moved on without you.'

I wince. 'I'm so close to succeeding I can taste success! Leaving Prince Burger will give me the final push I need. I'm planning to start typing out my submission to the Clay Mathematics Institute early this week.'

'I'm sorry. I didn't mean it to sound like a criticism. I think it's great you've dedicated so much of your life to this mathematical theory. It takes real sacrifice – no one can ever accuse you of not being fully committed.'

'Hmm. Thanks.'

'Look, this has forced your hand, *finally*. Now is the ideal time to seriously consider what career you want to embark on. Find a *professional* job while you work on your submission. Attempt to dip your toes into academia – or at least update your bloody CV and bring out some of the positives you've gained from Prince Burger, like your team-building and people skills.'

'I suspect that being fired after throwing a cup of Coke Zero at a customer proves once and for all that I have no people skills.'

'Well, other things,' William says in exasperation. 'Look, you're the expert in the service industry, not me. You'll have to give it some thought, obviously.'

'*Obviously.*'

'Simon—'

Quickly, I cut in and enquire about the health of Victoria and the kids, which William fails to realize is an ironic demonstration of my people skills. He says she is hovering and wants to pin me down about Christmas, but I make my excuses, citing my mathematical research. Wearily, I cut him off. I don't feel like speaking to anyone. I slump further into the armchair.

I lied to my brother.

I'm not glad I left Prince Burger. Being sacked is even harder than I expected. Already, I miss Ed's laughably bad alien comparisons and the background noise: the hum of machinery and activity that allowed my mind to relax and focus on other tasks. Most of all I miss the company – the conversations with Pam whenever she picked up fries on her break, and Jodie cornering me at quiet moments to ask for interview technique tips or advice about the exam.

I'd felt needed for the first time in my life.

37

JODIE

'I WANTED TO SAY HOW sorry I am that you took all the blame and got fired.' I blurt out the apology as soon as Simon cracks open his front door.

I've swung by with Zak early evening, after the usual Saturday chores. I couldn't leave it another day without apologizing in person. Simon hasn't replied to any of my messages and Pam hasn't been able to get hold of him either.

'This was my choice.' Simon shrugs.

His lip is swollen, and the surrounding skin bruised. He has darker-than-usual rings beneath his eyes. He's not slept, probably because his lip is painful. I'm sure he's also worrying about how he'll find another job that fits around his research.

'Can we come in?'

I'm half expecting him to slam the door in my face or make an excuse about how busy he is, but he steps aside silently.

'No messing with Post-its while we talk,' I say under my breath to Zak. 'Behave yourself. Remember, we're a team?'

He nods and follows me into Simon's hallway.

'Brrr.' Zak shivers, folding his arms around his anorak. 'It's like the North Pole in here, Mummy.'

'Shhh.'

'Do you want a cup of tea?' Simon says, backing away. 'I think I may have milk that's not off.'

'Sure. Sounds great!'

I follow him into the kitchen while Zak drifts off, clutching his lightsaber.

'I wanted to thank you for sticking up for me like that,' I say, as Simon peers into the fridge. 'No one's ever done that before.'

'It's OK.'

'No, it isn't. I feel terrible.'

Simon straightens up and turns around. 'Why? Did Ed fire you too?'

'No.' I glance away, reddening.

'Well, that's good. I'm glad. Otherwise this would have been for nothing.'

His voice isn't reproachful. He sounds like he genuinely means it, which makes me feel even guiltier.

'I admitted throwing the drink but Ed wouldn't listen. His mind was made up from the moment I walked into his office.'

'You couldn't have helped me escape from a statistical certainty.'

'A what?'

'I was on probation and Ed had given me a number of warnings. This mathematical result was inevitable.'

His explanation is clinical, his voice emotionless. I wish he'd yell or call me a coward, because that's what I am. I'm ashamed of myself for not walking out in protest at the way he was treated. But despite repeatedly arguing Simon's case, I couldn't bring myself to accept Ed's offer of a reference. I wasn't prepared to lose my job, our security for . . . For *who* exactly? My tutor? A friend? Or an accomplice? Probably the latter after I forced him to become Clyde to my Bonnie.

'Anyway, you've become a total legend at work. Everyone says—'

'Can you feed Archie for me?' he says, cutting in. 'He'll be wondering where I am. I can give you tins. I've got plenty in the cupboard.'

'Yes, of course.'

How can I refuse?

'Mummy! Come quick! It's an emergency!'

'Oh God, I apologize in advance.' I run out, praying to not find Post-its scattered in the hallway.

As I burst into the lounge, Zak points at a flat-screen TV.

'Is that the emergency?'

'Yes! Simon's finally joined the twentieth century.'

'Twenty-first,' he corrects, walking in. 'I took your advice, Zak, and purchased it along with Netflix before . . .' His brow furrows.

'This is great!' Zak beams. 'Now you should move your sofa to point towards the TV, the way normal people do.'

'Would you like to see what's on?' Simon hands him the remote control.

'Why don't I make us a drink, while you do that?' I offer.

I head to the kitchen and double-check the fridge; there's a dribble of out-of-date milk in the bottom of the carton. The shelves are bare except for half a lemon. I open the cupboards one by one. Simon only has enough pasta for a meagre helping. A couple of teabags remain in the packet and congealed coffee granules are glued to the bottom of the jar. However, Archie's shelf is well stocked.

I shut the cupboard, feeling worse. This is my fault – Simon has blown his savings on a new TV, possibly to please Zak. Now, he hasn't enough money to buy food. His flat is colder than before – probably because he can't afford to heat it, rather than out of choice. I feel sick. I have to find a way to make this up to him.

In the hall, I check my purse, hoping to discover an unexpected windfall. *As if.* I've got £20 for food shopping and that's supposed to last us all next week; I'm short again after buying shoes and a backpack for Zak.

What should I do?

I touch the wall, which is covered with a wet slick of damp.

I did nothing when Simon was fired from Prince Burger; I didn't walk out in solidarity because I was shit-scared of what would happen to Zak and me.

But I can't stand by and do nothing today. I remember the loan company I looked up on the library computer; the interest rates were exorbitant. I'd be racking up even more debt. Will I ever be able to repay it?

I can't worry about that now.

I have to help Simon get on his feet.

I'm unpacking shopping in the kitchen after popping out with Zak to buy the ingredients for spag bol – the first recipe I was taught to cook in the home. Simon doesn't know it yet but I've also stocked his cupboards and fridge with enough groceries to last a week. If he asks where I got the money from, I'll pretend I had a win on the scratchcards. While I was in the supermarket, I rang the loan company. I have to fill in a form online, but I've been given initial approval for a month-long £200 loan, which has an interest rate of 1,200 per cent. *Holy shit*. I don't want to do the maths.

After getting Zak settled in front of the TV again, Simon returns and stands on the chairs, searching the top cupboards. He discovers an ancient, dusty bottle of wine.

'Do you fancy a drink?'

'I never say no!' I reply. 'So Simon, have you thought . . .'

'Let's not talk about me.' He opens the bottle and pours us each a glass. 'What did your tutor say about your essay? Have you heard yet?'

'It was OK.'

I take a large gulp of vinegary wine, picking at my bandage. Monica's voice drifts back to me from our phone call this morning: *Where are your opinions and arguments? You need to rediscover your voice if you're going to get into Cambridge.*

I'd given her a first draft of my essay on 'Use of Memory in the Narrative Technique of *David Copperfield* and *Great Expectations*' to see if I'm on track. I'd experimented with the techniques I'd planned to use in the Cambridge exam – using a list of literary devices to compare one text against another. But I'm way off target. It won't get high marks in a formal assessment – and I need to do brilliantly. *If* Lucy Cavendish gives me a conditional offer in January I have to achieve a distinction in every assessed unit of my diploma course to take up the place.

'The essay was only OK?' Simon asks.

I don't want to kick him when he's down. I can't tell him his rote-learning method isn't working for me; it might be successful in maths, but English needs something completely different to memory and logic. Literature goes straight to your soul – it's feelings over facts, freedom to express yourself over rules and structures and new, exciting colours over rigid black and white. Somehow, I have to combine what Simon has taught me with my own instinct for writing essays.

'It needs more work,' I admit. '*A lot* more work.'

'How so?' Simon presses. 'Tell me exactly what needs to be done. It will take my mind off yesterday.'

I look around the kitchen for something to distract him before I cave and tell him what Monica said. My eyes settle on a copy of *New Scientist*.

'Why don't you sit down and relax? Have a read of this while I cook the best spag bol you've ever tasted!'

He shrugs and takes the magazine off me. I turn back to the stove and lean over the hob.

'How do you turn this thing on?'

Crack!

I spin around. Dark red wine pools, bloodlike, around the broken wine glass at his feet.

'Simon?'

He's white-faced, swaying.

'What's happened? Did you cut yourself?'

He slumps into a chair, throwing *New Scientist* across the kitchen.

'It's worse than that. Another mathematician has beaten me to it – he's solved the Riemann Hypothesis!'

38

SIMON

I'M LYING IN BED. It's 9 a.m. on Sunday, hours past my usual rising time. The radio presenter excitedly announces that it's December the first – the countdown to Christmas has finally begun. I reach over to the bedside table and hit the 'off' button on my clock radio before picking up the *New Scientist* again. The words had swirled devilishly around the page last night and I couldn't focus. I take a deep breath and reread the article carefully and clinically. An eminent mathematician has held a press conference, claiming to have made a breakthrough with the hypothesis. However, fellow mathematicians contacted by *New Scientist* have refused to comment on his so-called proof. That's encouraging! A colleague is quoted off the record, saying he is 'sceptical' about the new theory due to its 'vagueness'. The article states that the claims will now be checked. The Clay Mathematics Institute has refused to comment.

I breathe out slowly. Perhaps I overreacted last night. Claiming to have solved the Riemann Hypothesis and actually doing so are two very different things. Many mathematicians have made important breakthroughs over the years, edging closer and closer, but never reaching the finishing line. This does not spell the end for me. If anything, I can turn this to my advantage by proving that *my* theory is the correct one! I must move faster and begin typing out my submission at once.

I force myself out of bed. I need a strong coffee before continuing work. The dry ingredients are still on the counter where Jodie laid them last night; dinner was interrupted by the news in the magazine. She tried to calm me down but in the end she reluctantly left, despite loud protestations from Zak, complaining he was starving. Opening the cupboard, I reel backwards. Every shelf is packed with tins and packets of dried pasta and rice. I peer in the fridge; it's also brimming with fresh vegetables, fruit, meat, eggs and milk.

Jodie did all this for me . . . I feel a small, unfamiliar twinge in my chest.

I retrieve my phone and text a combined apology and thank you, suggesting we rearrange for tonight. She messages back within seconds.

No worries. Had a win on the scratchcards. Glad u r feeling better. Can't do tonight, sorry. Zak feeling worse – might have chest infection. But Arthur has pre-quiz team meeting at lunch-time. I gave him yr number. He's texted u. Go!!!

I find Arthur's text, which I'd missed earlier.

Fancy helping us today?

I sigh. How can I join their team? I'm hardly good company and I need to start typing out my submission. I force myself to sit at the kitchen table, retrieving the relevant file on my laptop. I close my eyes, trying to concentrate. Silence echoes painfully through my Memory Palace, threatening to force me into dark corners. Not a single voice will reverberate through these empty corridors all day. If I were on shift at Prince Burger today, I'd hear the whir of Fro-Bot stirring to life and the hum of voices. I'd feel the comforting warmth of Archie's fur beneath my fingertips during my break and possibly a hand accidentally brushing against mine as I pass an order.

I open my eyes and type out a message to Arthur on my phone.
Happy to help you. See you later.
Best wishes, Simon.

En route to The Rising Sun, I scoop up one of Zak's missing toy posters from the gutter and reattach it to the lamppost. It flaps miserably in the wind.

'LOST!
CAN YOU HELP
FIND THIS TOY?'

I'm trying, I promise.

I've deliberately taken a detour to enable a further hunt for Dog. I leave the sad, peeling posters behind and carry on with my journey. The pub sits at the junction of Cinder Street and Waterford Road and is accessed at the rear via a narrow alleyway, which is easy to miss. The smell of urine, alas, is not. It sports a fine stained-glass window above the rear door, featuring an orange sun and an out-of-proportion tree.

Arthur and his teammates are sitting at their usual table. They're studying a newspaper, no doubt catching up on current affairs. This is a staple subject in quizzes here. Arthur jumps when he sees me heading over. Trevor and Winston exchange looks before picking up their pints.

'You came!' Arthur pushes the paper to one side. 'How are things?'

'My neurons are firing superbly, and you?'

He nods, tilting his pint towards me.

'Oh yes, we're fine,' Winston says.

'So,' Trevor says, sighing. 'We're all . . . well, we're sorry, Simon.'

'About what?'

'That damned story.' Trevor shrugs his shoulders. 'But you know what everyone says – today's news is tomorrow's chip paper.'

I stare from one to the other, bewildered. 'What are you talking about?'

'Oh dear.' Arthur picks up *The Herald* from the seat next to him. 'We thought you must have read it already.'

An icy chill sweeps over my body.

'You might want to take some time alone,' Arthur says, jerking his head towards an empty table. 'Or maybe sit down?'

I can't move, I can't think.

He passes the paper. 'It's on page three.' He coughs. 'Like Trevor said – we're all very sorry.'

Hands shaking, I open the newspaper.

Staring back is a large colour photo of myself holding a packet of fries in Prince Burger.

WHERE ARE THEY NOW?

Ahead of the reboot of *Little Einsteins: Britain's Brainiest Kids* we've revisited the original bright sparks who astounded audiences with their intellect eighteen years ago. Did they become astronauts? Physicists? Neurosurgeons?

```
Let's find out!
First up is Simon Sparks.
```

Arthur's lips are moving as I read on, but I can't hear what he's saying. Blood rushes to my ears; my vision swims wildly, but I can't even blink.

I retreat into my Memory Palace. I imagine myself closing doors and bolting them. But it's too late. The damage is done. It can never be repaired.

The newspaper slips from my fingers.

My terrible secret is out, for the whole world to see.

39

Easter 2005

SIMON

ANOTHER BONFIRE RAGES, LARGER and more powerful than the one Father had created to destroy my guitar last week. Our next-door neighbour has threatened to contact the council. From the landing, I hear Father rudely dispense with him before returning to his model railway in the garage. I find Mother, crying, in the bedroom.

'What's happened?

She fumbles with a tissue, using it to dry her eyes then wrapping it around her picked, bleeding finger like a tourniquet.

'I'm being silly.'

'You're not silly or thick or whatever Father's called you this time.' I pick up her small, cold hand. 'Tell me. Please.'

'I'm just thinking how much it means to me having you here. I must make the most of you while I can.' She forces a smile.

'Things are going to change and I just have to get used to it.'

I squeeze her hand. 'Me too.'

After finals this term, I wanted to continue my postgraduate studies at Cambridge so I could be closer to William and home, but Father ignored my pleas. He applied to Princeton on my behalf, as that is the university he'd always wanted to study at in his youth. I'm due to begin the four-year applied and computational math PhD before Christmas while William continues at Cambridge. After that, Father has told me to complete a post-doc at Harvard or MIT rather than chase a big salary in Silicon Valley. He has planned my whole world out, but I don't control or even have possession of the map. I cannot attempt to wrestle it back without causing repercussions for Mother.

'But you won't be alone in this house for long,' I stress. 'We've talked about this. I've arranged it all – you'll come over to the States. We have enough money for your flight and living costs.'

Father gives her money sufficient to cover only household expenses; she's not allowed a bank account of her own. However, we've been secretly saving up for the hotel stay in New Jersey a couple of weeks into my term. I've siphoned off money from all the prizes and scholarships I've won over the years along with the monthly funds Father has paid into my bank. I've set up a new account he doesn't know about.

The end goal is that she'll return to the UK, feeling sufficiently strong enough to break free from Father and secure a place in a women's refuge, hopefully in Cambridge. I've done all my research. As a last resort I could ask my tutor, Dr Spencer, for help; he's a kind man and appears well connected. Friends and colleagues frequently drop by his office; they may be able to suggest or provide temporary lodgings.

She covers her eyes with her hands, weeping softly.

I feel a steely fist strike my heart. *Oh God.* 'He's found out, hasn't he?'

She doesn't look up. 'I don't think he knows about the savings account, but he senses something. He says I don't need a passport. He's burning it in the back garden.'

'No!' I grip the edge of the bed.

Father *can't* win again.

'We can solve this.' I open the front door to my Memory Palace, ready to mine it for clues, any answer that can stop this house of cards from collapsing. 'You can apply for a new passport.'

'I don't think I'll be able to go through with it when you're not here,' Mother says, sobbing. 'I won't be able to follow you.'

'You will. You're stronger than you think.'

'No, you're the strong one – all the things you've had to endure over the years. I'm weak. I always have been.'

'Those are Father's words, not yours. You *can* do this.'

My tone is firm, but secretly I'm unsure. Father has drilled it into her that she's useless for so long she's almost totally dependent upon him. She has no friends to confide in or turn to – he has driven them away over the years. But that doesn't cut the toxic ties that bind them together – she's unable to imagine life without him.

'When I'm alone, without you telling me what I should do, I know I'll crumble. He'll be watching me. How will I get a new passport or go to the airport without him finding out?'

'We'll bring our plans forward. Why wait until December when we can leave tonight?'

Mother's shoulders begin to shake. 'That's impossible . . . Where would we go?'

'Somewhere. Anywhere. Does it matter as long as it's away from here?'

'Where are you both going?' William has silently appeared by the door. 'Does Father know you're leaving?' He looks from me to Mother, worriedly. 'What will he do to you both when he finds out?'

I tell my brother to be quiet; his fretting isn't constructive. Mother is wavering. We help her pack a small holdall. We'll all leave at 7 p.m. when Father goes for his habitual run. Together.

Father hovers over me reading my notes and workings out after spending most of the day with his model railway.

'You're not concentrating properly on the task in hand.' He slams his hand down onto the desk, making me jump. 'What's going on?'

I swallow the lump in my throat that threatens to choke me. 'Nothing.'

I try to focus on revision, but my mind races frantically.

How will I get the Volvo keys off Father? Where will I drive Mother to later? Should I find a women's refuge online or take her to a cheap hotel until we figure out what to do? Will I still remember how to drive?

I passed my test a month ago but have been on the roads only once.

Father checks his watch. 'When I get back from my run, I want to see more progress otherwise you'll be pulling an all-nighter.'

I keep my head down as he walks towards the door. A floorboard creaks as he stops and the back of my neck prickles.

I try to push my shoulders down and control my breathing, forcing my trembling pen to make believable loops on the page.

The door shuts with a treacherous click. The bolt slides into place firmly.

No! I grip the desk as the walls close in on me.

Father has guessed something is wrong and locked me in.

How can I help Mother escape?

40

JODIE

'Have you seen the Prof this morning?' Pam asks. 'Or spoken to him?'

The breakfast rush is almost over and we're serving bacon buns and hash browns to the last stragglers. Ed has juggled the schedule around so Pam can work an early shift and take her husband to chemo later this afternoon.

'Simon doesn't stay over, you know! We're only friends,' I say hastily.

'OK,' Pam chuckles, 'no need to be so defensive.'

Talking of Simon, I must remember to sneak out and feed Archie later. I've promised to become the cat's new surrogate mum. It's the least I can do after everything Simon's done for Zak and me. I'll hand in my revised essay on Wednesday after finally getting to grips with it.

'I know you're not a couple, Jodie, you just seem closer to him than anyone else here. And I'm worried. He's a sweet guy beneath his odd ways and IQ talk. He didn't deserve any of this.'

I sigh and struggle to concentrate on an elderly man's order, making a mistake as I tot up the till. I realize I've forgotten to turn my phone back on in the rush to get out this morning. I was up half the night with Zak hacking and coughing and had to dose him up with medicine before dropping him off at Sandra's; he's not well enough for school. I felt pretty bad as her ankle's not properly healed yet and she's in pain, hobbling around, but I didn't have any choice. Ed's read us the riot act about calling in sick; he's a person down after firing Simon.

Pam nods towards the tables. 'Look, four o'clock, act busy, Jodie.' Ed's striding over with a face like thunder, clutching a newspaper in his hand.

'You're friends with the Prof, right?' he asks, throwing a copy of *The Herald* onto the counter.

It sounds like an accusation, but I'm no Judas.

'Yes, we're friends. We've stayed in touch after you fired him. *Unfairly.*'

His cheeks redden. 'Please tell him I'm sorry.'

'About sacking him?'

'Well, that was unfortunate – my hand was forced. But this too.'

I turn to Pam as Ed stalks off. 'What have I missed? What the hell's going on?'

'Take a break,' she says softly. 'The story's on page three.'

I scoop up the paper and retreat to the deserted crew room. I flick through the pages. My gaze settles on a photo of Simon smiling and holding a bag of fries. I scan the text. It's a 'Where Are They Now?' feature written by showbiz journalist Pippa Huxley about the original contestants from *Little Einsteins.*

I ignore the other case studies and focus on:

SIMON SPARKS

This 12-year-old child genius made it to the *Little Einsteins* final, but crashed and burned on a question about Charles Dickens, weeping on stage when his dad chastised him for getting it wrong. Simon said he wanted to solve the Riemann Hypothesis when he grew up, but never fulfilled his early potential.

As one of the youngest ever undergraduates at Cambridge, Simon dropped out of his mathematics degree course shortly before finals without graduating. After bouts of homelessness and years of unskilled, low-paid jobs, including shelf stacking in supermarkets, he ended up working at Prince Burger in West London. He was recently sacked for allegedly assaulting a customer.

Simon remains estranged from his family after they were struck by tragedy in March 2005. He was present when the body of his mother, Sylvie Sparks, was found by firefighters following a suspicious blaze in the family's garage.

The police investigated suspected arson and murder at the time but no one was ever charged.

Harold Sparks, a retired surgeon, has since remarried and lives with his second wife in Buckinghamshire. He was unavailable for comment last night.

A hand grips my chest, squeezing out all the air. I can barely breathe.

His Cambridge degree . . .

The car crash that killed his mum . . .

And his dad . . .

I can't believe it, *don't want to believe it*, but there it is in black and white.

Every single thing Simon has ever told me is a lie.

41

SIMON

'**WELL, THE SHIT'S WELL** and truly hit the fan,' William says gruffly. 'Father's finally crawled out of the woodwork.'

I'm sitting on the bedroom floor, covering my head with my hands. I'd left William a message to give him the heads up about the newspaper story – it was only fair.

'I can't quite take it in.' I quiver. 'Do you think I should try to contact him?'

'To say what? You're sorry for existing? Jesus, have some pride. He hasn't wanted to have anything to do with us for years.'

I close my eyes as my heart contracts.

'Oh God. Tell me what to do . . . I don't know . . . I can't . . .'

His tone softens. 'Breathe in. Breathe out. Keep your head between your knees.'

Stay calm . . .

This is awful, but it's not the end of the world . . .

'You're right,' I say, when I'm no longer light headed. 'Maybe I could ask the newspaper to print a retraction?'

William clears his throat. 'To be fair, they didn't report anything false. The reporter cobbled together something from those old stories, probably because she couldn't get hold of Father. But I'm afraid you also made it easy for the journalist, Simon – I found your photo on the Prince Burger website within a few clicks.'

'That's not my fault. Ed insisted I had it taken when I joined. All the staff photos are up there.'

A defensive note has crept in my voice.

'Sure, but I've been far more careful than you over the years. I have no digital footprint – no pictures on the hospital website or social media. Not that the journalist would have been interested in me, anyway, since I'm in the US. I had a lucky escape!'

William's chortles are like nails dragged down a blackboard.

'That's typical! You always get off lightly. It's like you're made of Teflon.'

'What? You think this is easy for me?'

'Of course I do!'

'But—'

Anger bubbles in my chest as I interrupt him.

'I hate that you ran away to America and left me to deal with all this, that I always get painted as the villain while you get off scot-free!'

'That's not true.'

'Isn't it? You've never taken responsibility for anything since we were children.'

William's tone hardens. 'That's where you're wrong, Simon. I have to take responsibility for *you*.'

I clutch my chest. 'Wow! Am I such a burden?'

'Stop shouting.'

I lower my voice. 'Well?'

He hesitates. 'You're not a burden. But let's face it, I always have to support you, keep you from going over the edge. I spend my life skirting around your secret while trying to come to terms with my own grief for Mother. It's tough sometimes.'

My whole body shakes as my anger boils over. 'You're responsible too! You pretend it's my fault entirely, but you know that's not true. We're both to blame. Why can't you just admit it for once in your life?'

I've wanted to say this to him for years, but he's not listening. He's talking to someone else in the background.

'*He's very upset. I know, I know. Let me try.*'

William's voice becomes clear once more.

'That was Victoria, asking about you. We're both worried by how distressed you sound. We think you're deteriorating again. Have you thought about seeing a doctor?'

A rapping at the front door cuts off the expletive that's on the tip of my tongue. The buzzer sounds.

'I have to go. Someone's here.' I steady myself against the walls as I walk into the hall and peer through the spyhole.

'You make that bloody excuse all the time when you want to escape from the real world and hide away in your Memory Palace.'

'There really is someone on my doorstep. Someone who doesn't blame me for everything, *all the time*!'

'Look, I'm your brother, for God's sake. We need to talk about this calmly and without interruptions from other people.' He pauses. 'Anyway, who else do you have to confide in after this monumental clusterfuck? You have no friends.'

'That's not true. I think I may finally have one.'

He falls silent for a few seconds as the buzzer rings a second and third time. A fist bangs on the door.

'Wait – don't tell me you mean that little Cambridge wannabe? The one who was pestering you to tutor her?'

'I followed your advice and gave her some lessons. We've bonded, I think.'

'Oh, Simon. Don't you remember what happened at school? Classmates used to pretend to be your friends because they wanted you to do their homework. They abandoned you as soon as it was handed in.'

'Jodie's not like that. She won't desert me. She'll understand when I tell her I had my reasons for lying.'

'Get real! She's *not* your friend. Now she knows you never even graduated, she won't want your help with the test or interview. You're no use to her. Mark my words – she'll drop you, like those kids did.'

'She won't!'

'Your judgement is clouded because you're angry, but you have to remain on guard,' he says sharply. 'Whatever you think of me right now, deep down you know I'm the only person you can really trust. No one else will ever understand. Not even Victoria. She'll want to keep you away from our kids if I tell her the truth about Mother. She'll withdraw your Christmas invitation.'

Jodie leaves her finger on the buzzer.

'The problem is, William, I don't trust or forgive *you*.'

I throw my phone at the wall, smashing its screen.

42

JODIE

'I'M NOT LEAVING UNTIL you open up! I know you're in there! I can hear you shouting at someone on the phone.'

I knock loudly on Simon's door again and keep my finger on the buzzer. Time's tight. I've dropped Zak off at school and have to get to college to sit a practice Cambridge exam and officially hand in my essay. First, I must see Simon. I tried calling him a few times yesterday, but his phone was switched off.

Eventually, I hear the bolts and chains shifting and the door opens a crack. I catch a glimpse of hollowed eyes; the shadows beneath them are bruised damsons.

'Can we talk?'

'I'm sorry. It's not convenient.' The door starts to close, but I stick out a foot.

'Are you OK? Everyone was asking after you at work on Monday – even Ed. We're all worried after reading that shitty article.'

Gently, I push against the door. He doesn't resist and I step into the hallway, bracing myself for the usual plunge in temperature. Simon is shivering in a thin sweater. His pale cheeks are emaciated. He's clutching his mobile; the screen is cracked.

'Simon?' I reach out and touch his icy hand.

He snatches it away, avoiding my gaze.

'You look terrible.'

'Thanks for your feedback. I'll be sure to file it in a useful place.'

'That came out wrong, sorry. What I meant to say is you look poorly. Can I ring anyone for you? Maybe I could let your brother know what's happened if he doesn't know?'

'We've fallen out again. I don't want to talk to him.'

'I'm sorry.'

He doesn't respond.

'Is there anything you want to tell *me*?' I ask.

He shakes his head. A frosty silence stretches between us. He's never felt more unreachable.

'Simon?'

'For God's sake, Jodie! Can you stop pestering me for once in your life?'

'But—'

'There's nothing to discuss!'

'Really?' My eyes narrow. 'How about we talk about your dad who is, hello, still alive and living in Buckinghamshire? Or how about the fact your mum died in a fire, not a car crash? Maybe we could discuss yet another lie – that you never graduated from Cambridge? Which one would you like to pick first? Your choice.'

Simon sniffs and looks down his nose at me the way he did the first time we met, as if I'm some undereducated idiot and he's far superior.

'No comment,' he says eventually.

'I'm not a journalist!'

He retreats further into his flat. 'But you're not family either. This is none of your business. I'd like you to leave now, please.'

'This *is* my business!' I follow after him, grabbing his sleeve. 'Is it true?'

'Which part?'

'That you never graduated from Cambridge? I need to know – you gave me a reference!'

'That's what you're worried about?' He smacks his forehead sarcastically. 'Of course! How could I be so short-sighted? My life is falling apart, but everything still revolves around you and bloody Cambridge.'

'I'm sorry you've been turned over, but this affects me as well. Cambridge could pull my application because I've used you as a personal referee. The tutors will ask about you – that's if I even manage to get to the interview now. They could reject my application because of your lie.'

He wrenches his arm free, trembling violently.

I continue. 'This has repercussions for you too, Simon. Do you think the mathematicians at the institute you keep going on about will take you seriously when they find out you've lied about your qualifications? You've lied to everyone!'

I'm gathering momentum now; I can't stop, it's like a serpent unleashed.

He sways gently, scarecrow-like, and leans against the wall.

'Say something. Anything! Why did you lie to me about your degree? Were you trying to show off as per bloody usual? You wanted to pretend you're better than everyone else at Prince Burger, right?'

'Please leave. I don't want to say something I might regret later.'

My blood's fizzing in my veins, I can't hold it in.

'Don't talk to me about regrets! I regret giving you a second chance after Brick-gate. I regret introducing you to Zak and asking you to prep me for Cambridge. I regret begging you for a reference and trying to help you make friends. All this time you were fishing for sympathy by lying about your parents. You thought you could get away with it because I'm a dumb nobody from a shitty children's home. Right?'

'That's not true! You *made* me write the reference, remember?'

'You could have said "no".'

'I did, repeatedly! But you never take "no" for an answer. You forced me into it, the way you bulldoze through absolutely everyone to get your own way.'

'Well, give me some answers now. Tell me one single thing about your life that's the absolute truth.'

He breathes in deeply. 'You won't want to hear it. That's a lesson I should have taught you from day one – the truth is painful.'

'Screw you! I'm done with your lessons and this whole *My Fair Lady* routine you've got going on. You're not Professor Higgins and I'm no Eliza fucking Doolittle so spit out whatever it is you want to say.'

'You've been wrong about Zak all this time,' he says quietly.

'What the hell does he have to do with any of this?'

'You wanted to hear the truth, however painful. Well, it involves your son.'

My heart beats wildly as he continues.

'He talked to me about his father that day in the playground when I was supposed to take him to the Charles Dickens Museum. He said he couldn't talk to you about him because you'd get upset. You think he was too young to remember what

Jason did to you, but he wasn't. He said his father used to turn up the music whenever he hit you, but he heard your cries through the bedroom door. He remembers you lying on the sitting room floor after Jason hurt your back. He thought you were dead because he couldn't wake you up. He dialled nine-nine-nine.'

I feel utterly winded, as if he's punched me in the stomach.

'No!' I gasp. 'That's not true. A neighbour called for help.'

'It was Zak. He told me.'

'You're lying, the way you've lied about everything else.'

'It's the truth. You told me to read between the lines, but you can't do the same. If you had, you'd realize that's why Zak asks about new boyfriends. He's terrified you'll find someone else who is a carbon copy of Jason. Why do you think he carries that lightsaber around? He wants to protect you. He knew that Jason had been in touch; he saw some of his text messages on your phone.'

'No.'

'He's still wetting the bed, isn't he? He's seen a man who looks like Jason doing building work near his school. That's enough to give him bad dreams. He thinks he's lurking around and he's petrified. That was one of the wishes he wanted to make with your birthday candles – to never see him again.'

'Why are you only telling me this now?' I scream. 'I had a right to know!'

'I'm a robot, remember?' he yells back sarcastically. 'How could I possibly understand such complex emotions!' His chest is heaving, his fists clenched. He takes a breath. 'Zak begged me not to and I couldn't break his promise. He doesn't want to make you feel bad.'

He takes a step towards me, but I edge away.

'I'm sorry. I never meant to hurt you or Zak. I can't tell you why I said the things I did about my parents but I hope, as my friend, you'll understand that I had my reasons, the same way that Zak had his reasons for not talking to you about Jason.'

'How dare you use my son against me like this? I'm not your friend! I don't understand! I don't want to bloody know!'

He stares at me. 'Of course. That was *my* misunderstanding. I'm your *former* tutor. Wait, no. One-Star Simon. That's what you call me behind my back, isn't it?'

I catch my breath. I want to deny it but I can't.

'You've conveniently raided my Memory Palace and no longer need me,' Simon says coldly. 'You use Sandra too. When was the last time you visited her for a chat and asked how she's doing instead of scrounging for childcare? You should be looking after her, but you're still begging for favours when she's elderly and can barely move with her ankle. But I guess you think that's what myself and Doormat Sandra exist for – to service you.'

'That's not true!'

'Isn't it? Maybe you should focus on being a friend and a mother instead of Cambridge. It's not the only thing in life and it's certainly not the most important.'

I step forward, my fist clenched. Instead of backing away, he moves closer, goading me.

'Do it. You know you want to. You can get revenge for Brick-gate.'

I relax my fingers. 'Fuck you, Simon, and fuck your Memory Palace. You don't get to lecture me about being a mum when you can't bring yourself to tell the truth about *yours*. What kind of son lies about his mum's death?'

Simon's face whitens. His bottom lip trembles.

'Get out of my flat! Get out of my life!'

I lurch blindly towards his front door, eyes brimming with tears. I never want to see *One-Star* Simon again.

'You want the truth?' he yells after me as I run down the corridor. 'I killed my mother. That's the kind of son I am. Are you happy now?'

43

SIMON

Goodbye, Jodie Brook.

I slump to the floor, tears spilling down my cheeks. I don't attempt to brush them away. That's the last time I'll ever see her. I've lost the one person who almost became my first true friend.

I'll never be able to see Zak again either. Jodie will never let me take him to the park or help with his maths or the bullying now she knows the truth about Mother. The Three Wise Men won't ask for my assistance; Pam will no longer send text messages, checking up on me. I have no job or prospect of getting another one. Who would employ a liar who fabricated their CV and has been fired from Prince Burger? I think of Mother – gone. My father – estranged. And who knows if William will talk to me again? I'm completely alone in the world.

I pull myself up and slowly walk to the bedroom, my hands skimming over the walls. Is Jodie right? Have I damaged her Cambridge application? I'll never be able to forgive myself if that's true.

My mind flits to the Riemann Hypothesis. Will the Clay Mathematics Institute take my submission seriously when they realize I don't have a degree, let alone a PhD? Snobbery is rife in the mathematical world, but surely my findings will take precedence over reservations about my lack of qualifications?

My fingers fumble to open the laptop on my bed. I pull up the document and stare numbly at my figures, comparing them with the calculations on my flipchart in the corner of the room. I glance back again. This can't be right. I must have read the equation wrong. I squint again at my numbers on the screen, trying to make sense of them.

What . . . ? How . . . ?

Sharp pains stab my chest. I gasp for breath, bending over double. I clutch my head tightly.

No, no, no, no!

The beautiful pattern I once saw has disintegrated into random chaos. Prime numbers swirl chaotically around the screen and the chart, refusing to slot into the right order. Eventually, they slip away into arbitrariness.

I have *nothing*.

History won't remember me when I'm gone.

No one will.

I hurl my laptop against the wall, kick over the flipchart and sweep the medals and trophies off the shelves followed by the family photos. I claw at the walls, pulling off the Post-its in great handfuls. I throw them into the air and they flutter around me like dying butterflies.

I think of the *Sparks' Family Guidelines for Success.*

Only cold showers allowed.

I head to the bathroom, lock the door and remove my clothes. I turn on the shower and curl up foetus-like beneath the jet of cold water. Father would approve – perhaps it's only what I deserve.

I've locked myself in the toilet cubicle, but Father hammers on the door until I come out. He makes me shake hands with the winner of Little Einsteins, *Francesca Briley, and her parents. I fix a smile on my face to match Father's rictus grin, but inwardly I want to die. William is sulking somewhere, after she knocked him out too.*

Father's yell from the audience after I had fluffed the Charles Dickens' question still reverberates in my ears: You idiot!

After hearing Father's reprimand, I couldn't move from the stage. An assistant had to help me off as I sobbed uncontrollably. A psychologist reassured me afterwards, but I know my public humiliation is complete. Father's reaction won't be left on the cutting-room floor because it makes good TV.

'How could you get Great Expectations *and* David Copperfield *mixed up?' Father slaps the steering wheel hard as the car stops at traffic lights on the way home. His grip tightens as if he's trying to squeeze the life out of it.*

'Yeah, Simon,' William mouths as I glance across at him.

'If you'd got up an hour earlier than usual to study literature, you could have got the answer right,' Father continues. 'We should have taken home the trophy! Anything other than first place is a failure. I've told you before, the world is only interested in winners, not losers.'

I stare at his whitened knuckles and back at William who whispers, 'Loser.' He's escaped censure after setting his alarm clock to rise at 3 a.m. to cram in more revision.

'Simon can't get up any earlier,' Mother protests weakly. 'Look

at the shadows under his eyes. All this studying and pressure is making him ill. You need to let up on him.'

'Nonsense, Sylvie. This means Simon has to work even harder.'

Back home, I'm sleepy from the stressful day and journey. The energy drinks Father had told me to drink ahead of the sudden-death round have worn off. He insists I take a shower to wake me up, but I know it's a punishment. He forces me to stand under the cold water for eight minutes – three minutes longer than usual.

When his hand stretches through the shower curtain and turns off the tap, I silently sink to the bottom of the bath and curl up into a ball, shivering. I hear him return downstairs, switching on the radio in the kitchen.

'Simon?'

William has silently entered the bathroom and locked the door. Often, he finds me in here and whispers soothing words in my ear, but today's final has changed him. Beating me has brought out an unfamiliar ruthless streak. Perhaps nothing will ever be the same again.

'Lazy boy! Father doesn't think you've been punished for long enough.'

He turns on the tap. The water slashes my body with knives.

I'm shivering too much to shout for help. Eventually, I feel nothing. I don't even notice the cold. William watches as my naked body turns bluish grey.

44

JODIE

I RUN OUT OF THE classroom, slamming the door. Monica, my tutor, follows.

'Where are you going?' she calls after me. 'You've still got thirty minutes left. We've discussed exam technique before. You've got to take all the time available to scour through your essay in detail and build a strong conclusion.'

I ignore her and sprint down the corridor. I burst through the doors into the pouring rain without bothering to pull on my coat. I'd messed up from the moment I'd turned over the practice paper. Monica will have no choice but to grade it as a band four. I'd tried to focus on reading each extract slowly and picking the pair with the most interesting features. But I kept changing my mind and swapping back and forth as the clock ticked, the way I did in my GCSEs. I barely managed to string together coherent sentences, let alone analyse the extracts in depth.

It all went wrong as soon as I saw the subject matter. Monica had picked the paper asking the student to contrast different literary portrayals of mothers. My mind wound back to what Simon had told me this morning.

I killed my mother.

I can't, *don't want to*, believe it, but he sounded so anguished – as if he really meant it. He seemed genuine when he told me about Jason too. Sure, Simon's lied about his past, but why would he make something up like that about Zak? What if he's right? I thought I was protecting Zak by never discussing Jason, but apparently that has been having the opposite effect. Zak has been shielding me from the truth all this time, carrying those terrible memories on his little shoulders.

Why couldn't I see what was staring me in the face?

Zak may not have visible scars, but he's still damaged. He's scared of all men, apart from Simon and his teacher, Mr Silva.

I have no idea how to make things better.

Where do I start?

Simon warned me I wouldn't like the truth; it could be too painful to bear. Unfortunately, he was bloody well right as usual.

From the end of the corridor, I notice our bedsit door is ajar. We'd been in a rush this morning and Zak must have forgotten to shut it when he went back for his woolly hat. My heart beats quicker as I draw closer. Splintered white wood juts out from the frame and I realize this isn't anything to do with Zak. Our door's been kicked in . . . My stomach flips; shivers ripple up and down my spine.

Fuck, fuck, fuck.

It has to be a junkie looking for cash and jewellery to flog, right? I mean, at least three other bedsits in this block have been hit recently. This isn't personal, it's just another random break-in.

I'm screwed if the leftover cash from my loan has been nicked; I've hidden the roll of notes in my dressing-gown pocket.

I step inside, scrabbling around for my phone and bracing myself for carnage: wrenched-out drawers and clothes dumped on the floor. But then ice travels down my spine. I look up to see a big, hulking figure. The room lurches, the walls close in around me. A man is rifling through my files on the table. The mobile I've pulled out from my handbag falls from my grasp as Jason turns around.

'This is a surprise. Shouldn't you be in college?' He holds up my timetable.

Fear crackles in my chest, snatching my breath away. I stare back numbly, rooted to the spot.

'I wasn't expecting you until later tonight – after tea with Zak at Prince Burger. Now you've bailed on class I'm guessing you'll pick him up from school instead of your friend – the one who lives in the flats down the road. Sandra, isn't it?'

I lick my dry lips. 'You followed me home from the hotel last week.'

'You should be more careful, particularly when it comes to looking after my son. You never know who might turn up on your doorstep and rob you.'

Jason's eyes flicker to my dressing gown on the floor. That's the first place he'd look for cash; my old hiding place. Next to it is my phone. I glance up again. He shakes his head slowly, a smile twisting on his lips.

'Let's have an uninterrupted chat. What do you think?'

My ears buzz, my stomach heaves. I'll never be able to reach down and grab the phone fast enough.

'Cat got your tongue?' He smirks, dropping my timetable.

He grinds his heel into the piece of paper until a ragged hole appears. His fingers slip into his jeans pocket and pull out a packet of fags and lighter.

'Don't . . .' The sentence dies in my throat.

'Sorry, what?' He touches his ear. 'I can't hear you.'

Jason lights the cigarette and turns to the table. Laughing, he picks up the prospectus. 'Is Lizzie still banging on about Cambridge? She turned you into a right stuck-up little cow with airs and graces – always thinking you were better than the rest of us when you're not.'

He blows smoke in my direction. 'You realize you're a pet project to her, right?' he spits. 'She'll move on to someone cleverer when you get rejected from . . .' He studies the brochure. 'Lucy Cavendish.'

I try to stay emotionless, keep a poker face. He doesn't know Lizzie's dead. Jason always hated her for trying to get me back into education. She'd come round to our flat while he was out to lend books and encourage me to return to college to get my A-levels. He destroyed all the application forms and college prospectuses she gave me when he discovered them under the bed.

'She always was an interfering old bitch.'

'Don't you dare call her that,' I mean to shout, but something has happened to my voice.

'Oooh, sorry!' He raises his hands in mock horror. 'But honestly, I can't believe you're still into this education crap. You've got as much fucking chance of getting into Cambridge as I have.'

'Get out!' I say, trembling.

'That's not a very warm welcome.' He saunters over to the mantelpiece, picking up a framed picture of Zak. 'Think I'll keep this. I don't have a recent photo of my son.'

'No!'

I dart forwards and try to grab it off him. His hand shoots out and grabs my throat. 'You don't get to tell me what I can or can't have, you stupid little slag. When are you ever going to understand that?'

'Please.' My hands scrabble with his. 'Can't. Breathe.'

'Are you shagging that guy from the hotel in here or do you go back to his place?'

I shake my head vigorously.

'Do you think I'm dumb? That wasn't your solicitor last week. He was your bit on the side, thinking he could intimidate me by spewing Latin shit.'

I gasp for breath as he lets go, turning his attention to my books.

'Where is it? It must be here somewhere.' Jason crouches down. 'Aha. *To Kill a Mockingbird.*' He grabs the novel, flicking through it. 'Here he is – Atticus bloody Finch.'

He shoves the open book in my face. 'Weird name. Knew it rang a bell. You bored me to death about him when you were nagging on about going to college.'

He rips a page out and screws it up, tossing it on the floor.

'Don't, please,' I beg.

'You met him at college, right? I'm guessing he's a book geek like you.' He tears out another page, and another. 'But the Latin's thrown me off. Is he a history or a languages nerd?'

'Stop it! These are Lizzie's books!'

I'd promised I'd care for her collection. This is all I have left of her.

I lunge for the novel, but his fist crunches into my stomach. I can't breathe. The room tilts and blurs. I crumple to the floor, eyes watering.

'*These are Lizzie's books,*' he repeats, examining *To Kill a*

Mockingbird. 'This is what I think of that bitch.' He flicks open his lighter, slowly bringing it closer to the novel until the flame hovers an inch away.

'No!'

'Too late.'

I stretch up my hand, but I can't reach. I can't protect her book. Fire crackles and rips through the pages, tearing at my heart.

'Jason! Stop!' My breath is painfully ragged.

'I've barely started.' With his other hand, he pulls out a small can of lighter fluid from his coat and douses my stacked novels.

Dizzying, white-hot panic surges through my body.

He's come prepared.

I drag myself along the floor after him. 'Don't do this. I'm begging you. You don't have to go this far.'

He pauses, staring at the flames licking towards his fingers. 'You're absolutely right, Jodie. I don't have to.'

My heart leaps slightly. 'Please!'

'The thing is, I *want to.*'

He hurls the blazing novel on top of the towers of books. Flames shoot to the ceiling, licking across the walls and curling up the curtains. I haul myself to my feet, trying to get to the sink to fill a jug of water, but Jason blocks my path. The inferno spreads to the clothes and toys strewn on the chair. He picks up the Lucy Cavendish prospectus as smoke billows out of the room, setting off the fire alarm in the corridor.

'I'm not going to burn this. I'll let you keep it as a reminder that you're never, ever going to make it. I know it. Deep down, *you* know it.'

He throws the prospectus to one side and walks closer. His eyes are emotionless pools of blackness. I recognize that look.

I remember all the punches he's thrown over the years and the insults he's thrown at me.

No one will give a toss if you die.

You're a terrible mum.

You're weak.

You're a pathetic nobody.

But I'm none of those things.

I'm Jodie Brook.

I glance around for a weapon and move to the chest of drawers, my fingers curling around a handle.

'Remember *me* with this!'

I swing the iron, clobbering Jason on the left side of his forehead. He drops to the floor, blood streaming through his fingers.

45

That day

JODIE

I'M IRONING A SHIRT when someone bangs on the door. Luckily, it's only a package for a neighbour, not one of Jason's 'business associates'. I return to the lounge and find him standing by the ironing board, a towel around his waist. He puts the iron back in its holder and turns around, holding up his scorched shirt.

Ohmigod. What have I done?

His mouth curls into a smile that doesn't reach his eyes. 'Come here.' He opens his arms.

'I'm sorry!' My heart batters against my ribcage.

He beckons again, unnaturally calm. 'Of course you are.'

Slowly, I approach. He pulls me towards him, stroking my chin. 'It's OK. Why would I be cross?'

I hear myself babbling. 'I'll make it up to you. I'll buy another shirt, I promise.'

'Why would you think so little of me, Jodie? Accidents happen.' He pushes me away gently. 'How about you make us both a nice cup of tea?'

My eyes widen with surprise. 'Of course. Thank you. I mean, coming right up.'

'Jodie?'

I turn back. A tattooed fist flashes in front of my face. I scream as pain explodes in my cheek and I hit the floor. I claw at the sofa, dragging myself up, but he kicks me down. Pain detonates grenade-like in my ribs.

'Mummy?'

Zak must have woken from his nap in the bedroom. Stay there, I plead silently.

The lounge door slams shut, muffling Zak's cries. Techno music blasts out; the neighbour bangs on the wall. It's the same old pattern.

'Mummy!' Zak's voice is louder, more urgent.

I glimpse a flash of silver and hear the ominous hiss of the iron. Surely, he wouldn't go this far . . .

Jason rips off my top. No! Searing pain ripples up and down my arm as I try to gouge his eyes. He flips me over onto my front as if I'm as light as a child. I scream with agony.

I smell burning flesh. It takes a second for me to process that it's mine. I throw up over his trainers.

'Dirty bitch!'

The hissing, sizzling noise stops.

My eyelids flicker shut. Everything goes black.

A thousand tiny knives tear at my back. I open my eyes, blink against the light. What happened? All I know is I have to get away from Jason . . . *Help me* . . . I struggle to get up, but a hand gently presses me down.

'You're safe now. Let me put these wet towels on your back.'

I'm lying face down on an unfamiliar green sofa. Where am I? Where's . . .

'Zak!'

'It's OK. He's here. You're both safe.'

I push myself up. A neighbour, Jez, points to the chair. Zak is rocking backwards and forwards, clutching Dog. His eyes are open wide and blank.

'Someone called the police,' Jez says. 'We got you both out before they got here.'

I've woken up in Jez and Karen's flat, five doors down. He tells me they'd heard Zak crying and the wail of a police car. Jez had carried us here to safety. He knows I'll never dare tell the police what happened; neither will any neighbour.

Jez takes me to A&E while Zak stays with Karen. I tell the junior doctor I passed out and fell awkwardly onto the iron. He doesn't question me; he's knackered and wants to go off shift. I tell Zak the same lie when we return later.

'I fell over and hurt myself, but it's OK.' I wince. 'That's what you must say if anyone ever asks you. Mummy's just clumsy. OK?'

Zak slowly nods his head.

He looks from me to Jez as we discuss getting our stuff from the flat once the police have stopped knocking on doors.

'What's happening? Do we live here now?'

He eventually falls asleep, holding Dog close.

46

SIMON

I OPEN MY EYES. VAGUE blurry shapes dance above my head. A bright light flashes into my pupils. A mask covers my nose and mouth. My arm itches; a tube crawls out of it. I try to pull it, but a firm hand stops me.

'Simon? Can you hear me, Mr Sparks? You've been admitted to hospital. Your neighbours raised the alarm. We're treating you for hypothermia.'

I look down. Pads are stuck on my naked chest. I'm covered by what looks like a gigantic inflatable duvet.

'We're trying to warm you up with this Bair Hugger. You need to keep still, OK?'

Another voice chimes in.

'Who is your next of kin? The paramedics said you were talking about your dad and brother. Can we contact them?'

I remove the mask and mumble the barest of details before attempting to pull off the chest pads.

'Please stop. We're trying to monitor your heart.'

I shouldn't be here. I don't want to be saved. I have nothing.
No one.

I scream and thrash about, clawing at the tube in my arm. A different, colder pair of hands restrains me. I see a syringe and feel a sharp stab in my thigh.

Insidious grey mist swirls around the corridors inside my Memory Palace, dulling my neurons. Lights turn off one by one in the rooms inside my head. I have to get away from the Dickensian smog. I spot a door opening and picture myself hurling through it. But I've picked the wrong escape route.

The door slams shut behind me.

I try the handle, but it doesn't move.

I'm stuck inside room thirty-six.

47

Easter 2005

SIMON

I'M STILL TRAPPED INSIDE my bedroom. I try to shoulder the door as soon as Father leaves for his run, but the lock doesn't budge.

'Mother! Let me out!' I press my ear to the door. 'Mother? William? Are you there?'

The house is frozen; not even the squeak of a floorboard dares betray the silence.

I check my watch. I don't have much time. I glance around for tools. I seize a ruler and scalpel from my desk, but both snap as I scrabble to remove the screws from the door handle. I'm still struggling to twist a coin into the tiny slots when I hear Father return. Early.

No!

I bang my forehead against the door.

This. Cannot. Be. Happening.

It's too late. I can't get Mother away tonight. I have to come up with a new plan, when Father is out for longer. After half an hour, he taunts me by loudly announcing that dinner is ready. My stomach growls treacherously as footsteps head down the stairs. I pace up and down, tearing at my hair and slapping my face.

Time slips away.

I must have fallen asleep, because I hear the bolt on the door slide. My eyes fly open. It's 10 p.m.

'William?' I whisper.

Heart beating rapidly, I tiptoe out onto the dark, empty landing.

Is this a trap?

When I was little, Father used to wait, ready to punish me all over again if I ventured out without asking 'formal permission' after he'd slid open the lock. I press my back to the wall, holding my breath. The radio blares out downstairs with a debate on euthanasia. I exhale slowly. This is Father's particular area of interest.

I pad over to the master bedroom, gently knocking on the door. I find Mother sitting in a chair by the window. The contents of her holdall are laid out neatly across the bed; bottles of sleeping tablets are among the toiletries. Her insomnia must have worsened.

'What happened?' I run over, kneeling beside her. 'Did he hurt you?'

'No, we just talked.'

She adjusts the sleeve of her blouse over her wrist, before I can check for bruises. She's trying to protect me from knowing the worst, as usual. I grasp her hands, squeezing them tightly. 'I'm so sorry. It's my fault.'

'No, I'm the one who should apologize.' Her voice breaks. 'He got it out of me, the way I knew he would. I told him everything – all about our silly plans.'

'No . . .'

'Don't worry! I told your father it was my idea, not yours. When he calmed down, he explained how my plans are selfish and will destroy your future.'

'That's not true. What did he say?'

'If we leave tonight, he won't let you study for a PhD in America. He'll email Princeton and cancel your application. He says he'll tell them to give the place to someone more worthy of their resources.'

'I don't care! Let him!'

She gently cups my face in her hands. 'Going to Princeton will set you up for life. The tutors could help you make a breakthrough with the Riemann Hypothesis. I know how much that means to you – therefore it means everything to me too. I can't risk that being snatched from you.'

'You're all that matters. I have to get you away from here. I don't care about the Riemann Hypothesis or Princeton!'

Mother looks at me uncertainly.

'I mean it. They mean nothing compared to keeping you safe.'

'But your studies . . .'

'Don't you see? This isn't *my* life. It's Father's. He's picked the university for me, my career . . . everything.'

I dig my fingertips deep into my aching temples. My Memory Palace is crumbling under the pressure. *Everything is spilling out.* I beat my forehead with my palms, until Mother takes hold of them.

'Don't hurt yourself. It breaks my heart to see you in pain like this.'

I hang onto her hands. 'I feel the same about you. I'll take you wherever you want to go, but we have to escape.'

'I can't let you sacrifice—'

'I'm not going to Princeton, Mother!'

'*Yes*, you are, Simon,' a voice barks.

Our hands spring apart as Father appears at the door. His jaw is clenched; his eyes glitter with fury. William joins him, standing shoulder to shoulder. His eyes plead with me to forgive him before they lower.

'I'm sorry, Harold.' Mother stands up shakily. 'I was trying to make Simon understand how—'

The china ornaments on the dressing table shiver as he bangs the doorframe with his fist.

'This isn't up for negotiation. The only thing Simon has to understand is that this is *my* house. *I* pay the bills, *I* make the decisions.'

I glance at William. He looks up and shakes his head slightly, but I ignore his warning.

'I said no.'

Father takes a step closer. 'You'll do as you're told, Simon, otherwise there will be consequences.'

He stares at Mother until her gaze flickers and eventually lowers to the carpet. 'For *everyone*.'

'I'm sorry,' William whispers.

He's quietly slipped into my bedroom. It's 3 a.m. The house is deadly silent again. I'm staring up at the skeletal white moon through the open curtains.

'Go away.'

I turn over and burrow my head deep into the pillow.

'Simon, please! Talk to me.'

'What's the point?' I say, peering out. 'Where were you when I needed to talk earlier? Oh that's right, taking sides with Father as usual.'

'I had to—'

'I said, go away. I don't want to speak to anyone. Not you, not Mother.'

'Don't blame Mother. None of this is her fault. We both know that.'

'I blame Father.' I throw the pillow aside and sit up. 'He's destroyed everything – Mother's passport, my guitar, our old soft toys.'

'Jesus. You're still harping on about *them*?'

I ignore him. 'Worst of all he's crushed Mother's hope. She looks so resigned, frail. She'll never get away from him.'

'Unless we show her she can seize back control.'

I look up at William, his eyes glinting in the moonlight.

'What can we do? We're powerless.'

He appears to grow bigger in stature as he draws his shoulders firmly back and lifts his chin.

'No, we're not.' He doesn't glance back at the door as usual. 'I'm done trying to keep Father happy all the time. Why don't we punish *him* for a change?'

'How, exactly?' Slowly, I swing my legs over the side of the bed.

'Let's destroy something *he* loves.'

My jaw slackens. I picture Father's precious model railway in the garage; it's worth thousands. He's spent years building termini, designing back scenes and lovingly painting and restoring vintage locomotives.

Could we? Should we?

I rub the back of my neck, which is suddenly slick with sweat. My armpits too.

'Come on, Simon. You know deep down it has to be his railway.'

'I'm not sure I can do this,' I say quietly.

'*We* can.'

Heart thumping, I look at his outstretched hand.

'We have to,' he insists. 'Let's do this for Mother. *Together.*'

I inhale, filling my lungs. When they're about to burst I reach out. He grasps my hand and hauls me up without hesitation.

'Together,' I confirm, breathing out slowly.

William's hand pulls away first. We head down the stairs, my heart pounding to the rhythmic hum of Father snoring. The spare keys for the garage are on the table by the door; he keeps the other set by the side of his bed. I snatch them up. William grabs his coat.

'We'll have to be quick,' he says. 'You know he's a light sleeper.'

We slip through the rear door, which is unlocked, and head around the front. The gravel betrays us by crunching loudly beneath our feet.

'That's odd,' William says, pointing ahead.

The garage is still lit up; Father has been using a temporary paraffin light after the switch fused. He must have forgotten to extinguish it. I unlock the double doors with the fob on the key ring. They slide up silently. Father has ample space for his tracks in here. The space is divided into two, with a curtain separating his pride and joy – a thirty-foot model railway – and the Volvo.

I sway slightly at the sight of the meticulously arranged tracks. The glass in the carefully crafted stations and houses glare back. Dozens of tiny enamel figures fiercely line up against us, squaring for battle.

I glance across at my brother. His hands are stuffed in his pockets, making his shoulders hunch. He looks smaller now we're standing side by side; his expression is unreadable.

'William? Ready?'

His pale cheeks flush unnaturally scarlet.

'We *have* to do this,' he says, without breaking his gaze from the tiny army. 'When Mother sees what we've done, it will give her the strength to stand up to Father too.'

I nod vigorously. 'You're right. We don't have a choice.'

'Grab a mallet or whatever weapon you can find. Be quick.'

I find a hammer on the workbench and turn around expectantly, but William's hands remain empty.

'You have to go first, Simon.' He squeezes my shoulder. 'It's only fitting. Father's punished you the hardest, made you suffer the most.'

'Are you sure?' I wipe my wet palms on my pyjamas. My heart is rattling in my ribcage, my stomach shifting uneasily.

He nods, helping me to lift the hammer above my head as I hesitate.

'Close your eyes and think of all the terrible things he's done to you.'

I obey.

I feel the stinging slashes of cold showers and bring the hammer down.

Smash!

As I open my eyes, coaches, wagons and buildings shatter beneath my blow. Adrenaline surges through my body, knocking me off balance. I steady myself on the table.

'That was amazing!' William cries. 'Do it again!'

I bring my weapon down a second time.

Crash!

Rolling stock splinters, stations split into two.

Joy ripples through my body. I feel so light I'm sure I'll float away if I let go of the handle.

But I can't. I haven't finished yet.

This is for Mother.

Sweat drips from my forehead as I pound Father's special collectors' edition of a Midland Pullman train. Two cars break off. That's not enough. It has to be destroyed; reduced to tiny pieces that he'll never be able to put back together again.

I raise the hammer high above my head and take another swipe.

Crack!

I glance down at the glass scattered around my feet. My brain scrambles to keep up.

Lamp. Broken. Fire.

Whoosh.

'Watch out, Simon!'

Flames climb up the curtain, higher and higher. Frantically, I look around for water and grab a tray containing liquid. I throw it at the curtain but it explodes into a ball of flames. *Bright sparks create fires.*

'That's accelerant, not water, you moron!' William exclaims. 'Can't you tell the difference?'

Oh God. What have I done?

We back out, coughing. I close the garage doors, panicked.

'I'll fetch a bucket of water,' I gasp. 'I can put it out.'

'It'll need more than that,' William shouts. 'Ring the fire brigade!'

He watches, transfixed, as the flames lick up against the glass. I run back to the house. The front door's already opening.

Fear claws at my throat as Father tears out in his coat and pyjamas. He stuffs a piece of paper into his pocket, pulling out his phone.

My knees weaken. I stumble backwards.

'It was an accident!' I say hoarsely. 'I promise.'

He grabs my shoulders, shaking hard. 'We have to save her, she's—

'Save who?'

Father's face is white with panic. He lets go and clutches his chest, as if he's having a heart attack.

'Your mother!'

I turn towards the blaze, horror struck.

Father staggers towards William, speaking rapidly into the phone clamped to his ear.

'The garage is on fire. I think my wife could be in the car.'

Blood drains out of my body.

Colours blur and merge, form spectres and melt away into darkness.

I turn around, tripping and flailing on the gravel. Stones stab my fingers as I scramble to my feet. My legs won't work.

I fall again. Move forwards.

I've almost reached Father and William. Flames shoot out of the garage windows, smashing the glass.

'Keep back!' Father yells.

He pushes me to the ground before wrestling with the handle.

I reach for William, but he recoils.

He joins Father's side, turning his back on me.

'Mother!' I scream. 'Mother, *please.*'

What have I done?

48

JODIE

WHAT HAVE I DONE?

I scoop up a mushy pile of novels reduced to pulp from the firefighters' hoses: *Mrs Dalloway, To the Lighthouse* and *A Room of One's Own.*

Provoking Jason has left us with nothing.

I'm sorry, Zak.

You too, Lizzie.

Virginia Woolf's beautifully constructed sentences have blurred into bluish-black bruises. I'd hoped a few books would be salvageable, but everything is destroyed. I pick up the blackened copy of *Wuthering Heights* and shove it into the bin bag, along with *Jane Eyre* and *The Poems of Katherine Mansfield.* This was Lizzie's final legacy – all I have left to remember her by except for the photo, which is safe in my handbag, tucked inside *Great Expectations.* During my final visit to the hospice, Lizzie had squeezed my hand and begged me to make a promise:

Read my books, give them a good home and pass them on to someone else.

I swore I would, but only managed one out of the three: reading each text, some of them twice or more. After Lizzie died I'd cleared her flat, as she had no family to do it for her. It had taken two journeys to shift her novels back to our bedsit – the way I was forced to carry all my stuff between foster and children's homes as a kid, using bin bags.

Feeling like rubbish, treated like rubbish.

But Lizzie wasn't trash. Nor were her books, even though they stayed packed in their bin bags for months because I'd mistakenly thought the council would move us on to a permanent flat. I'd dusted them every night and made sure the covers weren't scuffed or bent over and the pages remained smooth despite the damp. I was never able to give them a bookshelf or *a good home*. But I couldn't bear to pass them on to someone new either. How could I give away Lizzie's presents?

They meant far more to me than the pale yellow envelope containing a few pictures of Mum and me when I was tiny. They've survived the fire, along with my Prince Burger uniform, which is apparently indestructible. Superheroes, not fast-food employees, should wear it. But Lizzie's last gifts to me have perished, one by one. I've failed to fulfil her deathbed wish. I dump *Beloved* and *Love in the Time of Cholera* into the bag, together with Zak's new backpack and shoes. His lightsaber is ruined along with the library books, the bag of guinea pig food and the secret Lego Star Wars set I'd hidden under the bed, bought using cash from the loan.

I sweep up the ashes of my birthday card from Zak. I'll never forgive myself. I can't shake off the feeling this is a punishment not only for letting him and Lizzie down, but also for thinking these books could be a part of my life. How could I believe that I was the type of person who should read and cherish them? The towering piles of novels gave me hope, providing the offer of escape from our life. Now that ladder's been snatched away and it won't be put back beneath my feet.

I fill another bag with the rest of the wrecked books and my sodden college notes and essays, gagging as I finish. I slump against the wall. There's hardly anything to salvage and move to the B&B. I have no sheets or duvets to put on the bed or spare clothes for either of us. Most of our possessions that were untouched by fire have had to go into the sacks; they stink of smoke. I tuck the sole surviving photo of Zak and me into the rucksack I borrowed from Sandra. The council placed us in an emergency B&B yesterday, but Sandra invited us to stay with her for a night or two until I've managed to clear up in here and get our new room straight. I remembered Simon's accusation about using her and tried to refuse but she insisted, pointing out that her ankle was pretty much healed and she'd appreciate the company.

My phone vibrates. For a second, I think it's a text from Simon, but I remember the awful things I said to him on Wednesday. He'll never speak to me again. I can't blame him. I was a complete cow. I scramble through the mess, finding the mobile beneath a pile of blackened clothes and toys.

It's Sandra: *Zak's woken up. He's crying. Can you come?*

I reply, saying I'm on my way. I message Simon as I swing the rucksack over my shoulder.

Sorry about the things I said. I didn't mean them. Please forgive me.

I'm not expecting a response tonight; I'll try again tomorrow. I drag the largest bin bag filled with charred and sodden books to the door, stuffing in an old newspaper on my way out. I stop as I notice the prospectus for Lucy Cavendish lying on the table, next to the Cambridge practice papers I'd printed off in the library. The glossy cover shines less brightly; it reminds me of Jason and all the mistakes I've made in my life. I should never have enraged him. Now Zak will pay the price for my mistake; he's more traumatized than ever after losing everything.

I close my eyes.

I no longer have Lizzie's voice in my head, telling me I can do this and that I mustn't give up. All I hear is that doubting inner voice condemning me for destroying her legacy.

I've let down Zak. It was my job to protect him and I've failed. *Horribly.*

I also hear a new voice in my head – Simon's.

Maybe you should focus on being a friend and a mother instead of Cambridge. It's not the only thing in life and it's certainly not the most important.

I stare at the brochure. I'm done fighting. It's too hard. I have to be realistic. I messed up the practice test badly. The real test and interview is just over a week away. What was I thinking?

I don't need Jason to tell me this is a mistake. People like me don't end up in places like that; it was stupid and naïve to think I could. I can't waste any more time on a foolish pipe dream that's never going to happen.

Zak needs me more than ever. *Here.*

I ram the prospectus and test papers into the sack and firmly tie the handles.

'I've tried to comfort him,' Sandra says quietly, as she opens the door. 'But he only wants his mum, bless him.'

I struggle out of my coat and hang it on the rail. 'Thank you again. For everything.'

My eyes fill with tears as I turn around. Simon's accusation had stung, but he was right. I have used her. 'I also want, I *need* to tell you I'm sorry.'

'What on earth do you have to apologize for?' Her shocking pink flamingo earrings swing as she shakes her head.

'I've depended on you so much and taken you for granted.'

'No, Jodie—'

I plough on through her protests. 'But most of all, I'm sorry that I've never told you how much our friendship means to me.' I take her hand. 'I don't want to leave it too late, the way I did with Lizzie. I never got to tell her how I felt about her. But you're my family, Sandra. The best family I could ever ask for.'

'Oh, pet. You're mine too.' Sandra's voice is a quiet sob. 'Now go to your son.'

'Did you find my lightsaber? Or my guinea pig food?' Zak's bottom lip wobbles as he sits up. 'Anything?'

I sit down on his makeshift bed on Sandra's sofa. 'I'm so sorry. We've . . .' My voice breaks. 'Everything's gone. Apart from this.' I pull out the photo from my rucksack – a framed selfie of us together on his birthday earlier this year. Zak's huge gappy smile as he stares at his birthday cake makes my heart split in two.

'Oh, Mummy!' He bursts into tears. 'This is my fault.'

His sobs cause even deeper wounds. 'Of course it's not! Don't ever say that!'

'Think I accidentally left my pyjama bottoms on top of the flowerpot. The tealights were lit inside. *I* caused the fire.' He covers his eyes with his hands.

'No!'

'Look at me.' Gently, I raise his chin, removing his hands and wiping the tears from his cheeks. 'This has nothing to do with the flowerpot or *you*.'

'How do you know that?'

What should I tell him? Usually, I'd gloss over the worst details to spare Zak, but he's far more aware than I ever thought. Simon's also shown me that lying can be more damaging than being honest. I owe him the truth.

'Your dad did this deliberately.'

Zak weeps again as I describe how Jason had discovered where we live after getting out of prison.

'*He* set fire to our bedsit.'

Briefly, I explain that his dad did a very bad thing but he's gone now. The police have taken him away.

'What if . . . the police let him go and he finds us again?' Zak takes large gulping breaths.

I rub his back. 'That's not going to happen. Your dad will be locked up for a long time for everything he's done. He won't bother us ever again. I'm going to make sure of that, I promise.'

Tomorrow, I'm giving a full statement to the police about our relationship. I'll finally admit how Jason terrorized me for years, hurling words like sticks and stones, kicking me, punching me, and branding me with an iron.

'Can you ever forgive me?' I place my arm around his little shoulders. 'We're a team. I should have talked to you about your dad being back instead of pretending nothing was going on. I promise I'll be more open with you from now on.'

He manages a brave smile. 'I forgive you, but I'll *never* forgive Daddy.'

I hug him. 'We still have each other and that's the most important thing.'

'And Dog,' Zak whispers. 'Don't forget him. He didn't die in the fire. He's just lost. And I'll still have the guinea pigs when we get to Cambridge.'

My cheeks blanch. Despite my promise, I can't bring myself to tell him about my decision yet. It will break his heart all over again.

For now, all I can do is hold him tighter. I don't want to ever let go.

49

SIMON

A HOSPITAL ORDERLY CLEARS AWAY the detritus from breakfast; I haven't touched it. She frowns at the waste and explains how the radio, TV and telephone and answer service works on this ward. She'll return later with lunch; she says I've chosen options from the menu, though I don't remember picking anything. I've recovered well from mild hypothermia, but am now on the coronary care unit for continuous monitoring after doctors detected some cardiac disturbance. I long to rip out the IV line in my arm and remove the sticky pads on my chest, but I must cooperate if I want to be discharged today.

I'll receive another visit from a member of the psych liaison team later. They'll quiz me again about suicidal thoughts and I must be sufficiently prepared. I'd lied to the doctors in A&E, claiming I'd passed out in the shower before I could regulate the temperature. They didn't look convinced. I mustn't be transferred to a psychiatric unit. I have bad memories of those places.

I stare at the adjacent patient, who is locked in conversation on his bedside handset.

My heart sinks as I realize that William is also trying to get through.

'Thank God I've found you!'

'How . . . ?'

'You told the doctor about me when you arrived. Father too, apparently.'

'Did I? I don't remember . . . much.'

He sounds like he's at work; I can hear background noise. He's probably making early-morning rounds.

'I'm sorry about our quarrel, Simon.'

I flinch as I remember his accusation. *I have to take responsibility for you.*

I want to challenge him, but don't have the strength for a rematch.

'I'm sorry too,' I say, sighing.

'How are you? God, I've been worried sick.'

'I'm doing much better. There's nothing to worry about.'

'You say that . . . but you scared me half to death. That's why I was hoping I'd hear from you first.'

There's a tinge of recrimination in his voice.

'Sorry. I've been sleeping most of the time. Plus I've moved wards. I'm surprised you've managed to track me down.'

'Well, I'm glad we're speaking now. I wanted to jump on a plane as soon as I heard, but Victoria's away with her girlfriends. I've been left to look after the kids on top of work, but she's back on Sunday night. How about I come over and help to sort you out next weekend?'

'I don't need *sorting out*. I should be allowed home later. It was just a silly accident.'

'Really?'

William is no fool.

There's a pause. I hear a voice – someone is asking him for a signature. William never has been able to give me his full attention.

'How did it come to this?' he asks, after he's finished up. 'You used to need me. You relied upon me for everything. Yet we've never felt so distant, and I don't mean in air miles.'

I feel a dull ache in my chest.

'Be honest for once, William – you know we grew apart long ago. We haven't been really close since we were children.'

My heartbeat quickens as he protests. I feel myself spiralling back into the past.

'It's true,' I insist. 'I can trace it back to the day it happened – the *Little Einsteins* final. You turned on me.'

He sighs heavily. 'Can't you let that go? We were kids. You need to move on. It was years ago and you're still pointing the finger.'

'That was the start of most of my problems. If you want to help me recover, at least admit that one small thing.'

William's voice lowers.

'Fine. I haven't always been the best brother. I know you think I sided with Father, which is true, I guess. You have to understand that was self-preservation. I was safe when he focused solely on you.' He gulps. 'I hold my hands up. I made mistakes . . . I wish I could turn back time and do things differently, but I can't.'

I glance across at the monitor. 'Thank you for acknowledging that. Now I want you to go.' William spoke about self-preservation; it's time I took a leaf out of his book. I must look after myself.

'Of course. You're tired after the shock of what's happened. We can speak tomorrow when you're home.'

'I don't think so, sorry.'

'Well, I'll try anyway.'

'Please don't.'

'Simon—'

'Why won't you ever listen to me? I want you to leave me alone!'

I've put on a performance for Dr Atkins. After I spoke with William, I'd thrown my jug of water across the floor, crying out in frustration, and the nurses notified the psych liaison team. But I've managed to successfully convince them that I'm not an immediate risk to myself, or others. Dr Atkins didn't believe me when I said the shower incident was accidental, so I felt compelled to admit to some suicidal thoughts, claiming they have now dissipated. Dr Atkins stated he is happy for me to be discharged today, as the doctors also say my heart rate has returned to normal.

'My heart's not broken yet!' I'd joked.

I'm not sure he saw the funny side. Dr Atkins has offered a community-based approach to treatment, involving home visits from psychiatric nurses. I've agreed, but have no intention of answering my door should they turn up. I'm grateful for my game face and to NHS cutbacks. There's a rush to discharge patients like myself on Fridays to clear beds for the weekend.

'You must also make lifestyle choices that will minimize your stress levels – healthy eating, sleeping and regular, but not excessive, exercise,' Dr Atkins says. 'Try to incorporate relaxation techniques into your daily life. You cannot continue the four a.m. starts you mentioned. It was inevitable your body would tell you enough was enough – the slip in the shower was an accident waiting to happen.'

'Anything else, Doctor?'

I am playing the part of the model patient taking an active interest in my recovery. I know that's what he wants to hear, along with details of support networks in the community, which could help prevent readmission. Quickly, I describe William, Jodie and Zak, the Three Wise Men and my former colleagues at Prince Burger as evidence of my deep friendship bonds. Dr Atkins frowns and doesn't appear to be reassured.

'My problem is with William,' he says.

Ditto!

'The nurses told me how upset you were following your conversation earlier.'

As he gently broaches our destructive relationship I tune out, wondering whether I can borrow clothes and money to get home. The doctor isn't telling me anything I don't already know. I nod as he pauses, pretending to agree. He doesn't understand William the way I do. However much we argue, he'll never let me go. This makes me think of Mother and Father. *Bright sparks create fires*. But they also create toxic families . . . I'll never escape.

'Find a friend to confide in instead of relying on William – one of these other people you have mentioned. Perhaps Jodie?' Dr Atkins continues. 'Is she someone you can talk to about how you feel?'

I produce my best performance smile.

'I promise I'll ring Jodie as soon as I'm out of here. She won't let me down.'

50

JODIE

THE RADIO IN THE next room blares as I yank down the grey, torn nets; they'll get their first wash in about a million years. I stare out the window. *What a shocker!* The B&B owner has decided to cover up this amazing view – the wall of the neighbouring car repair workshop. I throw the curtains into a bundle in the corner and slop soapy water onto the blackened windowsill, scrubbing harder. After this, I'm going to attempt to remove the suspicious stains on the carpet – the whole room would probably light up like a firework display if a forensics team came in here with their equipment. They'd have to seal off the communal bathroom too.

I peel off the rubber gloves as my phone vibrates on the table. Has Simon accepted my apology? My heart leaps. I try to manoeuvre around the double bed with one glove sticking stubbornly to my fingers and trip over a sack of toys and clothes. *Dammit.* There's no space to put anything. How will Zak do his homework in here? Play?

How will we live . . . ?

I stuff the Three Wise Men's donations back into the bag and manage to step over a holdall containing spare bedding from Sandra and Pam without breaking my neck. Grabbing my phone, I discover two voicemail messages.

The first is from a woman at the emergency housing service.

'Thank you for your message. I'm sorry, but we have no other accommodation available at the moment except for this B&B.'

I cut off her apology; I'll keep pestering first thing Monday morning. This room is far grottier than our bedsit. I never expected to miss Hairy Mo – the man-shaped damp patch growing up our old wall.

The second voicemail message plays:

'Hi Jodie. Sorry to bother you on a Saturday afternoon. This is Dr Roberta Adams, director of admissions at Lucy Cavendish. I thought I'd give you a quick call about the personal character reference you emailed over.'

Half of me wants to hang up straightaway to spare myself the humiliation, but I force myself to listen.

'I thought I'd clear up any misunderstanding. We don't encourage – or want – personal referees. We've processed your college tutor's glowing academic reference. With that in mind, I have deleted your email. I'm sure you sent it . . . well, in error, and are now regretting including it in your application.'

She coughs, sounding uncomfortable. *Oh God!* She's definitely checked up on Simon's qualifications.

'Anyway, we're looking forward to seeing you a week on Monday. Please don't hesitate to contact us if you have any queries. Oh, and remember to turn up twenty minutes before your exam. Goodbye now, and best of luck!'

I replay the message, scarcely believing it. Dr Adams *knows* about Simon yet she still wants me to compete for a place. I listen to the message for a third time, but I've already made up my mind. I'm not going to turn up for the interview. I'll ring and apologize afterwards. I'll be lucky to finish my college course at this rate, let alone go on to university and teacher training. No way can I think about going to Cambridge.

I've got way too much going on. I gave my statement to PC Walker yesterday morning; Jason has been remanded into custody on charges including arson with intent to endanger life, coercive control, stalking and causing grievous bodily harm.

'Will you support the prosecution during a trial?' PC Walker asked. 'Are you prepared to give evidence against Jason in court if he pleads not guilty to all charges?'

'Hell, yes,' I replied.

I ran away years ago, but I'm facing up to him, *everything*, now.

I glance around the room at the grubby mattress and the bare light bulb hanging from the ceiling; the tilting single wardrobe that's missing a door and the repetitive knife marks scored on the legs of the table. I have to prioritize making this as habitable as possible. Most important of all, I need to look after Zak. I'm meeting up with Mr Silva next week to discuss seeing an educational psychologist. And when he gets back from his emergency play date at Billy's, I'll explain my decision about Cambridge. I'm dreading his tears over the guinea pigs, but, hopefully, I can make him understand why our Lucy Cavendish plans must be put on hold – for the time being, at least.

I stick the phone in my back pocket. I pull on my rubber gloves and return to scouring the windowsill. Still nothing from Simon. I feel worse with every brush as I replay our argument on Wednesday. I shouldn't have gone off on him like that, especially after he opened up to me about his childhood. I know better than anyone that people can have reasons for concealing their pasts.

I yank off my gloves again and throw them across the floor. I'm going to apologize to Simon in person.

Fingers crossed he will be as forgiving as Dr Adams.

I've been standing outside Simon's flat for the last five minutes, banging on the door and shouting his name. A neighbour has buzzed me into the building. I can't tell if Simon is in or not – I thought I heard someone moving about but it's completely silent now. An elderly man appears further down the corridor, carrying bags of shopping.

'He doesn't want to see anyone. I have tried, but he's politely asked me to leave him alone. He's been even more reclusive since the accident.'

Ice-cold fingers travel up my spine and the back of my neck. 'What accident?'

The man puts his bags down. 'Simon was taken to hospital on Wednesday. He's home now but hasn't ventured out, as far as I'm aware. I didn't know any friends or family to call.'

The handbag slips from my shoulder. That was the day of our blazing row.

'The neighbour on the floor below called the fire brigade,' he continues. 'Water from Simon's flat was pouring through her ceiling and he wasn't answering the door. Firefighters had to break it down. Then the paramedics arrived and they brought him out on a stretcher – he was hypothermic and shouting about lots of things that didn't make much sense.'

I shake my head numbly. 'Are you sure he's been discharged?'

'He knocked when he came out yesterday and I gave him his new key. He said he was going to bed. If he answers the door, tell him Aleksy sends his good wishes.' His voice wobbles. 'Simon's such a kind man; I'm lucky to have him as my neighbour. He's always offering to carry my bags or get my shopping when my arthritis gets bad. He got rid of my old TV.'

As the man disappears into his flat, I return to banging on the door.

Is this my fault?

I'm pretty sure I know the answer. Simon was distraught about his mum when I left. To my shame, I remember how I taunted him.

'Let me in. I'm so sorry about all the things I said.' I sink to my heels, repeatedly apologizing.

After a few minutes, I hear a noise behind the door.

'Simon?' I press my hands against the wood. 'Can you hear me?'

A floorboard creaks.

'Talk to me. Please, Simon!'

I sense he's still there. I wish he'd at least yell at me to go away.

His silence is far more wounding.

51

SIMON

*B*ANG, BANG, BANG.
     My time in hospital has blasted the foundations of my Memory Palace with the effectiveness of a bomb. I no longer remember the correct layout, the doors I must enter to access my prime number theories and those I must avoid entering at all costs. Memories lie shattered in the corridors, wounded with shrapnel.

Bang, bang, bang.

'Simon? It's Jodie again. I'm back. I'm not giving up on you.'

I glance at the clock radio by my bed. I've been lost for days in the corridors inside my head. I don't know how to find my way out.

I close my eyes and accidentally picture myself outside rooms housing my knowledge of Charles Dickens. A plaque reads: 'Facts Alone Are Wanted in Life'. I do not wish to linger with the horrors of Gradgrind in *Hard Times* and quickly locate a weathered oak door featuring the words 'Satis House' in gold lettering.

This room contains facts about *Great Expectations*. Inside, the clock has stopped at twenty minutes to nine – the time Miss Havisham was jilted on her wedding day.

Time drifts.

Facts merge.

Bang, bang, bang.

My eyes fly open again.

How predictable. Jodie's not giving up. This time, I retreat from my thoughts and shakily climb out of bed. My knees give way and I slump back down. When I feel strong enough, I try again. This time I manage to get up. Slowly, I haul myself out of the room and shuffle to the front door, steadying myself against the walls. Jodie is speaking, but I can't see her through the peephole. She must be sitting down. I sink to the floor, my hand pressing against the wood.

'I know you're there,' she says quietly. 'I can hear you.'

She taps on the door. It vibrates beneath my fingertips.

'You don't have to say anything. Just listen. I'm sorry I was more interested in my Cambridge reference than I was about your parents. And I'm sorry I hurt you and kept pressing you to talk. But I'm here to listen now, if you need me to. I want to understand what happened with your mum . . . I'll never judge you . . .'

She pauses, possibly because she's heard my stifled sob.

'You were right about Cambridge. My family and friends are more important than getting into university and I've neglected them. Horribly. I've taken advantage of people's kindness when I should have tried to help *them*. I'm sorry I let you down. That won't happen again. I promise.'

I lean against the door.

'Please open up. *Please* forgive me.'

I close my eyes. I can't bear to see her disappointment – or judgement. How can I face *anyone* in the outside world after my past has been exposed in print?

'People care about you – check your phone,' she continues. 'You'll hear messages of support from lots of people. Nobody cares about your past. They care about *you*, Simon Sparks.'

I wonder who has called. I haven't bothered to turn on my phone since I was discharged.

The letterbox rattles and something drops through, landing on the mat.

'Zak made this for you.'

I pick up the card. It's a stick man holding a stick boy and woman's hand. A toy dog sits at their feet.

Dear Mr Super Swot

Get well soon.

Luv Zak x

He's drawn a family.

My hands tremble. Tears form in my eyes and a knot tightens in my chest. Shakily, I stand up and reach for the handle. Fumbling with the locks, I let Jodie in. She opens her arms and this time I don't misinterpret the gesture. I let her envelop me in the hug. We hold each other tightly and I silently forgive her, the way I knew, deep down, I always would. In the kitchen, we drink tea and she tells me about Jason's attack and their homelessness. In turn, I describe my hospitalization. And – finally – I relay the events of that terrible night from all those years ago, the one that has blackened everything: our thwarted plan to spirit Mother away at Easter break.

'We wanted to wreck Father's model railway as revenge for his abuse, but instead . . .' I shake my head. 'It's too terrible . . .'

'You can tell me.'

My heart thuds painfully. 'I need a minute.'

Jodie nods. 'Of course. Take as much time as you need.'

I breathe out slowly, bracing myself.

'We accidentally started a fire that killed Mother,' I say, choking on the words.

I close my eyes and see flames dance malevolently behind my lids.

'Father ran out of the house. When he saw the burning garage, he clutched his chest as if he were having a heart attack. You see, he knew Mother was in the car . . .' I gulp, my tongue feels too thick in my mouth, but I have to press on. 'Father later told me she'd left a note saying she was leaving, but she'd fallen asleep in the driver's seat due to her medication. The firefighters managed to rescue her from the car, but the smoke was so bad . . . It was billowing out of the garage in huge clouds. They tried to . . . They tried really hard but couldn't revive her. Neither could the paramedics. She died before she could be taken to hospital.'

'Oh, Simon.' Jodie's eyes glisten with emotion. 'I don't know what to say. I'm so sorry . . . for all of you.'

'I've spent most of my life being sorry.' I bend over, cradling my head in my hands. 'Mother would probably have woken up in time if she hadn't taken sleeping tablets to help with her insomnia. She'd have heard us in the garage before the fire took hold.'

'It's terrible. I wish I could somehow take all your pain away.'

'You have enough from your own childhood.'

Jodie takes my hands again. My fingers curl around hers.

'Father was taken to hospital and checked over – he had heart palpitations due to shock, nothing more serious. I was arrested on suspicion of arson and murder. On the journey to the police station, I knew my life was over. Not because I couldn't go back to Cambridge or do my PhD. But because Mother was gone. And she was all I had. I was screaming for Mother and blaming William. I only recall fragments after that – the duty psychiatrist saying I was unfit to be interviewed. I was sectioned at the station and taken to a psychiatric unit. By then, I was out of my mind. I wanted to kill myself and hurt William too.'

Jodie shuffles closer, narrowing the gap between us. I close my eyes, breathing out slowly.

'I had a psychotic episode and was hospitalized for six months. I don't remember much. Quite honestly, I don't want to either. I'm told I couldn't function – not even to talk, feed or dress myself for some of the time. When I was finally allowed home, William wasn't there; I suppose he'd gone away before term recommenced. Father had cleared the house of every keepsake of Mother's – her clothes, books and even her jewellery. Only a few photos remained. He told me that the police had pursued the case initially *with vigour*, but had decided not to proceed with any charges due to my fragile mental state and a lack of evidence of deliberate or reckless intent.

'Father said, *You've been judged not guilty by reason of insanity, but you and I both know the truth, Simon. You killed your mother. She'd still be alive if it hadn't been for your wanton act of vandalism.*'

Jodie's mouth falls open. 'Putting all that guilt on you . . .' Her voice trails off as she shakes her head in disbelief. 'It's just horrendous . . . I have no idea how your dad could possibly think something like that, let alone say it.'

'He meant every word. Even with everything that had happened, he was still furious with me for the destruction of his precious model railway and for the waste of my education – I'd missed sitting my finals and was too unwell to think about rescheduling. I couldn't take up my Princeton place. Can you believe he mourned those losses more than Mother's passing?'

She shakes her head again. 'I can't even begin to imagine what it was like for you having a dad like that.'

'It wasn't for much longer. The next day he packed my suitcase, putting the *Sparks' Family Guidelines for Success* on top. I managed to smuggle in a couple of framed family photos before he kicked me out. I ended up on the streets for a while before managing to find accommodation.'

'How could a dad do that to his son?' Jodie's voice is thick with emotion.

'I'll always remember what he said: *Your life is a total car crash, Simon.*'

'Is that what was going through your mind when you lied about what happened to your parents?' she asks quietly.

I bite the inside of my cheek hard until I can taste blood.

Car crash; bright sparks create fires.

Those words have haunted me since Mother's death.

'It was easier to bury the truth than admit it – even to myself.'

When I've managed to get the words out, Jodie holds me close again.

'The trouble is, I don't know who I am now the truth is out – the real Simon Sparks,' I say over her shoulder, 'not the pretend one who supposedly graduated from Cambridge and wants to light up the mathematical world by solving the Riemann Hypothesis. I've realized that's probably never going to happen. I think I was mistaken – I'm nowhere near solving it. But who am I if I don't even have that?'

'*I* know who you are,' she says softly. 'You're my friend and

Zak's. I'm not just saying that because I was . . .' Her shoulders tense up. 'I mean, about Cambridge and everything. You're our friend.'

I wrap the word 'friend' around me, like a comforting blanket. No one's ever called me that before.

'You have friends at Prince Burger, and Arthur and his team-mates are also here for you. They want to see you again. They keep asking when you'll be well enough to join them. We both missed last week's quiz and they lost the sudden-death question.'

I sigh. 'I guess you're trying to tell me that the Three Wise Men need my help?'

'No, in all honesty, Simon, I think you need *them*.'

52

JODIE

I PUSH OPEN THE DOOR of The Rising Sun and plough
through the drinkers towards the bar where Arthur's buying
a round. Zak's at Billy's birthday sleepover and I'd promised to
come. Simon was noncommittal but I hope he turns up. I'm still
worried about him. At least he's answering his phone and Aleksy
has arranged for another neighbour to do a food shop. He looked
ill on Tuesday night, terribly thin and pale-faced. I'm not sure if
he's well enough to come out tonight even though the company
might do him good.

'You came, my dear!' Arthur kisses me on each cheek. 'One
vodka, lime and soda coming right up!' He signals to the bartender.
'It's kind of you to join us when you're so busy. I completely
forgot – your Cambridge interview is on Monday. How exciting!'

I look down at my feet. 'Actually, I've decided not to go. This
isn't a good time for Zak or me.'

Arthur's eyes widen as he pays for the drinks. 'What do you
mean?'

I pick up his tray and we head over to the table. 'Zak says he's doing OK, but he's still traumatized by Jason and the fire. He's lost everything . . . apart from me. He really needs me to be here for him.'

'Don't you think this is even more of a reason to go for it? This could be the start of a better life for the two of you.' Arthur sits down heavily in the chair, leaning on his stick. 'It's important to hang onto the dreams you spoke so passionately about. You mustn't give up when you've come so far.'

I slide into place next to him. 'It doesn't have to be forever. I could try again when Zak's older but, at the moment, being his mum is my priority. He needs me to be one hundred per cent present, not distracted by other stuff.'

'Yes, but—'

'So a jest, a witticism and a quip put on masks and hold up a bank together,' Philip, the quizmaster, booms into the mic. 'This robbery is no laughing matter.'

Arthur explodes into giggles, which are swiftly drowned out by groans across the bar. I'm glad of the distraction. Cambridge isn't a subject I want to answer questions about tonight.

Someone approaches and grabs the chair next to me.

'That's taken, sorry,' I say, leaning over to grip the side of the chair.

'There isn't room for one more?'

I glance up. 'Simon!'

He's not wearing his usual competition waistcoat, just a sweat-shirt and jeans that hang off his gaunt frame.

'Does anyone have a spare pencil I can borrow?' he asks shakily.

We all cheer as he sits down, blushing.

*

The quiz has played to our strengths. Simon has answered all the science and mathematical questions, Winston the geography and Zak would be impressed by Trevor's knowledge of football. Arthur's turned out to be a whizz at history and I've supplied answers on Shakespeare and Keats. I'm sure they're correct. I look over my shoulder at members of Team Victorem. They appear confident as usual, high-fiving each other.

'They're still the team to beat tonight.' Arthur leans closer as he notices me checking out the opposition. 'They're ex-Oxbridge.'

'How do you know?'

'I've spoken to a few members. They might have mentioned it once or twice.' He winks. 'Or a few hundred times.'

I scan their faces and clothes. What does a typical Oxbridge graduate look like? They don't swan around in blazers, clutching teddy bears like characters from *Brideshead Revisited*. Maybe it's a subtle difference – their education provides an innate confidence that becomes a part of their DNA.

'Where did you all go to university?' Simon asks the team.

They dissolve into laughter.

He looks around the table, bewildered. 'You've lost me.'

'We went straight from school at sixteen onto the production line in the factory,' Winston says. 'I ended up in quality control, Arthur became an operations manager and Trevor was an engineering leader.'

'Did you study for degrees in your spare time?' Simon presses.

Trevor swivels a large gold ring around his middle finger. 'None of us has degrees. We're self-taught.'

'Really? Well, I'm impressed.' Simon takes a sip of his drink. 'You're so knowledgeable about your chosen subjects, I presumed you'd all been through higher education.'

'I wish I'd been given the choice,' Arthur says. 'Back in the day, university wasn't a consideration for the likes of me. I failed the eleven-plus and was shoved into a secondary modern. I went down a different route to classmates who got into grammar schools. My life was decided for me as a kid, but your generation is lucky.' He fixes me with a hard stare. 'You can make your own decisions. I'd love to study history. I might still do a degree by distance learning. It's never too late to learn.'

I silently beg him not to bring up the fact that Cambridge is off the table. I haven't told Simon yet. I don't want to make him feel worse, realizing he's wasted all this time on me. I push the beer mat around with my finger as they discuss how family background also helps determine how well you do. People like me don't have parents who can buy houses close to top schools to get into their catchment areas or pay for tutors and private education. When you're not born into money, choices are snatched out of your hands. I've been sent down a different path, the way Arthur was at eleven and again at sixteen. I don't have a choice either.

'We've got more practical skills in our little fingers than that lot have combined,' Arthur continues, nodding at Team Victorem. 'Giving up when things get tough isn't in our DNA, is it, lads?'

I flush, picking up my handbag. I pretend I need to use the toilet – any excuse to avoid his lesson in uncomfortable truths in front of my ex-Cambridge tutor.

I was right to be upbeat about our answers – we've topped the leaderboard, knocking Team Victorem into second place by five points. Philip has given us a short break to get another round of drinks and decide if we're going to take the English Literature sudden-death question.

'Here we are again,' Arthur says. 'Are we ready?'

I detect a shudder in Simon's shoulders.

'I vote we go for it,' Trevor says.

Winston nods. 'We do it now, with Simon and Jodie's help.'

'Are you sure you want to take the risk?' Simon asks, frowning.

'Everything in life is a risk,' Arthur points out. 'But the only thing we should be worrying about is how to spend the winnings.'

'I'm booking a mini-break for my son and the grandkids,' Winston says, putting his pint down. 'They haven't been away for years.'

'I'm planning a dirty weekend away with the missus.' Trevor winks.

'There's life in the old codger yet,' Arthur says, slapping his leg.

'What about you?' Winston asks.

'I'm undecided,' Arthur replies. 'Maybe I'll put it towards a weekend in New York. My wife has always wanted a shopping trip and walk around Central Park.'

'You could recommend the best scenic route, Simon,' I say.

His eyes have a faraway expression. 'W-w-what? Why?'

'You've been there. I've seen the picture of you and William's family on Gapstow Bridge, remember?'

'Oh that,' he says, waving his hand dismissively. 'The bridge is at the northeast part of the Pond. We didn't circuit the whole park. The children were hungry and wanted to visit a diner.'

I could kick myself as he shifts uncomfortably in his seat and clears his throat. Bringing up William was a mistake; they're unlikely to arrange another visit any time soon after their latest falling-out.

'Well, anyway,' Arthur says, glancing between us. 'The only

thing I feel certain about are our new friends – they're going to take us all the way this time. I can feel it in my bones.'

Simon's eyes mist up. I can't deal with kindness either – I'll dissolve into an emotional puddle, especially now I'm on my third vodka, lime and soda.

'No pressure!' I say, with a small laugh. 'I wish I'd brought a lucky charm or something to help us get through this.'

'My granddaughter found this a while ago outside a newsagent's in Shepherd's Bush and insisted I brought it tonight for good luck.'

Arthur pulls out a familiar threadbare toy from the inside pocket of his jacket and places it on the table.

'Dog!' Simon shouts.

'I can't believe it!' I almost knock over the drinks. I snatch up the toy, turning it over as my eyes well up.

The team stares at us, bewildered.

'It's Zak's favourite toy!' Simon explains. 'He lost it on the way home from my flat three weeks ago. We'd given up hope of finding it.'

My voice chokes with emotion. 'This will make Zak's day – probably his whole year.'

'So this *is* a lucky mascot,' Arthur muses.

'How can we lose now?' Trevor asks.

I laugh, clutching Dog to my chest. Half of me wants to gatecrash Billy's sleepover party to give Zak his lost toy straight-away, but I know I must see this through.

'Are you ready?' Arthur asks, putting a hand over Simon's.

Gently, he removes it. 'If you don't mind, I'd rather not put myself through the pressure again. I've realized that sudden-death questions on English Literature aren't exactly my forte. You should listen to Jodie. She's the expert.'

'Really?' I ask. 'I'm not sure . . .'

'I believe in you,' Simon says. 'You're good enough to get into Lucy Cavendish *and* win the sudden-death question.'

My cheeks redden.

'It's time to believe in yourself,' Simon says. 'That's my final – and most important – lesson.'

Arthur offers me his hand. I take it, clutching Dog, and stand up next to him. My palms are sweaty and the alcohol is hammering tiny holes in my forehead. I don't have time to ask for a drink of water or try to find a painkiller in my handbag.

Holding hands, we turn to face Philip who pretends to drum-roll before staring down at his piece of paper.

'For the sudden-death question and the record-breaking eighteen-hundred-pound jackpot, can you name the comic novel written by Charles Dickens, which was referred to in the following private letters? The author told his friend, John Forster, "You will not have to complain of the want of humour as in the *Tale of Two Cities*. I have made the opening, I hope, in its general effect exceedingly droll. I have put a child and a good-natured foolish man, in relations that seem to me very funny." He also wrote about the same book: "I can see the whole of a serial revolving on it, in a most singular and comic manner."'

Philip tosses the mic from hand to hand as Simon groans, placing his head in his hands.

'Not Charles bloody Dickens again,' he wails.

'Do you have any ideas?' Arthur whispers.

'I can think of lots of funny characters in Dickens' novels. But I can't think of a solely comic book – not one with a child and a "good-natured" fool in the first few chapters.'

'Perhaps it's *Oliver Twist*,' Winston says. 'The little boy, Oliver, must be introduced in the first chapter, surely?'

'But it's not funny,' I point out.

'I'm going to have to ask for an answer,' Philip says.

'I hate to say it, but what about *David Copperfield*?' Simon asks. 'I memorized some famous lines years ago in preparation for the *Little Einsteins* final, but I never read the whole novel. Is it amusing, Jodie?'

Team Victorem pound their glasses in an attempt to put us off. It's working. I'm struggling to concentrate as other tables join in with the drumming.

'I'm trying to remember what you taught me about your Memory Palace.'

Quickly, Simon reminds me about the importance of visual and spatial memory. I picture the house Zak and I will live in one day. It has three bedrooms, one of which I'll use as a study, and a big garden where Zak will play football. Upstairs, in the study, I see the novels of Charles Dickens on a shelf, in order of publication, from *The Pickwick Papers* (serialized 1836–37) to *The Mystery of Edwin Drood* (1870). I stare at *A Tale of Two Cities* and the famous novel that followed it. Could Dickens have been referring to *this* book? It would make sense that he was discussing his work in progress, but it wasn't a comic novel. *Far from it.*

'I need an answer!' Philip booms.

'Let's go with *David Copperfield*,' Arthur whispers.

'I don't know about that,' Simon says quickly.

'It's the best we can do.' Arthur raises his voice. 'We have the answer, Philip. The comic novel by Charles Dickens is . . .'

I open my eyes. 'Stop!' I straighten my shoulders and push my chin up, ignoring the jeers from Team Victorem. 'It's not *David Copperfield*. It's a trick question. Dickens set out to write a comic novel after *A Tale of Two Cities*, but changed his mind. Instead, the first few chapters feature a frightened, abused boy who witnessed something terrible.'

I hold Dog closer. Simon stands up and takes hold of my other hand.

'That's fascinating background detail, but I haven't got an answer yet,' Philip says. 'Do you have the name of the novel? If not, I'm going to have to call time.'

Team Victorem laugh and chant: 'Time, time, time!'

'I've never been more certain about this – about me, about *anything*. The answer is *Great Expectations*.'

The pub falls silent. All eyes rest on Philip.

Simon and Arthur grip my hands tighter. Trevor and Winston sit on the edge of their seats, shoulders tensed.

'The answer is correct!' Philip shouts. 'Table five, you have *finally* won the sudden-death question. Many congratulations!'

The pub erupts into whoops and cheers.

'You did it!' Simon exclaims.

'*We* did it!' I gasp. 'I can't believe it! I've never won anything in my life!'

Arthur's voice shakes. 'I knew you wouldn't give up. We're cut from the same cloth, you and me. We're fighters. We always get there in the end even if it takes us a little longer.'

Winston and Trevor stand up. We have a group hug, before locking arms and launching into an out-of-tune rendition of 'We Are the Champions'.

Many, *many* singalongs and drinks later, Simon announces he's heading off. I don't try to argue with him; he's swaying like a ghost and has dark bruise-like shadows beneath his eyes.

I pull at his sleeve to make him lean closer; the music is deafening.

'I'm glad you were brave enough to join us,' I say into his ear.

I inhale fresh soap and a lovely warm, woody scent.

His eyes crinkle at the edges. 'Me too. Zak will be happy to get Dog back.'

'Yes!'

I'm about to suggest he helps give the toy to Zak tomorrow, but he's already backing away. He mouths something incomprehensible. I raise my hands, frowning. He smiles sadly and gestures to the door before manoeuvring around the drinkers.

My heart feels suddenly heavy. I thought the quiz would help, but it's obvious Simon is still suffering. I wish I could think of a way to ease his pain. Not tonight though, my brain's zonked. I should go too. Billy's mum said his nanny would take all his sleepover friends on to school, but I could turn up early and show Zak his lost toy.

I manage to find Arthur chatting to the enemy: members of Team Victorem.

'Come and have a drink with me and Robert!' Arthur cries, tucking his arm into mine. He whispers into my ear: 'He's not as much of a nob as I first thought. You might like him? He's single too. Unless you and Simon . . . ?'

'No!' I cut in. 'Absolutely not, we're just friends!'

He shakes his head. 'If you say so. In that case, let me introduce you. Robert can give you some advice about the Cambridge interview on Monday and who knows where it could lead?'

'I'm good, thanks. I've got to go.'

'In that case hold fire while I rally the troops.'

He extracts himself and returns a few minutes later with Winston and Trevor, who also look worse for wear.

'This is for you and Simon.' Arthur tucks his hand into his waistcoat and pulls out a white envelope. 'We want you both to have it.'

'Oh no, I couldn't. I told you – we agreed we wouldn't take a share of the winnings.'

'Look inside,' Winston says.

I open the envelope and stare in disbelief at the thick wad of £50 notes. I flick through them.

'But this is the whole jackpot,' I gasp. 'Eighteen hundred pounds.'

'You and Simon deserve it,' Trevor replies. 'You both helped us, more than you'll ever know. We proved that we're as good, if not better, than Team Victorem.'

'Seriously, getting Dog back is enough of a prize. I couldn't possibly take it.'

'You can and you will,' Arthur insists.

'No way!' I touch Winston's arm. 'What about the mini-break for your son and grandkids? And Trevor, you could have that weekend away with your wife! Arthur – think about New York!'

'Tashina agrees with me for once,' Winston says. 'I feel her approval right here.' He taps his handkerchief.

'You can't argue with his late wife,' Trevor points out. 'No one ever used to win against her, including Winston!'

I manage a small laugh.

'Simon must fix the water damage to his flat and you can put the winnings towards your studies at Cambridge,' Arthur says. 'It's bloody expensive, or so I hear.'

'I told you, I'm not going to the interview.' I attempt to press the envelope into his hands, but he resists.

'In that case, put your share into a savings account for Zak and start a university fund so he can afford to go when he's older. God only knows what the fees will be when he turns eighteen.'

'I'm not sure . . .'

'Or use it to get on your feet after the fire, and to buy that lad of yours some Christmas presents,' Winston says. 'Either way the money is Simon's and yours to do with as you wish. We can win other jackpots. We're in agreement that you've both earned this. You both *need* this, far more than we do.'

'I don't know what to say . . .'

I think of the horrendous debt I'm racking up from the interest rates on that £200 loan – I have to repay £400 in total this month, but if I can't come up with the cash, it will be £600 the month after and then a never-ending cycle of debt. This could help me to clear it *and* put aside money for Zak.

'Say you'll take it and make a group of old codgers happy,' Arthur says.

I break down into tears as I put my arms around him. 'Simon will be really touched. I am too.'

'This is the beginning of both your lives not the end,' he whispers in my ear. 'Promise me you'll think again about Cambridge?'

I hug him tighter, but remain silent.

Despite everything Arthur and his teammates have done for Simon and me, I can't bring myself to make yet another promise I'll fail to keep.

53

JODIE

BILLY'S HOUSE IS ONLY a short walk away from our B&B, but it may as well be in another continent. His street even smells better than ours; there's not a single overspilling rubbish bin or a piece of litter. It's lined with Mercedes, Range Rovers and Teslas instead of abandoned, wheel-clamped wrecks. The house is far bigger than the ones I used to clean in Clapham. It's a five-storey building with white-shuttered sash windows and a shiny black door with a lion's head knocker. This is what I imagine Simon's Memory Palace looks like. Empty flower boxes sit on the sills, ready to be planted with spring bulbs.

Billy's mum and dad are lawyers – highly successful ones. I'm still gobsmacked that Billy goes to a state school, but Mrs Devine says she 'doesn't agree with private education'. Her family comes from a long line of socialists. Champagne socialists, more like. She aloofly describes where they live as RBKC, which stands for the Royal Borough of Kensington and Chelsea, rather than just saying Kensington, which makes it sound even more posh. But

I must stop being such a snarky bitch. She's dug me out of a few childcare holes.

Margaret, the housekeeper, is expecting me; I texted ahead and said I'd call round at 7.30 a.m. She lets me in, explaining that the nanny has popped out to buy vegan croissants and pains au chocolate for the boys from the nearby bakery as a treat before school. *Of course she has.* I inhale the sweet scent of money as I step into the gigantic hallway; I bet the diffusers are from Jo Malone. A gigantic Christmas tree reaches towards a chandelier, which cascades in a glittering waterfall from the top floor.

'Impressive, isn't it?' Margaret says. 'The interior decorator deliberately designed the tree decorations to look like frozen jewels.'

'Doesn't everyone?' I say, with a small laugh.

She frowns as she leads me up the marble staircase. 'Zak's still in bed, but the other boys are playing Xbox with Billy in the games room.'

'Wow!'

A games room isn't a surprise in a house like this, but Zak not taking up residence inside it is a real shocker. She shows me to Billy's bedroom before retreating downstairs. It's three times bigger than the room we're living in, with built-in wardrobes and an en suite. I recognize a Millennium Falcon Lego box among a heap of presents on the floor; that gift alone cost at least £100. Zak didn't bring anything for Billy, but Mrs Devine had said not to worry. She understood our *difficult circumstances.*

'Hey, little man. What are you doing?'

Zak's propped up against a pillow, in a camp bed and sleeping bag. Billy's lightsaber is next to him.

'Reading. *Obviously.*' He puts down *The Wimpy Kid* and places his arms in a strange position by the side of his body.

'Cheeky!' I lean over and plant a kiss on the top of his head, which he immediately wipes off. 'I thought you'd be in the games room with the others.'

Zak shrugs. 'Didn't want to play with them.'

I frown. He doesn't look happy, but it must be tough for him seeing the way Billy lives. How can he not compare this mansion to our grotty little room? Zak can't ever invite friends over to us.

'Well, I thought I'd pop in early before you get ready for school. I've got some fab news.' I pause, distracted by the way he's sitting. 'Why are you sticking your arms out like that?'

'I'm holding Dog here.' He jerks his head towards his right armpit.

'Really?' My hand reaches into my handbag, feeling for his lost toy.

'*I'm* not stupid.' He rolls his eyes as if *I* am. 'I know Dog's gone, but he's left a hole right here.' He points at the space between his body and his arm. 'This is where he belongs.'

'Well, guess what I found last night at the pub?'

'A winning lottery ticket?'

'Better than that.' I pull out Dog and tuck it under his arm. Zak lets out a loud yelp.

'You found him!' His eyes fill with tears and his bottom lip wobbles. He hugs his toy closely and sniffs the material. 'Yeuch! He smells bad.'

'He might have got splashed with someone's beer. He spent the night partying in a pub.'

'Bad Dog! No more drinking!' He presses the toy to his face. 'But I forgive you because I missed you *so, so, so, so* much.'

'Don't worry. I'll give him a wash and he'll smell normal again.'

'What was he doing in the pub?'

'Arthur's granddaughter found him outside a newsagent's in

Shepherd's Bush. He brought him along as a lucky mascot for his quiz team. And boy was he lucky!' I pull out the envelope. 'Look what we won thanks to Dog!'

Zak's mouth widens as he touches the notes. 'Wow! Are we rich now? Can we buy a house as big as this? Billy has an indoor swimming pool and a cinema room. There's even a separate floor where the nanny and cook live.'

'Not that rich – we have to split this with Simon – but it's more cash than I've ever held.'

'Me too.' Zak touches the notes before hugging Dog again and tucking him under his right armpit. 'What are you going to buy? How about a motorbike?'

I stare at his left arm. It's still jutting out as if he's making the shape of a teapot, the way he used to in music class at play-group when he was little.

'Maybe you could choose a new toy to put under that arm?'

'Nah.'

'How about a lightsaber – a proper one with flashing lights like Billy's? Or you could have a big Lego Star Wars set?'

Zak shakes his head sadly. 'My gap isn't for a toy.'

'Is this about pocket money? Perhaps I can give you some now, if you're good.'

He looks under his arm. 'This is to make room for Emmeline Squeakhurst.'

'Who?'

Zak sighs heavily. 'I can't believe you've forgotten her. She's one of the guinea pigs at Lucy Cavendish, but I've lost her too.'

'She's not lost. She lives in her hutch with the other guinea pigs.'

'But *I* can't play with her!' He folds his arms crossly. 'That's why I don't want to go on the Xbox with the others – well, one of the reasons, anyway. I'm in a bad mood because you still lie to me.'

'That's not true! I admit I tried to protect you from the truth about your dad, but that's not the same thing as deliberately lying.'

He shakes his head. 'This is something else. You always say we're a team, but you lied about *that*. You decided not to go to the Cambridge interview without asking my opinion. Now, I'll never get to feed the guinea pigs again. I can't look for a black squirrel or a muntjac deer either. I have nothing to look forward to. I'll never have a pet because of you.'

I try to take his hand but he brushes me off.

'Zak!'

'You tell me my dreams will come true if I work hard at school and never give up. Well, that was another lie! You've given up and made me give up. You're a coward and a scaredy cat!'

I touch my chest, feeling a physical pain as sharp as if he's jabbed me with Billy's lightsaber.

'It's not that I don't want to try, but sometimes grown-ups have to make hard decisions. I have to concentrate on looking after you instead of spending my time trying to get into Cambridge – something that may or may not happen.'

'If you don't try, it's never going to happen.' Zak sniffs. 'That's what Simon said and he's a genius. He's *my* friend. He talks to me about maths and other things, like I'm a grown-up, and doesn't mind if I ask questions. He always answers them. You've taken him off me. I know you've had an argument with him. I've seen your text messages, apologizing for being mean.'

I'm pretty astounded by Zak's insight. Talk about seven going on twenty-seven.

'At some point we need to talk about respecting other people's privacy. But, in the spirit of being honest, we're friends again. I saw him last night at the pub quiz.'

'Hmm.' Zak eyes me suspiciously. 'When can I see him?'

'I don't know.'

Quickly, I explain that Simon is not fully recovered and doesn't have family to look after him; he's fallen out with his dad and now his brother.

'We should help them make up. Mr Silva says that talking is the best way forward. You have to try to understand the other person's point of view and tell them how *you* feel.'

'I don't think that's possible. Families are, well, complicated.'

'Everything in life is possible. Simon told me that, too, the day he took me to the playground.'

'Well, when you get older you'll find out it isn't that simple. You can't have everything you want.'

'Why not?'

'Because that's not the way it works. For a start, you probably won't be able to afford to buy a house as big as this when you grow up.' I wave my arm around the room. 'I know that's hard to accept when your friend has all this.'

'He's not my friend. He's a jerk. He only invited me because his mum said it would be good for him to learn about how other children at his school live. *Poor kids.* They feel sorry for us. His mum asked how often we visit the food bank in front of the other kids when Billy refused to eat his pizza last night.'

'Oh, Zak! I had no idea.'

My cheeks burn as he shakes his head.

'I don't care what Billy and his mum think. I don't want pocket money or a lightsaber or a Lego set. I have Dog back. I *want* to make Simon feel better and I *want* to live in Cambridge and play with the guinea pigs every day. Both of those things are possible, so don't tell me they're not. *I'm* not giving up.'

I take a deep breath, putting Dog into my bag for safekeeping. 'There is something I could do for Simon, I guess. Not today though – I suppose I have to go into college and discuss . . . preparations for the Cambridge interview with my tutor.'

A grin spreads across Zak's face.

He punches the air with excitement. 'Yes!'

'But, maybe I could do something for our friend tomorrow.'

'What?'

'I'll beg someone else to help Simon.'

54

SIMON

I'M LYING IN BED, flicking through the prize money in the envelope. Picking apart my errors and miscalculations on the Riemann Hypothesis has left me exhausted and demoralized. Jodie presented me with my half of the winnings earlier this morning. I'm overwhelmed by the generosity of Arthur's team. It will help my dwindling finances until I can summon the energy to search for another job.

I jump at the knock on the front door. I'm not expecting anyone after Jodie's visit. Maybe she's forgotten something. I head to the hallway.

'Has Arthur changed his mind and asked for the cash back?' I call out, fumbling with the locks. 'I haven't spent it yet!'

I throw open the door.

'Ed!'

I grip the frame to steady myself. The mathematical probability of my former Prince Burger boss turning up must be around one in two million, yet here he is, standing on my doorstep. He looks startled by my appearance. Nervously, I rub my cheeks, attempting to bring back some colour.

'Simon, hi. Can I come in?'

'I wasn't expecting visitors. It's a bit of a mess in here, I'm afraid.' I shoot a look over my shoulder at the wrecked bathroom. 'I'm, er, in the middle of redecorating.'

'I don't mind. I've probably seen worse. I run a fast-food restaurant remember?'

Before I can ask what's going on he strides in, eyes flickering left and right.

'OK, I take it back. I haven't seen worse. Why is it so cold in here?'

He shivers, pulling on his coat, which he'd half taken off. Tucked under his arm is a card and present; maybe he's called in on the way to a birthday party.

'Which way to the kitchen?'

I point and follow after him. 'Is something wrong?'

Ed peers into my fridge before sitting down at the table.

'Yes, Simon – you're out of milk and can't offer me a cup of tea.'

He pulls out a chair. 'Take a seat. Make yourself comfortable. As much as you can when it's freezing in here. You look way too pale and skinny by the way . . .' His eyes narrow as they rest on the *Sparks' Family Guidelines for Success*.

Only Ed could march in here, uninvited, insinuate I look like death warmed up and order me to sit down in *my own flat*. Half of me wonders if I'm hallucinating and he's not really here.

'Are you planning to fire me for being a bad host?'

'Touché.'

I raise an eyebrow.

'Yes, I can use words like that despite my *unfortunate IQ level*.'

I blush; I'm not imagining this encounter; I know that's definitely something I've previously said about my former boss.

'This is for you,' Ed says gruffly, passing me the present and card. 'From your colleagues at Prince Burger.'

Today is becoming even more unpredictable. I open the Get Well Soon card, which features a UFO and has been signed by every member of staff, and an 'Employee of the Decade' certificate. Surely Ed is taking the mickey? Yet he remains straight-faced.

'Thanks.' I pull off the wrapping from the present and examine the alien-shaped green cushion. 'This is, erm, what I've always wanted.'

He shrugs. 'It's a small gesture of our appreciation. I had a chat with Jodie this morning. She told me what happened to you last week.'

Warmth creeps into my cheeks. Jodie's certainly been busy when she's supposed to be doing last-minute revision.

'The truth is you're a total fucking weirdo with all your IQ talk, but you're *my* fucking weirdo.'

'Well, that's nice to know . . .'

'And things haven't been the same at Prince Burger since you left.'

I raise an eyebrow.

'Carlos is terrible at stocktaking. He accidentally ordered five thousand gherkins and no frozen fries last week. Plus, something you care deeply about has had an unfortunate accident.'

'Oh no! Has Archie been injured?'

Jodie admitted he's been missing since I was fired; he hasn't taken any of the food she's left out.

'Who's Archie?'

'No matter.'

Now probably isn't the time to admit to Ed that I used to

feed the stray cat that stalks and attacks him, ninja-style, at every opportunity.

'I'm talking about the French fries machine you apparently named Fro-Bot. It died shortly after Carlos filled in for a shift. I'm sorry. I know it's possibly the closest personal relationship you ever experienced with anyone at Prince Burger, aside from Jodie.'

Wow! And he once claimed I had no people skills.

'The strange thing is that the day Jodie says you were admitted to hospital, the robot stopped working. It was almost supernatural. You hear about dogs pining when their owner dies, well Fro-Bot just gave up and malfunctioned. No one's been able to bring the machine round. I'll have to order a new one, which will cost thousands unless you come and fix it.'

My mouth falls open. 'Are you offering me my job back?'

'It's yours if you want it. The police tell me that The Worstomer is pleading guilty to all charges, so Prince Burger will be spared the embarrassment of you and Jodie having to give evidence at a court case.'

'I'm not sure . . .'

'I'm not stupid, whatever you might think about my IQ level. I know this isn't your dream job, but it will help you get on your feet. You're a good worker. Well, most, if not some of the time.'

I run my hand through my hair, which feels like it's sticking out in tufts. I certainly need the money.

'I'm not sure I can face everyone after that newspaper article,' I admit.

Ed shrugs his shoulders. 'It's yesterday's news. Anyway, I've always believed, whatever head office may claim, that Prince Burger is a family.'

'It's quite a dysfunctional one, if you don't mind me saying.'

'Aren't all families?'

I can't argue with that.

'We accept people for who they are and whatever mistakes they make,' Ed continues. 'And, most important of all, we don't turn our back on family members in their time of need.'

55

JODIE

Harold Sparks is next on today's hit list after persuading Ed to give Simon a second chance. Finding the address isn't too difficult – Simon once let slip that he'd lived at 36 Ember Lane, room thirty-six in his Memory Palace. There's only one such road in Buckinghamshire, but locating the actual house is trickier. I've walked up and down the street twice. On the third attempt, I take a punt on a driveway that's more hidden among trees and bushes. Ah yes, the plaque obscured by the dense shrubbery tells me that this is the one. The gravel crunches and grinds beneath my shoes as I head towards the house. It's large and rambling, the kind of place I'd pictured living in as a kid. But up close, cream paint is curling from the walls, exposing old brick, and the windows are dirty. It's impossible to see a reflection or sneak a look inside.

I wipe my sweaty palms on my jeans. Before I can change my mind, my hand reaches out and whacks the brass stag's head doorknocker.

Footsteps approach and the door cracks opens.

'Can I help you?' A sixty-something woman peers out. She's as small and frail as a bird, with a bluntly cut grey bob. Her chunky blue sweater swamps her.

'Mrs Sparks? Do you mind if I have a quick word?'

'We don't wish to talk to journalists.' She begins to close the door.

'Hey, please, just one moment. I'm Jodie – a friend of Simon's from work. I wondered if I could speak to your husband about him?'

Mrs Sparks' eyes widen. 'Harold isn't here.' Her gaze flickers to her watch. 'He'll be back soon, but he won't discuss family matters with you.'

She tries to close the door again but I can't leave without achieving anything. The train fare has set me back an arm and a leg; it's lucky I can dip into the quiz winnings to pay for the ticket.

'Do you mind if I use your bathroom? I've had a long journey and the toilet was closed at the station.'

She hesitates, fiddling with the strap of her watch before glancing up the driveway.

'Please.'

Mrs Sparks sighs heavily. 'If you must.'

She cracks open the door wider and I step into the clinically white hall; the temperature barely changes from outside. Bookshelves line the walls from top to bottom. The pristine novels, biographies and encyclopaedias are in alphabetical order; precisely lined up like soldiers reporting for duty. Were Simon and William ever allowed to read, let alone touch, them as children?

'Upstairs, first left,' she says.

The walls leading up to the first floor are cold and bare, stripped of all personality, along with those on the landing. Possessions and photos were never out on display in my old children's home either. A knot tightens in my stomach. At least I had a giggle with some of the girls, but I can tell this house has rarely heard laughter. After finishing up in the bathroom, I notice a door with peeling white paint on the landing. A bolt's fixed high up – only an adult can reach it. I peek inside. It's a tiny room with bare floorboards and barely space for a single bed.

Is this Simon's old bedroom?

On the wall is a charcoal drawing of a clown and an oil painting with the name John Nash in the corner. Beneath the pictures is a single shelf filled with books including *Encyclopaedia Britannica* and *The History of Space*, along with A-level maths practice booklets. I long to find each a better home.

'Jodie?' Mrs Sparks calls.

'I'm coming.'

She's almost at the front door before my foot reaches the last step.

'I don't suppose I could get a glass of water?' I say, faking a cough.

If Mr Sparks is a non-starter maybe I can get her to open up.

She steals another look at her watch, her brow furrowed. 'You'll have to be quick. Harold won't like it if he finds you here.'

Leading me through the lounge, she explains she needs to find her glasses. In the adjoining dining room, piles of private school and eleven-plus exam papers litter the table.

'Here they are!' She snatches up her glasses from the side-board.

Tests cover the floor along with application forms for junior language and maths competitions. A letter catches my eye. Addressed to Mr Sparks, it says his complaint has been considered, but no exceptions can be made: the minimum age for applying to next year's production of *Little Einsteins* is eight.

No way.

He's at it again, inflicting yet more misery, but this time, presumably, on someone else's child.

'Is your husband working as a personal tutor?'

I'm unable to keep the horror out of my voice as I join her in the kitchen.

Mrs Sparks' hand shakes as she turns on the tap and passes me a glass of water. 'Tutoring is Harold's life – bringing out young children's full potential – that, along with his model railway, of course.'

I touch the counter, feeling winded.

'I'm sorry to hear that nothing has changed,' I say quietly.

'What do you mean?'

'I think, deep down, you might know.'

She takes a sharp breath. 'What has Simon told you about my husband?'

'Do you really want to know, Mrs Sparks?'

She fiddles with a tendril of hair, pushing it behind her ear. 'You can call me Clare. And yes, I *need* to know.'

She sinks into a seat at the breakfast bar and gestures for me to sit down too. She presses her fingers to her mouth as I describe Simon's childhood – the years of drilling, stress and abuse followed by the fatal Easter holiday when everything came crashing down.

'That's why I'm here. I thought if I spoke to your husband, I could at least try to give Simon some closure. He's torn up with guilt after . . . after what happened to his mum. He's told me all about the fire – how he accidentally caused her death. It's terrible to watch his pain. It's ripping him apart.'

Her face pales. 'Oh my dear. Simon—' She freezes at a noise in the hallway.

'It's OK. I think that's just your radiator. What is it?'

'I can't.' She shakes her head vigorously.

'Yes, you can.' I reach out and take her hand; it's cold and trembling. 'Please help Simon – he's a good person. I'm sure you'd like him. He's kind and brave. He doesn't deserve to be this miserable.' I pause, holding her gaze. '*No one* docs.'

'You're right . . .' Clare's voice wavers. Lifting her chin, she clutches my hand tightly. 'It's time someone in this family finally dared to speak up and tell the truth.' She takes a deep breath. 'There's something Simon should know.'

56

JODIE

I HAVE TO TALK TO Simon, that's for sure. But this isn't the sort of thing I can text or blurt out over the phone. It has to be face to face – and when I think he's strong enough. He was on shift yesterday and too tired to see me after work. It's tricky but, for now, I need to focus on my Cambridge interview. I can't tell him and run off to get my train, leaving him in pieces. I have to finish getting ready.

There!

A stranger confidently smiles back from the mirror. I've scraped my hair into a neat bunch with a gold clip to flatter my horrendous roots, and taken out my nose ring. My makeup is 'barely there', thanks to an online tutorial. Instead of my usual heavy black-winged eyeliner, I've brushed pale brown eyeshadow on my lids. The pastel pink lipstick is apparently *my colour*, according to the woman on the beauty counter. Personally, I prefer bright red, but my nails are a matching pink too. They're short but I've miraculously managed to resist biting them for days.

My jacket disguises the inked birds fluttering up my arm. I tug at my thick black tights and skirt; they're as prickly as hell. I only ever wear jeans or leggings with trainers, but I've used some of the pub quiz winnings to buy this suit. I've kept the receipt. I'm returning it tomorrow; I'll never wear anything as formal as this again. But I had to make an effort. Even though the tutors didn't bat an eyelid at my appearance during the open day, today is different.

Dress like a Cambridge student. Become a Cambridge student.

I tuck my revision notes and good luck cards from Zak, Sandra and my college tutor, Monica, into my bag.

I look at my watch; I can pay a flying visit to Simon at Prince Burger before I head to King's Cross to get my train.

I take one last look in the mirror.

You've got this, Jodie Brook.

57

SIMON

A WOMAN IN A SUIT comes tottering towards the fry station on high, pointy stilettos. It must be a head office inspection.

'Welcome to Prince Burger! Can I tempt you with a delicious French fry? Or perhaps you would prefer a tour of the kitchens? They are cleaned to the highest standard.'

'It's me, you idiot.'

'Jodie?'

She smiles and winks.

'I scrub up well, don't I?'

'Hmm. Well, kind of. I guess.'

I stumble over my words as she tugs at her skirt. She looks like a cross between an investment banker and one of those well-groomed but terrifying women on beauty counters who aggressively offer sprays of perfume as you walk past. I'm not sure if she'll take that as a compliment.

'You certainly look dissimilar to your normal appearance.' I line up bags of fries.

She rolls her eyes dramatically, as she pulls out a pair of trainers from her bag.

'Wow! Thanks for the compliment. I can tell you're feeling better – you're almost back to your usual tactful self.'

'Sorry. It's a shock, seeing you look so different.'

'This is my interview look. Personally, I think I'm rocking it. Have you seen the height of these heels?' She holds up the shiny black shoes.

She looks disappointed when I don't fill the silence and slips the stilettos into her bag.

'Anyway, I know the suit isn't my best look, but I can return it and get a refund as long as I don't spill anything on it.' She produces tags on the jacket and skirt. 'And the heels were a bargain – only a fiver from a charity shop.'

'Are you ready for today?' I ask, frowning. 'And I don't mean fashion-wise.'

Jodie straightens her jacket. 'I think, *I hope*, I've done enough, but who knows?'

'You've worked hard. You deserve to get a place.'

'Thanks. Are you around later after work? We need a catch-up.'

'Sure. I'm dying to hear how the interview goes. Head over to mine when you're back.'

'We need to talk about some other stuff.' She doesn't meet my gaze.

'Oh, OK,' I say, a little flummoxed.

'I should go.' She turns to leave. 'Any last advice?'

'Be yourself!'

She snorts. 'No, thanks! The tutors want a much better version of me – the scrubbed-up version who looks and sounds like everyone else.'

360

She's wrong, but before I can argue she points at the smoke drifting from the fryer behind me.

'Save the fries!'

'Oh no!'

This batch is burnt and Marta's gesticulating, demanding more orders. Ed is on the prowl again. He can't see this. I scoop out the charred potato sticks and start over, talking nicely to Fro-Bot who I've managed to miraculously raise from the dead.

How best can I say this to Jodie without sounding unbearably patronizing?

She shouldn't have to pretend to be someone she's not to get a place. It's the university that should change, not her. She *is* different, but in the best possible way. No one I met as an undergraduate could ever match her drive and dedication. She's suffered much greater hardship too. She's come the furthest and I'm sure she'll go a greater distance than the students who have everything handed to them on a plate.

There's something else . . .

I've got my back to her but in my head I see her smiling, her arms wrapped protectively around Zak.

She has to know she's a wonderful mother and an incredible student. She's an inspiration to all the other kids in care who have been handed a shitty deck of cards in life and grown up being told they'll amount to nothing.

Most of all, I have to tell Jodie that I wouldn't change a single thing about her.

I turn around, taking a breath. 'The truth is, I think you're perfect.'

I catch a glimpse of her ponytail swinging as the door to Prince Burger closes behind her.

58

JODIE

WHY THE HELL DID I wear a suit? It's as hot as hell. The radiators almost scalded my hand when I arrived at Lucy Cavendish; they're on full blast. I turned up an hour earlier than necessary; I was worried about the train being late or getting on the wrong bus at the station. Now, I feel sweat pooling in my cleavage and under my arms. I'm dying to take off my jacket, but I've only got a white T-shirt on underneath and my tattoos will be exposed. I wish I'd worn a different top. I'll freshen the inside of my jacket with body spray when I get home otherwise I won't get a refund. I'm dying to put my trainers on.

I glance across the student common room. Lydia, a grandmother of two, is sitting cross-legged on the sofa, next to her shoes, reading *The Ode Less Travelled*. When the admissions officer brought me over from the Porters' Lodge, I'd expected to find competitive twenty-somethings in sharp suits pouring over notes. But only Lydia was waiting here, flicking through her book. She explained she'd worked as a PA in the City for her whole career before deciding to return to education.

'If you think this is bad, wait until you reach the menopause,' she says, looking up. 'I came prepared. I can't be without this.' She produces a small electric fan from her handbag and positions it inches away from her face.

I wish I had one. I try to picture waterfalls and plunging into sub-zero rivers to distract me from the furnace. Lydia is wearing jeans, a T-shirt (nothing fancy), and no makeup, which is a good move. My lips feel sticky and greasy and I'm overdressed. I feel distinctly uncomfortable.

The admissions officer returns to the room. 'It's time to go, ladies. Are you ready?'

'I don't think I'm ever going to feel ready.' Lydia uncurls her limbs from the sofa and shoves her feet into the shoes.

Me neither.

I hide my trembling hands in the suit pockets. I picture Lizzie wishing me good luck and Zak giving a thumbs up as I follow, balancing myself against the walls to make sure my vertiginous heels don't kill me.

The white-walled test room is in the college's Oldham Hall, on the right-hand side of the Porters' Lodge. It's modern and cheery, but it's also too warm. All the windows are shut. I sit down at one of the large, white desks, along with six other candidates, as the invigilator, a graduate student, goes over how long the test will take, instructing us not to talk or use phones. My heart is beating rapidly as she announces: 'You may begin!'

I wipe my sweaty palms on my skirt and turn over the paper.

The following extracts are all linked by the theme or imagery of relationships between brothers, both loving and destructive. Compare and contrast two, examining aspects such as imagery, mood, structure and language.

This could be a description of Simon's dysfunctional relationship with William – supportive one minute and debilitating the next. It's a harmful circle, which he says the psychiatrist in the hospital has urged him to break. I scan the extracts, which include *The Sound and the Fury* by William Faulkner; 'To His Dying Brother, Master William Herrick' by Robert Herrick; *The Brothers Karamazov* by Fyodor Dostoyevsky, *Brother* by David Chariandy; *Family Life* by Akhil Sharma and 'Brotherly Love' by Jhumpa Lahiri.

I stare across the room at Lydia, who's frowning and twirling a pen around her fingers. She looks down at the paper and starts writing. Three other women are making notes. I need to quickly pick my texts and get on with it. My instinct is to opt for *The Sound and the Fury* because I read the book years ago and also Herrick's poem – I vaguely remember what it's about, whereas I haven't come across the other extracts before.

Oh God. I'm not sure.

I reread the instructions, which I can recite off by heart after studying for weeks. I know the samples are *supposed* to be unfamiliar literary materials; marks will not be awarded for referring to other texts. The other candidates are in the same boat as me; they won't have an advantage even if they recognize every extract.

Keep calm.

Read the samples thoroughly.

Choose the passages that will best show off your skills.

I hear Simon's voice clearly in my head, but it doesn't help.

My mind is racing, skipping from extract to extract. I'm not reading anything properly. The words swirl treacherously before my eyes. My heart's pumping a million times a minute. Adrenaline floods my body and I feel myself going into fight-or-flight mode. I want to run out. I'll tell Zak I did my best when I get home. He'll understand, won't he?

But that would be a lie. You haven't tried. You haven't put pen to paper.

Simon's voice is in my head again. He's telling me to go over the samples, slowly, but the words continue to buzz around the paper like bees.

I'm going to throw up.

I scrape my chair back.

'Is everything all right?' The invigilator looks up from her desk.

'I'm not feeling well. I need to go. I'm sorry.'

I make a bolt for the door, but she's walking towards me, smiling and brandishing a bottle of water.

'Why don't you sit down and have a drink first?'

She leads me to my seat, unscrews the lid and pours me a glass.

'This is the best I can do,' she says quietly. 'I'm sorry I don't have anything stronger.'

I take huge, chugging gulps, draining the glass and another refill.

'Better?'

'I don't think I can do this.'

'I remember a young woman who said exactly that during this test four years ago,' she whispers. 'She reached the door. Guess what happened to her?'

'She ran out and caught the first train home?'

'*I* sat down and completed the exam and got through the

interviews. I was offered a place to study English here and I graduated with a double-starred first. I'm now studying for a Master's in Eighteenth-Century and Romantic Studies.'

She squeezes my shoulder and returns to her table.

Many of the things that happened to me have been out of my hands: being put into care, living in the foster and children's homes and the post-sixteen dumps.

But this is my decision: *stay or leave.*

The choice is mine.

I look down at the test paper, recalling Simon's lessons. I close my eyes and think about that day in the café when he'd explained how to arm myself with the information I'd need.

Assign a literary device to a place you can picture clearly and keep travelling. If you run out of locations, allocate a technique to a person you know well.

I'd been reluctant to follow his advice at first. But later, I began associating different techniques with places and people from my past.

Here goes.

I think of the council flat I lived in with Mum in Lichfield, Staffordshire. It's cramped and dirty, with rubbish and needles strewn over the floor.

Hyperbaton.

Aged seven, I'm taken to my first foster home, with Rob and Stella, eighteen miles away, in Birmingham. I remember how butterflies were attracted to the bush next to the red front door with the brass knocker.

Anaphora.

I'm moved on to the next foster home in Manchester. This time, I'm living with Lisa and Jenny in a semi-detached house with thin walls. I hear the neighbours' TV in the evening.

Polysyndeton.

It doesn't work out. I'm on the move again, with less than a week's notice, and end up with Sally and Graeme in Bolton. The front room has a green, flowery carpet.

Assonance.

Now I'm with Karen and Derek in a two-bedroom house in Wigan.

Synecdoche.

Aged eight, I'm placed in a children's home in Newcastle, more than 180 miles away from Lichfield. No chance my mum could ever afford to visit.

Metonymy.

I'm moving south and end up in London. I'm placed in a children's home in Camden, aged nine. I stay for around seven years.

Anapaest.

I'm shunted between six post-sixteen homes across the capital – often turning up late at night and finding only a dirty mattress on the floor and no bedding. My housemates leave dirty needles in their rooms and carry blades for protection. I'm too scared to sleep at night and can't concentrate at school.

I have thirteen literary devices in total from being a nomadic, unwanted child.

I move on, energized.

I'm given a council flat after becoming pregnant.

I'm homeless after signing away my tenancy agreement and leaving Jason. That means I have to sofa-surf between two friends' houses before fleeing with Zak to a women's refuge, where we stay for six months.

Four more devices.

Lizzie helps me to persuade the council I haven't made myself voluntarily homeless, by showing officials the texts and photos she received from me, detailing Jason's abuse. Zak and I are placed in emergency accommodation – a grotty hostel – for six weeks.

Two years ago, the council moves us on to a temporary home – the bedsit.

Now we're back where we started with the council in emergency accommodation, at the B&B.

Twenty literacy devices.

I've run out of locations and move on to people.

I recall the names of every social worker I had between the age of nine and eighteen and write down fifteen literary devices.

Fifteen! I've never added them up before.

So many people drifted in and out of my childhood, not counting all the key workers and the staff in the home.

I stare at my notes.

I've been through enough.

I know the names of thirty-five devices and poetic terms in total, but I have far more than that. I remember how far I've come but, more importantly; I know my journey is far from over. It's only beginning.

I remove my jacket, take out the hairclip and kick off the stilettos.

I choose two texts I've never seen before. They're brimming with potential, waiting for someone to give them a chance and help bring out the best in them.

I pick up the pen and plan my essay.

59

JODIE

LUNCH IN THE LUCY Cavendish canteen is over and I have another fifteen minutes before the interviews start. My college tutor, Monica, says they will pick up on the texts I've mentioned in my personal statement and the two essays we've submitted: 'Ideas of Home in Katherine Mansfield's Short Stories' and 'The Idea of Loss in Poetry', which focused on Elizabeth Bishop's 'One Art'. The first interview will be with the admissions tutor and a subject specialist. After that I'll study an 'unseen' text for fifteen minutes and face a new grilling.

My heartbeat quickens.

Be yourself, Simon said this morning.

I stare at my reflection in the mirror above the toilet sinks. Even though I haven't put on my jacket, I still look like an imposter. I trace a finger up the birds on my arm; they're on the cusp of freedom. I rummage around in my bag, looking for my trainers to change into and can only find one.

Dammit. I must have left the other in the Porters' Lodge, when

I slipped my heels on and waited to be taken to the student common room. I'll have to suffer these evil torture contraptions for another thirty minutes or so. I wash off the makeup, put my nose ring back in and apply black eyeliner. I fold my jacket and place it on the top of my bag, careful not to tear off the tags. I want to be accepted for myself.

Jodie Brook. I'm not ashamed of who I am or where I've come from. It's taken all those points in the journey to get me here today.

I smile at the mirror. *Finally*, I recognize myself.

I feel quite positive about the first interview; both tutors were dead friendly and put me at ease. They didn't ask weird questions and appeared genuinely interested in my views on chivalry and the distinction between bravery and wisdom in *Song of Roland*.

Clutching my extract of 'unseen' text, I head towards the staircase in College House. The second interview room is on the top floor. Even though my feet are killing me, I'm on a high. I can't believe how well everything seems to have gone so far and I even recognize the passage I've had to study for the last quarter of an hour.

'Excuse me?' a voice rasps. 'Wait! Are you Jodie Brook?'

I turn around. 'That's me!'

A woman with grey curly hair and red glasses coughs into a tissue.

'Are you OK?'

'I've got a stinking cold. I'm quite hoarse.' She waves her hand at her throat. 'Sorry, I'm Dr Reid from the English department. I'll be talking to you about that extract.' She points at my piece of paper.

I step forward to shake her hand.

'Oh no! You don't want my germs.' She splutters again. 'Do you mind if we delay the interview by, say, fifteen minutes? I need to make myself a hot lemon drink and pester building services to mend our radiators. The heat's making my throat worse.'

'Of course. It's boiling everywhere, isn't it?' I joke nervously.

She nods. 'There's a seating area upstairs or, if you prefer, you can wait in the interview room. It's on the far left as you go up the stairs. The door has posters about academic conferences and Master's courses tacked on it. You can't miss it.'

'Sure. I hope you feel better.'

She tries to answer, but is gripped by another coughing fit. I head upstairs, passing chairs and a glass table that has a copy of Oxbridge's poetry and prose anthology, *The Mays*. I find the right door to the interview room. I'm curious as I step inside, a fresh wave of heat hitting me. The room has a large, modern desk and comfortable-looking armchairs. It's empty apart from a woman dressed in a denim boiler suit and Doc Martens. Her pink hair is tied back in a messy ponytail. She's crouched next to the radiator, clasping a pipe. Rusty-coloured water pools beneath it.

'Sorry, you should wait outside,' she says, glancing over her shoulder. 'Your interview's been delayed – I'm trying to fix this bloody thing. It's leaking everywhere.'

'Yes, I met Dr Reid downstairs. She told me about building services. She said it was OK to wait in here.'

'I don't think—' Water sprays out of the pipe as the woman reaches for a spanner. 'Shit, shit, shit!'

'I can give you a hand if you want? I know all about dodgy radiators.' I slip off my shoes and walk over. 'What's the problem with the heating in this place? The student common room should be renamed Dante's Furnace.'

She sighs. 'It's a long-standing problem. I'm Kate, by the way.'

'Hey, I'm Jodie.'

I pass her the spanner and sling my extract and bag down next to her, inspecting the side of the radiator. 'It looks like some idiot's snapped off the regulator valve when they tried to lower the temperature.'

She frowns. 'Hmm.'

'Sorry, I guess you know that.' I point at the valve on the floor. 'Any ideas how we can stop the leak?'

'You've tried closing the isolation valve, right?'

She doesn't reply.

'You do know where it is?'

'Erm . . .'

'I'll check around for you.' I'm tempted to examine the titles in Dr Reid's bookcase, but instead move around the room.

'Thanks. How come you're so knowledgeable about plumbing?'

'The radiators were always breaking down in the children's home where I grew up and it took forever to call out tradesmen. I had to learn how to fix radiators, rewire plugs – things like that. It's useful now I'm on my own. Well, not completely alone – I have a son, Zak.'

'How old is he?'

'Almost eight. I guess I should teach *him* to fix stuff rather than wreck it as usual.'

Kate laughs. 'I don't have children, but my sister has a daughter of a similar age. She says it's never too soon to start learning . . . well, anything, really.'

'Or too late,' I point out.

'Is that why you're here?'

I nod. 'I fucked up school. I'm twenty-five now and I'm not going to make the same mistakes again.'

She opens her mouth to speak, but dirty water sprays out.

'Aagh!'

'You're not holding the pipe tightly enough! Don't let up on the pressure.'

'I'm trying! Sorry, I've got your paper wet.'

I scoop up the soggy extract from the floor. A few lines are blurred but I can still read them. 'It's OK. I struck dead lucky with this.'

'You know it?'

'Yep – it's Shakespeare's Sonnet one hundred and thirty.'

I frown, quickly running over in my head what I'm planning to say.

'Don't mind me,' Kate says. 'You can practise out loud if you want.'

'Well . . .'

'Go on.'

'I'll probably explain that Shakespeare was subverting Petrarchan sonnets, which idealized women. He wanted to show the female form with all its flaws.' I pause. 'I'm not sure if Shakespeare was a feminist or not. He might just have thought men should be able to shag whoever they wanted without being judged.'

'I'd maybe drop that last bit?'

'Ha ha!'

The radiator rumbles and makes a thumping sound.

'Dee-dum, dee-dum, dee-dum, dee-dum, dee-dum,' I say, almost under my breath. 'I must remember to mention iambic pentameter, too.'

'You know your Shakespeare *and* plumbing. I'm impressed.' Kate wipes her forehead with the back of her hand, before grabbing the pipe again. 'But I don't get it. Why study English Literature at university when you can just read books at home?'

I pause, thinking.

'I guess . . . I'm hungry to learn and I want to be taught by the best in the world. I think great literature is like a family dinner – you enjoy it much more when you share it with other people, right?'

'The power of a good book,' she notes.

'Yeah. Plus, I can't read as much as I'd like to at home. To bastardize Virginia Woolf, I don't have a room of my own. I have to share a bed with my son. Our bedsit burnt down and all my books, save one, were destroyed.'

'Which book?'

'*Great Expectations*.'

'I'm sorry. That's bad luck.'

'You're kidding, right? Dickens is one of the greatest writers in history.'

I explain how Pip from *Great Expectations* had made a huge impression on me as a kid.

'I reckon Dickens is still relevant now – just look at his views on middle-class hypocrisy, charity and poverty.'

'I meant bad luck about the fire and losing your books, not about Dickens,' she says slowly.

'Thank God for that! I was beginning to think you're a heathen!'

Kate's face flushes bright red. 'Are you any closer to finding that valve? My hands are cramping.'

'Sorry. I got carried away. Dickens is a pet subject. I'll take a peek outside.'

I follow the pipes down the corridor to an empty room, off the landing. The valve is stiff, but I manage to close it.

I head back to Kate, who's still hanging onto the radiator for dear life.

'You can let go now. I've turned it off.' I bend over, checking the radiator. 'It's all good – no more leaks.'

I help her mop up the mess with tissues from Dr Reid's desk.

'Thank you! I don't know what I'd have done if you hadn't walked in when you did.' She stands up, dabbing a wet patch on her knee. 'Oh, wait. I can see the tag on your skirt.'

Before I can tell her not to worry, she rips it off.

'There you go!'

'Shit!'

'What?'

'Oh, don't worry. It's just I was planning on getting a refund. I'm way overdressed and I can't really afford something I'm never going to wear again.'

'Gosh, I'm sorry. I had no idea.'

I sigh heavily, picking up the tag from the floor. 'It's OK,' I say, examining it. 'I think I can stitch it on when I get home. The store will never notice!'

'You're very resourceful.'

I shrug. 'I've had to be.'

Kate's phone vibrates in her pocket. As she checks her mobile, I grab my stuff and attempt to shove my feet into the stilettos, but they're swollen from the heat. I can't get them back on.

'Oh, don't worry about your shoes,' she says, looking up from her phone. 'They look horrendously painful. I dress casually around college, either trainers or barefoot in summer.'

'That's good to know! But, no offence, you're not trying to impress Dr Reid.'

She laughs. 'Sorry, I should have introduced myself properly from the start, but I was distracted by Radiator-gate. I'm Dr Kate Garwood, lecturer and director of studies in English at Lucy Cavendish. I'm leading your interview today with help from

Dr Reid, who picked the Shakespeare sonnet. My research interest is literature of the nineteenth century, particularly . . .' She coughs. 'The works of Charles Dickens.'

My bag slips from my shoulder. 'But . . . But you . . .'

I can't finish the sentence, I'm frozen to the spot.

'Yes, I'm the idiot who attempted to lower the temperature in here by fiddling with the regulator valve after Dr Reid went to fetch building services. I turned the spanner too hard and it snapped right off in my hand. I had no idea how much water could spray out of a single radiator! But then again, I'm no expert in plumbing.'

I feel the colour drain from my cheeks. 'I'm so sorry. I had no idea. Dr Reid said . . . I thought . . . I mean, you don't look like a tutor!' It's out of my mouth before I can check myself.

'So I've heard. I've never been mistaken for a plumber before – but I have been the key speaker at literature conferences and men have automatically assumed I'm one of the PR girls, or even a waitress because I'm this side of thirty and have pink hair. A man once asked me to fetch him a drink while he went to the toilet. I was tempted to throw it in his face!'

Shit. I've dug myself into a hole and don't know how to get out.

'I imagine we both have to fight stereotypes in different ways.' Dr Garwood walks around the desk and gestures to the chair nearest me. 'Shall we sit down?' She opens a drawer and pulls out a file, along with a pen and a handful of grips.

I watch, horrified, as she fixes her hair.

This is her room, not Dr Reid's.

I glance at the door. I'm tempted to run out. This is even worse than my interview at Prince Burger when Ed quizzed me about cucumbers. My cheeks flood with colour. I've blathered on and essentially called her a heathen for thinking she was dissing my favourite novel.

She's only a world-fucking-expert on Charles Dickens.

I explained iambic pentameters to her like I was talking to a child!

I die inwardly. Simon had told me to prepare for all eventualities, but even he couldn't have predicted this catastrophe.

'Unfortunately, it's only going to be me today. Dr Reid has just texted. She sends her apologies and best wishes, but she's not well enough to join us. She's decided to go home before she gives everyone her germs.'

I stare at her, speechless. *Double shit.*

'Let's start over, shall we?' Dr Garwood says, opening a file.

Is that possible? I've admitted I share a bed with my son and rip off stores by returning clothes after wearing them.

'Can you explain to me why you want to study English Literature?'

I choke back tears, picking at a fingernail.

'You likened great literature to a family dinner, which is more rewarding to share than experiencing alone,' she prompts. 'Maybe you could expand on that?'

I clear my throat, trying to remember what I've learnt by rote.

'You're willing to make sacrifices . . .' I falter and try again. 'You skip lunches so you can save up to buy a book or trudge through sleet and snow to reach the library; you stay up late to read one extra page or get up earlier to squeeze in another chapter before work. You want to talk about characters with someone else, hear their viewpoints and learn from their opinions.'

I continue stiltedly, describing how studying at Cambridge has been my ambition since I was a teenager and my long-term plan to become an English teacher at an inner-city state secondary school.

'Hmm.' Dr Garwood leans back in her chair. 'Did I mention that my sister works in recruitment? She says she gains far more unrehearsed responses from interviewees when she asks how their mothers would describe them. I'm not allowed to ask personal questions like that, obviously, but my advice . . .'

'Wait!'

I don't like talking about my family, but I have nothing to lose after such a disastrous start.

'I want to answer *that* question.'

'Oh no. I was simply trying to make a point about letting the conversation flow more naturally.'

'*Please.*'

She hesitates. 'Well, if you're sure you feel comfortable discussing something so intimate?'

She reluctantly gestures for me to go ahead after I nod vigorously.

'The truth is, Dr Garwood, my mum couldn't tell you a single thing about me because she was addicted to heroin. She won't remember walking me to school, reading a book, cooking a meal or tucking me up in bed at night. But I know where she's living now with her new family. I've found her address and I plan to visit *eventually.*'

I sit up straight, smooth out the wrinkles in my skirt and raise my chin. 'I want my mum to remember me walking through her door again with my degree certificate from Cambridge. I want her to know that I earned it without her love, support or even her kindness. I'm going to tell her that the path she forced me down as a kid, being forced to live with strangers and the low expectations of my teachers and social workers didn't destroy me.'

I glance down at the tattoos on my arm.

I'm not just going to rise above all of that. I will soar like these birds.

I look up again and meet Dr Garwood's gaze unwaveringly.

'I'm going to tell my mum that in the end, I won. I found English Literature – or rather it found me. It's something in life that I love and I'm good at. I'll tell her that I got my degree and I'm going to become a great English teacher who inspires rejected kids like me to read every book they can get their hands on and to make something of their lives. I'll tell her I didn't listen to the people who told me I couldn't and I never would. I listened to Lizzie, my old friend.' My voice trembles. 'And, most importantly of all, I listened to the voice inside me that says . . .'

'Yes?'

She's probably going to think this sounds ridiculously twee, but I'm past caring what anyone thinks.

'You can, you must, you definitely will!' I say loudly.

Dr Garwood bends down to put something in the bin. When she eventually straightens up, her eyes are shining with emotion.

'Thank you for sharing that.' She coughs and shuffles her papers for a few seconds. 'Now, let's get back on topic. Can you tell me about the two narrative strands in *Bleak House*?'

My mind goes blank so I jabber on about Dickens' portrayal of London. I attempt to compare and contrast it with William Blake's poem of the same name and the setting of Virginia Woolf's *Mrs Dalloway*. I suddenly remember a few points about the narratives, but I swear that Dr Garwood can tell I'm an imposter, making things up on the spot. She glances at her watch.

'That's very interesting, Jodie. I'd love to discuss this with you further, but we're out of time, I'm afraid.'

'But I was about to say . . .' I take a deep breath. 'And another thing . . . We haven't even got on to Katherine Mansfield's short stories or the Shakespeare extract.' I hold up the soggy, brown, stained piece of paper.

'Sorry, but I'm running behind after the radiator leak. I have to get through a stack more interviews on my own. I think I've heard enough.'

'But—'

'Thank you for coming.' Dr Garwood shoves her chair back and stands up. 'It's been enlightening. Good luck, Jodie.'

Enlightening?

That's not how I'd describe this interview. It was a clusterfuck from start to finish – so much for being able to shove a Cambridge degree certificate in my mum's face before walking out on *her*.

I pick up my shoes and scarper before I burst into tears.

Across the landing, a man wearing overalls with a building services logo is examining a radiator valve. I shake my head at my stupidity.

Is it possible to die of embarrassment?

I pass the next young woman waiting to go in, sitting by the glass table. She's well-groomed with small diamond studs in her ears. She stands up, holding a copy of Homer's *The Odyssey* and her old school file; the crest features a deer. I can just make out the name, 'Roedean'. I bet she wouldn't have mistaken the tutor for a bloody plumber. She looks self-assured, privately educated and, unlike me, must be a shoo-in for one of the six places up for grabs.

I'm totally screwed.

60

SIMON

'How did it go?'
I let Jodie into the flat; she's looking more like her normal self, albeit dishevelled after the train journey. Her trademark makeup is back, but she's tired; dark shadows have appeared beneath her eyes.

She throws her bag down and flops onto my sofa. I avert my eyes as her skirt rides up her thighs.

'Well?' I prompt.

'Yeah, yeah good . . . The interviews were actually really fun! Guess what happened? As soon as I walked through the door a tutor lobbed a brick at me to see what I would do . . .'

I raise an eyebrow. 'Really? In that case, I guess I did you a favour with Brick-gate.'

'No, I'm joking. That would have been assault, remember?'

My cheeks blaze; she's never going to let me live that down.

'So tell me everything. What were the interviews like? Did the tutors ask you any strange questions?'

Jodie suppresses a sigh. She examines a ragged fingernail, which has started to bleed.

'No, they focused mainly on the texts in my personal statement, like you said they would.' She shifts in her seat, picking another nail. 'I discussed Dickens with Dr Garwood, who's a world expert on the author. I think I made quite an impression on her. She won't forget me in a hurry!'

'That's great! It's important to make a personal connection.'

'Yes.' Her voice is flat. 'I think I really nailed both interviews. I didn't let you down. I remembered everything you told me, you'd have been proud of me.'

'OK, well, brilliant!'

Jodie's shoulders droop as she kneads her temples. She appears dispirited or maybe she's simply exhausted.

'It would appear my re-education of Jodie Brook is complete,' I say quietly.

She rolls her eyes dramatically. 'You might need a few more lessons from me, Professor Higgins.'

'You won't have time to improve my people skills when you're a Cambridge undergraduate. Terms are short but tightly packed.'

She fiddles with the hem of her skirt. 'I'd never have managed to get this far without your help.'

'I'm flattered you think that, but you'd have got here with or without me. You had it in you all along. It's time you finally realized that fact.'

Her voice is soft when she speaks again. 'Still, I don't know how I'll ever repay you.'

I take a deep breath.

'Me neither, but I learnt from you that *kindness isn't a debt to be repaid. It's a gift to give away freely to others without expecting anything back.*'

'I never thought I'd hear you say that!'

'Nor me.'

'Perhaps I was wrong and your re-education *is* complete, Simon. Mission accomplished.'

Is this her way of saying goodbye?

I bite my lip at the finality of her statement, gripped with an unbearable sadness that makes my chest tighten painfully. Of course, it's probably for the best. William says I drag people down with me; that's why he relocated to New York. He didn't want to be infected with my melancholy. Now Jodie is about to do the same. It sounds like she'll be offered a place at Cambridge and move there with Zak. She'll make new friends and gain support from her tutor at Lucy Cavendish. I'm being replaced, the way I was when William married and had a family.

Will Jodie let me say goodbye to Zak? Will she at least try to keep in touch?

'Simon?'

'Sorry. Did you say something?'

'I was asking if you're feeling OK?'

'I'm fine. Why?'

'Well, you'll never guess what . . . the essay question and passages today were all about the relationship between brothers.'

'Oh?'

'Yeah, it got me thinking . . . Perhaps it's time you reached out to William – invite him over to London for a proper talk, you know, sort out your differences face to face.'

I exhale slowly, trying to ease the fresh wave of jabbing pains in my chest.

'No, thanks. That's OK.'

'I could be with you when you do it, the way you were for me with Jason.'

'And that worked out so well!'

She flinches, wounded, but I can't bring myself to apologize.

'What's this all about? Why are you asking me about William?'

'I have something to tell you, which you're going to find upsetting.'

I don't like where this is heading. She moves closer to me on the sofa, but I edge away.

'I thought, perhaps, when I was trying to find him online . . .'

My heart quickens. Every beat sounds deafening. 'You were doing what?'

'I've been checking Facebook and LinkedIn. I wanted to speak to William before I came round tonight, but I haven't been able to track him down yet.'

'That's because he's not on social media.' My jaw muscles clench.

'Look, what I'm trying to explain, *badly*, is that I wanted to talk to you both about your mum's death.' She pauses, biting her lip. 'I know you might not like this, but I went to your old house. I hoped to see your dad.'

'What?' I leap to my feet. 'Why the hell would you do something like that?'

'Because I want to help you.'

'By going behind my back? I don't want to speak to Father or William. You know that! You should have respected my wishes.' I glare at her, as she shifts uncomfortably in her seat. 'When did you go?'

'Saturday.'

'And you've left it until now to tell me?'

'There wasn't a good time to break it to you – I was worried you'd take it badly.'

'Well, I'm glad I lived up to your low expectations. I'd like you to leave now.'

'Simon!'

'I mean it. You've betrayed my trust.'

She slowly stands, picking up her bag. 'I'm sorry, but at least listen to what I have to say before I go. Your dad wasn't in, but I spoke to his second wife, Clare.'

I inhale sharply. There's a rushing noise in my ears. She walks over and tries to touch my arm, but I shake her off.

'I thought I knew you, Jodie Brook. I can't believe you'd do this. Get the hell out!'

I frogmarch her to the door and throw it open.

'Simon, please! I have to tell you what Clare said about your mum. Honestly, you need to listen to this.'

'How dare you mention that woman in the same breath as Mother! I have no interest in what she – *or you* – has to say. I won't forgive you for this. I hope you do get offered a place at Cambridge so I won't have to see you ever again.'

As she steps out, I slam the door shut.

61

SIMON

Istroke Archie as he eats his supper. After much coaxing, he's returned to the dustbins behind Prince Burger, but has clearly been mortally offended by my absence. My friend is refusing to blink at me or curl around my ankles as punishment for my perceived betrayal, but I will persist. He has become the one highlight of my day.

I thought I'd feel happy returning to Prince Burger but, this time, it all feels a little . . . empty. William was right: I've been burying my head in a dead-end job and I am no further forward with the Riemann Hypothesis after all this time. Prince Burger was once a temporary stopgap, but this is apparently who I am and always will be – not a world-famous mathematician, but a fry station assistant. Ed has been disturbingly friendly this week, restoring my two docked stars as well as awarding an extra one and playing 'We Are the Champions' over the loudspeakers twice in my honour. I haven't even done anything special, unless you count not burning fries for two consecutive shifts. I think I preferred it when he was rude – at least I knew where I stood. Meanwhile my colleagues are smiling at me more and making eye contact, but I lack the energy to strike up conversations with anyone.

'I have to get back, Archie.' I scratch behind his ears. 'Wish me luck.'

The cat stalks off, tail held high.

Jodie glances over her shoulder as I return to my post. She's on the late shift, along with Pam and Marta. Carlos' face reddens and he turns away, tending to his burgers. I reload Fro-Bot and open the doors to the facts in my Memory Palace in preparation for rejoining Arthur's pub quiz team in the New Year.

Selim I took control of the Ottoman Empire in 1512.

Fries stacking, facts shovelling.

In revolutionary France, Maximilien Robespierre led the committee of public safety.

Fries shovelling, facts stacking.

Time stretches and contracts, the way it always does.

At the end of the shift, I remove my apron as the last stragglers leave. Ed fastens the lock and puts the 'Closed' sign on the door. I'm about to follow Carlos, Marta and Pam to the crew room when Ed beckons me over.

'Can you take a seat over there, Prof?' He points to a table. 'We need a chat before you leave.'

I make my way over as Jodie loiters nearby, releasing her hair from its ponytail.

'Is something wrong?' I slide into a chair. Perhaps Ed has *finally* found out I'm feeding Archie.

I hear a knock on the glass and he opens up again even though we're officially closed. A man and a woman walk in. Breath catches in my throat. My heart feels like it's going to explode from my chest. My ears buzz and red dots twirl like fireflies in front of my eyes.

The man is stooping as if afraid of his height, he's thinner and older than I remember – his hair is completely white and his face is shrivelled and lined, prune-like.

Father.

I haven't seen him for thirteen years.

'You should have gone to the ladies' at the theatre,' he says sharply to the small, grey-haired woman with him. 'Are you sure we can use the bathroom in here? There's no way we're buying junk food.'

'It's OK, isn't it?' the woman asks timidly.

This must be his second wife, Clare.

Ed nods. 'Be my guest.'

My father turns around. His jaw drops. Time stands still. 'Simon?' His stare is cold and clinical, as if I'm a cadaver he wants to slice open. 'What the hell is this?'

I know exactly who must be behind this . . . I glare at Jodie. Her eyes plead silently for forgiveness. I want to leave. I try to stand up but my legs weaken.

'I'm Simon's friend,' Jodie says, stepping forward. 'I persuaded . . .' Her gaze flickers to the woman. 'I pretty much *forced* your wife to bring you here today because you *have* to speak to Simon.'

Father's glare switches to his wife. 'Clare? What have you done?'

She sways and mumbles something.

'Well?' he demands.

'This is the right thing to do,' she says quietly.

'Excuse me?' His knuckles whiten; his face is rigid with barely contained rage. 'How dare you!'

Clare flinches.

'Don't take this out on her!' Jodie says loudly. 'This was my idea.'

'I told you to stop interfering!' My chest heaves. 'You shouldn't have done this, Jodie.'

'Believe me, I had to. *We* had to. It took a lot for your stepmum to come here today, but we both want to help you.'

Clare gives me a small smile, before glancing up at Father.

'*Please*, Harold,' she says softly. 'You've got something to say to Simon.'

I hold my breath, wondering if we're going to find a rapprochement after all these years.

Father shakes his head. 'We have nothing to discuss. Our relationship – such as it ever was – concluded years ago. I have no desire to resume it.'

I flinch, as he inflicts a fresh wound. His rejection shouldn't hurt after all these years, but I'm ashamed to say it does.

'We're leaving,' he snarls. 'I don't appreciate being ambushed. Let's go, Clare!' Father stalks towards the door.

His wife looks down at the floor and doesn't move.

Ed steps forward, blocking his path. 'Sorry, the lock's a bit rusty. I can't seem to open it.'

'What? I'm being taken hostage now?' He spins around, scowling at Clare. 'Is this what you wanted?'

'I want . . . you need to tell Simon . . .' Her voice falls silent mid-sentence.

Jodie is already at Clare's side, giving her hand an encouraging squeeze. She mouths 'thank you', before turning to face Father.

'Tell him the truth about what happened to his mum!' Jodie cries. 'You owe him that.'

Ed folds his arms. 'We can stay here all night if we have to.'

Father shoots withering looks between Ed, Jodie and Clare,

before focusing solely on me. My shoulders automatically cave in, the way they always used to.

'Fine.' He sarcastically holds his hands up in the air. 'Let's get this over with.' He strides over and sits down rigidly in the opposite chair.

Jodie leads Clare over to the table, while Ed stands guard by the door.

'So?' Father says.

'Let's start with this,' Jodie says, sitting down next to me. 'You can't let Simon carry on thinking he's responsible for his mum's death. I won't let you! It's unbelievably cruel. Do the right thing and tell him the truth.'

'What . . . is she talking about?' I ask.

Silence.

'Father?'

He flexes his fingers. I can tell he's playing for time, the way he taught me.

Jodie glances at Clare, before focusing her attention on Father. 'Tell Simon *everything*, starting with the note his mum left.'

He bristles. 'That is private family correspondence and has nothing to do with you!'

I frown, rubbing my forehead. 'Do you mean the letter Mother wrote saying she was leaving us? You were holding it when you ran out of the house that night.'

He doesn't reply.

'You never let me read it,' I say slowly, 'but you told me that Mother had wanted to set off early before I woke up and tried to come with her. She got in the car, but fell asleep.'

He still won't look at me.

'Father?'

He sighs deeply, his forehead wrinkling. 'I woke up when I

heard your shouts outside. I discovered your mother's note on the dressing table. It was . . .' His voice trails off.

'Do it!' Jodie insists.

'It was . . .' He clears his throat. 'A suicide note.'

I grip the table tightly as the room spins. There's a terrible, whistling noise in my ears. My stomach pitches dangerously.

'And the rest,' Jodie prompts.

He runs his hands through his thinning hair. 'There was no evidence of smoke in your mother's lungs.' He takes a deep breath. 'The post-mortem examination revealed that she'd died of an overdose of sleeping tablets, not smoke inhalation as the paramedics had originally thought.'

'But—'

'Your mum was dead *before* you started the fire,' Jodie says bluntly.

'I don't understand . . . Father? You said I'd killed her . . . that the police weren't pressing charges because of my mental state.'

Jodie exchanges looks with Clare. 'There was never a case against you, Simon. The police closed the investigation once the toxicology results came back.'

'Is that true?' I gasp.

Father covers his eyes with his hands.

'The police contacted the psychiatric unit but you were too ill to discuss it,' he says in a small voice. 'Your psychiatrist said she would give you the update when you were well enough. However, there was a turnover of staff. She left suddenly and didn't provide a briefing note for her replacement.'

'But *you* could have told me. At any point!' My voice rises and breaks, forcing me to take another breath. 'You've deliberately lied to me all this time. You kicked me out as soon as I came home from hospital. Why did you torture me like that?' Tears slide down my cheeks. '*How could you?*'

He rubs his eyes, stubbornly refusing to meet my gaze.

'You can't bring yourself to apologize, can you? Or admit you did anything wrong. I've spent all these years believing I killed Mother. But it was you – you drove her to . . . to do what she did.'

Father's shoulders tremble as he weeps, but I feel no sympathy. 'Why? Just tell me why!'

He looks up, eyes glistening with defiance. 'You had to be punished! I was angry, *furious*, about the way you'd behaved.'

'All this pain and misery for a stupid model railway?'

'No.' He juts his chin out. 'You put ideas into your mother's head. You were encouraging her to leave me. She was *my* wife. You had no right to interfere!'

'I had every right! She was *my* mother and you treated her like dirt. You hurt her! I wish she had left you, I prayed for it every day. She might still be alive.'

Father puts his hand to his mouth, choking back a sob.

'Harold explained that your mother had sadly taken her own life,' Clare blurts out. 'I had no idea you didn't know . . . I'm so sorry . . .' Her voice disappears again.

'Thank you.' I manage to squeeze out the smallest of smiles.

'What do you plan to do with this information now?' Father asks.

'Of course! Your first thought is always self-preservation.'

He shrinks back in his seat.

'I *could* go to the police and give them a statement about how you gaslighted Mother into killing herself and mistreated me as a child. You *might* get a jail sentence – if you don't manage to wriggle out of it. But do you know what's worse than going to prison? It's being forced to live with what you've done every single day. This is a cell of your own making.'

'Simon—' he begins.

'You broke me, Father, but I'm rebuilding my life. You have nothing. You're no one.'

'He's right,' Jodie says. 'You don't have anything to fall back on. You're not going to make any more children crack under the pressure. Stop tutoring, otherwise I *will* persuade Simon to go to the police.'

Father's eyes widen, but he nods slowly.

'Simon has people who have his back,' she continues. 'We'll all look out for him.'

In the corner of my eye, I see Pam and Marta walking towards us, along with Carlos, who points a spatula threateningly at Father. They gather around me, making my heart swell in size.

'We should go.' Father reaches for Clare's hand.

'No,' she whispers, snatching it away.

'Pardon?'

She glances at Jodie before her voice rises, gaining in strength. 'I'm not coming with you, Harold. I should have left you years ago.'

Father's mouth falls open as she picks up her bag, hands trembling. 'Good luck, Simon. You deserve to be happy. We both do.'

Ed opens up quickly as she heads to the door.

'Wait!' Father cries. 'You can't do this!'

'Yes, Harold, I can,' she says, over her shoulder.

He pulls himself to his feet as she walks out. He opens his mouth to say something to me, but I turn away.

'This is goodbye, Father.'

62

JODIE

'ARE YOU OK?'
Ed has agreed to let us debrief in the storeroom before
he closes up for the night.

Simon turns around, white-faced. 'Yes . . . Maybe. I don't know.'

I squeeze his arm. 'You were incredibly brave back there.'

'Do you think?'

'*I know*. Zak would call you a superhero.'

His cheeks gain a slight pink tinge. 'I always thought I'd look
good in a cape.'

'You *might* be able to pull that look off, but I'm not one hundred
per cent sure.'

'Ha ha! Anyway . . .'

I open my arms. My heart flutters a little as he steps into my
embrace, but that's probably just the adrenaline still running
through my body.

'Thank you,' he mumbles. 'For everything.'

I hug him a little tighter.

'You're welcome. You needed to say those things to your dad. It took a lot to face up to everything in your past like that.'

He stiffens slightly beneath my touch.

'I'm proud of you. Zak would be as well. You were completely honest about your feelings. I've promised Zak I'll be more open in future – and he needs to be too.'

He pulls away, swaying slightly.

'Maybe you should sit down?' I nod at the row of cooking oil barrels. 'It's a lot for you to take in tonight.'

He sits down heavily on the nearest keg, resting his head on his hands.

'I know it's tough, but it will get better, I promise. We're all here for you when you need us.' I push a loose strand of hair behind my ears. 'And I really think now's the time to make up with William. He's the only family you've got left. Ring him. It doesn't matter what the time difference is.'

That sad, faraway expression has crept back into his eyes as he looks up. The old shutters have come down.

'You need to tell him what's happened with your dad. He has to know the truth about his mum. You owe him that, whatever he's said to upset you.'

'I can't. Please, Jodie . . .' His voice disappears into a strangled sound.

I crouch down beside him. 'Of course you can. It'll be a piece of cake compared to standing up to your dad. Give me your phone. I'll ring him and speak first – smooth the way for you, then I can step out if you like.'

'No, Jodie—'

'What is it?'

'Nothing.' His face is drained of colour again.

'Tell me. What's going on?'

He checks his watch. 'We should go. Ed needs to lock up. It's not fair to keep him waiting.' He shuffles and starts to rise.

'No! We need to stay and talk about this. *I know you.* There's something you're not telling me. No more secrets.'

A slight tremor ripples through his body as he sinks back down.

'What is it? Why won't you call William?'

His shoulders tense as he glances at the door.

'Tell me. And be honest. What's really going on?'

He takes a deep breath, his hand running shakily through his hair.

'Simon! Just come out with it!'

He looks up at me; his eyes wide, as if already begging for understanding.

'There is no William.'

'Ha ha. Very funny!'

I wait for him to break into laughter, but the corners of his mouth don't even twitch.

'There never has been a William.'

My lips make an 'O' shape. Eventually, I force myself to form words and break the stunned silence.

'I'm not following,' I say, trying to sound calm. 'William's your brother.'

'No, he's not. I'm an only child.'

Simon chews his lip and fiddles with the label on the side of the drum. 'You must be angry . . .'

'No, I . . .'

I want to yell: *what the actual fuck?* But I don't want to make things worse, the way I did with the newspaper article.

'I'm confused. Explain this to me. Please. *Make* me understand.'

His shoulders rise and fall. 'I created William as a young child to help me cope with Father.'

I try to rearrange the shock on my face as his gaze flickers up from the floor.

'William comforted me, to begin with, anyway. Father, of course, hated that I talked to him, but Mother accepted him as a part of the family. She made me feel that it was OK to have a make-believe companion. She just wanted me to be happy – or at least as happy as I could be.'

My eyes widen as I try to make sense of what he's telling me.

'But William beat you in *Little Einsteins* and rubbed your nose in it. He always got you into trouble with your dad.'

He shakes his head. 'No, I blamed an imaginary brother for forcing me out of the final. I couldn't admit the truth to myself: that I simply froze under the pressure. After that public humiliation, something just broke inside me. I punished myself even more for my failure. William became far more critical as a result.'

I grab another oil drum and perch on top as my mind races with a million questions. I'm trying to hold onto tiny grains of truth before they slip away forever.

'What about the cuts on your wrists? You said William was responsible for those scars. He punished you when your dad wasn't around – forcing you to stay under cold showers.'

'I did it to myself – a regular self-flagellation, before Father could inflict it on me. I was damaged. Obviously, I still am to a certain degree. Dr Atkins, the psychiatrist in the hospital, told me that creating William was the only way I could cope with Father's abuse. I projected my feelings of guilt for causing Mother's death onto him too; it was the only way to survive.'

I stare at him, my brain still playing catch-up.

'William's life – his career and family . . . It all sounded believable. I saw the photos in your bedroom . . . pictures of you and

William as children . . . at your graduation and with his family in New York.'

His face flushes a deep scarlet. 'I know.' He sighs.

'I don't understand . . .'

He won't meet my gaze.

'Simon?'

'I faked the graduation photograph. I faked *all* the pictures.'

'But why . . .' I fight to keep the judgemental tone out of my voice. 'Why would you do something like that?'

'I *know* it sounds crazy.' Simon rubs his neck, crossing and uncrossing his legs. 'But, in my head, I know exactly what William and his family look and act like, down to what they wear, eat and how they behave and talk. They are a huge part of my world and I wanted to acknowledge their presence.' His voice drops. 'They were the only company I had for a long time.'

His eyes mist up. I blink the moisture away from mine too. I have so many questions, but I need him to explain this in his own time. He fiddles with his shoelace, before beginning again.

'I digitally altered photographs of myself to create William and placed us together in the frame in all the childhood photos. I constructed the graduation picture – giving myself a gown and William, a suit.'

'Holy shit!' I blurt out. 'I thought there was something odd about that photo, but I couldn't put my finger on what was wrong.'

He runs his hand through his hair again. 'It wasn't the greatest photoshop. I couldn't get the filter right.'

'And the other photos?' I raise my eyebrows to stop a frown from appearing.

'I doctored my image of William to make him match my age, but I made him fuller-faced in adulthood, the way I pictured him. For Victoria and the children, I found photos online

– strangers who resembled the way I imagined they'd look. I edited them into pictures of myself and fake William in places like New York.'

A gasp escapes from my lips.

'That explains why you acted so oddly when I suggested giving advice to Arthur about a walk in Central Park.'

'I've never actually been,' he says sheepishly.

'I . . . I'm not sure what to say . . .'

'Like you said before – it's a lot to take in.'

That's the understatement of the year.

I tap my foot on the ground, mulling over his confession.

'I guess it makes sense now I think about it. I couldn't find William when I Googled neurosurgeons with his name in New York. Or when I looked on social media. He didn't exist.'

Simon buries his face in his hands. 'Yet he's always felt so real to me. That's hard to explain to anyone, so I've never tried before. I couldn't face . . . Anyway, now you know everything about me. You must think I'm mad. I'm so sorry.'

'You don't have to apologize.'

He grips the shelf to lever himself up, his neck mottled with red patches.

'But I want to . . . You see, William had everything I always wanted – a successful career, friends and a wife and children.' He inhales slowly. 'It was the life and family I might have had if I hadn't grown up with such a bullying father.'

I stand up too. My hand reaches out shakily to comfort him.

I'm about to tell him he could still have that life – it's never too late to go after the things you want.

But he's already bolted out the door.

63

SIMON

THROUGH THE HALF-OPEN CURTAIN, I watch snow-flakes flutter against the frosted windowpane. Archie is asleep, draped over my face and snoring loudly. Before fleeing Prince Burger, I'd headed to the dustbins to explain to my furry friend why I wouldn't be around over the festive period. Archie followed me onto the bus and all the way home. I tried to shoo him away, but was secretly glad of the company. I was too embarrassed to look Jodie in the eye after I confessed to making up William. I couldn't bear the thought of seeing the hurt or anger in her eyes or, worse still, discovering she was laughing. My cheeks flush at the thought.

I gently place Archie on the pillow. My bedroom is warm enough, even for him. I don't plan to move from here; the sooner Christmas Day is over the better. I had no energy to shop for food yesterday and the fridge and cupboards are bare. If I squint at the Post-its left on the walls, I could almost mistake them for twinkling golden stars. I haven't decorated the flat; the decorations looked forlorn and fragile when I unpacked the boxes.

Last year, I'd volunteered for the most unpopular shifts to avoid the loneliness, but Ed was having none of it this year. He insisted I have two weeks off with full pay while I was going through a rough patch. I'd tried to object, but he wouldn't budge. He thinks he's doing me a favour.

This could be the worst Christmas ever.

I can't even talk to William later or picture his family's traditional festivities to keep me company. A new hollow emptiness has opened in my chest; I have no idea how to fill the growing void. I'm looking forward to the weeks when discarded fir trees will appear on the streets, sorrowfully dropping needles that will signal the end of the festive period. I check my phone. I have no messages from Jodie, anyone at Prince Burger or the Three Wise Men. I understand they're busy with their own families.

A sharp rap at the front door makes me jump.

I ignore it – it must be someone at the wrong door – and scoop up my deck of cards from the bedside table, shuffling them.

But there it is again. The buzzer rings, waking up Archie. He yawns extravagantly.

I'm alert now.

I hear a loud chorus. Carol singers have mistaken my address for that of someone who celebrates and enjoys Christmas. It's a truly awful din. Archie howls. As they launch into another verse of 'We Wish You a Merry Christmas', I realize they will not desist unless I pay them to move on and torment another unfortunate neighbour.

I roll out of bed and search for my wallet, banging my head

on the wall as I stumble. My limbs refuse to obey the instructions my mind is giving them.

Unsteadily, I walk into the hall, followed by Archie, and move towards the discordant voices.

64

JODIE

'WE WISH YOU A Merry Christmas, we wish you a
Merry Christmas, we wish you a Merry Christmas and
a Happy New Year!'

Zak bellows out the lyrics, jigging from foot to foot and waving
Dog.

Simon looks pale and dazed as he opens the door, clutching
his forehead. A ginger cat curls around his ankles, hissing angrily.
It looks suspiciously like the vicious one from Prince Burger that
thinks it's a tiger.

'You took your time!' Zak exclaims. 'Surprise Happy Christmas,
Mr Mega Swot!' He throws his arms around Simon's waist, before
looking down. 'Have you got a new pet?'

'Careful, Archie doesn't like . . .'

The cat zooms off inside, followed by Zak.

'W-what are you all doing here?' Simon's eyes glitter with tears.

He stares at the group on his doorstep. Arthur, Trevor and
Winston have swapped their smart suits for jumpers – a polar

bear, a snowman and a Santa. Arthur and Trevor's wives are here too. Sandra's dyed her hair back to red for the festive period. She's wearing sparkly bauble earrings and reindeer antlers on her head; she's helped me organize today. Her youngest son is taking her to a big family reunion in Kent later tonight. Marta and Carlos were supposed to fly out to their respective parents, but both their flights were delayed until tomorrow. Pam's husband, Clark, felt unwell and couldn't travel to their friend's house in Manchester so they've joined our festivities, along with Simon's neighbour, Aleksy. Even Ed is here, wearing a festive alien jumper, although he looks like he's regretting it now he's realized that his feline nemesis is lurking around.

'You're not doing anything, are you?' Arthur asks. 'We needed somewhere to host Christmas lunch and Jodie thought your sitting room would be the perfect place – after we've spruced it up.'

He brushes past Simon, carrying a pre-cooked turkey. 'How does your oven work? We need to reheat the veggies and spuds.'

We've each brought a dish together with Christmas decorations after I'd described Simon's flat as having the atmosphere of a morgue. We all chipped in cash to buy the food. After paying off my loan debt, all the interest *and* my credit card, the remaining £300 is going into Zak's new savings account for university.

'I c-can't believe you're all here,' Simon stutters, stepping aside.

Carlos is carrying a flat-pack table and everyone else has fold-up chairs.

'Your friends want to spend Christmas with you,' I tell him. 'We're not easily driven away.'

*

Within an hour, Simon's flat is more sparkly and festive than a grotto. His temporary dining table groans with turkey, roast potatoes and veggies. Laughter rings out, glasses clink firmly together and streamers shoot out from party poppers. Marta finds plastic mistletoe in her cracker and kisses Carlos on the lips. They're going to the next London Comic Con dressed as Khal Drogo and Daenerys. Across the table Sandra and Winston are bonding over their love of swimming and TV quiz shows. Simon pulls another cracker with Zak. He puts the paper hat on his head, grinning broadly. He's the happiest I've ever seen him after laying all his ghosts to rest, in Prince Burger, of all places.

He gets up when Zak knocks his fork off the table and heads to the kitchen. I follow and find him standing by the fridge, staring at the *Sparks' Family Guidelines for Success*.

'Isn't it time you get rid of that?'

'You're right. I should have done it years ago.'

He pulls out a box of matches from a top cupboard and offers them to me. 'Do you want to do the honours?'

'I think it should be you.'

He lights the corner of the sheet over the sink. The flame slowly creeps up. We both watch the peeling, melting plastic form grotesque shapes: a twisted screaming molten mouth, now a monster's face. The acrid smell irritates my nose and throat, making me cough. He drops the plastic in the sink and turns on the tap.

'There, it's done. I'm getting rid of the fake photos of William too. Dr Atkins said I need to rely on friends in the real world.'

'You have plenty of those.'

His cheeks blush. 'Are we OK? I mean . . . about William? And all the things I told you?'

I nod. 'It was a huge shock, admittedly, but I understand why you did it. I'm just glad you've learnt to tackle your past.'

He takes a deep breath. 'And I'm glad we don't have any more secrets between us.'

My cheeks smart, but I don't contradict him. I still haven't admitted how badly my Cambridge interview went, but that can wait for another day.

'I want to also tell you how—' he begins, stepping closer.

Zak tears into the kitchen, clutching Dog. He grinds to a halt, looking up at the ceiling. A huge bunch of mistletoe dangles above our heads.

'Yeuch. You're not going to kiss Mummy, are you?'

Simon springs away, his cheeks rosy. 'No, of course not.'

'I hadn't even spotted the mistletoe!' I say, laughing.

Zak rifles noisily through the drawers, searching for a fork.

'What were you going to say?' I ask Simon above the clatter.

'I wanted . . .' He stops, frowning. 'Is something burning, apart from my father's guidelines?'

'Holy crap! I forgot the parsnips!'

I pull the incinerated vegetables out of the oven and flap the towel at the fire alarm to stop it going off. When I turn around, Simon has left the room.

We're all completely stuffed after helping ourselves to Sandra's famous plum pudding, which we covered with brandy and set alight. Zak watched the glowing blue flame, transfixed.

He takes the last spoonful of pudding and holds his bowl up to Simon. 'Please, sir, can I have some more?'

We laugh, as he dishes up the last serving and sits down.

'Speech!' Arthur cries, tapping a wine glass. 'Do you want to say a few words, Jodie?'

'No, thanks!'

Simon coughs awkwardly. 'Can I do it?' He stands up, almost knocking over his wine glass.

I'm grateful he's saved me from being the centre of attention; I hate doing presentations at college.

'So . . .' He runs a hand through his hair. 'Some thoughts were percolating in my brain, pertaining to . . .'

'Get on with it!' Ed shouts. 'In plain English, preferably!'

'This is the best day of my life,' he blurts out.

'Me too!' Zak cries.

Simon straightens up a little as everyone cheers.

'I want to thank all my . . . *friends* for being here today. This is a new experience for me. I think . . . I *know* that in the past, I haven't been kind to many of you. Well, probably all of you. I didn't try to help . . .' He steals a look at the Three Wise Men. 'But Jodie taught me the error of my ways.'

He turns to face me. 'I thought I was educating you, but I've slowly, *belatedly*, realized that it was always the other way around. You've re-educated me, Jodie. You'll never know how incredibly grateful I am for all your life lessons. Thank you for everything. To quote – and finally *understand* – Charles Dickens: *Family not only need to consist of merely those whom we share blood, but also for those whom we'd give blood.*'

He lifts his glass. 'To Jodie!'

More toasts and cheers ripple around the table.

'Hear, hear! To Jodie!'

'To Jodie and Simon!'

'To life lessons!'

Zak slings his arm around Simon's waist. They both beam back at me.

'To my family,' I say, raising the wine glass.

65

SIMON

ARCHIE DOESN'T CELEBRATE CHRISTMAS, apparently. Judging by the murderous look in his eyes, he's on the verge of scalping Ed. I collect a few things before taking him downstairs. As he gracefully leaps up and over the fence, I put the burnt remnants of the *Sparks' Family Guidelines for Success* in the communal bins at the back of the block of flats.

There's one more thing I have to do before returning to the festivities. I turn around. My brother is waiting for me. Victoria, Harper and Lucy wave and stand at a respectful distance to give us space to talk in private. William stares thoughtfully at the bin.

'Is this it?' I can't hide the tremble in my voice.

'This is Act Five, my final scene.'

'It doesn't have to be. I'm feeling much better and I'm not just saying that, the way I used to. I've talked to my GP and to the psychiatric nurse who visited last week. They're helping me come to terms with everything that happened. I'm learning better coping strategies, healthier ones, instead of retreating into my Memory Palace.'

William shakes his head. 'We can't write an Act Six. Shakespeare would turn in his grave.'

'No, maybe not, but we can still talk now and then, can't we?'

'I agree with your support team, Simon. We need a clean break. We can't risk falling into old habits.' William stares up at the window as bursts of laughter and singing drift down from my flat.

'In all honesty you don't need me.'

'I can't imagine my life without you, without being able to discuss my Memory Palace and . . . well, everything.'

'If you don't mind me saying, that was always your problem – relying too heavily on me and trying to create new structures inside your head.'

'But—'

'The world is waiting for you to discover it. I can guarantee it's not locked behind a door in your Memory Palace. Life isn't a list of facts to be regurgitated. Life is out there!' He throws his arms out expansively. 'Start living your life and find your own family. Stop relying on mine.' He winks.

'I think I've found a family. It's not *my* family; it's Jodie's. But it's a good one, a kind one. It's more than I ever had growing up.'

William raises an eyebrow.

'I don't have great expectations, but I'm OK with that. I want to remain a part of hers and Zak's lives, however that may turn out. I see my future with them in some shape or form.'

'Basically, you want an equilateral triangle but don't know if she does?'

'Are you trying to read my mind again?'

He laughs. 'I'm *in* your mind, remember?'

'Touché!'

'But seriously, you have everything you need.' He jerks his head up at the window. 'My hunch is it'll all work out fine. You'll be happy, *finally*.'

A comfortable silence falls between us.

'I've dreamed of telling you to permanently leave me alone for so long, but now it's about to happen I want you to know I'm going to miss you so very much.' A tear slides down my cheek.

'That's only to be expected when I'm the cleverer, better-looking, most successful twin.'

'I take it back,' I say, laughing through my tears. 'I'm not going to miss you at all. You're a total shithead.'

'Right back at you, brother.'

I move towards him and feel the warmth of his embrace. His voice is kind and gentle.

'It's time. We both need to let go.'

I dig around in my pocket. I pull out the box of matches and one of my decks with the king of diamonds on top. Squatting down, I pick up the card. My hand trembles as I strike a match. As the flame licks closer to my fingers, I set fire to the king of diamonds and flick it onto the ground. William doesn't flinch when I light another match and the jack of diamonds meets the same fiery fate.

I close my eyes.

The flame flickers inside my Memory Palace. I let it engulf the painful memories of my childhood. Another fire breaks out in the rooms that contain my research into the Riemann Hypothesis. I could stop its spread, but I don't think I want to. Maybe I'll solve it one day, maybe I won't. However, explaining the joy of maths to Zak that day in the playground made me realize that I could inspire other children. If I finally complete my Cambridge degree and train to become a maths teacher, perhaps one of my future pupils could grow up and crack the puzzle. It won't earn me a place in the history books, but it would be something to be proud of.

As the rooms continue to smoulder, I create new compartments that are comfortable, warm and forgiving. Inside one is a guitar. I plan to take up the instrument again. Further along the corridor is space for my colleagues at Prince Burger, the Three Wise Men and my elderly neighbour, Aleksy. I have a whole floor devoted to Jodie and Zak, of course.

I open my eyes and stand up as Victoria, Harper and Lucy head over to say their goodbyes. They walk away, but William remains with me for one final Sparks' family ritual. Together, we recite Father's mantra: *Bright sparks create fires.*

'Now finish it,' William says.

I tuck the queen and jack of hearts into my jacket pocket because I don't want to lose them; they belong together. I toss the rest of the cards into the bin, along with all the fake photographs.

'Goodbye, William.'

'Goodbye, Simon.'

His voice is a whisper now, a memory evaporating.

I don't need to watch William walk away to join his family. I can feel him leaving my life with each beat of my heart.

'Who are you talking to?' a voice asks. 'Please don't say "fairies" because that would be beyond lame.'

I spin around. Zak is standing behind me, hands planted on his hips.

'How long have you been standing there?'

He shrugs. '*For ever.*'

'I was talking to myself. There's nobody else here.'

'Are you sure?'

'Absolutely.'

'I promise not to laugh if you can talk to dead people. That would be cool.'

I laugh. 'I don't have that particular super power, unfortunately.'

'Mummy said to come find you. We're playing charades. Are you going to join in?'

I am, I am, I am.

I'm no longer a bystander, watching from the sidelines. I'm a part of this silly, painful yet wonderful and totally amazing thing called life. It won't be easy without the safety net of William and his family to rely on, but that's OK. The cards are stacked in my favour and I'm willing to take the gamble.

Zak reaches out his hand as he turns to go inside.

I take it.

I don't look back.

66

Late January 2019

JODIE

'YOU MIGHT THINK THAT maths is only in the class-room, but you'd be wrong. Maths is everywhere!' Zak beams at the parents and teachers in the audience, throwing his arms out expansively. 'You can learn about it in playgrounds by experiencing the gravitational force of swings. Most of all, I love looking for maths in nature. Did you know you can see fractals in the shapes of snowflakes, flowers, trees and lightning bolts? Fractals are even inside us, in our lungs, kidneys and blood vessels.'

Simon nods encouragingly as Zak clicks through the PowerPoint presentation with his zapper. They worked on this together for the assembly while I drafted my latest essay, which should hope-fully score another distinction. I never thought Zak would be confident enough to do a Show and Tell in front of the whole school; he'd refused point-blank last term. Discussing his love of maths without embarrassment is an even bigger surprise – he's no longer afraid to talk about his passion for the subject; I have Simon to thank for that too.

I'm bursting with pride as he explains that fractals are never-ending patterns that can be found across the universe and natural world. I think about the patterns *we've* created, as all our lines have intertwined, shattered and come back together.

Zak is like a new child compared to last year. He came top of his maths test a fortnight ago and is now putting up his hand in class. We're still on the waiting list to see an educational psychologist, but the nightmares and bedwetting are less frequent. I'm encouraging Zak to talk to me – or draw pictures – when he's worried about something instead of keeping it locked inside his head. And I'm opening up more – I've told him how Sandra has agreed to care for him if anything ever happens to me. This safety net has helped ease his anxiety, along with knowing that his dad will remain behind bars for a long time. The police believe Jason could plead guilty to all charges, but he'll still receive a hefty sentence later this year.

I'm concentrating on finishing my latest assignments – Monica says I'm on track for a full house of distinctions. The letter hasn't come through from Cambridge yet, but I know I've blown it. Plan B is to wait for my final college results in July and apply somewhere else. Maybe I'll follow Simon's old advice and do a distance-learning degree while continuing to work at Prince Burger. It's not so bad – I love my colleagues and we have a laugh. Even Carlos is friendly now he's out of the kitchen and serving customers alongside Marta. I've earned five stars on my badge *and* a pay rise after becoming a senior counter assistant.

I thought about celebrating by getting a large new tattoo to cover the scar on my back. I made it as far as the parlour near college but didn't go inside. I've decided I'm not going to conceal my past. It's a part of me and I have nothing to hide. Simon is moving forward too. He's applied to Cambridge to finish the final year of his maths degree and is waiting to hear. If he gets accepted, he'll move away this autumn. I can't imagine not seeing him every day. I try to refocus on Zak as my eyes mist up. He's finishing up by showing beautiful images of fractals in the world: ferns, river deltas, romanesco broccoli and flowers.

He smiles broadly. 'Maths is beautiful; maths is life! I love maths, I love life!'

Simon and me rise to our feet, clapping and cheering, as the hall echoes with applause.

'Well done!' Simon shouts. 'I couldn't have said that better myself!'

Zak blushes. He sits down on the bench next to his classmates who clutch lightsabers, seashells, telescopes and books. The head teacher, Mrs Beddall, reads out sports fixtures and is about to announce which class is this week's recycling winners when my phone vibrates in my bag. I dig it out, my heart racing as I see the email strapline: 'Lucy Cavendish College'.

Oh no.

I don't want to ruin Zak's assembly by reading my rejection. I'm about to put my phone away when Simon catches my hand.

'Read it!' he hisses, staring at my mobile.

'I can't!'

'How can you wait? Do it!'

'Later!'

Mrs Beddall shoots a look in our direction.

'Open it,' Simon whispers.

I sigh. I've steeled myself for failure and *can't* embarrass Zak by bursting into tears in front of his teachers and classmates.

I take a deep breath and click on the email. It has six attachments.

'What does it say?'

'I don't know. There are so many attachments. This one's about an open day. Do you think they're inviting me to reapply?'

Simon reads over my shoulder. 'This is an *Offer Holder Day*. That must mean you have an offer!'

'No! It can't be!' My voice rises into a strangled tone.

'Please can parents refrain from talking or using their phones until the end of the assembly?' The head teacher is staring directly at us.

This is agony. I have no choice but to slip the mobile into my bag. Could I really have a place? My heart's beating so fast, I feel like I'm going to pass out. The pupils stand up and file out. Eventually, only the Show and Tell kids are left on the stage.

'You may congratulate your children on their hard work before you leave,' Mrs Beddall says.

The kids scatter across the hall.

'You were amazing!' I say, as Zak sprints over. 'I'm so proud of you!'

'Congratulations to you both!' Simon exclaims.

'Why? What's Mummy done?' Zak glances up.

'I honestly don't think I've done anything.'

'Check your phone again while the head teacher's not looking,' Simon says.

I dig out my mobile. My hands are shaking but I manage to click on the right attachment. It's from Dr Adams, the director of admissions.

Dear Jodie
I am delighted to write to offer you a place to study for a
BA degree in English at Lucy Cavendish College. The
condition of this offer is that you achieve a distinction in
each module of your Access to Higher Education Diploma.

'I don't believe it!' My eyes scan the rest of the email. I reread it again and again, in case I've made a mistake. The words slowly sink in.

'You did it!' Zak exclaims, bending over to read the attached letter. 'This is amazing! We knew you would, didn't we, Simon?'

'Absolutely. I never had a doubt.'

'Cambridge here we come, Mummy!'

'Well, I have to get the grades first,' I point out.

'You will!' Zak and Simon cry in unison.

'And you're going too, Simon!' Zak says excitedly. 'We'll all be together. This is the best news *ever.*'

Simon looks down at Zak, smiling. 'Well, I don't know that for certain either, but I hope with all my heart—' he begins.

'I'll have my own pets!' Zak cries, jigging about. He throws his arms around me. 'Can we buy guinea pig food to celebrate?'

'I don't see why not.' I beam and turn towards Simon, who's shuffling from foot to foot.

He's standing at a short distance, even though he brought us all together: the three points of an equilateral triangle.

'*We* did it!'

I open my arms and he joins the group hug. He starts to say something, but stops himself. I don't break away, but I can't think of the right words to say either.

We simply hold each other.

*

Simon has headed off to Prince Burger but I need to stay on to talk about Zak with Mr Silva. I have time to kill as his teacher is tied up with a kid's nosebleed. I head to the library while I wait. The book collection has grown since I was last in, thanks to parents' fundraising. The email slowly sinks in as I browse the shelves. *Cambridge*. I could soon be following in the footsteps of Wordsworth, Coleridge, Byron, Sylvia Plath and Zadie Smith among other literary giants! Me, Jodie Brook, who was once told she'd never amount to anything.

I run my fingers over the books.

I feel Lizzie here with me.

When I turn around and look for her in the corridor, she's in the periphery of my vision. I sense her watching and waiting with bated breath for what comes next. Within months, Zak and I could be saying goodbye to Sandra and the rest of our friends and moving into one of the college's two-bedroom family flats.

Family.

That word takes time to process. For years, our family was only Zak and me but after meeting Sandra and Simon it's grown bigger. Pam was right – Simon does have hidden depths. I don't know what *we* are yet – that's the question I can't answer. I only know I don't want to say goodbye to him. He's a part of our lives. If we both begin our studies in Cambridge this October, we won't have to think about parting. He'll be close enough to see Zak and me regularly – and not because I'm looking for childcare.

Who knows where things could lead? I'm done guessing because life will surprise me, the way he has.

Mr Silva appears. 'Thanks for waiting. Would you like to come in here?' He points to an empty classroom.

'One minute! I have to take this.'

I pretend to answer a call as he heads inside.

There's one last thing I must do while I'm here.

I dig around in my handbag and pull out *Great Expectations* – it's the first book Lizzie ever gave me, and the last surviving novel from her collection. I find the photo of us together between the pages and slip it back into my bag.

It's time to keep my promise to an old friend.

'We finally got here, Lizzie. We made it to the last page.'

I slip *Great Expectations* onto the library shelf for the next child to find.

ACKNOWLEDGEMENTS

Firstly, a huge thank you to everyone at HarperCollins for being so enthusiastic about my book and supporting me every step of the way towards publication. I'm very lucky to have two amazing editors: Martha Ashby and Charlotte Brabbin. Both have an incredible eye for detail, which has helped make me a better writer. I'm extremely grateful for their hard work, support and dedication. It's been a joy to work with both editors, along with the hugely talented, wider HarperCollins team, including Fliss Denham and Becca Bryant. A particular shout-out goes to Caroline Young who designed my gorgeous cover.

Thank you, as always, to my wonderful agent, Jemima Forrester, who believes in me and continues to be a huge source of support and inspiration. This wouldn't have been possible without you. I also owe a big debt of gratitude to the foreign rights' team at David Higham Associates and my film agent, Georgina Ruffhead.

When I first came up with the idea for this book, I knew I had to find an extraordinary Cambridge college that would make a huge impression on Jodie. I discovered Lucy Cavendish, a truly inspiring place that accepts students from all walks of life. A massive thank you to its former press officer, Kate Coghlan, who gave me a tour of the college and answered my endless questions. Lucy Cavendish has such a warm and friendly family atmosphere – I genuinely felt this was somewhere my character would be accepted and flourish. Thank you to its former admissions director, Dr Victoria Harvey, who helped with the admissions process and Dr Isobel Maddison, who assisted with all aspects of the English undergraduate course. I'm hugely grateful to Bonnie Samuyiwa, who was an English undergraduate at the college and indispensable during my research. Thank you also to James Hardy, acting director of communications at Cambridge.

For this book, I'd wanted to highlight how children in the care system are too often let down. As a freelance education journalist, I frequently read reports warning how children in care slip through the cracks in the education system – and society in general. As I write this acknowledgements page, I find it appalling that children – like Jodie – continue to be dumped in unregulated accommodation, often left to fend for themselves in unsafe surroundings. Jodie manages to turn her life around with a great deal of help, but in reality too many will never be given a chance. This *must* change. However, some people are making a difference to these young people's lives – thank you to Sam Turner, at Become, a charity for care leavers, and Bev Costello, a children's advocate, for your help and advice, along with a care leaver who did not want to be named.

Ruth Ehrlich, a policy officer at Shelter, answered my questions around Jodie's homelessness and lawyer, Andrew Moxon, kindly assisted with my legal queries.

Thank you to consultant psychiatrist, Dr Chetna Kang and GP Dr Matt Kurian for answering my medical questions around Simon's health problems. Matt – you were very generous with your time! Thank you yet again to Graham Bartlett, a police procedural adviser, who is totally indispensable when writing about crime.

As part of my wider research, I visited the Charles Dickens Museum in London and found books including *Charles Dickens: A Life* by Claire Tomalin particularly useful. I also discovered that teacher Eddie Woo makes mathematics fun and accessible – his TEDx talk is inspirational.

I'm very grateful to early readers Lindsay Galvin and Victoria Crook, and for the support of authors including Sarah Govett and Faye Bird.

Many thanks to you, the reader, for taking the time to pick up my book – I hope you enjoyed it. Finally, thank you to Mum, Dad, Rachel and Maureen for always being there for me. Much love and thanks to Darren, who has read this book more times than he wants to without complaint and my wonderful sons, James and Luke. I may force them to read it one day!

Newport Community
Learning & Libraries

PILLGWENLLY.

Y041654